MARIA V.
SNYDER

'Maria V. Snyder tantalises readers with another complex, masterful story set in a magical world so convincing that she'll have you believing that it's actually real.'
—YAReads.com on *Storm Glass*

'A compelling new fantasy series'
—*SFX* magazine on *Sea Glass*

'Wonderfully complex…
Opal finally comes into her own in *Spy Glass*.'
—*Fantasy Book Review*

'This is one of those rare books that will keep readers dreaming long after they've read it.'
—*Publishers Weekly* starred review on *Poison Study*

'Filled with Snyder's trademark sarcastic humour, fast-paced action and creepy villainy, *Touch of Power* is a spellbinding romantic adventure that will leave readers salivating for the next book in the series.'
—*USA TODAY* on *Touch of Power*

'Maria V. Snyder is one of my favourite authors, and she's done it again!'
—*New York Times* bestselling author Rachel Caine on *Inside Out*

SHADOW
STUDY

MARIA V.
SNYDER

Published in Great Britain 2015
by MIRA Ink, an imprint of Harlequin (UK) Limited,
Eton House, 18-24 Paradise Road,
Richmond, Surrey, TW9 1SR

© 2015 Maria V. Snyder

ISBN: 978-1-848-45363-0
eBook ISBN: 978-1-474-01318-5

47-0315

Harlequin (UK) Limited's policy is to use papers that are natural, renewable and recyclable products and made from wood grown in sustainable forests. The logging and manufacturing processes conform to the legal environmental regulations of the country of origin.

Printed and bound by
CPI Group (UK) Ltd, Croydon, CR0 4YY

THE TERRITORY OF IXIA

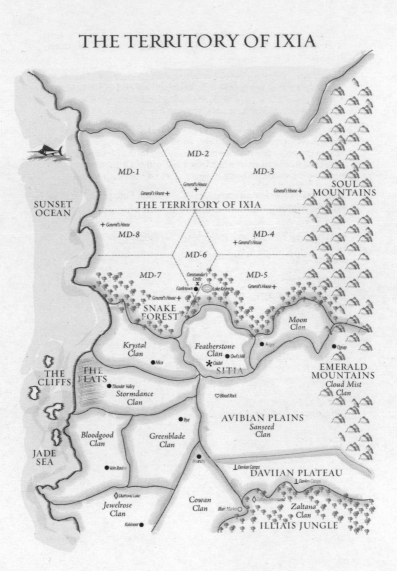

SHADOW
STUDY

This book is dedicated to all my loyal readers
who asked for more books about Yelena and Valek.
This one is for you. Enjoy!

1

YELENA

Ugh, mud, Kiki said as she splashed through another puddle. The wet muck clung to her copper coat and dripped from her long tail. It packed into her hooves and coated the hair of her fetlocks with each step.

Through our mental connection I sensed her tired discomfort. *Stop?* I asked. *Rest?*

No. Images of fresh hay, a clean stall and being groomed formed in Kiki's mind. *Home, soon.*

Surprised, I glanced around the forest. Melting piles of snow mixed with black clumps of dead leaves—signs that the cold season was losing its grip. Rain tapped steadily on the bare branches. The light faded, turning the already gray woods leaden. For the past few hours, I'd been huddling under my sopping-wet cloak, trying to keep warm. With my thoughts fixed on my rendezvous with Valek, I'd failed to keep track of our location.

I scanned the area with my magic, projecting my awareness out to seek life. A few brave rabbits foraged in the soggy underbrush and a couple of deer stood frozen, listening to the squishy plodding of Kiki's passage. No souls haunted these woods. No humans within miles.

That wasn't a surprise. This remote area in the northeastern Featherstone lands had been chosen for that very reason. After Owen Moon ambushed us about four years ago, Valek and I had decided to move to a less well-known location near the Ixian border.

I leaned forward in the saddle. We were getting close and my wet cloak no longer pressed so hard on my shoulders. At this pace, we'd reach our cozy cottage within the hour. Valek's involvement with our friend Opal's rescue from the Bloodrose Clan and the aftermath had kept him busy for months. Finally we would have a few precious days all to ourselves before he reported back to the Commander. He should already be there waiting for me. Visions of sharing a hot bath, snuggling by a roaring fire and relaxing on the couch once again distracted me.

Kiki snorted in amusement and broke into a gallop. Behind the clouds the sun set, robbing the forest of all color. I trusted Kiki to find the path in the semidarkness as I kept a light magical connection to the wildlife nearby.

In midstride, Kiki jigged to the right. Movement flashed to the left along with the unmistakable twang of a bow. Kiki twisted under me. I grabbed for her mane, but a force slammed into my chest and knocked me from the saddle.

Hitting the ground hard, I felt all the air in my lungs whoosh out as pain erupted. Fire burned with each of my desperate gasps. Without thought, I projected again, searching for the... person who had attacked me. Despite the agony, I pushed as far as I could. No one.

Kiki, smells? I asked. She stood over me, protecting me.

Pine. Wet. Mud.

See magician?

No.

Not good. The person had to be protected by a magical

MARIA V. SNYDER

null shield. It was the only way to hide from me. Null shields blocked magic. At least it also prevented the magician from attacking me with his or her magic since it blocked magic from both sides of the shield. But it wouldn't stop another arrow. And perhaps the next one wouldn't miss.

I glanced at the shaft. The arrow had struck two inches above and one inch to the left of my heart, lodging just below my clavicle. Fear banished the pain for a moment. I needed to move. Now.

Rolling on my side, I paused as an icy sensation spread across my chest. The tip had been poisoned! I plopped back in the mud. Closing my eyes, I concentrated on expelling the cold liquid. It flowed from the wound, mixing with the blood already soaked into my shirt.

Instead of disappearing, the poison remained as if being refilled as fast as I ejected it. With pain clouding my thoughts, the reason eluded me.

Kiki, however, figured it out. She clamped her teeth on the arrow's shaft. I had a second to realize what she planned before she yanked the arrow from my chest.

I cried as intense pain exploded, blood gushed and metal scraped bone all at once. Stunned, I lay on the ground as black and white spots swirled in my vision. On the verge of losing consciousness, I focused on the hollow barbed tip of the arrow coated with my blood, reminding me of the danger. I remained a target. And I wasn't about to make it easy for my attacker to get another shot.

Fix hole, Kiki said.

I debated. If I healed myself now, then I'd be too weak to defend myself. Not like I was in fighting condition. Although I still had access to my magic, it was useless against arrows and, as long as the assassin hid behind the null shield, I couldn't touch him or her with my magic, either.

Kiki raised her head. Her ears cocked. *We go. Find Ghost.*

I groaned. How could I forget that Valek was nearby? *Smart girl.*

With the arrow still clutched in her teeth, Kiki knelt next to me. Grabbing her mane, I pulled myself into the saddle. Pain shot up my arms and vibrated through my rib cage when she stood. She turned her head and I took the arrow. It might give us a clue about the assassin's identity.

I crouched low over Kiki's back as she raced home. Keeping alert for another twang, I aimed my awareness on the surrounding wildlife. If the animals sensed an intruder, I'd pick up on their fear. A sound theory, except I'd been in contact with the deer when the arrow struck. I'd be impressed by the assassin's skills if I wasn't in so much pain.

It didn't take long for us to reach our small stable. The main doors had been left open. A warm yellow glow beckoned. Kiki trotted inside. The lanterns had been lit and Onyx, Valek's horse, nickered a greeting from his stall. Kiki stopped next to a pile of straw bales. Relieved to be safe, I slid onto them then lay down.

Kiki nudged my arm. *Lavender Lady fix hole.*

After Ghost comes. I suspected I would drop into an exhausted sleep once I healed the injury and I knew Valek would have questions.

She swished her muddy tail and stepped away. *Ghost.*

Valek appeared next to me. His confusion turned to alarm as his gaze swept my blood-soaked shirt. "What happened?"

No energy for a detailed explanation, I filled him in on the basics and handed him the arrow.

All animation dropped from Valek's angular face. Fury blazed in his sapphire-blue eyes as he examined the weapon. For a moment, I remembered our first meeting when he offered me the job of the food taster. Poisons had brought us

MARIA V. SNYDER

together at that time, as well. But I'd never expected it to last. Then I'd wanted nothing more than to escape from him as quickly as possible.

Clear liquid dripped from the hollow shaft. He sniffed it. "Did you expel all the poison?"

"I think so." Hard to tell for sure, but I wouldn't add more fuel to his anger. Valek's hard expression already promised murder.

He smoothed the hair from my cheek. "How bad is it?"

"Not as bad as it looks. Now go, before the assassin gets away." I shooed.

"I'm not leaving you unprotected."

Kiki huffed and flicked her tail, splattering mud on Valek's black pants. I yanked my switchblade from its holder, triggering the blade. "I'm far from unprotected. Douse the light before you go."

"All right. I'll station Onyx outside the stable. Stay here." Valek opened Onyx's stall and the black horse trotted out. After he extinguished the lantern, Valek disappeared into the blackness.

I lay there listening for any sounds. My shoulder and left arm throbbed. Each inhalation caused a sharp stab of pain in my chest. To ease the discomfort, I pulled a thin thread of magic from the blanket of power that encompassed the world. A mental picture of the injury formed when I focused on the wound. My clavicle had been broken. The arrow had sliced through my muscles on impact, and the metal barbs in the arrow's head had ripped chunks of skin when Kiki had yanked it out. Lovely. I used the ribbon of power to lessen the pain— a temporary measure.

Once more sending my awareness into the surrounding forest, I kept a light contact with the nocturnal creatures. Too bad my bat friend was hibernating over the cold season. His unique senses would have helped with finding the assassin in the dark. The wildlife conducted their nightly hunt of food and showed no signs of agitation—not even from Valek. His immunity to magic prevented me from keeping track of him. I hoped he stayed sharp.

As time passed without incident, I wondered who had attacked me. That line of thought didn't go far as all I could deduce at this point was the person was a magician who had the power to form a null shield, who favored a bow and arrow, and who might have an affinity with animals. Either that or he/she was really quiet and had masked his/her smell.

Unfortunately, pondering why I was attacked generated a longer list. As the official Liaison between the Commander of the Territory of Ixia and the Sitian Council, I'd created at least a dozen political and criminal enemies in the past six years. As the heart mate of Valek, the infamous Ixian assassin, for the past eight years I'd been a target for anyone who hated Valek, which included most of Sitia and probably hundreds of Ixians. As a magician and Soulfinder, I made many people nervous, worrying that I'd turn rogue. These people were under the mistaken impression that I could create a soulless army when in fact all I did was find lost souls and guide them to either an eternity of peace in the sky or an eternity of suffering in the fire world, depending on their deeds while alive.

A slight squish jolted me from my thoughts. Careful of my injury, I sat up and swung my legs over the bales of straw. Then I slid off. Better to stand and fight than be caught lying down. The darkness outside was one hue lighter than inside due to the faint moonlight. It illuminated just enough to see shapes.

I kept alert for any movement, peering through the door. When Kiki stepped between me and the entrance, I startled. Even though she was sixteen hands high she could be really quiet. Her back was taller than me and she blocked my view.

MARIA V. SNYDER

Granted, I reached only five feet four inches, but she was a big girl like most Sandseed horses.

A few more squishes set my heart to beat in double time. I tightened my grip on my switchblade.

Ghost, Kiki said, moving away.

I sagged against the bales. A Valek-shaped shadow strode into the stable. He lit the lantern. One look at his grim expression and I knew he'd lost the assassin's trail.

"The guy's a pro," he said. "He used magic to erase his footprints. They just stopped. And without leaves on the bushes, it's harder to track him, especially at night. I'll go out again in the daylight."

"He? How do you know?"

"Big boots, deep prints. We can discuss it later. Let's go inside and take care of you."

"Kiki first." And before he could argue, "She saved my life. If she hadn't moved, the arrow would have pierced my heart."

Valek's shoulders dropped. Knowing I wouldn't leave, he worked fast. He removed her saddle and knocked the dried mud off her legs and stomach. After he cleaned out her hooves, she walked into her stall and munched on hay.

"Guess she's happy enough," Valek said, tossing the pick into a bucket. "Now, let's get you warm and dry, love."

I removed my muddy cloak and left it on the bales before I wrapped my right arm around Valek's shoulders. He wanted to carry me, but I worried he might jar the broken bone out of alignment and I wouldn't have enough strength to heal it.

The sharp pain returned by the time we reached the house. I made it as far as the couch. A bright fire burned in the hearth and a bottle of wine sat on the end table with two glasses and a plate of cheese. Valek must have arrived a few hours before me.

Tilting my head at the food, I said, "That's lovely."

"We'll indulge after you're healed and rested. Do you want to change first?"

Just the thought of moving my left arm hurt. "No."

"Then what are you waiting for?"

"A kiss. I haven't seen you in months."

Valek transformed when he smiled. The sharp angles of his face softened and warmth radiated from him. He leaned forward and pressed his lips to mine. Before I could deepen the kiss he pulled back.

"No more until you're better."

"Meanie."

"Yelena." His stern tone would have made my mother proud.

"All right." I reclined on the couch and closed my eyes.

Reaching for the power blanket, I gathered a thick thread of magic. I wound this ribbon around my broken clavicle, fusing the two pieces back together. A second thread knitted the muscles and a third replaced skin. The effort exhausted me. Drained dry, I passed out.

By the time I woke, afternoon sunlight flooded the living area. Besides the green plaid couch, a couple of oversize nubby brown armchairs and a matching love seat made a semicircle in front of the hearth. In the center, a dark brown deep-pile rug covered the floor—soft on the feet and...other body parts.

All that remained of the fire was ashy coals and half-burned logs. The wine and glasses waited—a promise for later. No sounds emanated from the rest of the cottage, but moving without a sound was second nature for Valek. I called his name just in case. No response.

I opened my mind to Kiki. *Is everything okay?* I asked.

Quiet. Nap time, she said.

If the horses could sleep, then all should be well. *Ghost?*

Out. Woods.

My left shoulder and upper chest ached. The muscles would be sore for a few days. I sat up and examined the wound. Purple bruises surrounded an angry red circle. Another scar to add to my collection. I'd stopped counting three…or was it four injuries ago? Stretching with care, I tested my range of motion. Not bad.

The cold had soaked into my bones. My blanket had fallen to the floor. A hot soak in the tub should cure it in no time.

Stiff with blood and poison, my shirt reeked. All the more reason to bathe. But first a quick check of the rest of the cottage. It wouldn't take long. I palmed my switchblade, but didn't trigger the blade.

The ground floor consisted of a living area, kitchen and washroom. The living area spanned the left half of the cottage while the kitchen and washroom occupied the right half. The hearth sat in the middle of the building so all the rooms could share its warmth.

I peered into the kitchen. A layer of dust covered the table and chairs, but the wash sink, cold storage box and water jugs had been cleaned. Nothing appeared out of place.

The washroom's entrance was to the right of the hearth. I smiled. Valek had filled the large water tank near the back wall. Hot coals glowed underneath—one of the benefits of having a stone floor. I tested the water with my finger. Almost perfect.

I climbed the stairs to the single bedroom in the loft. Our cottage was too small for company, another excellent reason to own it.

My red-silk robe and clean clothes had been spread out on the king-size bed. Valek had been busy. I resisted the urge to check under the bed as I undressed. I'd have to ask my cousin Nutty to repair yet another shirt. Despite a few mud stains, I could still wear my black wool pants. I donned the robe—a gift from Valek. Running my fingers over the smooth material, I verified all my surprises remained in place. Valek always included weaponry with his gifts.

Which reminded me. I removed the lock picks, releasing my long black hair.

After a quick peek outside to check for signs of intruders, I returned to the washroom. Steam floated from the water's surface. I opened the valve and the warm liquid rushed into the sunken tub. Turning off the water, I banked the coals, hung my robe on the hook and settled in, oohing and aahing until only my head remained above water.

Wonderful for about five minutes. Then the door squeaked and I lunged for my switchblade.

"Sorry," Valek said. He leaned against the door's frame as if it kept him from falling.

Had he been up all night? "Did you find anything?"

"He's gone. I found nothing except those boot prints. No doubt he's a professional assassin with magical abilities." He rubbed the stubble on his chin. "That will be the key to finding him. Not many people have that combination of skills. He's probably already a person of interest. I'll have to check my sources."

I resisted correcting him. What he called sources were really Ixian spies in Sitia, which as Liaison, I'd been trying to stop. Ixia and Sitia shouldn't be spying on each other. Instead, they needed to form a relationship based on mutual trust and respect.

"Unless he's a new assassin. Some young hotshot."

Valek straightened. "That's a possibility. And if that's the case, then he chose the wrong target if he wishes to grow old."

"After you find out who hired him."

"Of course. Any ideas who…?" He shook his head. "We

　　　　　MARIA V. SNYDER

should make a list of who *doesn't* want to kill you, love. It'd be shorter."

I'd be offended, but it was actually a good idea. "Let's not let it ruin our vacation. Join me."

He hesitated, frowning.

Oh no. Bad news. "Tell me."

"I have to leave in the morning."

"Not because of the attack?"

"No. The Commander ordered me to return earlier than I'd planned. He's been very patient. I've been in Sitia for most of the past year and he says I'm needed for an urgent matter. I'm sorry we have to cut our vacation a few days short."

Even though disappointment pulsed, I understood his loyalty to the Commander. And the Commander had been more than generous with Valek's time. Working with Opal and helping to stop the Bloodrose Clan, Valek had done more for Sitia than Ixia.

No sense moping about something I couldn't change. Suppressing my frustration with the time limit, I splashed Valek. "Come on in while the water's hot."

He grinned and peeled off his clothes. Scars crisscrossed his long lean muscles, and a faded C-shaped scar marked the center of his chest. Even after spending seasons in Sitia, his skin remained pale, which contrasted with his shoulder-length black hair.

"Like what you see, love?" Valek stepped into the water.

"You lost weight."

He huffed. "Janco's a lousy cook."

"Did Janco pout when you ditched him to come here?"

"Yes, but it was fake. He's more than ready to return to Ixia." Valek settled next to me. "Do you really want to talk about him right now?" His gaze burned hotter than the water.

"Who?"

"Exactly." He ran his thumb over my wound. "Does it hurt?"

"No." His touch drove the cold away as a fire ignited in my heart.

He closed the distance between us and our lips met. Another perk of stone floors: no worries about water damage.

Morning sunlight and chills woke me late the next morning. Memories of last night replayed and I remained in bed savoring them. We'd gone from the tub to the living area, drunk the wine, tested the softness of the rug, and then up to the bedroom. My lips still tingled from Valek's predawn goodbye kiss.

Another chill raced along my skin. Shivering, I pulled the blanket up to my chin. All my bones ached as if encased in ice. Unease swirled. Something was…off. Wrong.

Without warning, a wave of heat slammed into me. I yanked the blankets off and jumped to my feet. Sweat poured, soaking my nightshirt as dizziness threatened to topple me. I sank to the ground. The heat disappeared as fast as it had arrived, but the cold returned, seeping into my skin, freezing the sweat into a layer of ice.

Before I could pull the blanket over me, another hot flash consumed me. Memories of going through the fire to enter the fire world rose unbidden. The searing pain of my flesh burning all too familiar. I batted at my arms even though I knew my skin hadn't been set on fire.

Fear wormed through my chest. Maybe I hadn't expelled all the poison.

Between gasps of breath, the ice extinguished the heat. My muscles tightened and cramped. My teeth chattered hard enough to cause a headache. I curled into a ball, afraid I'd shatter like an icicle hitting the ground.

When the fire blazed again, I straightened as steam rose from my skin. Then the cold reclaimed me. And it kept going back and forth, hot to cold and hot again. Like I had a super-fast fever, which gave me no time to draw power to counter it.

I endured the waves. Each flip drained my strength. One of two things was bound to happen. I'd either pass out or the attack would stop. There was a third possibility, but I preferred to stay positive.

After hours…days…weeks…the seizures ceased. At first I braced for the next cycle. But as time progressed without an attack, I slowly relaxed. With no energy to stand, I groped for the edge of the blanket and pulled it down, covering me. At this point, even the hard floor couldn't stop me from falling asleep.

Darkness greeted me when I woke. Every single muscle ached as if I'd run here from the Citadel. My dry throat burned and my stomach hurt. I needed water, food and a bath. But first, I needed to ensure that I didn't have another attack. Had the poison run its course? Or was it still inside me? One way to find out.

I drew a deep breath and reached for the blanket of power. Nothing happened. Trying again, I concentrated on pulling a thread of magic.

Nothing.

Fear pushed up my throat. I swallowed it down, determined not to panic.

I opened my mind to Kiki. *What's going on?*

No response. Not even images.

Dead air surrounded me.

My magic was gone.

2

VALEK

He hated leaving her. Memories of last night's activities swirled in his mind, but he suppressed them. No sense torturing himself. Instead, he focused on the attack on Yelena as he saddled Onyx.

Valek had done another sweep of the area as soon as the sun had risen. No one in sight and no signs of anyone. Not much of a comfort, considering the bastard had been able to conceal himself so well. His identity remained a mystery for now. But Valek would find him. No doubt.

Mounting Onyx, Valek grabbed the reins. Kiki said goodbye with a sad little whinny.

"Please keep her safe," he said to Kiki.

She nodded. Her blue eyes shone with intelligence.

"Thanks." Valek clicked his tongue, spurring Onyx into a gallop. Kiki was the only reason he didn't insist on personally escorting Yelena to the Citadel. Yesterday, he'd taken Kiki to the spot where the assassin had waited. She'd sniffed the area and had the man's scent. Combined with Yelena's magic and her skills with her switchblade and bo staff, they made an impressive fighting team. Plus Yelena had assured him she'd recovered from the injury.

Of course, there was the possibility that since the assassin knew how to construct a null shield, he might also know Valek's biggest weakness, which would render him unable to protect Yelena. Valek could never forget that disadvantage. It was like a knife slowly piercing his heart in tiny increments. Each day it dug a little deeper.

Once his greatest weapon against magic, his immunity was now a drawback. If a magician surrounded Valek with a null shield, Valek would be trapped inside just like being caught in a bubble made of invisible steel. Weapons could cross the barrier, but he couldn't. Well, neither he nor Opal, who was also immune to magic. Her adventures last year had uncovered this particularly nasty weakness and, while the magical community promised to keep it quiet, Valek had learned the best way to distribute information was to classify it as secret.

Valek guided Onyx north toward the Ixian border. At this pace, they'd reach the checkpoint in three hours. Their cottage had been in an ideal location. Too bad they would have to move again. He contemplated retirement—not for the first nor the last time. And for a moment, he dreamed of a time when he and Yelena could disappear and never have to worry about assassins, intrigue and espionage again.

Except she couldn't retire from guiding lost souls. Perhaps she could wear a disguise. He imagined them dressed as an old married couple traveling from town to town. For half the year, they'd visit the local sights, try new foods and find souls. The other half would be spent together in a cottage, gardening, carving and going out for daily rides. It was a pleasant daydream.

A mile from the border, Valek stopped Onyx. He changed into his Ixian uniform—black pants, boots and shirt. Two red diamonds had been stitched onto his collar, marking him as an adviser to the Commander. He turned his cloak inside out, revealing the black material with two red diamonds instead of the gray camouflage. In Ixia, he had to wear his uniform with the Commander's colors of black and red. While in Sitia, he had to blend in.

Back on Onyx, he headed to the main checkpoint, hoping the soldiers would recognize him. It'd save time. Valek considered sneaking into Ixia, but the Commander's message said the situation was urgent.

The official border crossing between Sitia and Ixia was a cleared, one-hundred-foot ribbon of ground that stretched from the Sunset Ocean in the west to the Soul Mountains in the east. The border followed the contours of the Snake Forest, which also spanned the area between the ocean and mountains. At one point, Valek had asked the Commander to clear the entire forest. Even with the hundred feet of open ground, smugglers and refugees still managed to slip across the border. But now he found the forest convenient for his network of spies. Not that he'd admit that to Yelena.

The six border guards snapped to attention when he approached. A good sign.

"Welcome back, sir." The captain saluted.

Nice. "Thank you. Any news, Captain?"

"It's been quiet, sir. A caravan crossed earlier this morning, but they were on our approved list. A Sitian delegation is due to come through here in a couple days, but we haven't gotten the manifest for the visitors yet."

Interesting how the man mentioned the delegation as if routine. It was only eight years ago that the border had been sealed tight. No one in or out.

"Do you know why the Sitians are visiting?" Valek asked, wondering if the delegation was the reason the Commander had ordered him back a few days early.

"No, sir."

MARIA V. SNYDER

Ah. He'd have to wait. "Anything else?"

The captain smiled. "*Adviser* Janco informed us that a Sitian spy would attempt to cross this checkpoint today. He claimed this spy would be disguised as you and ordered us to attack first and ask questions later."

Valek suppressed his ire—he needed to have a little chat with Janco. "And why didn't you follow Adviser Janco's orders?"

"I was in basic training with the...er...Adviser, sir."

"My condolences, Captain."

The captain's soldiers all grinned at his deep laugh. "His pranks were endless, but he taught me more than our instructor."

Interesting and not that surprising. "You showed excellent judgment today. While being attacked by six skilled opponents would have been good practice for me, I preferred the friendly welcome."

They parted, letting Onyx through.

"Sir?" the captain called.

Valek turned.

"Papers, please."

Ah. Now the soldiers surrounded the horse. Smart move. Valek pulled a folded sheet from one of his cloak's inner pockets and handed it to the captain. "The Commander's orders."

Valek waited as the man scanned the fake document.

The pleasant expression dropped from the captain's face. His right hand slid to grasp his sword's hilt. Following his cue, his men tensed and grabbed the hilts of their weapons.

"This is a forgery," the captain said.

Valek noted he didn't say *sir*. "Just testing you, Captain."

"Dismount now."

Valek tsked. "What happened to your manners, Captain?"

The captain drew his sword in answer.

Good. The man followed proper protocol. If Valek didn't dismount soon, they'd rush him, yank him from the saddle and unarm him. How far should he push it? Not far. The Commander was waiting for him, after all.

Pulling the real orders from his sleeve, Valek held up his hands. The captain gestured to one of the guards who approached slowly, then snatched the parchment from Valek with one quick motion. The guard delivered it to the captain. So far, so good.

Peering at the letter, the captain relaxed. "This one is real. It was a test."

"And you passed. What is your name, Captain?"

"Broghan, sir."

"I'll make sure to mention this to your commanding officer, Captain Broghan."

"Thank you, sir."

Pleased with the border guard's actions, Valek urged Onyx north. They would reach the Commander's castle by late afternoon. Dirty, hard-packed snow covered the well-used trail. The surrounding forest showed no signs of green—all bare branches and bleak even with the sunlight streaming to the ground. Buds already coated the Sitian trees, and the southern half of the Avibian Plains would be lush with plant life and warm breezes by now.

Not that he missed the south—not at all. Just one specific southerner. Valek scanned the surrounding area seeking signs of an ambush. Memories swirled of the times he'd used the cover of the forest to hide his actions. Valek glanced up. Yelena had also exploited the Snake Forest's tree canopy to escape the Commander's men during a training exercise. It had been the day he learned she was far smarter than he'd thought. And more dangerous, too.

If only the Commander allowed magicians to live in Ixia,

MARIA V. SNYDER

then she'd be working with him instead of being the Liaison. Valek had argued about the benefits of having a magician on staff with the Commander for years, but he remained stubborn. Perhaps Ambrose had changed his mind about magic after Kade's demonstration. Valek had heard the Stormdancer had traveled north during this past cold season to harvest the energy from one of the blizzards that blew down from the northern ice pack. Kade's magic had transformed the killer storm into a regular old snowstorm. The Commander let Kade stay for the rest of the season, but Valek hadn't heard if Kade and his group of Stormdancers would be invited back next year. One thing was for sure: Valek and Commander Ambrose had a lot to catch up on.

When he arrived at the castle complex, Valek stopped at the southern gate. An immense stone wall completely surrounded the castle, barracks, stable and other support buildings.

Once again, he presented his fake orders and was pleased that these guards also followed the proper protocol.

After they allowed him entrance, Onyx automatically headed to the stables near the west gate and next to the dog kennels. Halfway there, they were stopped by a messenger.

"Adviser Valek, the Commander would like to see you in his war room right now. I'll take your horse to the stable and see that your bags are delivered to your rooms, sir."

He'd hoped to wash the travel grime off, but one didn't tell the Commander to wait. Dismounting, he handed the reins to the boy and followed the path to the western entrance.

The only thing impressive about the castle was its sheer size. With four tall towers anchoring the corners of the rectangular base, the palace spanned a half a mile in width. Other than that, the odd layers of squares, triangles, cylinders and whatnot perched atop the base looked ridiculous. Even after all these years, Valek still didn't know why the King had agreed to build a structure that resembled an uncreative child's tower of blocks.

Perhaps the first King of Ixia had thought the asymmetrical design would hinder assassins. It would only confuse the stupid ones. Valek had infiltrated the castle without trouble by posing as a hairdresser for Queen Jewel.

Picking up his pace, Valek cut through the servant corridors to save time. He arrived at the Commander's war room just as the kitchen servers left. They held empty trays. Ah, supper. His stomach growled in anticipation.

Located in the northwest tower, the circular war room was ringed by slender floor-to-ceiling stained-glass windows that spanned three-quarters of the wall. When the afternoon sunlight shone, a rainbow of colors streaked the large wooden table that occupied the center.

Lanterns had been lit, sending sparks of colors in different directions from the windows. Ari and Janco shoveled food onto their plates and the Commander sat at the head of the table, waiting as his food taster slurped and sipped his supper. A small stack of files had been piled next to the Commander's plate.

The food taster, a skittish young man, shot Valek a nasty glare as he slipped past. Valek actually missed the old taster, Star, but she'd been too difficult to work with and keeping track of all her schemes had grown tiresome. So he'd slipped a dose of My Love into the Commander's drink to test her poison tasting skills. Star'd failed the test and paid for that error with her life.

The Commander crinkled his nose at his messy plate, but didn't comment as he speared a piece of beef.

"Well, look who decided to show up—the Ghost Warrior," Janco said. "Have any trouble at the border?" He smirked.

Valek stared at Janco with the promise of retribution.

MARIA V. SNYDER

Unaffected, Janco elbowed his partner, Ari. "See? I told you he'd get through."

While Janco was all lean wiry muscles, barrel-chested and broad-shouldered Ari was solid muscle. About a foot taller and wider than Janco, Ari also had more common sense.

"He told me about it later, Valek," Ari said. "Nothing I could do at that point." His long-suffering tone said more than his words.

"Your prank failed to work." Valek ladled stew into a deep bowl.

"Oh?" Janco didn't sound convinced.

"Captain Broghan recognized you from your basic-training days."

Janco stabbed his fork into the air. "I knew he looked familiar, didn't I, Ari?"

"You said he resembled your second cousin."

"Close enough. So Broghan made captain." Janco tapped the fork against his teeth.

"Is he worth looking into for my corps?" Valek sat on the opposite side of the table from the power twins—Ari and Janco's nickname.

"He's smart and a fast learner, but he has no finesse."

"Not everyone can be a drama queen like you, Janco," Ari said.

"I'm insulted." Janco pouted, proving Ari's point.

"Go on," Valek ordered. "No finesse?"

"Yeah, no spark…imagination. He'll follow orders and protocol, but if a situation goes well beyond the protocols, he'll be stymied."

"Stymied? Who uses that word?" Ari teased.

"Those who know what it means. Please excuse Ari. His vocabulary is limited to fifty words—most of them curse words."

Ari drew breath to counter, but the Commander leaned forward and stopped the banter with a hard gaze from his gold, almond-shaped eyes. Time for business.

The Commander's uniform matched Valek's except he had two real diamonds stitched onto his collar and his was wrinkle-free. His steel-gray hair had been cut close to his scalp.

"I have two matters I wish to discuss," the Commander said. "The first is regarding smugglers. The reports of illegal goods being stopped at the border have slowed to a trickle. However, black-market goods are still in ample supply."

Valek considered. "That means they've found a new way into and out of Ixia."

"Correct." The Commander pushed his plate away.

"Are we still allowing some smugglers to slip by?" Valek asked. Following the caravans of illegal goods to the source was a sound strategy.

"No. The few who are attempting to cross illegally are so inept, they're being caught right away."

"Decoys," Ari said. "To make us think they're still trying to sneak through the Snake Forest."

"Which means they're organized," Janco added.

"Organized how?" the Commander asked.

Janco scratched the empty place where the lower half of his right ear used to be. "If it was just one or two smugglers using the new route, then the others would continue as they have been. But with the decoys, it means all the smugglers have gotten together and figured out a way around the border guards."

"A smuggler convention?" Ari asked with a touch of humor. "Thieves don't usually play well together."

"Maybe a big bad arrived with a new way of doing things."

"A ringleader?" Ari asked.

"Exactly. Some scary dude who has taken over. He's probably all 'do it my way or...'"

"It's a possibility," Valek said while Janco cast about for a proper smuggler threat.

"Regardless. I want the three of you to figure out the new route and the new players. The sooner the better," the Commander ordered.

"What about Maren?" Ari asked. "Will she be helping us?"

Maren had teamed up with Ari and Janco, and the three of them had beaten Valek in a fight, earning the right to be his seconds-in-command.

"She's on special assignment," the Commander said. "You can recruit if you need more assistance."

Unease nibbled on his stomach. Valek knew nothing about Maren's assignment and, from the Commander's closed expression, he wouldn't be learning more about it from his boss.

"Tunnels," Janco said. "They could have dug tunnels underneath the border."

"They'd have to be miles long. Otherwise, they'd pop up in the Snake Forest and someone would have seen them," Ari said. "Who has the ability to build a tunnel like that?"

"Miners," the Commander said in a quiet voice.

No surprise the Commander mentioned them. His family had owned a mine in the Soul Mountains bordering what was now Military District 3 until they'd discovered diamonds. The King of Ixia had claimed ownership of the gemstones and "allowed" the Commander's family to stay and work for him. The King's greedy move had started the rumblings of discontent and turned a brilliant young man into the King's number one enemy.

"We'll look into the possibility of a tunnel," Valek said.

"Boats on the Sunset Ocean." Janco held up his napkin. He had folded it so it resembled a sailboat.

"Not practical," Ari said. "Between the storms and the

Rattles, we haven't had any problems with people using the ocean as an escape route."

The Rattles extended from the coast of MD-7 out to at least a hundred miles into the Sunset Ocean. With submerged rocks, strong and unpredictable currents, and shallow areas that moved, the Rattles were impossible to navigate. Sailing around them took too long plus sailors ran the risk of hitting dead air and being stranded for months.

Valek tapped a finger on the table. "When did the decoys start?"

The Commander flipped through a few papers in the file on top of his stack. "End of the cooling season about sixty days ago."

Valek calculated. "Prime storm season. It's suicide to be on the ocean at that time of year."

"I will leave the detecting to you. As for this other matter…" The Commander pulled a letter from underneath the folders. He scanned it then turned his gaze to Valek. "An unfortunate development, but one that we will *not* get involved in. Do you understand?"

"Yes, sir." Valek kept his expression neutral, bracing for the bad news.

Ari and Janco exchanged a concerned glance.

"Do you remember Ben Moon?"

He couldn't forget the man who had tried to murder Yelena in revenge for the execution of his brother, Owen Moon. Only the fact Ben remained locked tight in a special wing of Wirral Prison for the past three years kept the man alive. So why was the Commander… A sick feeling circled his chest. "He escaped?"

"Yes."

MARIA V. SNYDER

3

YELENA

Don't panic. Don't panic. Don't panic. Clutching the blanket in tight fists, I repeated the words. *Don't panic. Don't panic. Don't panic.* Except it failed to work. Panic burned up my throat. I gasped for breath. The words transformed to *no magic. No magic. No magic.*

The darkness pressed against my skin, sealing me inside my body, blocking me from the warmth and light that was my magic. All my senses had been stolen along with my magic. Sounds, sights and scents gone. A bitter taste all that remained.

No magic. Cut off from the lost souls, disconnected from the wildlife and severed from my colleagues, I'd been rendered useless. No magic.

I stayed on the hard floor of our bedroom huddled under the blanket. My thoughts buzzed with misery. When the sun rose, a bit of relief eased the chaotic terror that had consumed me. My vision worked after all.

A loud bang on the door broke the early-morning quiet and Kiki's piercing whinny cut right through my conviction that all had been lost. Hooves pounded on wood and I staggered to my feet.

I'm okay, I said. No response. My heart twisted.

"I'm okay," I shouted over another barrage.

Kiki stopped. But for how long? I grasped the handrail and eased down the steps. Sharp hunger pains stabbed my guts, but I aimed for the door. Kiki's mostly white face peered through the window. A patch of brown circled her left eye.

As soon as I opened the door, she barged in, almost knocking me over. Not hard to do since I hadn't eaten in over a day.

I wrapped my arms around her neck. "I'm fine." Leaning my forehead against her soft hide, I opened my mind to her. Nothing. I breathed in her scent—a mix of dry straw, cut grass and earth.

"I can't... I don't have..." Why was it so hard to say? "My magic...is gone. I can't talk to you."

Kiki snorted.

"Yes, I know I'm talking to you, but we can't *communicate*."

She pulled away and gazed at me. And while her thoughts didn't sound in my mind, I understood her sarcastic, what-do-you-call-this look. Then she nudged me with her nose as if prompting me to explain.

Her actions snapped me from my scatterbrained panic. Logic wrestled raw emotion aside and I considered. What happened before my magic disappeared? A lovely evening with Valek, but we'd had a number of them throughout the years without consequences.

And before that? I touched the still-tender area on my upper chest. "The poison! How could I be so stupid?"

Kiki nodded in agreement.

"Thanks," I said drily. "Now I just have to figure out what poison blocks a person's magic." Curare fit, except I'd have been paralyzed and I would have recognized its crisp citrus scent. "The arrow." Perhaps a few drops of the poison remained.

Kiki followed me to the stable. Poor girl hadn't been fed grain in over a day. I filled her feed bucket before searching

MARIA V. SNYDER

for the arrow's shaft. It didn't take long to figure out Valek must have taken it with him.

Valek. Should I join him in Ixia? It'd be safer. And without the taint of magic, the Commander would welcome me with open arms. Ambrose's aversion to magicians started back in his childhood. Even though he had a female body, he insisted he was male. He dressed as a boy and changed his name. Terrified that a magician would "see through" him, he banned them from Ixia and executed any found within the Territory when he gained power. Plus it didn't help that the corrupt King was also a magician who had abused his power.

When I accepted my Soulfinding abilities, I discovered the true nature of the Commander's dual personality. His mother died in childbirth, but she'd refused to leave her newborn son. She had just enough magic that her soul remained with Ambrose, turning him female. I'd offered to guide her to the sky, but the Commander felt her presence aided, not hindered, him. For now.

The Commander's stance on magicians in Ixia had loosened a bit since he learned of his own magical beginnings, but he still had a long way to go.

Besides, traveling to Ixia wouldn't help me discover what happened. My condition could be temporary and if so I was freaking out for nothing.

Searching my memories, I reviewed the list of poisons Valek had taught me when I'd been the Commander's food taster over eight years ago. None of them had side effects that matched my symptoms. Then again, Valek wouldn't have been worried about a substance that blocks magic. But would he know if one existed? Possible.

How about the Master Magicians? I groaned. First Magician Bain Bloodgood! His knowledge of history and magic was unparalleled, and if he didn't know about this poison, he'd hunt through his stacks and stacks of books until he found it.

Feeling much better, I returned to the cottage to eat and pack. I checked the hearth and coals in the washroom, ensuring all had been properly extinguished. When I closed and locked the door, a pang of regret vibrated in my chest. Because of the attack, Valek would insist on moving. I rubbed my fingers on the stones. Fond memories swirled. The distance to the stable seemed to stretch, growing longer with each step.

Once I reached the stable, I saddled Kiki. We didn't use reins or a bridle and normally, I'd forgo the saddle, but the saddlebags were stuffed with enough food and supplies to last a week. I paused. Had Valek and I ever had a full week to ourselves? No.

Kiki grunted, jarring me from my thoughts.

"What's wrong?"

She jerked the girth's latigo strap from my hand. I'd pulled it too tight. It took me a moment to understand. It was easy to saddle a horse that instructed you on how tight to make the saddle. I wondered how many other things I would need to relearn—a dreary prospect.

I fixed the girth and mounted. "Back to the Citadel as fast as possible, please." That remained the same. I'd always let her find the best way and set the pace.

She galloped through the mud. The bright sunshine of midmorning failed to lift my spirits. I scanned the forest, seeking predators. A bird screeched and I ducked. I drew my switchblade when I caught movement out of the corner of my eye. And I flattened, hugging Kiki's neck when a thud sounded behind us.

After a few hours, Kiki stopped for a rest. I stayed by her side, keeping my back against her and my switchblade in hand. Invisible dangers lurked in the forest. A whole army of am-

MARIA V. SNYDER

bushers could be waiting for us downwind and I'd have no warning.

Panic simmered. I was weak, vulnerable and an easy target. When Kiki stopped for the night, I didn't light a fire, and the few uneasy hours I slept were spent between her hooves.

By the time we reached the northern gates of the Citadel two days later, I started at every noise. Never had I been so glad to see the white marble walls that surrounded the Citadel reflecting the sunlight. The guards waved us in and I worried. What if the guards conspired with a group inside? What if we were mugged?

I twisted my fingers in Kiki's copper mane as we crossed through the rings of businesses and factories that occupied the center of the Citadel like red circles around a bull's-eye. A bustling market lay at the heart of this section. Skirting the crowded stalls, Kiki headed toward the Magician's Keep, located in the northeast quadrant.

People hustled through the streets, talking, laughing, arguing as they attended to their morning chores. I stared at them. No thoughts or emotions reached me from the crowds. To my senses they had no souls. A horde of walking dead.

I leaned forward and whispered to Kiki, "Faster to the Keep, please."

She increased her pace, weaving through the busy streets. The logical part of me understood that the shouts and curses following our passage did not come from soulless dead people. However, that knowledge didn't stop my trembling hands or rapid pulse.

Shocked, I realized my magic had influenced how I viewed the world. I barely remembered how I had interacted with my world without magic. I wouldn't have thought I relied on my power so much or used it to connect to the people around me in the past six years. Yet, I felt as if I'd been wrapped in a thick black cloth from head to toe. The cloth had holes for my eyes, ears, nose and mouth, but the rest of me remained swaddled.

I eased my tight grip on Kiki's mane when the Magician's Keep's grand entrance loomed. Elegant pink marble columns supported scalloped arches that framed the two-story-high marble doors. The doors were always open, but they were guarded by four soldiers, a magician and a wooden gate.

They straightened as we approached.

"Good morning, Liaison Zaltana. Back so soon?" asked the sergeant in charge.

"Yes, Mally, an urgent matter has cut my vacation short. Is Master Bloodgood in his office?"

She turned to the magician…Jon from the Krystal Clan.

Jon peered at me, questioning. "Can't you—"

"Not right now," I said between clenched teeth.

"Oh…kay." His gaze grew distant. "Yes, First Magician is in his office." Then he met my gaze. "He's with a student right now and says to come by in the early afternoon."

I had no intention of waiting and no desire to tell Jon. Instead, I thanked him. Mally moved aside, but didn't raise the gate. Kiki jumped the heavy wooden barrier in one easy stride, showing off just like she always did.

The Keep's administration building sat directly across from the entrance. A few blocks of peach marble marked the yellow structure and a set of grand marble stairs led up to the first-floor lobby.

Kiki stopped at the base of the steps.

I dismounted and patted her sweaty neck. "I'll catch up with you at the stables and give you a proper grooming."

She butted my palm with her soft nose, then trotted toward the stables located in the northwest corner of the Keep right next to Irys's tower. The Magician's Keep had four towers stationed in each corner. They rose high into the air. Each

MARIA V. SNYDER

Master Magician lived in a tower. Right now, only two were occupied. Second Magician Zitora Cowan had resigned her position to hunt for her missing sister and no other magician had the power to be a master. So far. There was always hope that one of the new students at the Keep would mature into master-level powers.

I raced up the steps and into the administration building. And just like its name implied, the structure housed the administrative staff who handled the day-to-day accounts and bills and the details involved in running a school for future magicians. The Masters all had offices inside and the infirmary was located on the ground floor.

Ignoring the staff in the hallways, I headed straight toward Bain's office. I opened the door without knocking. Not surprised to see me—no one could sneak up on a Master Magician—Bain frowned at my rude intrusion. But one look at my expression and he ushered his student from the room.

Once the girl left he turned to me. He tapped his temple with a wrinkled finger. "Why didn't you answer me?"

"I can't. It's gone. My magic is *all* gone!" Panic spun in my chest. Tears threatened.

His face creased with concern. He stepped closer and spread his hands. "May I?"

"Yes."

Bain grasped my shoulders and closed his eyes. I braced for… What? I'd no idea. However, nothing happened.

His eyes popped open in surprise. "You are correct."

Bain's confirmation hit me like an avalanche of rocks tumbling down a mountain. Unable to keep it together any longer, my body trembled as tears gushed with each sob. First Magician guided me to an armchair, pressed a handkerchief into my hands and muttered soothing words until my bout of self-pity ran its course.

Ringing for tea, he sat in the armchair next to mine and waited for his assistant to arrive. Deep in thought, he smoothed his white hair. Or rather, he tried. The curls resisted and sprang back into their positions, sticking up at odd angles.

I wiped my eyes with his handkerchief and scanned his messy office. Contraptions in various stages of completion or dissection littered the floor, shelves bowed with piles of books, rolls of parchment covered his desk and numerous shades of ink stained…just about everything, including Bain's deep blue robe. The scent of jasmine mixed with a tangy aroma filled the room. I wondered if the large arrays of candles scattered throughout were the source of the smell.

When Bain's assistant arrived, he brought tea and Second Magician Irys Jewelrose, my mentor and friend. Bain must have mentally communicated to her about my arrival. I stood, but she kept her distance as the man poured three cups of tea and set the steaming pot down amid the clutter on the table.

"Do you require anything else, sir?"

"No, thank you."

He left and Irys rushed over to embrace me. "Don't worry. We'll figure this out."

Tears welled, but I calmed as I breathed in her comforting apple-berry scent; more crying wouldn't solve anything. I squeezed her back and moved away. Her emerald-green eyes held concern and a promise.

Bain gestured for us to sit. Two more armchairs faced the ones Bain and I occupied. Irys handed out the cups before settling in. I clasped mine in both hands, letting the warmth seep into my fingers.

Bain gazed at me over the rim of his cup. "Tell us."

Starting with the attack, I told them everything that had happened. They sat in silence, absorbing the information. Then the questions started. I answered them as best as I could.

"Do you know of a poison that robs a magician of her power?" I asked them.

"No," Irys said.

After a few moments, Bain said, "I do not know of a substance that has that ability. If it exists, it would be a formidable weapon against magicians."

"What do you mean *if*? Do you think I'm making this up?" I put my cup down. It clattered on the saucer.

"No, child. I'm merely considering other possibilities besides poison. Perhaps there is another reason for your condition."

"Oh. Like a null shield?"

"Correct. Except it is not a shield."

"How do you know?"

"I can sense your surface thoughts and my magic helped soothe you. Which also means you are not immune to magic."

I sucked in a breath. Bad enough to be without magic, but to be at its mercy... This was just getting worse and worse.

"Perhaps your magic was siphoned," Irys suggested. "Opal no longer has the ability, but there's a chance another magician has learned the skill. There was a gap in time between the arrow strike and your bout of...fever—for lack of a better word."

If that was the cause, my magic was gone forever. Unless there was a vial of my blood around, which I doubted. So far, no one could duplicate Opal's glass magic, but Quinn Bloodrose's magic was also linked to glass.

"What about Quinn?" I asked.

Irys considered. "He's attending classes here. I don't think he's left the Keep. However, we can talk to him. And I can contact Pazia Cloud Mist to see if she has any ideas. Her magic was accidentally siphoned and since then she's been working with glass, making those super messengers."

A queasy unease roiled. "I don't want word to spread about me. I've too many enemies."

"I'll be discreet and won't mention you," Irys said. "I'll check the logbook at the gate. If Quinn left the Keep, there will be a record of it."

The vise around my chest eased a little.

"And I will scour all my books for information," Bain promised. "I am sure Dax will be happy to translate the languages I am unfamiliar with."

I smiled at Bain's word choice. My friend Dax would be *happy* to complain and whine nonstop about the task, but he was trustworthy.

"What can I do?" I asked.

"I suggest you visit Healer Hayes," Irys said. "There's a chance you're sick or he might have some information about what is causing your...condition."

All good ideas. I leaned back, sinking into the cushions as exhaustion swept through me.

"Does Valek know?" Irys asked.

"No. He left before my symptoms started. I don't want to alarm him. I'll message him when I know more."

"We must search for the assassin, as well," Bain said. "I'll contact the security chief. He—"

"No," I interrupted.

"Then who do you suggest?"

I considered. No doubt Valek's spies would be hunting for my attacker, but they didn't have magic or intimate knowledge of Sitia's back alleys. Two people came to mind—one had magic while the other had the knowledge.

"Leif and Fisk. I trust them both."

"Would they be willing to work together?" Bain asked.

"They have before. Remember the gang of scam artists that plagued the Citadel a few years ago?"

"Ah, yes. A nice bit of detecting." Bain tapped his fingers on the edge of his teacup. "However, this assassin may not be from the Citadel or have ties here."

"Fisk has been branching out to other cities." I smiled, remembering the dirty street rat who had begged me for money. I'd emptied my pouch into his small hands, but when he approached me a second time, I'd hired him to help me navigate the overwhelming market.

Eventually he founded the Helper's Guild and recruited other beggar children to help shoppers find good prices, quality merchandise and to deliver packages, all for a small price. His network of guild members also had the unique ability to gather information on the criminal element.

"I didn't know he's expanding," Irys said. "That little scamp. I shouldn't be surprised." She sipped her tea. "Well, he's not so little anymore. It's a good idea to ask them."

If they had time. "Is Leif out on assignment?"

"Not right now," Bain said with a significant look.

Meaning the Sitian Council might have a job for my brother soon, which led to another question. "Should I inform the Council of my condition?"

Bain ran a gnarled hand down his sleeve. Since becoming the First Magician, he'd aged more than just the natural passage of time. His duties included overseeing the Keep and being a member of the Sitian Council—same as Irys. She, too, had aged. Gray streaked her black hair and a few more wrinkles etched her face.

"Not about your lost magic," Irys said. "Not until we know more. However, we should tell them about the attack. They might have intel from their clans."

Each of Sitia's eleven clans had one representative on the Council, and, along with the two Masters, the Council governed Sitia.

Bain straightened in his chair. "I believe we have a plan of attack. I will liaise with the Council and do extensive research. Irys will check the gate logs and talk to Quinn and Pazia. Yelena will visit Healer Hayes and talk to Fisk and her brother, Leif. Did I miss anything?"

"No." For the first time since the morning I'd woken without my magic, my chest didn't hurt. Too bad it didn't last.

"Yes," Irys said. She leaned forward. "Yelena, you need to keep a very low profile. If you interact with the Keep's students, they'll figure it out eventually and then it will be impossible to keep your condition a secret. Plus you're vulnerable. Whoever did this to you knows magic can influence you. What if they use you to get close to one of the Councilors or the Commander and Valek? Or turn you into an assassin? I'd suggest you ask Leif to weave a null shield into your cloak and, once you've talked to Fisk, you need to go into hiding. That's the safest thing you can do right now."

Run and hide? That was so not my style.

MARIA V. SNYDER

4

VALEK

Ben Moon escaped with help? Who could have broken him out of Wirral Prison? Most likely a group of rogue magicians. They'd have to be intelligent, resourceful and powerful in order to get through Wirral's supertight security. Valek dug his fingernails into the chair's armrests, but kept his expression neutral as the Commander relayed the information. His first impulse—to race to the Citadel to warn and protect Yelena—throbbed against his hollow chest.

"As I said, we will not be getting involved in what is strictly a Sitian affair," the Commander said, not fooled by Valek's calm demeanor.

"How long ago did this happen?" Valek asked.

The Commander stilled. "It is not our concern."

Valek chose his next words with the utmost care. "Not directly, but Liaison Zaltana was ambushed and shot with an arrow two days ago."

"What…? How…? Why didn't you tell us?" Janco sputtered in outrage.

Concern hardened Ari's face.

"She's fine," Valek assured them. "Kiki sidestepped and

the arrow missed her heart." He explained what had happened.

"And you think this attack is related to Ben Moon's escape?" the Commander asked.

"It would depend on the timing, sir."

"I see." Commander Ambrose scanned the parchment.

Valek suppressed the desire to snatch it from the man's hand.

"The incident happened ten days ago. Not enough time for Ben to set up the attack on Yelena."

"Unless his buddies planned it and all Ben had to do was show up and hide behind the null shield and wait for her," Janco said.

Good point, except the Commander failed to appear impressed.

"Regardless, we will let the Sitian Council handle the investigation. After all, she was ambushed in Sitia." The Commander gathered his files.

"May I send a message to Yelena, warning her about Ben?" Valek asked.

"She probably already knows, but if you feel it's necessary, then go ahead." He stood. "I expect daily reports on your progress regarding the smuggling routes." The Commander paused. "Valek, stop by my rooms later tonight."

"Yes, sir."

He nodded and left the war room.

Valek stared at the door, wondering why the Commander made a point to order him to visit his rooms. It had been their routine since the takeover to touch base before bed. Valek and the Commander had spent many late nights together discussing strategy and talking through problems, seeking solutions.

Perhaps the Commander thought Valek would skip tonight due to all the work that no doubt piled up while he'd been in Sitia. The stack of reports wasn't nearly as concerning as

MARIA V. SNYDER

Commander Ambrose's indifference over Ben's rescue, which was the opposite of Valek's reaction. Usually they were in sync and the Commander shared all his information. But he hadn't let Valek see that letter, which made him suspect the Commander had lied or hidden something. Why?

If Yelena had been assassinated, the relationship between Ixia and Sitia would be affected. Probably not enough to cause a war, but it would further strain an already uneasy truce. While Valek agreed the new smuggling routes needed to be discovered, the impact of black-market goods on Ixia was minor in comparison.

Perhaps the Commander wished to sever relations with Sitia and he planned to confer with Valek about it tonight.

"You know, the Commander didn't specify *which* messenger you could send to warn Yelena," Janco said.

Valek waited.

"*We* could deliver that message to her," Ari said, catching on. "Then hang around and investigate the *smuggling* operation."

"Oh yeah. The best way to discover the new routes is to infiltrate their operations. In fact—" Janco slapped the table. "I still have a few contacts in Fulgor. They might have some leads to the *smugglers*."

Janco had worked undercover as an officer at the Wirral maximum-security prison, which was located in the city of Fulgor in the Moon Clan's lands.

"I thought you were looking forward to being in Ixia and away from all that 'magical muckety-muck,'" Valek quoted.

Janco pished. "Discovering the *smugglers* is more important."

True. However, rushing off into the unknown never sat well with him. He preferred to gather information, collect data, observe and then infiltrate before making an arrest. Yelena had her magic, and she'd promised to return to the Magician's

Keep after he'd left. No doubt the Masters would inform her of Ben Moon's status and ensure that she'd be well protected.

Anger flared for a moment. He should have killed Ben right away. Valek had slipped inside Wirral once before to tie up a few loose ends. And Ben Moon was definitely a loose end. Too bad Ben hadn't been caught in Ixia like his brother. Owen had attempted to steal the Ice Moon from a diamond mine in Ixia, coercing Yelena to help him by kidnapping Leif. A smart and powerful magician, Owen had almost succeeded, but was outsmarted and executed four years ago. Ben blamed Yelena and, a year later, had tried to cut her throat.

Valek considered. Despite the Commander's orders, he didn't plan to leave it to the Sitian authorities.

"Before we do anything, I'll check with my network in Sitia," Valek said. "One of ours may already have eyes on Ben and his cohorts. Same with the new smuggling routes."

"What do you want us to do in the meantime?" Ari asked.

"Go shopping."

"Shopping?" Janco perked up. "I could use a new dagger and a short sword and a set of sais. I've been drooling for a pair since Opal—"

"Not that kind of shopping, you dolt," Ari said. "He wants us to shop for black-market goods."

"Correct. And see if you can…persuade the sellers into revealing their sources."

"Yes, sir. We'll go first thing in the morning." Ari stood.

Janco groaned. "What's wrong with going in the afternoon? We'll avoid the crowds and I can catch up on my sleep and it's warmer."

Ari ignored his partner and headed for the door.

Janco trailed after. "I've been working undercover for the past two years. It's hard to rest when you might wake up to a

MARIA V. SNYDER

knife at your throat. I should visit my mother. I haven't seen her in—"

The door closed on Janco's prattle. He might be annoying and have a short attention span, but he could be counted on when a situation turned serious. Then he was focused and deadly with his sword.

Valek sat a moment longer, savoring the quiet. He needed to review the piles of reports that waited for him on his desk so he could prepare for his meeting tonight. The Commander's stiff manner during supper warned him it wouldn't be pleasant.

As expected, stacks of files filled every square inch of his desk. Although Maren had kept his office clean of dust while he'd been in Sitia for most of the past year, the room smelled musty and a stuffiness pressed against his skin. Valek wove through the piles of books and heaps of stones that littered the floor, lit the lanterns and candles ringing his desk, opened the window a crack and settled in his chair.

Maren had been in charge during his absence. Again he wondered what mission she'd been assigned and how long she'd been gone. Perhaps he'd find out tonight. Practical as always, Maren had organized the reports into three categories—general updates, important and action required. Notes written in her loopy handwriting accompanied each one. Handy, it would make it easier, but still time-consuming since the reports from his network of spies had been written in code that had to be deciphered.

Sneaking into Wirral and helping the Bloodrose Clan win their freedom was more appealing than sifting through all the files. However, years of experience had taught Valek that golden nuggets of information resided within these piles. He'd just have to dig through them one at a time.

Hours later, a light knocking on his door jolted him from a detailed description of the Hunecker quarry operations in MD-4.

"Yes?" he called, grasping the handle of his sword with his right hand and palming a dagger with his left.

A guard entered slowly.

Smart man.

"Commander Ambrose has retired for the evening, sir."

Valek studied the man's face, committing the guard's features to memory. "Thank you...?"

He straightened. "Sergeant Gerik, sir."

"You're new. How long have you been with the Commander's security detail?"

"Three seasons, sir. I was assigned by Adviser Maren."

Ah. "Has anyone else been promoted in my absence?"

"No, sir."

"Thank you, Gerik. You're dismissed."

Gerik did an about-face and left. Valek added the man's name to the list he'd written of items he needed to follow up on. New personnel in the Commander's detail were not unheard-of, but Valek performed a complete background check on each candidate before he or she was assigned. Perhaps the paperwork for Gerik waited in one of the stacks he had yet to peruse. Those would take another couple of days to complete.

At least Valek had found a few clues that might lead them to uncovering the new smuggling routes. And, even better, he had an action plan to report to the Commander.

Valek swept up a few files, extinguished the lanterns and candles, and locked his office door. The three complex locks prevented most intruders from gaining entry. However, a professional could pop them in minutes.

Heading to the Commander's suite, Valek passed a few servants and soldiers, recognizing them all. He nodded at those

MARIA V. SNYDER

who met his gaze. A few returned the gesture while others kept their gazes on the floor.

Two massive wooden doors guarded by two soldiers Valek knew well blocked the entrance to what had once been the King's royal apartments. The guards opened the doors, allowing Valek to pass into a short hallway.

When the Commander's forces took control of Ixia about twenty-three years ago, Ambrose divided the King's expansive rooms into two suites, one for him and one for Valek. The hall had only two doors opposite each other. Valek knocked on the one on the left and waited.

A faint "come in" sounded. Valek entered the Commander's main living room. The Commander's living space matched the rest of the castle. In a word, utilitarian. After the takeover, Ambrose had stripped the castle of all its opulent decorations. Paintings were removed, tapestries shredded and statues crushed. If it didn't have a specific or useful purpose, it didn't stay.

Instead of sitting in his favorite armchair near the fireplace, the Commander sat behind his desk facing the entrance. He still wore his uniform. A bad sign. Valek approached.

"Sit." The Commander gestured to a hard chair with his quill. "Report."

Valek perched on the edge. "Ari and Janco are going to sniff around the markets tomorrow and see if they can get a lead on the suppliers of the illegal goods. Once we've identified them, we'll follow them and see where they cross back into Sitia."

"A good start. Anything else?"

"No, but—"

"You're dismissed." The Commander returned to his work. Valek didn't move.

The Commander ignored him. Valek studied his boss. Thin, clean-shaven despite the late hour, and with a couple more wrinkles than the last time Valek'd been in Ixia. They'd been working together for the past twenty-four years. Cold fury emanated from Ambrose, and Valek wasn't going to leave until he discovered why.

The top of the desk resembled the rest of the room: neat, spartan, and no ink stained the wood. However, a single decoration stood out amid the starkness. A ylang-ylang flower crafted from small multicolored stones glued together. Probably a gift from Yelena. Her clan, the Zaltanas, had a number of artists who created those figurines.

"You're disobeying a direct order, Valek. Do I need to call for the guards and have you arrested?"

"Permission to speak freely, sir?" Valek asked.

"And if I say no?"

"Then you'll need to call the guards."

The Commander set down his quill. "You have one minute."

"Spit it out, Ambrose. Why are you so upset with me?"

The silence stretched.

Valek waved a hand, indicating the two of them. "This isn't going to work. If we no longer have an open rapport with us batting ideas back and forth, then fire me or arrest me."

Nothing.

Last try. "Our relationship has always been based on complete trust and—"

"And I trusted you to tell me *everything*."

Ah. There it was. Valek had kept one thing from the Commander. He reported all his adventures in Sitia, and obtained permission to render aid, but he had failed to inform Ambrose about the disturbing fact that a null-shield bubble could trap him. The reason? Initially to keep the knowledge from spreading. But in omitting the Commander from the list of

MARIA V. SNYDER

those in the know, Valek acted as if he didn't trust the Commander, which wasn't true at all. So why didn't he tell him?

"I'm sorry."

How did the Commander find out? Who did know? Those fighting in the Bloodrose revolt—Opal, Devlen, Ari, Janco, Quinn, Kade, Heli, Nic and Eve. Quite the list. Who had opportunity? Anyone could have sent a message, but why would they? Only three people had been in Ixia since then: Ari, Janco and Kade.

"Not good enough, Valek."

"You're right." He stood. "I'll go collect—"

"Sit down."

Valek resumed his seat.

The Commander studied Valek. The force of his gaze had broken many people, rendering them into a quivering mess as they begged forgiveness or confessed to every crime. It was impressive. And Valek suspected the Commander used a form of magic even though Valek had never felt it. To him, magic pushed against his skin like molasses. The stronger the power, the thicker the air around him. The Commander's appraisal certainly held enough weight. The C-shaped scar on his chest burned in response.

"Why?" Ambrose asked.

Digging deep within himself, Valek considered the question. His immunity to magic was not only a part of him, but a protection. Years of practice had honed his fighting skills, and experience with spies, criminals and schemers had given him a sharp mind. To be trapped in a null-shield bubble and encased within an invisible force field of magic galled him. A silly thing to have such dire circumstances. But his weakness meant he could no longer be… What? Invincible? Did he have that huge of an ego? Or was it another thing altogether…?

"Fear," Valek said into the silence. "That once you found

out, you'd no longer need me. I am getting older, and Ari and Janco could—"

"Drive me insane. No, thank you. Do you really think I'd replace you because of one drawback? Actually, two."

"Two?"

"Yelena."

"I think she's an asset."

"Until her life is compromised. That would be the easiest way to hurt you. Or influence you."

True. "I guess I just need more time to…adjust to my predicament."

"Time is an excellent way to gain perspective. I trust this won't happen again."

"Yes, sir."

The Commander pushed away from his desk and swiped a decanter of brandy before settling into the cerulean suede armchair. He waved Valek into the other chair and poured two drinks.

Valek sipped the spicy liquid. Blackberry. A pleasant warmth spread into his stomach and he smiled, remembering when he'd taught Yelena how to detect poisons in various flavors of brandy. She'd gotten drunk at the General's brandy meeting and tried to seduce him. Talk about self-control. Valek had deposited her in her bedroom and bolted before he ravished her. Worry had trumped desire. She might have regretted it when she sobered, and he'd wanted more from her than a drunken one-night stand.

With the tension between him and the Commander gone, Valek asked how he'd found out about the null shields.

"Janco mentioned it before you arrived. He'd assumed I knew and I didn't correct him. And during his monologue of prattle, he remarked that he has a certain sensitivity to magic. Is that true?"

MARIA V. SNYDER

"Yes, he's pretty good at seeing through magical illusions."

"Useful. What about Opal Cowan? After all that training, is she going to join your corps?"

"Not quite." Valek swallowed a mouthful of brandy. "She offered to assist us if we need her." He set his glass down. "And she sent you a present."

"One of her glass animals?"

"No. She no longer is able to make her magical messengers, but what she can now do is far more useful to us."

"Oh?"

"I'll be right back." Valek dashed across the hall and grabbed the package from his saddlebags that had been delivered as promised. He returned and handed it to the Commander.

Unwrapping the cloth, Ambrose uncovered a lifelike glass snow cat. He examined the hand-sized statue. "Her artistic skill has improved, but it doesn't glow with an inner fire." He raised a slender eyebrow, inviting Valek to explain.

"That fire was her magic trapped inside." And only visible to magicians and the Commander. "What's inside that snow cat is a bit of her immunity. What you're holding is a magic detector. When a magician uses magic near that cat, it will flash with light, alerting you to its presence."

"Clever. Is she mass-producing these for the Sitians?"

"The Councilors all have one for protection, and in case a rogue magician tries to use magic to influence them. Regarding mass production, I don't know what Opal plans. The Sitian Council wishes to be in charge of the distribution, but Opal won't give them control. I think she's letting her father handle the allocation of the detectors."

"Wise." The Commander tapped a finger on the glass. "And our spies can purchase more of these for us, evening the playing field a little between Ixia and Sitia."

"They still have those super messengers."

Ambrose frowned. "Those put us at an extreme disadvantage."

Valek agreed. The messenger was a glass cube with a magic-charged black diamond at its heart. The cube allowed magicians to communicate over vast distances instantly. An indispensable tool, and one that would give Sitia a big advantage during warfare.

"We can hire magicians and they would no longer have the upper hand," Valek said despite the Commander's deepening scowl. "You know how versatile magicians are and how many ways they could aid Ixia."

"Better to stop the Sitians from making the super messengers. If we assassinate Quinn Bloodrose, Sitia couldn't produce any more."

The thought of killing Quinn didn't sit well with Valek. "Not quite. They could still charge the blacks with magic and encase them in glass, but once the magic is gone, it'd be useless. Quinn's the only one who can recharge them without cracking the diamond."

"Then we need to steal the diamonds and sabotage their mining operations."

Once they'd won their freedom, the Bloodrose Clan kept dredging the sand for the black diamonds, going deeper into the sea with each sweep. Soon they'd have to use boats.

"It would be difficult." His stomach soured.

"Look into it after you find the new smuggling route." The Commander finished his drink. "I need to write a note to General Rasmussen and have him check his beaches for black diamonds." He returned to his desk.

Valek held up his glass. The light from the fire reflected off the amber liquid. An odd shuffle-step sounded behind

MARIA V. SNYDER

him. He jumped to his feet, yanked out his dagger and spun in one fluid motion.

A figure dressed from head to toe in black pressed a knife to the Commander's throat.

5

YELENA

"Other than needing a full night's rest, you're healthy," Healer Hayes said. He'd examined me using both his magic and a mundane physical check. Opening a file with my name on it, he jotted a few notes.

How could good news be bad? I sat up, clutching the sheet to my chest. "Are you sure you didn't detect a poison?"

"All your body systems are working properly. I didn't sense any taint or rot or infection. I'm very sorry."

Frustration grew. "Do you know or have you heard of any substance that would cause my problem?"

I'd explained the entire story to him when I'd arrived at his office in the infirmary an hour ago. Hayes had listened without interruption, then led me to an examination room. Located on the ground floor of the administration building, the infirmary had a number of private rooms for recovering patients as well as an open area of beds for those who needed only a few hours. Unfortunately, I'd spent more time under Healer Hayes's care than most.

"No. I can read through my medical books and see if there is a mention of such a substance. It's a long shot, Yelena. If someone had discovered this poison before, it would have caused trouble and been reported by now."

"Unless it had been forgotten like Curare. That had been mentioned in a history book about the Sandseed Clan and, combined with the knowledge from a Sandseed healer, my father had been able to find it in the jungle." I gasped then groaned over my own stupidity. "My father. He's discovered many medicines and substances in the Illiais Jungle. He might know about this magic blocker."

"A good idea."

I hopped off the table.

"Before you rush off, I need to update your file."

As I dressed, he asked a bunch of questions.

"How old are you?"

"Twenty-seven." Although most people assumed I was younger because of my five-foot-four-inch height. I twisted my long black hair into a bun and used one of my sets of lock picks to keep it in place. Despite being in the Keep, I couldn't let my guard down. Especially not now.

"When was your last blood cycle?"

I paused and glanced at him. He kept his gaze trained on the file in front of him.

"And this is relevant how?"

"Your last dose of Moon potion was close to a year ago. You're due for another, but the timing is critical."

Oh. Since Valek and I hadn't even discussed marriage let alone a child, I needed to take the Moon potion. I thought back. "Twenty days ago or so."

"Here." He handed me a vial full of a white liquid. "Drink this right after your next cycle."

"All right." I put the potion in my backpack and left the infirmary. Disappointment over his prognosis stabbed. While I hadn't thought Healer Hayes would have the cure, I'd hoped for more. At least I still had other avenues to explore.

Perhaps my father had heard of the poison. Esau had given me a field guide to help me identify plants to use in healing. After I discovered my healing powers, I no longer needed it, but I'd kept it. I would read through it tonight.

Hungry for the first time in days, I headed to the dining hall located right behind the administration building. Remembering what Irys had said about not interacting with the students, I grabbed a couple of sandwiches and bolted, nodding at a few people I recognized on my way out.

I found a quiet sunny spot in the gardens—the green center of the Keep—to eat my dinner. The two apprentice wings bracketed the gardens to the east and west. From the top of Irys's tower, the buildings resembled parentheses. I considered my next move.

Bain wished for an investigation into the identity of the assassin who'd attacked me. I needed to talk to my brother and Fisk. Also Leif had helped our father with his jungle research, and he might know about the poison. I could search for Leif or I could ask the one person who would know where Leif was—his wife, Mara.

When I finished my meal, I strode northeast through the campus. A few students milled about and others dashed between buildings. The sunlight warmed the air and in a few months color would invade the Keep along with the warm season, and the gardeners would plant flowers with vicious delight.

As the manager of the glass workshop, Mara would no doubt be overseeing the student magicians who learned how to work with glass. I wondered if Quinn charged the black diamonds used for the super messengers here or in his rooms. Since he was an older student who'd already learned how to

MARIA V. SNYDER

use his magic, he'd been assigned to the apprentice wing just like I had been six years ago.

Any glass artist could encase the diamond in glass, but only Quinn could charge them with his magic. He was in the same position Opal had been when she'd manufactured her animal-shaped messengers—one of a kind and vital to Sitia. Loads of pressure for the young man to bear. That intensity had almost crushed Opal, but she proved to be as strong and versatile as the glass she loved and now she easily bore the responsibility of being the only person able to create those magic detectors.

If I couldn't reclaim my magic, I'd need to purchase a detector in defense. Lovely. What else would I need? Chain mail and body armor? Bodyguards? I rolled my stiff shoulder. My magic hadn't saved me from the assassin's arrow. Small comfort.

White smoke billowed from the stack atop the glass workshop. When I entered, the heat pushed against my skin like a wet wool blanket. The roar of the kilns rumbled deep in my chest and through the soles of my boots. Students sat at gaffer benches, spinning their iron rods to shape the molten glass gathered on the end. Others blew into pipes and the glass expanded into bubbles.

I scanned the activity, seeking a familiar face. In the center of the bustle stood Mara, instructing a student. A beautiful woman with a heart-shaped face and the sweetest soul. My brother had done plenty of stupid, annoying and crazy things, but marrying Mara had been the smartest thing he'd ever done.

Her tawny-colored eyes lit when she spotted me. A kerchief tied back her golden-brown hair. Dirt smudged her cheek and her apron had seen better days. She gestured to her office and held up two fingers.

Understanding the signal, I wove through the glassmaking equipment and entered the relative coolness of her office. Glass vases, paperweights, bowls and tumblers littered the room. Student efforts or Mara's, I couldn't tell. Did my sister-in-law even have time to produce her own work? The Council hoped another magician would develop an affinity with glass like Mara's sister, Opal, and Quinn, so a steady stream of first years arrived for their mandatory glass lessons. Those who enjoyed it continued to study the art during the rest of their five-year stay at the Keep.

I settled in the chair next to her desk, considering how much had changed since Opal's glass magic had been discovered. It gave me a bit of comfort. Despite Bain's lifelong quest to learn about magic and magicians, he'd never heard of Opal's particular skills. Therefore, there was no reason to panic because he hadn't heard of a magic-blocking poison.

Mara bustled in with a swish of skirts and I stood.

She embraced me. "Yelena! What a wonderful surprise. I didn't expect you back so soon." Then she pulled away and frowned. "Is something—"

"Nothing's wrong. Valek had to leave early. The Commander's patience had finally run out."

"Oh dear, I hope he's not in trouble."

"*In* trouble? No. Causing trouble? Always."

Her musical laugh warmed me.

She closed the door to her office, reducing the noise of the kilns and ensuring privacy. "Would you like some tea?" Mara lifted a glass teapot by its handle.

"Yes, please."

She poured two steaming cups and then sat down.

"Is that—"

"One of Quinn's hot glass pieces? Yes. It stays hot for days. A marvel! He's a darling boy and gave it to me when I cleared two hours each evening just for him. Poor boy doesn't like working

MARIA V. SNYDER

with a crowd drooling over his shoulder. Who would?" Mara sipped from her cup. "And I had to ban the kitchen staff, too. They love his hot and cold glass and had been pestering him for more pieces. Who knew keeping meat cold keeps it from spoiling longer?" Wonder touched her voice.

"Has he discovered any other glass abilities since coming here?"

"He's been concentrating on the messengers and the temperature glass. Opal told me he could attach a null shield to glass and other…" Mara swept her arms out as if searching for the right word. "Emotions. But between his classes and his work, the poor boy hasn't had time to experiment."

Interesting about the null shield. "He's here every night?"

"Except for one night a week."

Keeping my tone neutral, I asked, "Which night?"

Mara gazed at me. "Why? Is it important?"

Shoot. She'd been spending too much time with Leif.

"Just curious."

"Uh-huh." She waited.

"Oh all right. I want to talk to him."

"Better. Let's see…" Mara checked a ledger on her desk. "He was here the last couple of nights… His night off was four days ago."

The timing matched the night of the attack. My heart thumped. "What does he do on his nights off?"

"He has riding lessons."

Oh. Still, he could have missed his lesson. I needed to talk to the Stable Master.

"Is that the reason you stopped by?" Mara asked.

"No, I was looking for Leif." Only after I said it did I realize how it must have sounded. "And to visit you." Weak.

"How nice." Her tone didn't match her words.

"Sorry. It's just…something came up and I haven't been sleeping…" Weaker.

Concern softened the hard lines around her mouth. "And it's probably some political problem that you can't tell me. Between Leif and Opal, I'm used to being in the dark."

From the way her shoulders drooped, I knew she was far from used to the idea, yet she put on a brave front. I drank my tea and reflected. Leif and Mara hadn't even been married a year yet. It had been a lovely wedding and she had glowed with pure joy. She was part of my family. Kidnapped from Sitia at age six, I'd grown up in Ixia believing I had no family. Dreams of a fictional loving family had helped me through the dark times. And now I planned to enlist Leif's help, taking his time away from Mara. Not very nice.

"The reason I need to talk to my brother is…" I filled her in on what had happened.

Mara clutched her apron, gathering the fabric into a tight bunch, but she didn't say a word. When I finished, she slid off her chair and hugged me.

"Oh, Yelena, that's terrible." She squeezed tight then let go. "What can I do to help?"

"Help?" I hadn't thought about it.

"Of course. I'm sure you have a plan of attack. And don't tell me to keep it quiet. I'm not an idiot."

True. "Can you find out if any of the students are able to siphon magic? Opal had done it with glass, but perhaps there is another magician who can do it with another object."

She brightened. "I can. I know all the students and they like to brag about who can do what." She held up her hand. Burn scars marked her fingers and wrist. "Don't worry. I'll be discreet. Are you going to talk to Opal? She might have some ideas."

I groaned. Another possible avenue that I'd missed. "I will."

"Good. Now go get some sleep. Leif's at the Council Hall this morning, but he'll be in the training yard later this afternoon, helping Marrok teach the juniors how to defend against a machete."

"Thanks."

She escorted me out the door and then remained on the workshop's steps, ensuring I headed in the right direction. Another knot in my stomach eased as I skirted the pasture that occupied the space between the glass shop and the stables. Telling Mara had been the right thing to do.

When I entered the large wooden barn, Kiki whinnied a welcome. She looked over the Stable Master's broad shoulder as he bent to clean dirt from her hooves. Her copper coat shone, her mane had been brushed and her whiskers were trimmed. Oh no.

"I was planning on—"

"Yeah, yeah." The Stable Master cut me off. "Always the same. In a hurry with urgent business to attend to. I've heard all the excuses." He moved to her back feet. "She was a muddy mess," he grumbled. "Keep taking advantage of her and one day you'll come out here and she'll be gone."

Not unless he stopped feeding her his famous milk oats. I sighed. The Stable Master lived and breathed horses. To him, nothing was more important. And he had a point.

"I'm sorry." I draped my cloak over a stall door, picked up a comb and worked on untangling her tail. Then I helped him clean tack and muck out stalls until he no longer muttered quite as much. Which was as good of a mood as possible for him.

Before he left to order more feed, I asked about Quinn's riding lessons.

"Strong as an ox, that boy," the Stable Master said. "He

don't look it, but all those years of diving for oysters honed his muscles. See that bay?" He pointed through the window.

A horse with a deep garnet-colored coat and a black mane and tail trotted around the inside of the pasture's fence. "Yes."

"Flann's a son of a bitch—stubborn, spirited and strong. Quinn's the only one who can ride him."

"A Sandseed horse?" Sandseed horses, like Kiki, were picky about who they allowed to ride them.

"Nope. One of those new Bloodgood breeds. I was gonna send him back because he's been a real pain in my ass, but he took a liking to the boy."

"Is Quinn enjoying his lessons?"

"I don't care. He shows up on time and has improved. That's all I care about."

"Did he miss his last lesson?"

"No. Why?"

And there went another lead. "Flann looks like he needs a workout."

"Tell that to the Master Magicians. Quinn's too busy to do more." The Stable Master hooked his thumb toward the bay. "You're welcome to try." He patted Kiki's neck with affection. "I'm sure Kiki here won't mind. Will you, girl?" He slipped her a milk oat then left without saying goodbye.

After he left, I scratched Kiki behind her ears. She closed her eyes and leaned closer. Sadness panged deep inside me, radiating out with pain. The loss of our connection hurt the most. And I cringed at the thought of riding another horse. It would also be an unnecessary risk. Kiki rested her chin on my shoulder as if consoling me.

"I'll figure this out," I promised her.

She nipped my ear playfully then left the stable. I followed her out. She hopped the pasture's fence, joining the other horses. I scanned them. Silk, Irys's horse, and Leif's horse, Rusalka, nickered a greeting to Kiki.

Exhaustion clung to me, but horse hair and slobber coated my clothes and hands. I stopped at the bathhouse to wash up before I trudged to my apartment in Irys's tower.

Each Master Magician lived in one of the four towers of the Keep. Irys occupied the northwest tower and Bain had the southeastern one. The northeast tower belonged to Zitora Cowan, Second Magician, even though she'd retired. We all hoped she'd return. The southwest tower still remained empty. Roze Featherstone, who had been the First Magician, had lived there until she betrayed Sitia. After the Warper battle, she was killed and her soul trapped in a glass prison.

When I was no longer considered a student of the Keep, Irys offered me three floors of her tower to use. A generous offer. My few belongings had all fit on one floor, but I had since expanded to another, setting up guest quarters for visitors. So far, only my parents had used the space.

I lumbered up the three flights of steps. At least I hadn't been gone long enough for my bedroom to be coated with dust. I glanced around. The single bed, armoire, desk, chair and night table all appeared to be undisturbed. My footsteps echoed against the hard marble walls. I hadn't had time to install tapestries and heavy curtains to absorb the harsh sounds. Good thing since now I'd need to hear an intruder in order to wake up in time to defend myself.

Bending down, I checked under the bed and then opened the armoire. Yes, I felt silly and paranoid, but sleeping would be impossible unless I ensured no one hid in my room.

Satisfied, I tossed my cloak over the chair and crawled into bed. The chilly air swirled as I drew the thick blankets up to my chin. If I had any energy, I would light the brassier nearby. Instead, I drifted to sleep.

And for the first time in years, I didn't dream.

★ ★ ★

I woke a few hours later when the late-afternoon sunlight streamed through my window and touched my face. Without thinking, I reached for my magic and encountered deadness. The desire to curl into a ball and remain in bed pulsed through my heart. But I refused to give up. Plus I needed to speak to Leif. I flung my blankets off.

The training yard was located next to the glass shop. I leaned against the fence and studied the various matches. Most of the students held wooden practice swords or wooden machetes since they were only in their third year at the Keep. They wouldn't use real weapons until their final, apprentice year.

Leif sparred with a tall lanky student. I smiled at the mismatched pair. His stocky, powerful build, black hair and square face were the opposite of his opponent—a lean, lithe, blonde woman with a pointy chin. She used her longer reach and sword to stay out of his machete's chopping zone. Moving with the quick grace of a Greenblade, she dodged Leif's strikes.

However, experience won over fancy footwork and Leif ducked low and rushed her, knocking her down while unarming her. He grinned and helped her to her feet, then explained his strategy.

I waited as he wrapped up the session and lectured the group on where to focus.

"Don't stare at their eyes or shoulders," he said. "Watch your opponent's hips to anticipate his next strike. You've seen how a machete can counter a sword with the right moves and tactics. Do you think a machete can fight an opponent with a bo staff?"

A resounding no sounded from the students. Leif's eyes gleamed and he picked up a five-foot wooden staff that had been lying next to the fence.

"Yelena," he said and tossed the bo at me.

Instinctively, I caught it in my right hand.

"Let's show them how it's done." Leif set his feet into a fighting stance. "Unless you don't want to be embarrassed in front of a bunch of juniors?"

His challenge cut right through all reason and logic. It was physically impossible for a younger sister *not* to rise to her older brother's bait. Shedding my cloak, I hopped the low fence.

I faced Leif and slid my hands along the smooth grain of the staff out of habit. The action helped me find that zone of concentration that allowed me to sense my opponent's movements. This time, my fingers rubbed an ordinary piece of wood. No connection flared to life.

Could I still fight without my magic? Everyone had gathered to watch the match—not the best time to experiment. And Irys's comment about keeping a low profile rose in my mind too late. Oops.

Leif stared at me with an odd expression. His nose wrinkled as if he smelled an offensive odor. Great. Guess I'd have to rely on my training, my experience and the thousands of hours of practice I'd sweated through. My magic couldn't be that vital in my fighting. Could it?

Despite my worries, I clutched my weapon at the third points and twirled the bo into a ready position. As soon as the match started, I advanced, swinging the tip of the staff toward Leif's left temple. He backpedaled and blocked my attack. I aimed for his right temple, then left. Right. Left. Feint right. Rib strike. Leif countered with ease.

"Predictable," he said.

"I'm just getting warmed up."

My next series of attacks aimed for his ribs, then temple. Rib. Temple. Rib. Chin strike. Leif jumped back with a laugh. Then he advanced. I scrambled to keep his thick blade from chopping my bo in half. When he swung at my neck, instead of blocking the weapon, I ducked and swept his feet out from under him. He landed with an oomph.

Pleased, I relaxed my guard. Big mistake. Leif grabbed my ankle and yanked. I joined him on the ground. And the advantage of having a longer weapon ended there. From that position, his machete had a greater range of motion, and within a few strikes, he disarmed me.

Far from being triumphant with his win, concern creased his face. I shook my head and signaled for him to keep his mouth shut. Valek had taught us both hand signals to communicate when talking would give away our hidden positions or our plans to an enemy listening nearby.

He sprang to his feet and gestured to me while addressing the students. "See? A machete can defend against a bo staff if you can get in close. Yelena let me take her down in order to demonstrate to you one way to gain an advantage. Normally, she isn't so easy to beat. That's it for today."

The students picked up the training swords and talked in groups as they returned the weapons to the armory connected to the yard. I wiped dirt from my pants.

Once everyone left, Leif turned to me. "Okay, spill it. What's wrong? You smell…"

Leif's magic smelled people's intentions and emotions. He frequently helped with solving crimes due to his unique ability to sniff out criminals. When we'd been reunited after fourteen years apart, he'd proclaimed to our entire clan that I'd killed and reeked of blood. Nice, eh?

"What do I smell like?"

"You smell like death."

6

VALEK

Valek studied the figure standing behind the Commander. Five feet eight inches tall, about one hundred and forty pounds, either a young male or female—hard to tell when the only thing not covered with black was the assassin's light gray eyes. Armed with a dagger, which was currently pressed against the Commander's throat, but Valek guessed the assassin carried more than one knife.

The Commander frowned with annoyance.

"Impressive," Valek said, sipping his brandy. He tightened his grip on his knife, suppressing his anger at the Commander's security detail for not stopping the intruder. He'd deal with them later.

"Move and I'll slit his throat," the assassin said in a gravelly voice.

Not a natural tone, and Valek suspected the person wished to hide his or her true voice. It was an empty threat. If the assassin had wanted to kill the Commander, he'd have been dead before Valek had turned around.

"I'm not the one you should be worried about," Valek said.

Ambrose moved, grabbing the attacker's wrists, yanking the blade down and away from his body. He spun, trapping the assassin's arm. Within a minute the knife clanged to the floor and the Commander had the intruder at his mercy.

"Good show, old man," he said even though Ambrose was only about seven years older than Valek. "You still have the best knife-defense skills in the Territory. Do you want me to dispose of...that for you?" He set his drink down.

"No," the assassin cried in a higher-pitched voice this time. "I have the right to challenge you to a fight!"

"As soon as you climbed through that window, you gave up all your rights." Valek moved closer and yanked the hood off the intruder.

Unafraid, a young woman glared at him. "You know I had the drop on him. How many others have sneaked in here? None. Come on. Let me show you what I can do with a knife."

"Fine by me. Commander?"

The Commander released her. "Don't take too long, Valek. I've an early meeting." He settled behind his desk.

She glanced from him to the Commander and back.

"Don't worry. He won't interfere."

"How about when I'm about to gut you?" she asked.

"If you can gut him, go ahead," the Commander said.

"Such love. I'm touched." Valek patted his chest. "Pick up your knife," he said to the intruder. He switched his dagger to his right hand and turned his body sideways, keeping the weapon close to his stomach. He bent his left arm and held it in front of him to block any incoming strikes.

She mirrored his stance except she held her knife in her left hand. Ah, a lefty. Interesting. They circled and she slashed. He blocked. She shuffled forward and stabbed. He sidestepped. Recovering quickly, she spun and aimed for his throat. He ducked.

Valek remained on the defense as she tried all her offensive moves. She had learned an impressive number of them

MARIA V. SNYDER

and he'd gotten a few cuts during a couple of her combination strikes. He had to admit, she was fast. Her style of fighting seemed eerily familiar.

A slight swirl of unease brushed his stomach. Knife fighters tended to let their guard down when striking, believing their opponent would be too busy protecting himself to counterstrike. Not her. She stayed tight.

Without warning, Valek switched to an offensive series of jabs and kicks, bringing the level of the fight up a notch. She dodged, blocked and kept up with the speed of his attack.

As they fought, he tested her weaknesses and found little. When she executed a perfect feint and lunge, he cursed as the tip of her blade jabbed his gut. Pain burned and blood seeped, but Valek increased the pressure. After she snaked past his defense again in another near miss, Valek recognized her fighting style.

"You're a student of Hedda's, aren't you?" he asked.

"Save your breath." She advanced with a Janco-like flurry of jabs.

He wasn't winded. But if she kept this pace, he'd be sucking air. Concern grew. He'd managed to slip past her blocks a few times, but years of experience showed him how this fight would play out. It didn't look good for him.

As the fight continued, her style of attacks changed. She fought more like the Commander. Perhaps she had two teachers—a deadly combination. He needed to end this match. The sooner the better.

Fortunately, he had a few tricks up his sleeve. Well, not tricks exactly—he yanked another knife from his right sleeve and attacked with both.

She floundered for a bit, backing up. Then she sidestepped and drew a second knife, as well. While competent with two, she didn't have the same precision and speed.

After a few minutes, Valek lunged and slashed at her mid-section, knocking the weapon from her right hand. He pressed his advantage before she could pull another blade, keeping her arms busy. If Hedda had trained her, she would have three or four more daggers hidden in her clothes.

As the fight continued, she managed to grab another knife. By that time, Valek'd had enough. He stepped back, flipped his weapons over, grasping the blades, and threw them. The hilts slammed into her wrists, numbing her hands. She yelped and her knives clanged to the floor.

Then he shuffled in close and punched her. Hard. With a whoosh, she fell back. He followed her to the floor and pressed one of his favorite daggers to her throat.

"That's..." she panted "...not...fair."

"Hedda must have gotten soft in her old age. When she trained me, the words *not fair* were not part of her vocabulary."

She grimaced. Ah, he'd hit a nerve. Perhaps the young assassin didn't agree with all of Hedda's philosophies.

"Did she send you?" he asked.

Clamping her mouth shut, she stared at him.

"Who trained you?"

The Commander stood and yawned. "While that was entertaining, I must get to bed. Clean up the mess, Valek."

"Yes, sir."

The assassin sucked in a quick breath, showing her fear. Hedda hadn't driven all emotion from the young woman. Which made him wonder if this young pup had finished the training.

"Why are you here?" he asked.

"To kill you and take your place."

That would explain why she hadn't slit the Commander's throat. But he couldn't trust her. He yanked a dart from his belt and jabbed it into her arm.

MARIA V. SNYDER

"Listen up. If what you said is true, then I'll lock you in the dungeon. Escape and find me and we'll talk. There's no need to kill me to take my job. Just show that you're smart, capable, resourceful, cunning, trustworthy, loyal, ruthless and are willing to give your life for the Commander's and the job is yours."

She opened her mouth, but instead of words a soft "oh" escaped her lips as the goo-goo juice pumped through her body. Valek stood, gathered all the weapons and pulled her to her feet. She swayed. He grabbed his drink and downed it in one gulp.

What a night.

Picking up a lantern, he led her to his suite so their conversation didn't bother the Commander. She plopped into a chair and scanned the room with a bewildered expression. "So... much...junk! Are you an assassin or a crow?"

Crouching next to her, he asked, "What's your name?"

"Onora. I'm an assassin. Shh...don't tell anyone."

"How old are you?"

"Twenty."

"Which Military District are you from?"

"MD-2. I escaped."

"Escaped from what?"

"The captain. Shh...don't tell him I'm here."

"Captain who?"

"Cap-pa-tain Timmer, thinks he's a winner, and we must all obey," she sang.

"Why are you here?" he asked again since it was almost impossible to lie while under the influence of the goo-goo juice.

"To kill. *You*, of all people, should know that! King killer."

No doubt Hedda had trained her. "Did Hedda send you?"

"Hedda smedda. Crazy old bat. Stubborn. Stupid. Gone. Gone for good."

"You killed her?"

"I...stopped her. No more assassins."

Ice coated his heart. "She's dead?"

"Right-o! Dead to the world."

Valek stood and fingered his dagger. Hedda had taught him the skills that had kept him alive all these years. Anger and sorrow melted the ice inside him and Valek aimed the tip of the knife at her throat.

He buried the blade into the cushion next to her head. Onora jumped. He could always change his mind. Perhaps after he'd wrung every bit of information from her.

"How did you get into the castle?"

Onora explained in a roundabout rambling way how she slipped past the gate's guards, climbed up the side of the castle, jimmied open a window. "Easy as pie in the oven."

"How did you know where the Commander's suite is?"

"Gotta friend working inside. Shh...sweet soul doesn't know."

"Doesn't know what?"

"Doesn't know I know. I tricked. Have to protect... Have to protect..."

"Protect who?"

She shook her head. "Have to... Have to...protect."

Even with the goo-goo juice, Onora wouldn't say the name of her friend. Frustrating. At least it sounded as if the friend had been an unwitting accomplice.

When Valek was satisfied, he pulled her up and towed her to the guards outside the main door.

"I found an intruder in the Commander's suite," Valek said, handing her over.

The guards straightened as the color leaked from their faces.

"Ha," Onora said. "I found him!"

Valek gestured to two of the men. "Take her to the dungeon. Have Lieutenant Abira strip-search her, check every inch

MARIA V. SNYDER

of her skin for putty, comb her hair for weapons and dress her in one of our coveralls before incarcerating her. Understand?"

"Yes, sir."

"We will discuss this *incident* in the morning."

"Yes, sir."

Before they left, Valek pricked Onora with another dose of goo-goo juice to ensure she'd remain incapacitated until morning. It would be interesting to see if she was resourceful enough to escape the dungeon.

Returning to his apartment, Valek picked up the lantern and searched the first floor. Aside from being filled with boxes and clutter, the three rooms off his living area were empty of intruders. Valek paused at the threshold of the bedroom that had been Yelena's. He'd kept her close to him with the pretense of protecting her. And while she attracted trouble like a sweet cake drew ants, the true reason had been that he had been fascinated by her and wanted her near.

Back then he couldn't touch her and they were together all the time, but now...they were heart mates and apart most of the time. The dusty air scratched at the back of his throat. What if Onora had succeeded and killed him? He'd never see Yelena again. Unless she visited him in the fire world. He huffed with dry amusement. He'd taken Hedda's teachings to heart. His soul was destined for an eternity trapped in the fire world.

He shut the door and climbed the steps to the second floor. It mirrored the first floor with three rooms to the right of a sitting area. More boxes, books and piles of rocks littered the floor. After a quick peek inside the bedrooms, he retreated down a long hallway to the left of the sitting area. A few more chambers lined the right side of the corridor. A stone wall ran along the left. More packed rooms. Empty of threats. The only organized area was Valek's carving room.

Stone dust covered the grinding wheels, worktable and pyramids of the gray stone he used for his carvings. The lumpy rocks were dull and lifeless, but with a chisel, grinder and sand, they transformed into beautiful black statues with flecks of silver. The hours he spent in here not only honed his artistic skills, but his mind, as well. Many times he'd enter with a vexing problem and leave with a solution.

He unlocked the door to his bedroom, then secured it behind him. No windows in this chamber. Glancing under the bed and in the armoire, he relaxed for a moment. Then Valek stripped off his shirt. The cut in his stomach had stopped bleeding. Good. He changed into his black skintight sneak suit. He wouldn't be able to sleep until he checked the castle walls for spiders.

Alighting on the balcony outside his apartment's first-floor living area, Valek flexed his fingers. The combination of climbing up and down the cold stone walls plus the fight with Onora earlier had stiffened his muscles. He had found no other intruders—the good news—but he'd also discovered how Onora had reached the Commander's room—the bad.

The lapse in security would be addressed in the morning. Valek glanced to the east. The sun would be up in a few hours. He headed to his bed, peeled off the sneak suit and slid under the blankets.

Exhausted beyond measure, Valek still couldn't sleep. He stared at the ceiling, mourning Hedda's death. After his brothers had been murdered, he'd searched for a teacher for two seasons. During that time, many people took advantage of him, selling him bad information, tricking him, or outright knocking him down and stealing the money he'd earned when he'd worked at his father's tannery. A hard lesson on whom to trust. No one.

Hungry, sick and drained, he'd spent his last coin on the

MARIA V. SNYDER

slim chance that the street rat did indeed know the location of a teacher. Valek found the remote complex along the rocky coast of MD-1 at the beginning of the warm season. The gates had been secured for the night and he sat on the stoop and waited in the cold damp air that smelled like salted fish. The irony of having searched all of Ixia for a teacher only to end up within miles of Icefaren, his hometown, was not lost on him.

Eventually he passed out on the hard stone for hours or days—he didn't know nor care at that point. Cold water splashed, jolting him awake. The sun was high in the sky. He blinked, wiping his eyes.

A woman in her midthirties with long red hair peered at him through the gate's bars. "You're persistent, I'll give you that." She set the bucket down.

"Are you the mistress of this school?"

"I am. What do you want?"

He stood to face her. His legs shook with the effort, but he met her hard gaze without flinching. "I. Want. To. Kill. The. King."

She studied him. "Ambitious."

At least she didn't laugh at him. A good sign.

"Can you fight?"

"No."

"Have you killed anyone?"

"No."

"Do you have any family?"

"No." His parents had pleaded with him to stay at home and not ruin his life by seeking revenge. He ignored them. When he left, they told him never to return. He was no longer their son.

"Do you have any skills?"

"No."

"Money?"

"No."

"How old are you?"

"Thirteen."

She shook her head. "Scrawny, penniless, homeless and without any redeeming qualities. Why should I accept you as my student?"

"Because I *will* kill the King. And the claim that *you* trained the man who assassinated the King will be a nice feather in your cap."

The humid air thickened around Valek, pressing against his skin like a sticky syrup. She pursed her lips as she stared at him. "Ten days."

"Ten?"

"To prove yourself."

"Thank you."

"Don't thank me yet. If you don't prove yourself—"

"Save it for the next applicant. I won't fail."

Hedda opened the gate and he followed her up a narrow winding path to a sprawling complex of buildings atop a cliff overlooking the Sunset Ocean. The stone walls resembled the grayish-white rocky outcroppings surrounding the complex. The few people working outside wore subdued tunics and pants that also blended in with the landscape.

She made a grand sweeping gesture, indicating the buildings. "Welcome to the School of Night and Shadows. How many people do you see?"

Valek scanned the area, counting. "Ten."

Hedda whistled. Movement exploded and figures jumped, crawled and slid from various nooks and shadows around the complex.

"Now how many?" she asked.

"More than ten."

"Correct. The best assassins are invisible. No magic needed."

MARIA V. SNYDER

When they drew close to the biggest structure—a four-story-high building with balconies facing the sea—Hedda called to a man. "Fetch Arbon. Tell him to meet me in my office."

"Yes, sir." The man dashed away.

Hedda led him into the main building and to an office on the ground floor. Out of the bright sunlight, Valek studied the woman. She wore a soft gray-green tunic and matching pants. Long red eyelashes framed light green eyes.

Gesturing to a chair, she settled behind a pristine desk. Nothing occupied the surface. He glanced around the room. A few tapestries hung on the gray-white-black walls. The color reminded him of seagull droppings. No fire burned in the fireplace. The sparse furnishings held no warmth and he guessed this wasn't her true office, but a place to conduct business with outsiders.

"What is your name?" she asked.

"Valek."

"Tell me why you want to kill the King."

"Does it matter?"

"Very much."

"His men murdered my brothers." Red-hot agony burned in the center of his heart as an image of their bodies flashed in front of him, but he clamped down on his emotions.

She studied him. "Then why not go after them?"

"Oh, they will die, too."

"But that's not good enough?"

"No." He spat the word out. "They murder in his name. The King's corruption has gone too far."

"Did you know the King is a powerful magician?"

"Yes."

"And that he's well protected?"

"Yes."

"And you still believe you can kill him?"

"Yes."

"How much time are you willing to dedicate to this endeavor?"

"As long as it takes. If my last breath is one second after the King's last gasp, I will die a happy man."

Hedda grinned. "One thing at a time. Let's see how long you last, King Killer." She glanced over his shoulder. "Arbon, come in and meet Valek."

A young teen around Valek's age slipped into the room. His black hair had been shorn close to his scalp.

"Take him to the medic then feed him and show him around. He can have Pyo's cell."

"Yes, sir," Arbon said.

"Valek, I'd suggest you concentrate on getting healthy. Once you begin training, luxuries like eating and sleeping are not guaranteed."

Valek smiled at the memory. He had used that phrase—*eating and sleeping are not guaranteed*—a thousand times with the men and women he had trained for his corps. It was as true today as it had been twenty-eight years ago. Of course, then he'd been a stupid kid and had no idea that lack of sleep and missed meals would be the least of his problems. Ah, youth.

Still unable to sleep, Valek pushed off his covers, dressed in his uniform and ghosted down to the dungeon to check on the newest occupant.

The guards snapped to attention and followed protocol to the letter. Everyone was worried about the consequences of the midnight assassin. As well they should be. Valek planned to demote them to privates and send them to guard the diamond mines in MD-3.

A thought occurred to him. What if the new guy...Gerik, was Onora's friend and he'd inadvertently tipped her off to

　　　　　　　　　　　MARIA V. SNYDER

the lapse in security? Even if that was the case, the members of the Commander's detail had been chosen for a reason and their system of double checks should have revealed the gap.

Sleeping off the goo-goo juice, Onora sprawled on the cell's metal bed, which had been bolted to the bars. Her brown braid had been pulled apart and her hair fanned around her face like a messy mane.

"Keep a close eye on her, but don't alert her to the extra security," Valek said to the guard.

"Sir?"

"I want to see if she tries to escape."

"And if she does?"

"Let her go. I'll have one of my corps in place to follow her."

"Yes, sir."

Satisfied, Valek swung by the kitchen to swipe a couple of apples before waking up Qamra and assigning her babysitting duties.

"How good is she, sir?" Qamra asked.

"Don't let her get close to you. Bring your darts and blowpipe."

"Yes, sir." She hopped from her bed.

He left and headed to his office. Qamra had the best aim in his entire corps. He'd put her through the paces, thrown every obstacle and distraction in her way, and she never missed. Valek wished he could say that about all his operatives. Blow in Janco's ear and he'd miss every time. But that was the beauty of training—it exposed the strengths and weaknesses of his corps so he could match jobs to agents.

At Hedda's school, though, she hadn't allowed weaknesses. Every skill had to be mastered before learning another. When Valek had been a student and he'd regained his health, his training began in earnest.

Arbon had shown him the long narrow one-story building then left Valek there without a word. An instructor gave Valek a stone about as big as his thumbnail. The man pointed to a target at one end of the building, then swept an arm out, indicating a series of red marks along the floor.

"Stand on the first mark, closest to the target. When you hit the bull's-eye with that stone at that position ten times in a row, move to the next one. Repeat. When you can hit the bull's-eye from the last mark, you will go back to the first mark and practice hitting the target with a knife. Understand?"

"Yes, sir."

Who would have thought hitting a bull's-eye with a stone would be that difficult? Hours turned into days and, determined to succeed, Valek only stopped when it was too dark to see. Hedda's training methods were simple and effective. No one taught you how to throw the stone. Repetition and practice until calluses coated your hands and you figured out the best way to hit a target.

Valek wished he had the time to train his corps the same way. However, time was always an issue. Back in the days before the Commander's takeover, he had sent promising individuals to Hedda's school to be trained. After the takeover, the Commander wished to incorporate her school into his military. She refused and had retired. Or so she claimed. Obviously she'd lied, and there might be more assassins in Ixia. Yet another detail to investigate.

He unlocked the door to his office. Even with the first rays of dawn creeping in through the square window, it remained too dark to read. He lit the lanterns. Searching through the files, he found the one on Gerik and read through the man's dossier. Nothing popped out at him. Maren had performed a thorough background check.

His door banged open. Valek stood and drew both knives without thought.

"Easy there, boss," Janco said, spreading his hands wide.

"I said to knock. Not to knock the door down." Ari entered.

"I barely touched it. It wasn't latched tight."

Valek returned his knives to their hidden locations and sank into his seat. "Come on in."

They drew closer.

"Is it true?" Ari asked him.

Nice to know the castle's gossip network still worked with lightning-fast precision. "Yes."

"Son of a snow cat!" Janco slapped his thigh. "Did you kill him?"

"Her. And no, I didn't."

Ari and Janco glanced at each other in amazement.

"But she reached the Commander." Janco's voice held outrage.

"He wasn't her target." Valek leaned back in his chair.

Ari smiled. "Possible recruit?"

Or replacement. But Valek wouldn't say that aloud. "We'll see if she escapes the dungeon."

"You want us to hang out near the dungeon, catch her in the act?" Janco asked.

"No. Continue with your assignment, and I'd also like you to nose around and see if you can dig up anything on Sergeant Gerik. He's a transfer from…" Valek consulted the file. "MD-2 about a year ago, and managed to impress his commanding officer enough to be promoted to the Commander's security detail."

"Seems sketchy to me," Janco said.

"Maren approved it. Do you know where she is?" Valek asked.

"No," Ari said. "No one does. She slipped out of here without a word a month ago, leaving Mannix in charge, but all the poor guy's been doing is sorting reports into piles."

"Keep asking around. See what you can discover."

"Yes, sir."

They left and Valek returned to the files. After a few hours, a light tap broke his concentration.

"Yes," he said.

Gerik poked his head in. Strain lined his haggard face, but he kept his voice even. "The Commander wishes to see you in his war room, sir."

"Now?"

"Yes, sir."

Valek straightened a pile of files then followed Gerik out. He locked his door and strode to the war room. Gerik didn't say a word as he trailed behind. The guards waiting near the entrance flinched when Valek approached. White-faced and with eyebrows pinched tight together, he sensed there was more going on than their fear of being reprimanded.

They pulled open the double doors. Valek entered the room.

Onora sat at the table with the Commander, eating breakfast.

7

JANCO

"You know what I can't figure out?" Janco asked. He leaned against the wall despite the grime. They hid in yet another garbage-strewn alley that reeked of piss, tracking potential suspects. Ah, the life of a superspy.

"How to tie your laces?" Ari asked.

"Funny. What I want to know is why sell black-market goods this close to the Commander's castle? Castletown is crawling with soldiers and spies. Why not sell their illegal wares in MD-7 or MD-5 since both are closer to the border?"

"Who says they're not selling there, too?" Ari crossed his arms. "This is a big city full of people. Criminals like to hide in plain sight."

"Yeah. They can be smart until they're stupid."

Ari's mouth opened, but then he closed it. Too bad. Janco enjoyed provoking his partner. It helped pass the time. When they did stakeouts that required silence, it killed him to keep quiet. Worse than magic. No, scratch that—nothing was worse than magic.

"There's the guy with the funky mustache." Janco pointed to a tall man unlocking one of the warehouse doors. "Could be going to get more of those illegal Greenblade cigars."

"Or he's going to warn his boss about the guy who had asked too many questions about those potent cigars," Ari said drily.

"No way. I was smooth. Subtle. More than subtle." He pouted.

"I think you're too recognizable. You should have worn your cap."

"It itches."

Ari sighed. "We'll see what happens next. If they start packing up, we'll know you hit a nerve."

Janco fidgeted. He studied the building. "Why don't we jimmy open that second-story window and slip inside? Better to hear what's going on than guess."

"We've no idea what's inside."

"Exactly."

"What if there're guards?"

"So? Not like we can't handle a couple—"

"And tip them off? By the time we fight our way in, they'll scatter."

"Oh, all right." A few minutes passed without incident. "How about *I* slip inside and you watch for Funky Mustache?"

"No."

Janco groaned. He was a man of action. All this sneaking about… Yes, it was necessary and patience led to results. Usually. But give him a fight over this any day.

Hours, seasons, years must have passed while they watched the door. An ordinary green door with paint peeling from the wood, revealing a yellowish-gold color underneath. Curled chips of paint lay on the ground right in front. Probably from when they installed the lock. A shiny knob and keyhole looked out of place on the weathered wood.

Smart until they're stupid. Install a new lock, but don't bother

MARIA V. SNYDER

to paint the hardware to match the age of the building or bother to clean up.

Janco's hair turned gray as another few years passed—or so it felt to him. According to Ari, two minutes equaled two years in Janco time.

Ari touched his arm as the door swung open. They melted back into the shadows of the alley. Two men exited. Funky Mustache and a big burly brute. They parted, with Funky heading back to the market and Big Brute cutting through the alley to the other side.

"I'll follow the new guy," Ari whispered. "Now's your chance to sneak inside. Watch out for guards. If you see anyone, don't engage. We can always come back later tonight. I'll meet you at the Black Cat Tavern."

"Get inside, avoid guards, don't get married, meet at the Cat. Got it," Janco said.

Ari shot Janco his I-don't-know-why-I-put-up-with-you look and followed Big Brute. Giving Ari a few minutes to catch up to Big B, Janco showed considerable sense by waiting a handful of months.

Janco slipped off his boots, tied the laces together and swung them over his shoulder. Not bothering with the door, he scaled the wall, finding finger- and toeholds in the crumbling mortar of the old brick structure—his favorite type. His least favorite—the marble walls of the Sitian Citadel; those buildings were slick as ice.

When he reached the second-story window, he peered inside. The sunlight reflected off the glass and made it hard to see beyond the sill. Clinging to the bricks with one hand, Janco shielded his eyes until they adjusted to the dimness. The room had a few pieces of office furniture, but was otherwise empty.

After a few minutes, he pushed on the window, testing it. The pane slid up without trouble. Rookie mistake, thinking you were safe on the upper levels of a building. No floor was unreachable. All a thief had to do was climb up or use a rope to climb down.

Janco eased into the room. Puffs of dust tickled his nose and he held in a sneeze. Memories of another sneeze that had revealed his and Ari's hiding spot rose unbidden. He'd never seen Ari so angry. No, wait. There was that other time… His eyes watered as laughter threatened to bubble up his throat. He sucked in a deep breath and focused on the task at hand.

After a quick scan of the abandoned room, he put his boots back on, then grasped the door's knob and slowly twisted. The metal creaked. He paused and listened. Nothing. When the latch cleared the jam, he pulled the door open an inch. Beyond the room was a walkway with a half wall on the opposite side, and past that, thick chains hung from pulleys attached to the ceiling.

No voices echoed or footsteps neared, so he poked his head out and glanced to the left. A few more doors led out to the walkway before it ended. To the right, two more offices and then metal stairs. Lantern light from below flickered on the walls. He ventured onto the walkway and peered over the half wall. Stacks of crates lined the space downstairs. A few had been opened and their contents filled tables along the back wall. As he waited, no one appeared. All remained quiet.

Janco then checked the rooms to the left. All had a thick coat of dust and matched the room he'd entered. The same with the first of the two on the right. However, the door to the office closest to the stairs was locked. Kneeling next to it, he pulled his diamond pick and tension wrench from his pocket and popped the lock in seconds.

He slipped inside and closed the door. The dirty window let in enough sunlight to illuminate the desk, chairs, filing cabinet and liquor cabinet. No dust scratched his throat and

MARIA V. SNYDER

an area rug covered the floor. Nice. Invoices, inventory lists and billing receipts littered the desk. Janco scanned them, but nothing illegal was on the list of goods. No surprise.

Checking the drawers and then the filing cabinet, Janco didn't find anything incriminating. Too bad. He searched for a safe. None in this room. Janco read the labels on the whiskey bottles in the cabinet. Expensive. The man had good taste. He left the office, relocked the door and paused. No sounds from below.

Janco crept down the metal stairs. They creaked with his weight. He then explored the warehouse. Crates stacked three high didn't have any writing or labels on them. The big loading doors had been bolted shut. Wagon-wheel marks on the floor indicated where the four-foot-tall crates must be loaded and unloaded onto wagons by using those chains and pulleys. He found the back door with the shiny new lock. Other than that, nothing appeared out of the ordinary.

Time to check the merchandise. Peering into one of the opened crates, Janco saw bolts of Sitian silk. Another crate held small burlap bags filled with coffee beans. The boxes on the table, however, held a dozen Greenblade cigars. Made from dried honey-tree sap, kellpi weeds and crushed abacca leaves all grown in the Greenblade forest, the cigars caused quite a buzz and seemed to be very addictive. The Commander had banned them as soon as it became obvious they weren't your ordinary cigar.

Janco searched the other open crates, but he couldn't find any more cigars. Perhaps there were more in one of the unopened crates. He stared at a stack and again absently scratched at the place where the bottom half of his right ear used to be. Why fill a crate and risk it being opened and discovered by the border guards? Unless...

He returned to the one with bags of coffee and dug down until he reached the bottom. Nothing. Unless…

Measuring with his arm, he estimated how deep it was inside the crate. Then he straightened and compared it to the height of the box. Bingo! False bottom. Small enough to miss and big enough to fit those boxes of Avibian cigars. Janco suppressed the desire to dance a jig. He'd wait until he hooked up with Ari at the Black Cat.

A metallic snap cut through Janco's elation. Oh no. He dived behind a stack of crates as the back door opened. Strident voices quarreled. Janco counted. Two, three, four, five in all. Maybe they'd be so engrossed in their argument they wouldn't notice him sneaking out. Or maybe they'd all go up to the office and shut the door. And maybe Valek'd assign him to spend a season tanning on the beach. That would be just as likely as the other two.

Janco slid into a more comfortable position. He might be here awhile.

"…it doesn't matter whose fault it is," one voice yelled over the others. "Spread out and find him. He has to be here somewhere."

Then again, he might not.

8

YELENA

"I smell like death?" I asked Leif, trying to keep my panic from my voice. "Whose death? Mine? Yours?"

He tapped his chest and crinkled his nose. "No one's. I just…" Leif waved his arms as if trying to pull in the right word. "It's similar to death. It's a…loss. Something is missing. And there's strong grief, as if someone close to you has died."

Oh. That explained it.

"Are you going to tell me what's going on?" he asked.

Guess he hadn't talked to Mara yet. I glanced around at the training yard. A few students still lingered and a couple kept practicing. Some magicians had the ability to listen from a distance.

"Don't worry. It's not that dire. I'll tell you when I tell Fisk," I said.

"Fisk?"

"Yes, I need both of your help and it'd be easier if I only have to explain everything once. Do you have time now?"

Leif looked at the glass workshop with a wistful expression. "Mara knows."

He turned to me in surprise. "She does?"

"Yes."

"Thanks."

Not the reaction I'd expected. I'd figured he'd be put out because I told Mara first.

"I'm not that childish," he said, correctly reading my look.

I waited.

"At least not this time. I'm glad you confided in Mara. She always feels left out. She doesn't ever say it aloud or complain, but I can smell the disappointment."

"Must be tough."

"It is, but I've a duty to Sitia, and discretion is a big part of it. You should know all about that. I'm sure you can't tell Valek everything. Right?"

"If I said no, would you have me arrested for treason?"

"No."

"Nice to know you trust me."

He pished. "Trust has nothing to do with it. It'd upset Mara and that would upset Mara's mother and then I'd be cut off from the best food in Sitia."

"Ah, food trumps treason."

Leif laughed. "Every time." Then he sobered. "I need to tell Mara where I'm going and to take a quick bath. How about I meet you at the gate in fifteen minutes?"

I sniffed and crinkled my nose. "Make it thirty."

"Ha-ha," he deadpanned before heading toward the bathhouse.

I grabbed my cloak. Since I had the time, I stopped by Irys's office on my way to the gate. She called me in before I could knock. Her office was similar in size to Bain's, but much neater and not as many books.

A red-tailed hawk sat on a perch by the window. He squawked at me in greeting.

"Hello, Odwin. Who's the handsome fellow?"

The hawk flexed his wings, showing off.

MARIA V. SNYDER

"That's right, you are." I stroked his head.

"Don't encourage him. His ego is big enough," Irys said.

"Any news?" I asked.

Irys pushed a strand of black hair from her eyes and leaned back in her chair. "I reviewed the logbooks for the past two weeks, and Quinn hasn't left the Keep. I also talked to him between classes. He said he can't draw magic into the glass. Opal tried to teach him to use the empty glass orbs like she did when siphoning magic, but he couldn't. So far, all he's able to do is make his magic stick to the glass."

"Are you sure he was telling the truth? Maybe Leif—"

"I think I can spot a lie by now, Yelena."

"Sorry." More good/bad news.

"I'm glad he's not involved. And you should be, too. Quinn's a valuable asset."

"I know. I'm being…overly emotional." I huffed. "Do you know at one time I wished I didn't have *any* magic?"

"I'm sure you did. I did, too. We all have. Ask any magician and she will be able to tell you exactly when she wished to be ordinary."

Ordinary. Could I get used to the idea of being ordinary?

"Oh no. Cut that out," Irys admonished. "*You* will never be ordinary. Don't worry, Yelena. We'll find out what happened to you."

"The market closes for supper time. Fisk will probably be at his guild's headquarters," Leif said when he joined me at the gate.

"Is he still at—"

"No. He found a more secure location." Leif glanced around and then lowered his voice. "It's in one of the outer southern rings."

We headed west from the Keep's entrance.

"Let's take the scenic route," Leif suggested.

Ah. Leif wanted to ensure no one followed us.

As we entered the central business district, Leif cut through a couple of alleys and zigzagged through the streets. The sunlight disappeared behind the Citadel's walls and the lamplighters began their nightly ritual.

"Is Fisk still having trouble with that rival gang?" I asked.

"Yes. They're bold and have been trying to put him out of business. Fisk keeps telling me he's taking care of it, but I've heard many shoppers grumbling at the market stalls. Those interlopers cheat, steal and bribe merchants to give them better prices than they give Fisk's members."

A few people hurried past us. Probably heading home for supper. The majority of the Citadel's citizens lived in the northwest and southwest quadrants. However, a number of warehouses had been converted into apartments, which the Keep and government workers had snapped up along with a few business owners who wished to be close to their factories.

"What a shame. That rival gang could have joined his guild and all worked together." Why couldn't they just leave Fisk alone and let his guild operate in peace? Was it jealousy? Greed? Spite? Hate? Probably a combination of all of them.

"I think Fisk is in over his head on this one. Maybe I could ask my brother-in-law for a little favor."

"How can Mara's brother, Ahir, help?" I asked.

"Not Ahir—Valek."

"Valek isn't your brother-in-law."

"Why not? You've been together for... What? Eight million years. And he's, like…eighty by now."

I punched him in the arm.

"Ow!" He rubbed his biceps. "Oh, I see. He hasn't asked you. No wonder you're sensitive."

"Leif," I warned.

He ignored it. "Yes?"

I pressed my fists to my legs. "We've been busy."

"Doing what?"

"Rescuing a kidnapped brother, for one." I gave him a pointed look.

"Uh-huh. Too busy to get married. That's a new one. Does that mean he asked—"

"Drop it."

"Wish I could," he muttered.

And then I understood. "Who put you up to this? Mother?"

He ducked his head. "She just wants you to be happy."

"And why in the world would she think I'd be happier if I was married? If anything, it would make it *harder* to be apart from Valek."

"Maybe she sees how happy I am and wishes the same for you."

Oh.

"And I've been picking up quite a range of emotions from you, sister dear. You're never this easy to read." He turned to me as if he'd just figured it out.

"Wait," I said. "We'll discuss it with Fisk."

By the time Leif was satisfied no one had followed us, we had looped around to the south side of the market. Glancing over his shoulder, he slipped into a narrow alley. I stayed close to him and kept my hand near the hilt of my switchblade. The alley dead-ended.

"Are you lost?" I joked.

Instead of a sarcastic retort, he gaped at me, horrified. Without thought, I yanked my weapon and triggered the blade, turning.

"No one is there, Yelena," Leif said in a tight voice. "You just confirmed what I thought was impossible."

I faced him. He had discovered I no longer had magic. It

hadn't taken him long. Once again, Irys's advice about lying low rose in my mind. Smart woman. Perhaps I should listen to her.

Leif pointed to the side wall. "It's an illusion." He stepped right through the bricks.

Holding my hands out, I followed him. No tingle swept my arms as I entered a dark alcove. Leif rapped a series of knocks on the door and waited. A beam of light shone through a small peephole.

"Kinda late for a visit," a voice said.

"It's never too late to lend a helping hand," Leif said.

The door swung wide, allowing us in.

Momentarily blinded, I stumbled over the threshold.

Fingers grasped my elbow, steadying me.

"Lovely Yelena, always a pleasure to see you," Fisk said, releasing his grip.

My vision adjusted to the brightness. We stood in a foyer. Rooms branched out on three sides. Straight ahead, a fire burned in a small hearth. The enticing aroma of beef filled the air. Leif's stomach grumbled.

I gazed up at Fisk. No longer a boy, he towered over me by a good eight inches. His light brown eyes matched the color of his shaggy hair. Clean-shaven and muscular, he'd filled out quite a bit since I'd seen him last. Except for the impish intelligence in his gaze, he was a far cry from the malnourished, filthy street rat he'd been when we first met.

"Hello, Fisk. How's business?" I asked.

"Never better."

"Are you sure?" I gestured around. "You've moved again."

"That I did. However, we plan to stay here for quite some time. Let me give you a tour."

The room to the right opened up into a large area crowded with bunk beds. Members of the Helper's Guild either sat or

MARIA V. SNYDER

stretched out on the mattresses. Others huddled together, playing a game of dice, and some gathered in groups, talking and laughing. They all called a hello to me and Leif.

To the left of the foyer was a classroom.

"We still have weekly meetings and are always training new recruits." He pointed down a hallway on the other side. "There are a few more training rooms down there. Unfortunately, we had to teach everyone self-defense, and a couple of the older members are learning how to fight with swords and knives."

"That bad?" Leif asked.

"It's getting worse."

"We can—"

"No, thank you. I'm handling it. Once I find their leader, there won't be a problem." The steel in his voice ended that discussion.

I peeked down the hallway. "I'm guessing there are classes in information gathering, as well."

Fisk grinned. "Information can be a profitable business. In fact, I'm pretty sure that's why you're here."

Leif's stomach grumbled again.

Fisk laughed. "That and for a bowl of Amberle's beef stew."

My brother perked up. "If you insist…"

The kitchen and dining area filled the room opposite the foyer. Long wooden tables stretched in rows to the left.

"Wow, these rooms are bigger than you think. How much space do you have?" Leif ladled out a big helping of stew.

"My guild occupies the entire ground floor of this facility."

"Nice. Let's hope the owner lets you stay for a while."

"Oh, he will."

A gleam in Fisk's eyes gave him away.

"You own this building," I said.

"Yup. I'm converting the three upper levels into apartments."

"Wow, a landlord at… How old are you?" Leif asked between bites of stew.

"Seventeen."

Leif spat out a mouthful of beef. After sputtering and coughing, he gasped, "I…need a new job. Are you…hiring?"

"Always. Yelena, are you hungry?" Fisk filled a bowl.

"No, thank you. You were right about needing information. Is there someplace private we can talk?"

"Of course."

Carrying his dinner, Fisk led us through the classroom and down the hallway to the very end. He unlocked a door and ushered us into a large living space. The ceiling spanned two stories over half the room. It appeared a loft had been built over the other half. While a couch, armchairs and tables occupied the center, Fisk had converted the space below the loft into an office.

Fisk sat in one of the nubby red armchairs and cradled the stew in his lap. Leif flopped into the opposite chair without waiting for an invitation and I settled on the couch. A glass sculpture of two life-size hands spread out like wings with their thumbs together rested on the table between the armchairs.

"Is that one of Opal's statues?" I asked Fisk.

"Yes. Lovely, isn't it?"

I gazed at Fisk. Was it one of her magic detectors? The Councilors each owned one but, so far, the distribution of the detectors was limited. "Yes. It matches the design of the necklaces your members wear."

Leif grunted in amusement. He stared at the sculpture with a crinkled brow. Inside the clear glass a spark of light flashed in response to Leif's magic. "Handy."

"Yes, it is. And, yes, Opal gave it to me." Fisk smiled. "You've been hanging out with politicians too long, Yelena. No need to dance around a subject. I'll tell you the truth."

"Sorry. Some habits are hard to break." I gestured to the detector. "Are they available on the black market?"

"No. But fakes are showing up, which means the real thing is probably not far behind."

"Will you let me know when that happens?" Leif asked.

"Of course. Is that why you're here?"

"No." I traced the black-and-white diamond pattern of the couch's fabric with my finger. How to start?

"Then how can I help?" Fisk asked.

Might as well just jump right in. "Have you heard of a drug or poison that blocks a person's magic?"

Leif's spoon froze halfway to his mouth, but he kept quiet. Very un-Leif-like.

"You mean something like Curare?" Fisk asked.

"Yes, but without the paralyzing effect."

He rubbed a hand along his chin. "I haven't heard of anything, and considering it would be an effective weapon against magicians, I doubt the criminal element could keep it quiet for long." Fisk met my gaze. "Are you guessing about its existence or do you have evidence?"

Now who was acting like a politician? "I'm speculating." I explained about the attack.

Leif cursed. "It's worse than I'd thought. Are you all right?"

I gave him a flat look.

"Oh, right. Dumb question. Have you—"

Interrupting him, I filled them in on our efforts to discover the cause of my affliction. "…and we were hoping you might have information," I said to Fisk.

"Sorry, but this is the first I've heard about it." He set his half-full bowl aside. Fisk had stopped eating during my story. "I can make a few discreet inquiries."

"That would be great. What about the assassin? Do you know anyone who has those abilities?"

"Not operating out of the Citadel."

He had answered so fast I asked him if he was sure.

"Unfortunately. Assassins make a point to let my guild members know they are available for hire just in case we get a request. Not that we'd ever help a client hire an assassin, but we keep track just in case."

"Are you still expanding to other cities?" I asked.

He frowned. "No. That's on hold until I settle things here."

"I can help—" Leif tried.

"No." Fisk sighed at Leif's hurt puppy-dog look. "Thanks, Leif, but you're too well-known in the Citadel. I've a couple members on the inside and it's just a matter of time."

"You'll let us know if you need anything?" Leif asked.

"Of course."

Leif turned to me. "You should have told me sooner."

"I just arrived today."

He waved away my excuse. "You're vulnerable and unprotected."

I drew a breath, but clamped my mouth shut before Leif reminded me about our sparring match.

"I can weave a null shield into your cloak, but that's a temporary measure. I'll get you something that will work better."

"Than a null shield?"

Leif glanced at Fisk. "It's similar," he hedged.

Fisk grinned. "The new glass magician can probably make you a glass pendant to wear that will kept a null shield around you at all times."

Red splotches spread over Leif's cheeks. "How did you…? Oh, never mind. At least you didn't hear it from me. Right?"

MARIA V. SNYDER

"Right. You're a vault."

I suppressed a smile over Fisk's word choice. "Then who did you hear it from?"

"Ah, Lovely Yelena, I can't give away my sources. Otherwise no one would trust me."

A light tapping sounded. Fisk excused himself and answered the door. "I'll be right back," he called as he slipped out.

Leif stood. "Give me your cloak."

I shrugged it off and handed it to him. He spread it out on the floor. Kneeling next to the cloak, he stroked the fabric with the tips of his fingers, going from the top of the hood down to the hem, then repeating. The glass hands sculpture flashed and flickered as if agitated. Leif turned the cloak over and continued, touching every inch. A sheen of sweat covered his forehead. He sat back on his heels when he finished, pulling off his short cape. Lines of strain etched his face and sweat stains peppered his shirt.

Scanning the room, I spotted a pitcher of water and poured Leif a drink. He downed the cool liquid in a couple of gulps. When his strength returned, he lumbered to his feet, bringing my cloak with him.

Leif tossed it at me. "Use it for a blanket until I talk to Quinn. You also need a bodyguard. Perhaps Irys can assign—"

"No bodyguard."

He set his square jaw and crossed his arms—did they teach this to all the boys at a certain age?

"You're getting a bodyguard. If not one of the Keep's guards, then who do you suggest?" His posture dared me to argue.

Since he was so determined… "How about you?"

I'd surprised him, but he recovered within a heartbeat. "I can't because I'm going to track down the assassin."

"Leif—"

"Don't 'Leif' me. I have law-enforcement contacts all throughout Sitia. One of them has to have heard about this assassin."

"And you're going to travel to every major city in Sitia?"

"If that's what it takes."

So sweet and impractical. "It'll take seasons, Leif. Seasons away from Mara."

His shoulders drooped a bit.

"Perhaps we should wait until we have an idea of which direction to look. Valek promised to check his sources and send me any information on the assassin he finds."

Leif relaxed his arms.

"And in the meantime, you could be my bodyguard. Plus it wouldn't look strange for us to be together so much."

The stubborn line in his jaw disappeared. I kept my expression neutral. If I gloated, he'd insist on assigning me a big bruiser as a bodyguard.

Fisk returned. Concern creased his face. "I think I know who hired the assassin to attack you, Yelena."

But that was good news. Why did he look so grim?

"Spit it out, Fisk," Leif said.

"Ben Moon escaped from Wirral Prison."

Oh no. I sat on the edge of the couch. "How long ago?"

"Eleven days."

Not long enough to stage the attack.

"The authorities believe he had help," Fisk said as if reading my mind.

Leif and I exchanged a glance. We'd had dealings with Ben before. Not only was Ben a powerful magician, but he had inherited notes on magic from his great-great-grandfather, who had been Master Magician Ellis Moon. Perhaps somewhere in those notes was mention of a substance that blocked magic.

"We should inform the Council," I said.

Fisk's expression darkened. "They already know."

"That's good, right?" Leif asked.

A coldness settled over me. "How long have they known?"

"A few days after he escaped."

Ice crackled through my heart. The Council knew before I left to meet with Valek and they didn't bother to warn me.

9

VALEK

Valek's gaze jumped from Onora to the Commander. Ambrose appeared to be relaxed, unlike his guards who stood behind him with puffed-out chests and stiff backs. They glared at the assassin.

She ignored them as she picked at her food. Onora still wore the dungeon jumpsuit. She'd braided her long brown hair, and her feet were bare. Rough calluses covered her toes and scuff marks scratched her toenails.

"Join us," the Commander said to Valek.

Onora glanced at him as he sat to the Commander's right, but she didn't smirk or gloat. His reaction to her presence flipped between impressed and worried. Had the Commander invited her? Or had she escaped and managed to reach the Commander without encountering anyone?

"Relax, Valek. I stopped your agent...Qamra, is it?...before she could shoot Onora with a dart. I figured since Onora made it that far, she deserved breakfast."

"I was on my way to see you," Onora said to Valek. "Unless what you'd told me last night was bullshit?"

The Commander sipped his tea. His eyebrows rose a fraction, inviting Valek to explain.

"Seems this young pup is after my job. I told her if she demonstrates her abilities, shows cunning, resourcefulness, intelligence, and if she proves she is loyal, trustworthy and willing to die for you, then she could have it."

"And why did you tell her that?" the Commander asked.

"She has plenty of raw talent. Another year of training and she would have beaten me last night. But as I said, there's more to my job than winning a fight."

Again, Onora showed remarkable restraint in keeping her emotions under control. If Valek had told Janco he could have won a fight against him, Janco would have jumped on the table and danced a jig.

"Are you thinking about retiring, Valek?"

Was he? He'd been in this business for years. The thought of not having to worry... A nice thought. Of being with Yelena all the time... A wonderful thought. But he wasn't quite ready. "Not for a while. However, if someone comes along and shows he or she can take my job, I'd be content to let that person have it."

"Trust is the biggest issue right now," the Commander said, gazing at the young woman. "Why didn't you join the military and work your way up through the ranks?"

"Valek didn't have to go through all that. Why should I?"

"You've no idea what Valek did to prove himself," the Commander snapped. "A protocol has been put into place since I've been in charge. I see no reason for you to bypass it."

A brief flash of fear rippled her calm. Valek remembered a comment she'd made last night about escaping MD-2. "Captain Timmer," he said.

Onora jerked as if he'd stabbed her with a knife. Her reaction seemed familiar. It reminded him of how Yelena flinched every time she'd heard Reyad's name. The bastard had raped her and Yelena'd killed him. Saved Valek the trouble of hack-ing the man into tiny pieces and feeding him to a pack of snow cats.

"Tell me," he said.

"No. I'll join the local unit."

"And challenge me again after the first few training sessions? I think not. Plus it wouldn't earn you any trust."

"What can I do to earn your trust?" she asked.

Valek exchanged a look with the Commander. "A series of tests?"

"Do you think she's worth the effort?" the Commander asked.

He studied the young woman. She had been the first to sneak into the Commander's apartment, and she knew how to fight. Plenty of potential. Better to keep her close than risk her making another attempt. Perhaps she'd become a valuable member of their team. Stranger things had happened.

"Yes."

Ambrose dabbed his mouth with a napkin and stood. "I'll leave it to you, then, Valek." He left the war room.

"Tests?" Onora twirled a spoon in her left hand, spinning it through her fingers.

"Yes. You're now an official member of my corps. However, if I find out you haven't been honest about why you are here, you won't be locked in the dungeon. You'll be buried underneath it."

"An empty threat. You said so yourself—it's just a matter of time and I'll beat you."

"True. But if you double-cross us, you won't be fighting just me, but the Commander and a couple of my loyal people. You're good, but not good enough to go against four of us."

"Not yet."

Valek smiled. As Janco would say, gotta love the attitude. "And trust goes both ways, Onora. Something happened to

MARIA V. SNYDER

you up in MD-2. Something traumatic enough to send you to Hedda. I need to know that and how long ago you started your training. How did you convince Hedda to train you? It's all part of what needs to be discussed."

She stilled. "That's none of your business. I'm here to prove what I can do. My past is not relevant."

"Your past is what guided you here. It is your motivation, and I need to know everything."

Onora sprang to her feet. "Why don't you just prick me with that...poison and make me spill my guts?"

"It's called goo-goo juice and it's very effective. Last night you were a criminal. Today you are a new team member. Hard to establish a mutual trust using goo-goo juice."

She stared at him. "And if I don't satisfy your curiosity, you'll use it anyway."

"If this was about mere curiosity, you wouldn't be given this chance."

Lacing her fingers together, she pressed her arms tight to her body. "I'd bet you didn't have to explain everything to the Commander."

"The Commander knows me better than my heart mate. And if I were you, I wouldn't trust rumor and speculation. I didn't beat the Commander in our first fight. He won and could have easily killed me. He still can. With his knife or with an order. That isn't the reason I'm his second-in-command."

"What's the reason?"

"Pay attention and you'll find out. Come on." He strode to the door.

"Where are we going?"

He nodded at her jumpsuit. "To get you a uniform. Nice touch, by the way, hiding lock picks under your toenails." Valek mentally added *check toenails and fingernails* to his growing list of new procedures for the castle's guards.

She covered her surprise. "Thanks."

Valek guided Onora to the seamstress's quarters. Long wooden tables strained under the weight of piles of clothing. Dilana sat in her favorite spot by the window, hemming a pair of pants.

And just like she had done with Yelena, Dilana took the girl in hand and fitted her with the standard plain black pants, shirt and boots the members of his corps wore. After Onora had a stack of clothing, Valek showed her to an empty room in the wing used by his corps.

"Bedding is in the supply closet at the end of the hall," he said. "Meals are served in the dining room. Report to my office right after supper for your first assignment. If you don't know the way—"

"I know the way."

Valek ignored her little dig. "Good."

"What about my weapons?"

"They'll be returned to you tonight."

"And if I take off and disappear?"

"Then you will be considered a criminal again. But I'm thinking you're not the type to run. And besides, what else is out there? Since the Commander's been in power, there hasn't been much work for an assassin, and the few who have survived the takeover have moved to Sitia."

Then it hit him. Perhaps the man who attacked Yelena was an Ixian assassin. Before the takeover, magic was allowed in Ixia. Valek might have the name of her attacker listed in one of his files.

He left Onora and headed straight to his office. The haphazard stacks of files on his desk and the towers of dossiers on the conference table plus the general disarray might give a visitor the impression that he was disorganized. Not so. The mess had been arranged with care and, within the piles, Valek had implemented a system that would help him find the information he needed without having to search his entire office or suite.

After flipping through a heap of reports under the conference table, Valek located the dossier on known assassins. He settled behind his desk and read. Many of the names were familiar. During his years at Hedda's school, he'd met a few others who'd graduated.

When he'd first started his training, he'd known only Arbon. The boy had shown Valek around the complex and had answered his questions. Arbon had arrived at Hedda's a season before Valek and had been working on hitting the target with a bow and arrow, which came after perfecting your aim with a knife. They'd spent hundreds of hours inside the training building together and a friendly rivalry began.

"The knife is supposed to stick in the wood, not bounce off the target," Arbon said to him during one of their daylong sessions. "Can't kill the King let alone a bunny with that weak throw."

Valek ignored the jab and considered Arbon's comment. His throw had lacked power. He needed to strengthen his muscles. That night, Valek found the weight room. The air reeked of sweat and body odor. A few others worked out in the dim lantern light. He didn't know if the four men and two women were students or instructors and they didn't bother to introduce themselves. They mostly ignored him when he headed toward the barbells.

But there was always one big mouth. "Hey, skinny arms, do you want me to call my mother to help spot you?" he asked as the others laughed.

Valek stared at the man. Taller, heavier and with thick muscles, the bruiser would pound Valek into pulp. He kept his sarcastic retort about the man's mother to himself. But someday, he wouldn't worry about whom he'd pissed off. As he lifted the heavy weights, he focused on that future time.

The teasing stopped after Big Mouth realized Valek wouldn't react to his digs and when Valek continued to lift the heavy weights every night despite his sore and aching muscles.

"Gotta respect the dedication," the big bruiser said.

Arbon scoffed at Valek's efforts. "You'll burn out by the end of the warm season."

Curious, Valek asked, "What happens if someone doesn't complete the training?"

"Why? You thinking of quitting?"

"No. Just wanted to know where to send you my condolences."

Arbon's laughter boomed with a deep explosive sound. "Well, then, you roll up your note of sympathy, stick it into a bottle, seal it and toss it over the cliff. When you hear the splash, consider the message delivered."

Harsh. But that explained why information about the school had been hard to find. Those who failed became fish food. And those who succeeded kept the location of their home base a secret. In fact, most of the students kept a low profile and didn't make friends. Valek had no idea how many students trained here, or the number of instructors or graduates, for that matter. The lack of information intrigued more than frustrated him.

Valek's aim with the knife improved faster than with the stone. Arbon claimed Valek would never catch up to him despite the fact Arbon couldn't finish the requirements with a dart. It just added more incentive for Valek. After working with the weights, he grabbed a lantern and returned to put in a few extra hours of target practice. A couple of weeks later, he started dimming the light a little more each night. It made

MARIA V. SNYDER

sense to him. Assassins worked mostly at night. It'd be rare that he'd be aiming at a victim in the bright sunlight.

By the time Valek caught up to Arbon—both working with throwing darts—Valek was sleeping only four hours a day. No one had set a schedule for him, so he slept during the afternoons. Also there were no lessons in fighting or how to be an assassin. On occasion an instructor would arrive to test his aim, but otherwise no one bothered them.

"This is impossible," Arbon said. He stood about thirty feet from the target, but his dart didn't reach.

Valek's efforts to strengthen his muscles showed as he had struck the bull's-eye at thirty feet, but at forty feet the lightweight dart nose-dived five feet short of the target.

"Is this the last weapon?" he asked Arbon.

"I think so. We've done stones, knives, arrows, crossbow bolts and now darts. What's left?"

"Chains, whips, nunchucks."

"You practice with those on a dummy. I've seen the practice area. It's in the building along the edge of the cliff."

Valek hadn't spent too much time exploring the complex. He considered it a waste of time and energy. He'd been given a task and would accomplish it so he could move on.

After Arbon gave up for the evening, Valek continued to throw the darts. No amount of force made any difference. He mulled over the problem. Perhaps there was another way. Valek picked up a crossbow and tried using a dart instead of a bolt.

The force of the string destroyed the dart before it could launch. Valek laughed for the first time since his brothers' murders, and the burning pain that had seized his heart for the past year died down for a brief moment. He returned the weapons to the wall and left the training building, which Valek suspected was only used for the new students to see if the boredom and repetition would drive them away.

A warm breeze blew from the east for a change, carrying the dry scents of pine and earth. Even though it was the heating season, the chilly damp air from the Sunset Ocean kept the temperatures low.

He strode to his favorite spot along the cliff, where large gray boulders jutted over the ocean far below. From this height, the crashing water sounded muted and mild. The white tips of the waves glinted in the bright moonlight.

Smaller gray rocks covered the ground between the path and the outcrop. As Valek crossed them, he concentrated on keeping his weight evenly distributed so the stones wouldn't crunch under his boots. Success was spotty, but tonight he managed only a few cracks.

Grabbing a handful of the rocks, he settled on the edge. His feet dangled and he tossed a bunch of the stones out into the darkness. After a couple of heartbeats, a distant plunk sounded. He absently rubbed two of the rocks together as he pondered the problem with the darts. Nothing sparked. Not even from the heat generated between the stones. However, the action had scraped away the dull gray and revealed a darker color underneath.

Valek pocketed the two rocks and headed back to the target room. On the way, the wind rustled the long green stalks of bamboo that lined the complex's paths. A hollow wooden ring mixed with the shushing of the leaves. He stopped and cursed his stupidity.

After fetching a knife and a lantern from the training building, Valek cut a piece of bamboo from the plant and brought it to his room. Hedda had called it a cell, and if it'd had bars, he'd agree with her. The tiny space held a cot, a table, a chair. It had no windows, a dirt floor and no place to build a fire. By sleeping in the afternoon, Valek stayed warm, but he wondered what he would do in the cold season. Arbon stayed in a cell two doors down. The other three rooms in the one-story structure that resembled a long shed instead of a building were empty. Again Valek thought isolating the new students had been done for a reason.

He worked on his piece of bamboo until the sides were smooth and straight, and the inside was completely hollow. Sap coated his fingers and the blade of the knife, but he was careful to keep the sticky substance from getting into the center of the bamboo.

Once he was satisfied with it, he returned to the target room to test out his new blowpipe. Starting at the first red mark, he loaded the bamboo with a dart, aimed, then blew out a quick puff of air. He smiled. Much better.

When Arbon arrived after dawn, Valek hid his blowpipe. The boy had once again shaved his hair close to his scalp. White skin shone through the black stubble and looked odd on top of his round face.

"Did you get any further last night?" Arbon asked.

"To sixty feet," Valek said.

"Liar."

"How about a bet?"

"All right. What's the bet?"

They both owned nothing of value. "How about if I hit the target with the dart, you owe me a future favor, and I'll owe you one if I don't?"

Arbon agreed.

Valek stepped up to the sixty-foot mark, whipped out his blowpipe and hit the bull's-eye.

"That's cheating!" Arbon cried.

"No, it isn't. I never specified how I'd accomplish it."

"But—"

"But what, Arbon?" Hedda asked. Clothed in black, she stepped from the dark corner of the room.

Valek wondered if she'd been there all night. Did she often hide there? His heart rate increased.

"The task was to…" He stuttered to a stop as Hedda moved closer to him.

"To what?" she asked.

"To hit the target, sir."

"Exactly. Did anyone tell you *not* to improvise?"

"No. No one told us anything!"

"Are you not satisfied with the training?" A cold flatness settled on her narrow face.

"I'm…I'm…fine."

"I see." She turned to Valek. "So, King Killer, you're still here."

"Yes, sir."

"Let's see what you can do from the last mark."

He grabbed the weapons and demonstrated his skills, hitting the bull's-eye with the stone, knife, arrow, bolt, but not the dart. He didn't have enough air to send the dart that far.

"How would you make it go further?" she asked.

He sensed it wasn't an idle question, so he considered the problem carefully. More air would work, but his lungs only held so much and he doubted he could generate more force. A longer pipe would help improve aim, but again the amount of air remained the same. Then he remembered how his father rigged the water pipes coming into the tannery so the water pressure increased as the diameter of the pipe decreased.

"A longer blowpipe with a smaller exit hole," he said.

"Arbon, does that sound right to you?"

"Uh…I'm not sure, sir."

"Sounds like you need to do some experimentation. See if you can make his suggestion work in hitting the target from a hundred feet."

"Yes, sir."

MARIA V. SNYDER

"Valek, come with me." Hedda strode from the room.

Valek followed, staying a step behind.

"You passed the first test. Let's see how you do with the second." She led him to the main building and up to the first floor, which was a wide-open area filled with mats and people sparring with and without weapons.

Excitement built deep inside him, but he was careful not to let it show on his face.

"You'll start with self-defense techniques and basic moves. When you have mastered them, you will learn how to use a weapon. Tamequintin will be your instructor. If Tamequintin isn't happy, I'm not happy. Understand?"

"Yes, sir."

She called a young man over. He appeared to be in his early twenties. Tamequintin's long black hair had been braided into a single rope down his muscular back. He wore a pair of short black pants and nothing else.

Valek noticed his smooth gait. It reminded him of a snow cat about to pounce. Unfortunately, since he'd lived near the northern ice sheet, he'd seen plenty of snow cats.

Hedda introduced them and left.

Tamequintin studied Valek for a moment. "So you're the wannabe King Killer, eh? Hedda must be getting desperate for recruits."

Valek refused to rise to the bait. Instead, he waited.

The man grunted. "Call me T-quin. Everyone does except for Hedda and only because she earned the right." He scanned Valek from head to toe. "Do you know how to fight?"

"No."

T-quin grunted again. "You will, or..." He shrugged. "You won't. And then you'll be shown the exit. Be careful. That first step's a killer."

Valek remembered T-quin's black sense of humor. Of course,

he hadn't appreciated it when T-quin had beaten him over and over for weeks. Too bad Tamequintin had refused to join Valek's corps after the takeover. And when he'd gone after Yelena, Valek had to kill him.

Reading through the dossier of Ixian assassins, Valek found only one potential suspect. And that was his old friend Arbon. And Arbon still owed him that favor.

MARIA V. SNYDER

10

JANCO

Boots pounded on the floor of the warehouse. Janco pressed against the side of the shipping crate, considering his chances of getting away. Five of them to one of him and they knew he hid somewhere inside.

Not liking his odds, Janco scanned the area. Stacks of crates loomed behind him and the two stacks in front of him blocked him from view. But not for long. He glanced at the metal stairs across an open expanse a few yards away. Should he risk it? One of the men raced up the steps to search the offices. He liked the odds way better against one opponent than five.

"Here," a voice called from the right. Stepping around the crate, the man pulled his sword and advanced on Janco.

The stairs it is. He moved left until another man slid between Janco and escape. The new guy called for someone named Stig, and the guy who'd just been on the second floor clattered back down.

"Come on, buddy," Stig said. "You're surrounded. Put down your sword and let's have a chat."

Janco glanced over his shoulder. Big Brute had joined his friend. If Big Brute was here, then where was Ari? When he turned back to Stig, Funky Mustache stood with the others. Lovely. *Come on, Ari. Where are you?*

He tightened his grip for a moment, then sighed. Sheathing his weapon, he palmed a couple of glass balls. Janco leaned against the crate and crossed his arms. "What would you like to chat about?"

"Why you broke into our warehouse," Stig said.

"Oh that?" Janco waved a hand. "Just testing your security, gents. And I must say it sucks."

"Uh-huh. And why are you so interested in our cigars?"

"I like a good smoke from time to time. Just wanted to make sure the merchandise is genuine."

"He's lying," Big Brute said. "He's that Franco sneak from the castle. Kill him now or he'll report us to Valek."

"It's *Janco*, you moron. And Valek already knows all about your operation."

"He's bluffing." Big Brute inched closer. A pair of nasty-looking hatchets hung from his belt.

The smell of ripe meat assaulted Janco's nostrils. Ugh. Big. Annoying. And smelly. *Anytime now, Ari.* Janco shrugged. "Go ahead and think what you like. But if I'm not breathing when Valek shows up, he'll be extremely put out. I'm his favorite sneak."

"Yeah, sure you are." Stig strode toward him. "We'll let the boss decide." He reached for Janco's shoulder.

A loud crashed echoed. The men jumped. *About time.* Janco spiked the two glass balls into the ground. The chemicals inside the balls mixed and formed a thick white fog. Janco scrambled up the stack of crates, keeping above the cloud. He stood on the top and jumped up, grabbing the chains that hung from the ceiling.

Below him voices shouted. Janco swung from chain to chain, heading toward the exit. Ari guarded the broken door

MARIA V. SNYDER

with his broadsword in hand. One of the smugglers staggered from the smoke. Before the man could react, Ari stepped in close and knocked the guy out with the hilt of his sword.

When Janco reached another stack of crates, he dropped onto the top, then climbed down, landing within sight of his partner.

"Playtime is over," Ari said.

Big Brute rushed from the thinning fog.

"Awww, can't I stay just a little longer?" Janco pulled his sword with a flourish.

Yanking a hatchet from his wide leather belt, Big Brute aimed for Janco.

Janco jigged to the side as the weapon whizzed by his ear. "A hatchet? Really? You're taking this whole lumberjack thing way too seriously."

He pulled another, but then stumbled forward with a dart in his neck, collapsing onto the ground.

"Hey, no fair," Janco said to Ari. "He was mine."

"Take your pick." Ari nodded in the opposite direction.

Stig, Funky Mustache and the other man emerged from the dissipating fog. White tendrils of smoke clung to their clothes, and fury burned in their expressions.

"Ooh, I'll take Funky Mustache and Stig. You get that other dude." Janco slid his feet into a fighting stance.

Ari sighed. "Here." He handed Janco a couple of darts.

"You're no fun."

"I hurt my shoulder busting the door down."

Which had given Janco the distraction he needed. "All right. We'll do it your way *this time.*"

He aimed the darts and hit Stig in the throat and Funky Mustache in the cheek. Janco backpedaled as the two men continued to charge, ducking Stig's swing and countering Funky Mustache's sword thrust. After a few seconds the sleeping juice kicked in. They swayed on their feet, took a few wobbly steps and plopped to the ground.

"What took you so long?" Janco asked Ari.

Ari gave him a sour look. "They were onto us from the very beginning. The big guy lured me away so you would sneak in. Then he picked up some friends and doubled back. I waited to see if you'd give them the slip, but when you didn't climb out the window, I came in."

"Guess I should have worn my cap." He scratched his head. Just thinking about it made his scalp itch. Maybe Dilana could sew him another one with something…nonitchy.

"I don't think that would have helped. What did you find?"

Janco showed him the cigar boxes and the crates' false bottoms. "There's an office upstairs with lots of paperwork. It looked legit, but I'm not an expert."

"Let's report back and send a cleanup crew." Ari pricked the two men he'd knocked unconscious to keep them from reviving before the crew arrived.

Picking up the pieces of the broken door, Ari leaned them against the wall. It had split right down the middle. They searched for supplies to repair it at least temporarily. No sense having the local thieves clean the place out. By the time they'd left the warehouse and headed back to the castle, the sun had set.

One of Ari's comments nagged at Janco. "How did you know they were onto us from the beginning?"

Ari waited until a group of people passed out of earshot. "I think these guys and that warehouse are all part of the ruse. The smugglers want us to uncover this operation to keep us from finding the *real* operation."

"You think they had us marked as soon as we left the castle complex?"

"Yep."

MARIA V. SNYDER

"We need better disguises."

"And better intel. Let's see if Valek's discovered any new info."

Valek called, "Come," when they knocked on his office door.

Candles blazed, revealing Valek sitting cross-legged on the floor with file folders scattered around him.

"Organizing?" Ari asked, sounding doubtful.

Despite what Valek claimed about his filing system, Ari and Janco were not convinced there had been any logic applied to the piles.

"No. I'm searching for replacements." Valek flipped open a folder. "What do you think of Sergeant Hunter?"

"For what?" Janco asked.

"The Commander's new personal guard."

Ah. Time for the comeuppance. "He's a bit stiff, but dependable," Janco said.

"Smart and ambitious," Ari added. "He won't be content to be a sergeant for long."

"Hmm. I'll add him to my 'maybe' pile." Valek placed the folder on the middle of three stacks. Then he stood and wiped the dust off his black pants. "Do you have news for me?" He scooped up the three piles and carried them to his desk.

"Yes, sir," Ari said. He explained about the warehouse and smugglers. "I asked Deet to send a cleanup crew so we can interrogate them later. But overall, they were too easy to find."

"A fake operation?" Valek asked.

"No. They're selling illegal goods, but it's mostly minor stuff. We can see what the smugglers say, but I'm thinking we need an undercover operative that's not recognizable."

Janco pished. "A good disguise—"

"Won't be enough," Ari said. "They know us too well."

"As in, there's a mole in our operations?" Valek asked.

"That's always a possibility, but this seems more like they've been watching us and keeping track of our whereabouts. Like we do with the minor criminals that we don't arrest, but use to find the more dangerous ones."

"That matches what I've been thinking." Valek drummed his fingers on his desk. "And I may have the perfect operative to work with you. She's a complete unknown. That is, if she shows up."

Janco didn't like the sound of that. Not at all. "Who?"

Instead of answering, Valek picked up one of the files. "What do you think of Private Krist for the Commander's guard?"

Ari and Janco exchanged a glance. Valek would tell them whom he had in mind when he was ready. They discussed personnel and who had the best skills to protect the Commander until a light tapping on the door interrupted them.

Valek tensed before he invited the knocker into his office. Janco's fingers caressed the hilt of his favorite dagger as he turned to see who entered. A young girl approached. Seventeen—maybe eighteen. Her graceful strides seemed familiar. Her gaze flicked between him and Ari, sizing them up. Pretty with light gray eyes. However, no warmth emanated from them. When she neared, Janco changed his estimate of her age to twenty.

"This is Onora. She's going to be working with you," Valek said. "This is Ari and Janco, my—"

"*Current* seconds-in-command," she said.

The challenge in her voice pricked the hair on the back of Janco's neck. "Are we that desperate for recruits we need to hire children?"

She glared but didn't rise to the taunt. Too bad.

"Is she the one?" Ari asked Valek.

MARIA V. SNYDER

"Yes. And she's going to be working with you to find the brains running the smuggling operation."

"Seriously? What's she gonna find? A lollipop and Binky?" Janco laughed at his own joke.

Without warning, Onora palmed a knife and pressed it to Janco's throat in one quick motion.

His smile widened. "Ooh, I like her."

11

YELENA

Anger boiled up my throat as Leif cursed the Sitian Council.

He prowled around the couch and chairs in Fisk's sitting room. "Why wouldn't they warn you about Ben's escape? Are they insane?"

"Perhaps they believed he wouldn't have time to set up an ambush for Yelena," Fisk said. "He's running from the authorities. Even with help, their focus would have been on escaping and not revenge."

"And they promised Valek that Ben would be incarcerated for life in a special wing of Wirral built to block a magician's power," I said. "If they'd told me, I might have informed Valek."

"That's stupid," Leif said. "Why risk Yelena's life? She's valuable."

"Perhaps they thought in the unlikely event she is attacked, she is more than capable of protecting herself," Fisk said. "Plus you were with Valek, right?"

My fury eased a fraction. "Yes, but it happened before I'd reached him. And they wouldn't have known the assassin has this new...poison."

"Are you sure about that?" Leif asked. "They're already keeping secrets and that would be a giant secret. Think about it."

Fisk agreed. "The Council is afraid of magicians. They have been since Devlen switched Councilor Moon's soul with her sister's. They all have a magic detector to make sure no one is influencing them with magic. So it's not a big leap in logic to assume that if they've learned about this power-blocking poison, the group they keep the news from is the magicians."

Fisk's speculation rang true to me. We needed to find out how much they knew.

"Has the Council had any recent closed-door sessions without the Master Magicians?" I asked.

"That's illegal," Leif said. "All members must be in attendance."

"How about an informal get-together?"

"That's harder to determine. The Councilors frequently meet in small groups, but nothing official is supposed to be decided."

"And I haven't heard any rumors about secret meetings," Fisk said.

"What about our Councilman, Bavol Zaltana?" I asked Leif. "Would he tell us?"

"It would depend on how much we're willing to divulge to him," he said. "If he knows you've been poisoned, he'd probably give us any information he has. But if we're vague and ask about a potential substance, he might clam up."

Uneasy about having yet another person know about me, I considered my options. "The attack on me could have been sanctioned by the Sitian Council. They've always been leery of me and my abilities. If they neutralize me, they no longer have to worry about me. Although you'd think they'd've learned to trust me by now."

"Now you're being paranoid," Leif said. "We'll talk to Bavol. But we'll call it clan business."

"And why would it matter what we call it?"

"Loyalty to clan members is important to Bavol. Besides, the Council doesn't need to know about this poison right now as long as the Master Magicians are aware of it."

I'd argue we'd gotten into trouble before by not informing the Council, but the thought of them not warning me about Ben Moon didn't give me any warm and fuzzy feelings toward them.

"All right. Bavol should be back at his place by now. Let's go pay him a visit before we return to the Keep."

We said goodbye to Fisk. He promised to gather any information he could about the assassin and poison.

When I wrapped my cloak around my shoulders, it felt like putting on armor. Just knowing it protected me from magic eased my biggest fear. I resisted the temptation to pull the hood over my head. The night air wasn't that cold.

The lamplighters had finished their nightly task. Bright yellow pools of light painted the streets. Not many people lingered in the central business district after the market closed and the factories reduced their production levels for the evening. We navigated the quiet streets, heading east toward the government quarter, where the Council Hall and housing for the Councilors and their aides was located.

As we neared Bavol's town house, memories of the time I'd had to sneak into his kitchen rose unbidden. The Daviian Vermin had taken over the Sitian Council, there had been a price on my head, and I'd needed Bavol's help.

When we reached his front stoop, I kept walking, pulling Leif with me.

"But—"

"Let's go around back," I whispered.

"There's no one in sight."

I gazed at him.

"Oh, all right, but I still think you're paranoid."

"I prefer to call it being cautious."

He snorted, but followed me for a few more blocks. After a quick glance over my shoulder, I ducked into the alley behind the row of town houses and doubled back to Bavol's rear entrance.

I peered through the kitchen window. Petal, his housekeeper, scrubbed pots. Tapping on the door with my knuckle, I stepped back as she opened the door.

Petal's wide face creased with first alarm then concern when she recognized me and Leif.

"Oh my, you gave me such a fright!" Petal ushered us inside. "Come in, come in. What kind of trouble are you two in now?"

"Seems you have a reputation, dear sister," Leif muttered.

"I believe she was referring to you as well, *dear* brother." I turned to Petal. "No trouble. We just wanted to visit our clan's leader without alerting the entire quarter. You know how nosy the other Councilors and their aides can be."

"That I do. They're the worst gossips. But give an old lady some credit, child. An unannounced visit through the back door only means one thing. Trouble."

No sense arguing with her. "Is Bavol in?"

"He's in his office. I'll go fetch him. Would you like something to eat or drink while you wait?"

Leif opened his mouth, but I said, "No, thanks."

She led us into the front parlor and we settled on a pair of turquoise-and-silver armchairs while she ascended the steps to the second floor.

"You didn't need to answer for me. Petal makes the best jungle soup—even better than Mom's." Leif pouted.

"You ate at Fisk's. How can you be hungry?"

"It's not about being *hungry*. It's about the combination of spices and the explosion of flavors inside your mouth."

My stomach roiled just at the thought of jungle soup. One of the favorite dishes of the Zaltana Clan, it contained leaves and flowers from the Illiais Jungle, where our clan lived. To me, it tasted like pulpy rotten coconut mixed with vanilla and lemons. Yuck.

Bavol followed Petal into the room, his wide smile at odds with her worried frown. She clutched her apron in her hands before disappearing into the kitchen.

"What a pleasant surprise," Bavol said.

Gray had almost covered all his hair, and he was a bit stockier since I'd last seen him.

"Yelena, I didn't know you were back from your vacation already." Bavol sat on the couch.

"There was a change in plans." I studied his expression. Suddenly, I wanted to know if he'd tell me about Ben Moon.

"Oh?" His smile remained, but a slight wariness crept into his gaze.

"I was attacked on the way to our cabin."

"Oh, that." He brightened with relief.

Interesting reaction.

"I've heard. Nasty ambush." Bavol tsked.

"You heard I was attacked, but didn't know I had returned to the Citadel?"

Leif shot me a warning look. Bavol was the leader of our clan and I was cross-examining him like a criminal. Too bad. Bavol should have told me about Ben Moon.

"Yes…well…Master Magician Bloodgood reported the incident this afternoon, but I assumed you remained at your cabin with Valek. Er…how are you feeling?" Bavol asked.

MARIA V. SNYDER

"I'm fine. I wanted to ask you if you had any idea who might be behind the attack."

"No, sorry," he said too quickly. "We discussed this at the Council meeting. And while we listed a number of suspects, we didn't think any of them could have pulled it off."

Leif stiffened, but kept his mouth shut. Even I sensed Bavol had lied to us. Why? And did I call him on it or ignore it?

"Who were the suspects?" I asked.

"Uh...you know...the usual..."

Oh joy, I had *usual* suspects—I should write a letter to my mother. I waited for him to continue.

"You know...Valek's enemies, the relatives of the Cloud Mist men you arrested during that sting operation, and Lyle Krystal, who you exposed as a fraud."

"Oh yeah. I'm good at spotting liars."

Bavol squirmed.

"Okay, Bavol, what's really going on?" Leif asked.

"What are you talking about?"

"Come on. It's *us*. Besides, we already know about Ben."

He leaned forward. "That's classified. How did...? Did you read my mind?" Bavol peered at me. Suspicion narrowed his eyes.

"No." I stared at him. "Why didn't you tell me?"

"The Council—"

"I don't care what the Council decided. I needed to know. Why didn't *you* tell me?"

"I can't go against the wishes of the Council."

Again I waited. He'd gone against their wishes in the past.

Bavol sighed and sank back against the cushions. "Councilor Moon promised he'd be caught and they didn't want anyone to panic."

"And they didn't want Yelena informing Valek, right?" Leif asked.

He didn't answer, which meant we'd been right. The Council still didn't fully trust me despite all I'd done for them over the years.

"I keep Sitia's secrets along with Ixian secrets," I said in a tight voice. "I'd only alert Valek if I had information that Ben planned to travel to Ixia to hunt for the Ice Moon. Do you know if Ben targeted me? Or what he might do now that he's free?"

"We don't think he's behind the attack. As for his plans, he's too busy running and hiding right now."

"Anything else you *can't* tell us?" Leif asked. "Perhaps another escaped criminal? Or a new drug on the black market? Or an attack of rabid Valmurs?"

Bavol shook his head. "We've had an increase in black-market goods and haven't been able to track the source down yet. But other than that…just the usual crises and bickering between the clans."

I stood. "Thank you for your time."

Leif joined me.

"Wait. How did you find out about Ben?"

"Sorry, we can't reveal our sources," I said. "However, I will tell you that Valek probably already knows." I held up my hand. "Not from us or our sources but one of his spies in Fulgor. Despite all my efforts, there are still a few in all the major cities of Sitia. And after finding out the Council had kept vital information from me, I'm glad there's a network of spies that I can tap into."

I strode into the kitchen and said goodbye to Petal, who handed Leif a steaming bowl and spoon.

"You're the best, Pet." He pecked her on the cheek. "I'll bring the bowl back tomorrow licked clean."

She giggled.

I shook my head as we left. "Does everyone feed you?"

MARIA V. SNYDER

"Only the nice ones." He slurped the jungle soup as we headed to the Keep.

Exhaustion pulled on my muscles. My legs weighed a hundred pounds each. It'd been a long day and I wasn't sure if I'd accomplished anything or not. When Leif finished his second supper, I asked about his take on the conversation with Bavol.

"He doesn't know about the magic-blocking poison," Leif said.

"How did you figure that out?"

"When I listed those other threats, I didn't smell a reaction to the one about the new drug or the attack of rabid Valmurs, for which I am grateful—those little devils have sharp teeth."

Ah. Leif had used his magic. "But he did say there were more illegal goods for sale."

"Yes, and I think that's my next assignment from the Council."

Irys had also mentioned he would be needed soon. "Guess that means we need to leave town as soon as possible."

"Field trip to Fulgor?"

"Yes. We can also visit Opal and see if she has any ideas about my problem."

But first to bed. Leif and I agreed to meet at the Keep's stable at noon tomorrow. We both needed to wrap up a few things in the morning.

Irys wasn't in her tower, so I slogged up the three flights of stairs and collapsed into bed, covering my entire body with my cloak. I pulled my switchblade and slid the weapon under my pillow. Not paranoid. Just cautious.

The next morning, I visited Bain and surprised him when I opened his office door without knocking. He started and spilled a bottle of ink. I rushed to apologize and help clean up the mess. Nice to know the null shield woven into my cloak worked against a master-level magician.

He waved my apology away. "I am more glad you are protected than upset over another stain on my desk. As you can see, it blends right in. Now sit and tell me what you have learned."

I updated him on everything except for the news about Ben Moon. "In other words...nothing."

"That is not true. You've ruled out a number of possibilities. We are narrowing down the routes to an answer."

I asked him how the meeting with the Council went.

Bain played with the fraying threads on the sleeve of his robe. "Not as expected."

Good or bad? I waited.

"Of course they were upset and tossed about a few names of suspects. But no one offered to investigate through their clans. Odd."

I studied Bain, his white hair a messy cloud around his head. Did he know about Ben? "Do you think they sent an assassin after me?"

"Oh no, no."

"But how would you know? They're all protected by null shields during meetings. They can lie with abandon."

Bain straightened as if affronted. "My dear child, I can spot a liar without using my magic. And I can also sense when a person is holding information back." He gave me a pointed look.

"So I'm not supposed to withhold information, but you can if you call it Council business?"

"What are you referring to?" His hard gaze slid past my shoulder.

I turned in time to see Irys stride into his office.

Fury sparked in her eyes. "She is referring to Ben Moon's rescue."

"Who?" Bain asked.

As Irys explained, the tight lump in my throat lessened. Always a relief to discover that your mentor and friend hadn't been lying to you.

"The Council has kept this from us, Bain. And this isn't the first time."

He pulled at his sleeve. "No, it is not. But it is the first of this magnitude."

"We should ban null shields from our meetings."

"For what purpose? We are not allowed to rifle through their thoughts. It's against the Ethical Code."

Irys growled in frustration. "We need more master-level magicians!"

"While I agree there is always need for more, why do you think they would help in this situation?"

"They'd aid in changing the sentiment in the Council."

"What sentiment?" I asked.

Irys leaned against Bain's desk. "The anti-magician sentiment." She threw her arms wide. "With all the discoveries about how to neutralize us—Curare, null shields, voids—they believe we're weak and vulnerable and corruptible."

Her comment slammed into me almost as hard as the arrow. "How could...? What...?" Unable to pull together a complete sentence, I shut my mouth.

"The convenience of certain magicians, like healers, has been such a part of their daily life they don't consider them special anymore," Bain said. "And the troubles we have had with other rogue magicians like Owen, Kangom, Roze, Ferde, Galen, Walsh, and Devlen while he was addicted to the blood magic, have tarnished all our reputations."

Wow, that was quite the list. And what did it say about

my life that I knew them all? "What about the ones before I came to Sitia?"

"Oh, we've always had troublesome magicians," Irys said. "But it seems since the border with Ixia has been…opened, for lack of a better word, the incidents have increased."

The trade treaty with the Commander happened around the time I'd returned to Sitia after a fourteen-year absence. Had I been the catalyst?

Irys swatted me on the shoulder. "Stop furrowing your brow. You're not responsible. The rediscovery of blood magic and Curare also matches the timing of the Commander's treaty. So it would have happened if you were here or not."

I gave her a grateful smile. She knew me so well.

"And I suspect the Councilors are frustrated with not being in direct control of the super messengers and Opal's magic detectors," Irys said. "They believe both items should be considered property of Sitia. Two clans, Cloud Mist and Jewelrose, have been very vocal about it. I suspect their richer citizens have been pressuring the Councilors. And there have been rumors about the need to control magicians—to use us like an army instead of letting each be free to do our own thing."

"The problems created by the Council are never ending. That is not why Yelena is here," Bain said. "Did young Fisk have any ideas?"

"No." I filled them in. "Have you learned anything?"

"Not yet," Irys said. "I'll send a message to Pazia this afternoon."

"Where is her glass factory?" I asked.

"In her family's compound near Ognap. Why?"

Ognap was a five-day journey east of Fulgor. "Don't send that message. I'll pay her a visit."

Irys crossed her arms, waiting.

"You told me to keep a low profile, so I'm leaving for Fulgor today."

"My advice meant you should remain in your rooms, reading books, catching up on sleep and avoiding danger. Remember those things?"

"Yeah, well...that's not going to happen anytime soon."

"Do you really think you'll learn Ben's whereabouts when the authorities haven't?"

"Who says I'm chasing after Ben? I'm going to talk to Opal, see if she has any thoughts about my condition. Then I'll visit Pazia and my father."

"Uh-huh."

"I'll be protected. I'm taking Leif."

"The Council has an assignment for him. I'm supposed to tell him."

"Sorry, he just left. Guess you'll have to tell him when he returns."

"Not funny." She huffed. "I should go with you, too."

"You're welcome to come along."

Bain cleared his throat. "That would be ill-timed. We have—"

"Council business. I know. How about taking along another magician for added security?"

"Who do you have in mind?"

Irys covered her surprise. Guess she'd thought I'd give her more resistance. Normally, I would. These weren't normal times.

"Let's see... There's your friend Dax."

"No. I need him to help research Yelena's problem," Bain said. "Plus he's teaching classes."

Too bad. Traveling with Dax would have been fun.

"And Zebb won't leave Councilor Moon's side." Irys rubbed her temples as if she had a headache. "Hale's between assignments. He proved himself when Opal was having all that trouble."

"Does he have a Sandseed horse? We're planning on traveling through the Avibian Plains as much as we can." Plus the Sandseed's magic in the plains would prevent anyone from following us.

"I don't think so, but talk to the Stable Master and see if he'll allow Hale to borrow Garnet."

I gave her a flat look.

"Oh, all right, tell him I sanctioned it."

"I can't believe you're afraid of the Stable Master!"

"I am not."

I laughed at how childish she sounded.

Irys smiled back. "What else do you need from us?"

I sobered. "Just keep searching."

"You got it. And I'll tell Hale about his new mission. When do you plan to leave?"

"Noon." Which wasn't that far off. I said goodbye to Bain and Irys and hurried to finish getting ready for the trip.

I stopped in the message office on the ground floor of the administration building and sent a note to Valek. Using the code we'd developed just for this purpose, I informed him about Ben just in case he hadn't heard and listed my travel plans. There was no need to worry him about my condition. At least, not yet.

After I collected my backpack, I headed to the stable. When I arrived, Leif stood next to Rusalka. He smirked as he watched a man arguing with the Stable Master. The man had close-set eyes, short black hair and a high forehead. Probably Hale.

"...you can't have him, you idiot," the Stable Master said. "I don't care who you are or what you're doing. He's—"

I interrupted them. "Hale's coming with us on an important mission."

　　　　　　　　MARIA V. SNYDER

Leif made a choking sound. His smirk disappeared.

"Do you have any Sandseed horses he can...borrow?" I asked. "We're going to be traveling through the plains."

"Ah hell." The Stable Master ran a hand through his mane of hair as if smoothing it down. If anything, he made it worse. "Why didn't the...he say so?"

"He just received his orders from Second Magician, so I'm sure he's a bit out of sorts." I shot Hale a significant look.

The Stable Master stomped over to Garnet's stall. "If he'll let you saddle him, then he's up for the trip. If not, then you're out of luck." He scratched him behind the ears. His features softened as he gazed at Garnet. Then he glared at us and continued down the aisle, muttering under his breath.

"Hi, Hale," I said, shaking his hand. "Thanks for coming along. Did Irys fill you in on where we're going?"

"Uh...Irys?" Hale appeared to be a bit flustered.

"Second Magician."

"Oh, she said we're traveling to Fulgor and I was to protect you." His face creased in confusion. "I'm not sure why. You're already covered by a null shield. Plus you're the...Soulfinder." He said the word almost as if it left a bad taste in his mouth.

"I'll explain on the way. See if Garnet will stand for you."

"Okay." Hale approached the horse as if he'd never seen one before.

Leif pulled me aside before I could saddle Kiki.

"What's with the stiff?" his voice hissed in my ear.

"Irys thought I should have more protection. Seemed like a good idea."

"It is, but why Skippy?"

"Skippy?"

"Hale. Let's just say we don't get along."

Oh great. "Irys assigned him. Are you saying he's not trustworthy?"

Leif sucked in a deep breath. "No. He's loyal and has plenty of magic."

"Then what's the problem?"

"He's...annoying."

I laughed. "So are you."

He frowned. "I'm funny and lovable. He's...a snob and thinks our Zaltana magic is impure."

"I don't care what he thinks. Is he good in a fight?"

"Yeah." The word tore from Leif's lips as if it pained him to say it.

"Then we'll let Garnet decide if he's worthy. If the horse rejects him, we will, too. Okay?"

Another huff. "Okay." Leif pulled a thick silver chain from his pocket. Dangling from the chain was a clear glass octopus about the size of my palm. "Here." He handed it to me. "It's from Quinn. There's a null shield attached to it so when you wear it next to your heart it protects your entire body."

"Thanks." I looped the chain around my neck and tucked the lifelike octopus under my shirt. The cold glass sent a shiver through me.

Leif returned to Rusalka. The sorrel-and-white horse nuzzled his neck.

Kiki unlatched her stall with her teeth and stood by her tack. I stroked her neck. A sudden wave of grief rose in my throat, strangling me. Pressing my forehead to her shoulder, I endured the torment. I missed my connection with Kiki the most.

Eventually, she snorted and pawed the ground as if to say, "Stop wallowing in pity and get moving."

I saddled her and attached plenty of feed bags. The plains would have enough water. When I finished, I mounted and glanced around. Leif sat on Rusalka, looking dour, and Hale pulled himself into Garnet's saddle. Hale's expression from atop the tall horse was a mix of awe and terror. Sandseed horses had a reputation for being stubborn and willful and intelligent.

"Just follow us and you shouldn't have any trouble," I said to Hale.

"No trouble?"

"With the horse. I can't make any guarantees about the mission."

"Yeah, I heard that about you."

"Oh?"

"No disrespect intended. It's just you have a certain... reputation." Hale cleared his throat. "I'm honored to accompany you."

Leif rolled his eyes. "Laying it on a bit thick, aren't you, Skippy?"

Ignoring my brother, I spurred Kiki toward the Keep's gate. If we hurried, we could be in the Avibian Plains by nightfall. We left the Keep, then threaded through the afternoon Citadel traffic. We crossed through the southern exit without a problem and continued south. Once we reached the plains, we'd turn east before cutting north to Fulgor.

I really didn't expect trouble until we arrived in Fulgor. But minutes after we cleared the gate, the rumble of many horses at full gallop sounded behind us.

Leif glanced at me as we moved to the right side of the road. His hand rested on the hilt of his machete. Hale's face pinched tight. A small part of me hoped the riders were just in a hurry and would pass us. But a cold dread churned in my stomach, warning me.

Sure enough, the riders surrounded us. They stopped and blocked our path. Leif yanked his machete out, and in response, seven soldiers pulled their weapons and pointed them at us.

12

VALEK

As Onora threatened Janco with her knife, Ari stood, holding a dagger in each of his massive hands. Even though Janco was grinning, he'd palmed his switchblade.

"Save it for later," Valek said, stopping the inevitable. "You can spar with Onora in the training yard tomorrow." When no one moved, he banged a fist on his desk. "Weapons down. Now."

Ari and Janco returned their knives to various hidden holders without hesitation. Onora waited a few heartbeats before slipping the weapon into her pocket. Valek noted a few other telltale bulges, indicating a number of hidden surprises. She wore the uniform Dilana had given her, but she yanked at the collar as if uncomfortable.

"Onora, you must learn to ignore Janco's taunts. He's testing you. Being quick to anger is not a desirable trait in my corps," Valek said. He gestured to the empty chair. "Sit down."

Ari remained on his feet until she sat. Then he settled next to Janco, who lounged back as if he didn't have a care in the world. Except Valek knew better. Janco was far from relaxed.

"Ari, please update Onora on what we've learned so far,"

Valek ordered. He studied the young woman's body language as Ari detailed their investigation.

Onora perched on the edge of her seat. She listened with her head cocked slightly to the right and her hands clasped in her lap near another concealed knife. He hadn't returned hers, yet she was well armed. Interesting.

When Ari finished, Valek asked, "What's our next move?"

"Interrogate the smugglers, find out who their boss is and where their headquarters is located," Janco said.

"Let one of them escape and follow him," Ari suggested.

"Find another group selling black-market goods and infiltrate them," Onora said.

All good suggestions. "It's doubtful the location of their headquarters is still the same since the arrests. However, learning who is in charge will be a step in the right direction."

Janco puffed out his chest.

"I also liked the other ideas. The three of you will work together as a team and implement them."

Janco no longer looked so pleased. Ari frowned at Onora. They were going to be difficult about working with her.

"Your first team meeting is tomorrow after the morning exercises. We'll meet in the training yard for a workout session. Then you can plan a timeline and task list for finding the smugglers. You're dismissed."

They stood. Ari and Janco left after shooting a couple of glares at Onora. She lingered behind.

"Yes?" he asked.

"You promised to return my weapons tonight."

"I did."

She didn't flinch from his scrutiny. Cocky. He'd never been that cocky even in his prime. Then again…Valek had placed black statues he'd carved on his targets' pillows, warning them just to make it more difficult to assassinate them. Very cocky.

"Well?" she asked.

"You actually want me to check my locked drawer and find it empty? So you can smirk over getting one over on me? Considering that you've already recovered your weapons, it seemed like a waste of time."

Two small splotches reddened her cheeks.

Gotcha. "You shouldn't have threatened Janco. That tipped me off that you were armed."

Keeping her mouth shut, she nodded.

"Experience counts for more than you think." Valek rubbed his chest, remembering when he'd hunted Ambrose, believing it would be an easy kill. "I know you don't believe me. You won't believe me until you're standing here, facing some young hotshot determined to take your job."

"Are you saying you've just realized this now?"

He laughed. "Oh no. I've been facing young hotshots since the takeover twenty-three years ago. You are not the first to challenge me."

"No. I'll be the last."

"That has yet to be determined. Let's see how you do working with Ari and Janco before I turn over my office keys."

She moved to leave, then paused. "How...? What is the best way to work with them?"

Ah progress. "Listen to them. They've years of experience, but don't be afraid to speak up if you have a better idea. They might not like it, but they know a good idea when they hear one. Even Janco. He's used to listening to the voice of reason."

"And that's Ari's voice."

"Yes. Unless Ari's being emotional. Then he can be very unreasonable." Valek watched for a reaction.

Onora pressed her lips together. "Nothing wrong with emotion."

He'd hit a nerve. "Only at the right time and place." Yelena had taught him that. "But when Ari gets into his protective mode, he will rush into danger without a thought to his own survival."

"Why is that bad?"

"Since you have to ask, I'm guessing that was part of the training you didn't agree with Hedda about."

"Emotion gives us strength."

"At the right time and place."

She shook her head as if he couldn't possibly understand.

"It's the reason you lost last night."

"I lost because you cheated," she said, anger stiffening her posture.

"Keep thinking that. Then I won't have to worry about finding another job."

Onora spun on her heel and left without another word.

Valek returned to his desk. Contemplating their conversation, he dug through the reports. Onora's comment—*emotion gives us strength*—repeated in his mind.

During the second stage of his assassin training, Valek hadn't been able to beat T-quin in hand to hand despite hours of practice and lifting weights until his muscles shook with exhaustion.

In order to move to the next level, he had to win a match against T-quin. Their fights lasted longer and longer, but always ended the same.

"Pinned you, Wanna Be." T-quin pressed his knees into Valek's shoulders, proving his point. He released him and stood. Sweat coated his chest and soaked his hair. He puffed from the exertion, but offered Valek a hand up.

Valek ignored it as anger pulsed through him. He sprang to his feet ready to try again.

"That's enough for now, Wanna Be. I don't want to injure you," T-quin said.

"No. I almost had you. You can't stop now."

"All right, but don't go crying to Hedda if I break your leg."

They faced each other. Both stood in fighting stances. Dark purple bruises stained Valek's knuckles and circles of red, green and black bruising marked his chest, arms and thighs where T-quin had punched or kicked him.

T-quin shuffled forward and snapped his foot out. Valek blocked the blow with his forearm and countered with a round-house kick. T-quin sidestepped and received only a glancing blow. But Valek didn't wait for a counterstrike. He hooked his foot behind T-quin's ankle and yanked. T-quin hit the ground rolling. Valek chased him, but he sprang to his feet and, using Valek's momentum, flipped Valek over his head. His breath whooshed from his lungs as he landed.

T-quin laughed. "So predictable, Wanna Be. You've no imagination."

Fury gave Valek a surge of energy. He scrambled to his feet and rushed his opponent. T-quin once again dipped and threw Valek over his shoulder.

The match continued. T-quin taunted and Valek attacked only to end up on the ground.

"Pinned, again," T-quin said, digging his heels into Valek's hips.

Valek lumbered to his feet. Battered with bruises on top of bruises, he shuffled over to the water pitcher for a drink.

"Lose the anger," Hedda said.

He jerked in surprise. No sound warned of her approach, and he hadn't known she had watched his match against T-quin.

She regarded him with a frankness he'd learned to admire.

"But T-quin—"

"This has nothing to do with T-quin or your vendetta.

MARIA V. SNYDER

T-quin is baiting you on purpose. When you get angry, you make mistakes. Mistakes he can use to his advantage. And you are very quick to anger."

He drew breath to argue, but she had a point. Fury at the King, the soldiers and even his parents had fueled his desire to learn and improve his skills.

"Lose the anger, then lose all those other annoying emotions while you're at it. In order to be an assassin, you must be rational, logical, cunning, ruthless and emotionless. Those soft feelings have no place in an assassin's heart or head. They make you weak."

While he agreed with her, he'd been holding on to his passion for revenge for so long, he worried he'd lose his desire to see the King's blood on his hands.

"Determination, persistence, concentration, focus and drive are not emotions," she said. "Put your emotions aside or you will not succeed in this program. You have ten days." She strode away.

T-quin stood nearby. He raised his hand and then bent it at the wrist as he lowered it while making a whistling sound. "Hope you can fly, Wanna Be. Even if you miss the rocks, the current will drown you. Splash!" He laughed and returned to the training floor.

Arbon met Valek's gaze as he took a break from his match. He'd been working with another instructor for the past few weeks and showed an affinity for hand to hand. Arbon would soon advance to the next level.

Was competition an emotion? The thought of being pushed to his death failed to ignite fear in Valek's heart. The challenge of ten days did more for his motivation than anything else.

However, recognizing a weakness remained easier than overcoming it. Although Valek knew T-quin baited him, the anger boiled inside him, pressing to be released. If anything, his temper shortened. And the heating season's hotter temperatures didn't help, either.

Valek's matches with Arbon and some of the others had gone mostly in his favor until news about his weakness spread. After another frustrating, fruitless day of training, Valek dragged his battered body to his favorite spot overlooking the Sunset Ocean, which was awash in the pinks, oranges and golds cast by the setting sun.

He grabbed a handful of the gray rocks and tossed them one by one out into the sea, wishing he could throw his emotions away as easily. Or rather, evict the anger that had infested him. Valek imagined it as a black, oily rot flowing through his veins, pumping through his heart, twisting around his thoughts.

"Jump, Wanna Be," T-quin yelled. "Save Hedda the trouble of tossing your sorry ass over the edge herself."

Valek's grip tightened. The stones cracked in his hands and the desire to whip them at T-quin's head rose in his chest. He refrained from the action. Instead, he channeled his anger into the unyielding cold rocks cutting into his palms.

"What? No retort? Afraid I'll trounce you again?"

Valek stood and walked past T-quin without saying a word. When he reached his room, he sat on the edge of the bed and opened his hands. Blood covered the stones. The force of his grip had cracked them in half. Inside lurked a sleek blackness with glints of silver.

He reached under his bed for the stones he'd carried back during the first stage of his training. The gray outer coating had been scratched off and revealed the same black-and-silver interior.

Taking out his knife, he chipped away at the dull gray on one of the rocks. He concentrated on carving the stone, letting his rage and frustration disappear for a while. When it was too dark to see, he lit a lantern and continued. Instead of

MARIA V. SNYDER

reporting for training the next day, he remained in his room, working on the stones. Their inner beauty fascinated him and he scraped away the parts that didn't belong.

Odd that he saw a shape trapped within the stone. A figure that had to be released. He worked for hours, neither eating nor sleeping until he finished. Then he collapsed.

The sound of knocking woke him.

"Valek," Arbon called. "Are you okay?" He twisted the knob, but the door was locked.

"I'm fine," he called.

"T-quin's gonna be pissed. He bet Eden a gold you jumped off the cliff."

"I'm happy to disappoint him."

"Are you coming to training? You only have two days left."

Valek rolled over and gazed at his collection of rock statues. The crude figurines stood in a row. One wore a crown, three others held swords and a couple held hands. His father had done nothing to stop the soldiers from murdering his brothers. His mother had disowned him.

"Valek?"

"I'm not going."

"But—"

"Don't worry, Arbon. I'll be there for the test."

"You better. I've two silvers on the line."

"I'm touched you would risk so much."

"Who says I'm betting on you?" Arbon's booming laugh rumbled through the door.

Valek spent the next two days sleeping, eating and recovering his strength. The morning before his test fight, he stood at the cliff's edge holding the statues in his hands.

He whipped the king figure out into the air. Determination replaced anger. The three soldiers went over the edge one by one. Persistence would aid him as he hunted down these three murderers. Tossing the couple holding hands together, he sent the last of his weaknesses out into the abyss. If he cared for no one, then the pain of grief would never touch him again.

When Valek arrived at the training room, he squeezed through a press of people. Trainers, students and teachers had all come to watch the fight. A murmur spread as they spotted him.

As Valek warmed up, Arbon pushed his way next to him.

"Will ya look at this crowd," Arbon said. "I'd call them morbid, but they are training to be assassins or are already cold-blooded killers." He sounded cheery. "Guess there hasn't been anyone tossed over the cliff in a while."

"Your confidence in me is heartwarming."

Arbon slapped Valek on the shoulder and wished him luck.

Valek stretched his stiff muscles. At least they didn't ache as much. The rest had done him good.

"Are you ready, Wanna Be? I want to collect my winnings," T-quin called.

He faced T-quin. The oily blackness inside him had been purged and thrown into the Sunset Ocean. Nothing left but hard silver.

When the match started, T-quin attacked with a series of front kicks. His movements appeared crystal clear to Valek. Rage no longer clouded his vision. He almost felt sorry for T-quin, but sorrow was an emotion. And Valek had taken Hedda's advice to heart.

Valek blocked a side kick and a punch to his head, staying on the defensive.

"Come on, Wanna Be. Fight back or I might fall asleep," T-quin said.

The crowd laughed and cheered T-quin on. Valek ignored the noise, focusing on T-quin's attack pattern, analyzing his strikes for weaknesses. Even though they'd sparred so many

MARIA V. SNYDER

times before, Valek learned more about T-quin's fighting style in these five minutes than in the weeks before.

Valek waited for the perfect opportunity. When T-quin did his favorite shuffle side kick, backhand combo, Valek stepped in close and punched T-quin's exposed ribs. T-quin grunted and backpedaled.

"Lucky strike, Wanna Be."

"You wish."

The fight continued and Valek took advantage of every opening T-quin gave him. After a series of blows to his kidneys, T-quin dropped his guard and swayed on his feet. Valek spun, windmilling him to the ground, and knelt on his shoulders.

"Pinned, Tamequintin," Valek said.

Stunned silence filled the air until Arbon whooped. "Yes! You owe me two silvers, T-quin."

The crowd had recovered and dispersed. Valek had flexed his muscles, assessing the damage—a few sore ribs and a tender spot on his biceps.

Hedda had approached. "Not bad, King Killer. I should have given you the ten-day deadline sooner. You do well under pressure. Now let's see how you do with weapons training."

"Ten days?"

"Of course."

A knock on his office door jerked Valek from his memories. "Yes?"

Sergeant Gerik poked his head in. "The Commander has retired for the evening, sir."

"Thank you." Before the man could close the door, he called, "Gerik, come in here, please."

Strain whitened Gerik's face as he approached Valek's desk. All the members of the Commander's guard knew they'd be punished for letting the assassin through, but had no idea what was in store for them. Once Valek had assembled a new team, this team would be reassigned.

"Sir?"

"According to your file, you're a recent transfer from MD-2. Been here a year. How long did you serve up there?"

"A year, sir."

"Being assigned to the Commander's detail is an impressive accomplishment for someone who's only served a couple years. Most of these guys have ten or more years' experience. What do you credit for your success?"

Gerik hesitated.

"Feel free to speak frankly."

"I'm good, sir. Fighting hand to hand, or with weapons, is easy for me. I've a natural affinity for sparring."

"Fair enough. When you were in MD-2, did you know a Captain Timmer?"

The slightest flinch creased Gerick's face. "I've heard of him, sir."

"And? Again I'm looking for an honest opinion."

"He has a reputation for cruelty, sir."

"Cruelty?"

"The officers believe he's very strict and his troops are the best. No one has ever filed a complaint. It's just gossip among the enlisted, sir."

"If his troops are considered the best, why weren't you promoted to his company?"

Gerik frowned. "I was offered a position, but I turned him down."

Interesting. "Refused because of gossip?"

"Yes, sir."

The man was lying. Valek wondered why, but he wasn't going to push it right now. Some things couldn't be rushed.

MARIA V. SNYDER

"I also wanted to let you know that you're being reassigned, Private Gerik."

He straightened. "Yes, sir." Resignation laced his voice.

"It's a temporary assignment. If you do well, it might become permanent."

"Yes, sir."

"Report to the training yard tomorrow morning after exercise."

"Yes, sir." This time surprise tainted his tone.

"You're dismissed."

"Yes, sir." Gerik left in a hurry.

Probably worried Valek would change his mind. Valek read through Captain Timmer's file, but spotted nothing out of the ordinary. On his way to the Commander's suite, he visited one of his operatives, assigning the man to deliver a message to Yelena, warning her about Ben Moon.

"You give this directly to her. No one else. Understand?" Valek asked.

"Yes, sir," the man replied.

The tension in Valek's shoulders eased as he sent another agent to seek out Arbon and let the assassin know Valek wished to talk to him. Then Valek knocked on the Commander's door. He'd accomplished more than he'd hoped today.

"Come," Ambrose called.

Valek entered. A glass of blackberry brandy waited for him by the empty armchair. The Commander already relaxed in his.

"Did our young assassin show up tonight?"

"She did."

"And how did the boys react?"

"As expected."

Ambrose laughed. "Bared teeth and raised hackles, eh?"

"Tomorrow morning should be interesting." Valek explained what they'd learned about the smugglers.

"Good. Anything else?"

He reported about Captain Timmer in MD-2. "I need more information on him."

"Yes, find out about him. My officers are forbidden to abuse their positions."

Another reason Ambrose held Valek's loyalty. His insistence that his army always behave as professionals. No cruelty, no killing for killing's sake, no drunken brawls and no sexual harassment.

Valek sipped his drink. Molten spices rolled over his tongue, burned down his throat and warmed his stomach. "I'd like to investigate this Timmer personally."

The Commander stilled. "You've only just returned. Why not send an agent?"

"It's too important. He's the reason both Onora and Gerik are here and I suspect they're working together. Besides, an agent would have to infiltrate his squad and earn his trust. Time I'm unwilling to waste at this point."

"And you believe you can get answers faster?"

"Oh yes."

The Commander stared into the fire. "What about *my* safety?"

Good question. What about it? Ever since Onora had appeared in the Commander's suite, Valek had been mulling it over, viewing the entire night from every possible angle. He'd missed something vital. He'd no idea what, but he'd discover it eventually.

"I will ensure that the gap in security has been plugged, and that you have a new detail before I leave. Besides, if Onora has a change of heart, I'm quite certain you can handle her," Valek said.

"Quite certain?"

Valek met the Commander's amused gaze. "I haven't beaten you yet, old man."

"Experience trumps youth?"

"For now," Valek agreed.

"And when it doesn't?"

Valek laughed. "We team up. I'll knock him on the head with my cane and you aim for the groin with your bony feet."

The Commander chuckled and sipped his drink. They sat in companionable silence for a while.

"All right, Valek. Go and take care of this Captain Timmer. You have ten days."

All humor fled Valek. Ten days. Just like the inside joke between Valek and Hedda all those years ago. He'd never told the Commander or anyone about that. Coincidence? Or had the Commander talked to Hedda? And if so, why?

13

JANCO

Janco hated mornings. The bright sunlight, chirping birds and those obnoxious morning people just made his stomach churn. Unfortunately, since he'd been a soldier for forever morning exercise and training had been a requirement. He'd probably be a general by now if training was scheduled for a decent hour of the day.

Ari's white-blond hair gleamed in the sun, making it easy to find his partner in the vast training area. As in everything, Ari was the complete opposite of Janco. He was even one of those obnoxious morning people.

"You're late," Ari said.

"Yeah, well, I got behind a group of newbs while running laps. My grandmother could run faster than them."

"You couldn't just pass them?"

"And miss a chance to taunt them? No way."

"I see you've taken to heart Valek's orders to be a good example to the new recruits."

"Yep, that's me. A shining example."

"Speaking of examples…" Ari tilted his head.

Janco turned and groaned. "Here comes Little Miss Assassin. What have we done to get saddled with her?"

"It didn't help you were caught snooping in that warehouse. Some sneak you are."

"I was far from caught. I was just…biding my time." Janco eyed the young pup sourly.

Little Miss Assassin moved through the groups of soldiers with ease. No discomfort from being surrounded by armed men and women. She joined them without a word and warmed up. Her long brown hair was braided down her back. She wore a light-colored tunic and pants and her feet were bare! And people called *him* crazy.

He stretched and bantered with Ari until he saw *them*.

"Ari, look." He elbowed his partner.

"What? Oh, crap. This can't be good."

"Ya think?"

The Commander and Valek headed toward them followed by some grunt, who looked terrified. Didn't blame him.

Little Miss Assassin froze for a second when she spotted the threesome. Scared of Valek? Not from what he'd heard. The Commander? Ditto. A slight hitch in the big grunt's stride gave him away. She knew him and vice versa. Valek also watched the young pup's expression. Probably testing a theory.

But why was the Commander here?

Valek introduced the grunt—Sergeant something or other. Seemed he might be another member of their team. Oh, this day was just getting better and better. He should have stayed in bed.

"We're going to do some sparring," Valek said. "Janco versus Gerik, Ari versus Onora, then switch."

The Commander leaned against the wooden fence that lined the training yard. Better put on a good show.

"Weapons?" Ari asked.

"Your choice."

Janco sensed a trick. He glanced at his partner. Ari shrugged.

No help there. Janco studied the grunt. Taller than him, but not as broad as Ari. Best to wait until the grunt chose a weapon before he picked his.

Sergeant Grunt chose a bo staff. A surprise. Janco was sure he'd go for the sword. No worries. He'd learned a thing or three from Maren. Picking up his bo, he slid his hands along the wood of the staff and faced the grunt.

Valek refereed the match. "Go."

The grunt swung his bo, aiming for Janco's temple. He blocked and the loud crack of wood hitting wood vibrated in the air. The man meant business. Janco countered and soon all he heard was the rhythmic cracks of the two bos. His opponent was good, but Janco was better. Natch.

"The grunt can swing, but can he sing?" Janco shuffled close and jabbed at the man's groin.

He hopped back. "Hey! No blows below the belt."

"Who says?"

The grunt glanced at Valek. Oh, this was too easy. Janco poured on the speed. Rib strike, rib strike, temple, temple, feint to the ribs and then sweep the legs. Sergeant Grunt landed with an oomph and Janco pressed the tip of his bo just under the man's Adam's apple.

"Gotcha!"

Valek called the match. Janco refrained from smirking.

Ari slapped him on the back and almost sent him sprawling. "Nice."

Janco pulled Ari aside. "Watch out. She almost beat Valek, so she's probably very fast."

"That's why I'm not choosing a knife."

"Use your scimitar."

"Why?"

"No one in Ixia uses it. She'll be unfamiliar with what it can do. Plus it's intimidating as all hell."

MARIA V. SNYDER

"Great idea."

"Don't sound so surprised."

"Ready?" Valek asked.

Little Miss Assassin waited with her knives drawn. Ari approached, holding his scimitar in one hand. The thick, four-foot-long curved blade gleamed in the sunlight. The sucker weighed a ton, but Ari hefted it with ease.

Although she clenched her weapons tighter, Little Miss Assassin kept her cool. This ought to be good.

"Go."

She moved first, rushing Ari. A suicide move, except she cut to the right and sliced at Ari's neck. Ari just blocked her attack. Janco had been right—she was not just fast, but super-fast. And she used it to her advantage, snaking inside his strike zone and then dancing back.

Ari adjusted and used his scimitar to keep her from getting close. But she managed a few more strikes. The match lengthened. When Ari grabbed his hilt with both hands, she smiled, probably thinking she had worn him down.

Janco waited, and sure enough, Ari's lumbering swings, slow shuffles and heavy breathing lured Little Miss Assassin within striking distance. She stepped in, and he punched her in her solar plexus. Collapsing with a whoosh, she looked up in time to see Ari placing the tip of his very sharp blade on her neck.

"Gotcha!" Janco yelled, because Ari was too much of a gentleman to gloat.

Ari offered her a hand up, but she ignored it, rising to her feet. Indignation furrowed her brow and her mouth opened as if to protest. She shot Valek a sour look, but then pressed her lips together.

Wiping her hands on her pants, she picked up her knives and faced Janco. He chose the bo staff again.

"Go." Valek stepped back.

She attacked. Boy oh boy her speed was impressive. If he'd held a knife, the fight would be over by now. However, the longer bo staff kept her from getting close, and he was also known for his speedy little jabs. He worked on her ribs as her blades cut chunks from his staff.

"Little Miss Assassin is as slow as molassin," Janco sang.

"*Molassin?* That's not even a word," Ari called.

"Everyone's a critic. I'd like to see you find a word that rhymes with *assassin*." Janco backpedaled as the young pup came after him with a flurry of slices aimed at his throat and stomach.

The tip of her blade nicked his neck.

"This kitten has claws under her puppy-dog paws."

She growled and Janco bit down on a chuckle because her next series of attacks almost knocked him over. Impressive. He endured two more assaults. Then on the third, he planted the end of his bo in the ground and, using his momentum, flipped over her head. He landed, swept her legs, then followed her down, pressing the bo staff against her throat.

"Gotcha."

"The correct term is 'pinned,'" she said, panting.

"That's boring. Besides, we don't do 'correct' around here."

Ignoring his hand, she stood and brushed a lock of hair from her sweaty face. "I've noticed."

"Next," Valek said.

Sergeant Grunt faced Ari without a weapon. "Hand to hand?"

"All right."

"Bad move," Janco muttered.

"Why?" She moved closer to him.

"You'll see."

While the grunt had an impressive array of techniques, Ari

MARIA V. SNYDER

had spent the past ten years perfecting hand-to-hand fighting. In order to beat Ari, an opponent had to have brute strength, speed and to make no mistakes. Grunt gave a good fight, but his inexperience proved his downfall.

"Gotcha," Janco said when Ari pinned the grunt.

"Not bad," Valek said. "Final fight. Ari and Janco against Onora, using knives."

Janco had been about to protest until that last part. He sensed he and Ari were about to get their balls handed to them.

He hated when he was right. Actually, he preened and bragged when he was right, but being soundly beaten by Little Miss Assassin was a huge blow to his ego. And the Commander had watched it! Absolutely mortifying.

Ari wiped the blood and sweat from his arms. "Nice fight."

Janco glared at him. "Nice? That—"

"Oh hush, Janco. Can't you just admit when someone is better than you?"

"Obviously not." He pouted.

"That explains why Valek had such trouble with her. Be glad she's on our side."

He gazed at her. She talked to Valek while the grunt stood nearby. The Commander had left. Probably disgusted by their fight.

"Is she? Her and the grunt know each other."

"Probably why Valek brought him along today."

"He could be the reason she got into the castle without trouble."

"Could be."

"You don't seem concerned."

"I'm sure Valek has a plan."

"Humph." Janco moved closer to eavesdrop on their conversation.

"…obvious you never completed the training," Valek said to

the assassin. "You're deadly with your knives. Now you need to be deadly with a bo staff, a sword, hand to hand. These two can help you with that if you let them."

Ha. Not unless Valek ordered him. Or… Hmm. If she shared her knife-fighting techniques, he might be tempted to show her a few moves.

Valek called Ari over. Once they were assembled, he said, "I'm counting on the four of you to work together and find how the smugglers are transporting illegal goods into Ixia. Ari's the team leader for this mission. Keep me updated."

"Yes, sir," they said in unison.

While Janco wasn't happy with the new members, he suspected Little Miss Assassin was annoyed that Ari was chosen as team leader. She stood next to Sergeant Grunt as if waiting for Valek to yell *go*. Two of them against him and Ari would be interesting as long as she didn't have her knives.

"All right, chief. What's next?" Janco asked.

"Team meeting," Ari said.

"Here?" Little Miss Assassin glanced around at the clusters of fighters.

"Hell no. First meeting will be at the Black Cat Tavern this afternoon."

Sweet. "Ari, you the man."

MARIA V. SNYDER

14

YELENA

I scanned the four men and three women surrounding us on horseback. Most of them had drawn their hoods up over their heads. If I'd had my magic, I'd know exactly whom I dealt with and would have clouded their thoughts so we could continue on our way to the Avibian Plains. Instead, I told Leif to put his machete away so we could play nice. For now.

"Is there a problem?" I asked.

One person pushed his hood back and I recognized him as Captain Romas from the Citadel's guards.

"Yes," Romas said. "I'm here because the Sitian Council believes you're in danger."

Leif snorted. "And that's news?"

Romas ignored him. "Seems an assassin is after you, and we are to escort you back to the Citadel so we can provide you with additional protection."

Ah. "Please tell the Council that I appreciate the concern, but I'm quite safe. And I'm not returning."

"We're not here as a courtesy. We have our orders."

"I don't care. The Council cannot order me."

"Liaison Yelena, a word in private." Romas gestured and an opening between his riders appeared.

I considered refusing, but was too curious about what he had to say. Kiki followed until we were far enough away.

"The Council is more than concerned. They know *all* about the danger you're in," Romas said in a low voice despite our distance from the others.

Fear swirled and I gripped Kiki's saddle. Was he implying they knew about my magic? Impossible.

"And considering you're heading straight to the man who vowed revenge on you, it would be wise to return with us."

"Quit dancing around the subject, Captain, and tell me what exactly the Council knows."

Concern creased Romas's brow and he leaned forward. "The Council has recently learned that your magic is gone and you are unprotected."

His words burned into me like a red-hot pontil iron, but I used every ounce of will to keep my face neutral. "Interesting rumor. Who started it?"

He shook his head sadly. "I've my orders. Please cooperate or I'll be forced to take drastic measures."

"Such as?"

"We are armed with Curare."

I shrugged. "Go ahead and waste the Curare." As I glanced back at Leif and Hale, I tapped my fingers on Kiki's neck, signaling her. "Come on, guys. We're done here."

When Romas gestured for his men to stop them, I leaned close to Kiki's ear and whispered, "Ask the others to dump their riders and run home, please."

Seven horses bucked at once, throwing their riders onto the ground, including Romas. They galloped north.

"Let's go!" I yelled.

Garnet and Rusalka joined Kiki as we raced south. Darts whizzed by my head, but I stayed low until we were out of reach. Then we slowed so we didn't exhaust the horses.

MARIA V. SNYDER

"What was that about?" Leif asked, riding next to me.

"Tell you later." I inclined my head, indicating Hale.

"We really should have returned to the Citadel," Hale said when he joined us. His hair was windblown and two red spots spread on his cheeks. "I don't know if I can protect you against an assassin."

"Not to worry, Skippy. Did you see how Yelena gave them the slip? She's more than capable of defending herself. You're just here to be arm candy."

I almost laughed at Hale's pinched expression, but the thought that the Council knew about my condition still burned, sending sweaty waves of fear through me. How did they find out? The only people who knew were Irys, Bain, Leif, Mara, Healer Hayes and Fisk. All trustworthy.

Unless someone tricked the information from Mara. A sweet, lovable woman who was kind to everyone and would never suspect duplicity. Except she kept Opal's secrets and knew how important this was. Unless someone forced the information from her.

I stopped Kiki.

"What's the matter?" Leif asked.

"Give us a moment, please?" I asked Hale as I pulled my brother aside.

"Okay, now you're really worrying me."

I explained about the Council. It didn't take long for Leif to jump to the same conclusions. "I'd better contact Irys. Why didn't you tell me sooner?" He dug in his saddlebags for a small super messenger.

"We were a little busy fleeing the Council's guards."

"Oh, right." Distracted, Leif gazed into the square-shaped glass. After a few minutes he glanced up. "She's checking."

We waited forever. If Mara had been hurt because of me, I'd never forgive myself. Kiki shifted her weight under me as if she, too, worried about Mara. She probably did. Mara fed her apples on her way to the glass shop every morning. As far as Kiki was concerned, a daily apple equaled unconditional love.

Leif's attention riveted on the glass. Then he smiled. I relaxed.

"She's fine and a little angry we didn't trust her to defend herself," he said.

"She wouldn't last against a skilled opponent."

"I know, but she said she'd match her pontil iron against your bo staff any day."

That would be an interesting fight. "Tell her she's on."

We resumed traveling. Once again, my thoughts contemplated the encounter.

Who else knew about me? The assassin was well aware of what he had done to me. Did that mean the assassin worked for the Council, or was in contact with one of the Councilors or aides? A more likely scenario.

After a few hours, we reached the border of the Avibian Plains and headed east. The long stalks of grass had turned brown and brittle. Various shades of browns, grays and tans covered the undulating barren landscape.

"It's dreary during the cold season," I said to Hale. "You should see this place in the warm season. It's bursting with color and life."

"What about the Sandseed's magic?" Hale asked in a small voice.

"Stick with us, Skippy. The protection doesn't attack family. Oh, wait, you're not family. Too bad. Good luck finding your way home." Leif chuckled.

Even after the decimation of a majority of the Sandseed clan members, the protection remained strong, attacking intruders by convincing them they were lost. They'd wander the plains for days until they died of thirst.

MARIA V. SNYDER

"You're not family, either," Hale said.

"Distant cousins. You know that weird magic you teased me about in school? I'll bet you wished you had some of that now."

"Don't listen to him, Hale. Garnet will keep you from going crazy."

"Lovely," he muttered.

Garnet pinned his ears back.

"He didn't mean it, Garnet," I said. "He's just scared." I gave Hale a pointed look.

"Oh...ah...right." He patted Garnet's dark neck. "It's my first time in the plains. I'm a bit...skittish."

Nice word choice. I gave him a thumbs-up. "Okay, Kiki, you're in charge." It seemed weird talking out loud to her after years of silent communication.

"What does that mean?" Hale asked.

"It means Kiki will decide the route we take to Fulgor," Leif supplied. "And she'll stop when the horses are tired or hungry or thirsty. We're just along for the ride. Oh, and hold on tight. It's a ride like no other."

"You mean because of that gust-of-wind gait you talked about?"

"Yep." Leif grinned.

As if on cue, Kiki broke stride and, with a hop forward, launched into the gait I'd dubbed her gust-of-wind gait. It felt as if we rode on a river of wind. That was the easiest way to describe the feeling. Kiki's hooves didn't drum on the ground. I didn't have to match my movement to hers. We flew, covering twice the amount of ground as a regular gait.

The magical gait only worked in the Avibian Plains and only Sandseed-bred horses had the ability. Handy, considering the plains, which were located southeast of the Citadel, stretched east to the base of the Emerald Mountains and south to the Daviian Plateau. A nice chunk of Sitia that we used as a shortcut on many occasions.

Kiki stopped to rest a couple of hours later. We collected firewood and Leif used his magic to start a fire. With Hale in charge of cooking dinner, Leif and I groomed the horses as they munched from their feed bags.

Leif broke the silence. "If the Council didn't find out from Mara about your…ah…condition, how did they?"

"The only possibility that makes sense is the assassin or the person who hired the assassin told one of the Councilors or one of their aides."

"I don't like the sound of that."

"Well, would you like the sound of Irys, Bain, Healer Hayes or Fisk betraying my trust better?"

"No."

"I didn't think so."

"No need to be snippy."

"Leif, word is spreading. Fast. I need to find a cure before all my enemies come after me."

Hale called that dinner was ready.

Leif tossed the currycomb at me. "Good enough."

I caught it, then finished brushing the knots from Kiki's tail. He might be satisfied with "good enough," but my Kiki deserved perfection.

When I finally finished, Leif was asking Hale what he thought of the gust-of-wind gait between slurps of a bread-and-cheese soup.

"It was…incredible," Hale said, smiling for the first time since I'd met him. "Like nothing else."

"Not many people have experienced it. You're in rare company, Skippy."

His smile dimmed and Hale focused on his bowl.

"Leif, how old are you?" I asked.

He creased his brow in confusion. "You know my age. I'm two years older than you."

"Then act like it. Stop calling Hale names."

"Do you know how many names Mr. Hale called me while we were in the Keep together?" Leif asked. "Dozens."

"And you were an annoying teenager who hated the world," I reminded him.

"Doesn't mean I deserved it."

"*No one* deserves it. There just comes a time when you need to forgive and move past it. We're going to be together for weeks. Can you try to be civil?"

Leif pouted, reminding me of Janco. "I guess, but only if I can have another bowl of the soup."

If only smoothing relations between Sitia and Ixia was this easy. I could retire.

"Since we will be traveling for a while, perhaps this is a good time to share with you the extent of my magic," Hale said.

Leif opened his mouth, but I shot him a look and he wisely kept quiet.

"That would be helpful." I encouraged Hale to continue.

"It seemed only fair, considering I'm very familiar with Leif's powers and your...er...current situation, Yelena."

Warning signals rang in my head, and I moved my hand closer to my switchblade without thought.

If Hale noticed, he didn't react. "You see, while I'm able to construct null shields in record time, light fires and communicate with my mind, I'm also able to hear."

"Hear what?" I asked.

"Hear with my magic, meaning I heard your whispered conversation with Captain Romas and your discussion with Leif by the horses."

"Whoa, I didn't know you could do that," Leif said.

"After the Ixian takeover, the Master Magicians decided not to advertise all their students' powers in case the Commander attacked us or another one of our own attempted to overthrow the Council. Since spies are always a concern, it was a sound strategy."

I agreed, but if Hale had this ability, could he be the one who'd informed the Council about me?

"I only use it when necessary," Hale said as if he'd read my thoughts. "I believed the encounter with the captain might not go in our favor, so I listened to be ready to act."

Smart.

"And what he said made sense. I'd already determined something was very wrong. Why would you need to be protected by a null shield? You're the most powerful magician—"

"That would be Bain," I said.

He shook his head. "Who else calls Master Bloodgood... Bain?"

"Uh, Irys?"

"And who calls Master Jewelrose...Irys?"

Only Bain and me. "Okay, you made your point."

"Face it, sis. You're in elite company." Leif bumped my arm.

"You call them by their first names all the time." I swatted his shoulder.

"Not in their presence."

"This is a pointless argument. I'm no longer a magician."

"For now," Leif said.

"How did it happen?" Hale asked.

He had the right to know. We could be attacked again and both Leif and Hale could lose their powers. I explained about the arrow.

"Never heard of a substance with that ability." Hale worried his bottom lip.

"If you wish to return to the safety of the Citadel, go ahead.

MARIA V. SNYDER

I wouldn't blame you. We should have been up-front about it from the beginning, but I was too…" Terrified.

"I think I'm safer with you than at the Citadel," Hale said.

"I'm not so sure about that, Skip…er…Hale. She seems nice now, but wait until you're part of one of her crazy schemes," Leif said.

Here we go.

"One time, I was bait for a necklace snake—"

"What is it with you and that story?" I demanded. "You survived, didn't you? We rescued our father, didn't we? And as I recall, I was the one who ended up wrapped in the coils of an amorous necklace snake."

Leif huffed. "It's a good story if you don't ruin it with all those little details."

I gazed up at the stars, seeking patience with my brother. Moon Man, my Sandseed Story Weaver, was up there in the sky probably laughing his deep laugh. Despite the six years since his death, I missed him just as much now as I had then. He'd probably spout some cryptic advice on how to solve my problem. But this time, I would welcome it.

Two days later we entered the city limits of Fulgor. The city was the capital of the Moon Clan lands and also where Opal and Devlen lived and worked. The bustle on the streets was dissipating as the sky darkened.

"We can stay with Opal. She's like my mother-in-law and loves having company. Plus she can cook."

"Not a good idea," I said. "We might attract the wrong element."

"No problem. Opal's deadly with her sais, and Devlen knows how to swing a sword."

"And Reema, your niece? Or have you forgotten about her?"

"Ah, that little scamp knows how to stay out of trouble. One time she helped me finish a pie, but when Opal discovered us... Poof! Reema was gone. Snug in her bed as if she didn't have cherry juice staining her lips."

"I'm sure Opal won't be happy to see me," Hale said drily.

"True. If you weren't all stiff and haughty and nasty—"

"I wasn't there to be her friend. I had my orders from the Council."

"That's enough, boys." I glanced around at the buildings. Factories mixed with businesses and homes—typical Sitian hodgepodge. "I'd like to keep as low a profile as possible. Let's find an inn for the night and visit your in-laws in the morning."

Leif perked up. "I know the perfect place."

We stopped at the Second Chance Inn. I gave Leif a questioning look over the name of the place.

"Second-best chef in town works here," he said.

Figures.

"Who's the best?" Hale asked.

"Guy named Ian, who owns a tavern called the Pig Pen. We'll go tomorrow. Wait until you taste his beef stew. After a mouthful, you'll never be able to eat another's stew again because the rest will taste like crap in comparison."

I ignored my brother as I helped the stable lad with the horses. The stalls were clean and the air smelled of fresh hay. Happy that they would be well cared for, I joined Leif and Hale in the inn's common room. We rented two rooms, one for me and Leif and the other for Hale.

The next morning, we left Hale to make inquiries about the recent prison break from Wirral as we took a circuitous route to Opal's glass factory.

"It's a nice place," Leif said. "She has four kilns on the ground floor and upstairs are the living quarters. Of course,

MARIA V. SNYDER

it gets superhot in the warmer seasons, but they don't seem to mind the heat. I guess it's because she'd worked in a glass factory almost all her life and he grew up in the Avibian Plains."

Leif continued to prattle on while I kept an eye out for anyone following us. No visible sign of anyone. When we reached the factory, the outer door was unlocked. Inside a young woman sat behind a desk in a receiving area that had been a storefront at one point in time. "Can I— Oh, Leif. Nice to see you again. Go on back." She waved us toward a door behind her that said Employees Only. Fancy.

Leif opened the door and the roar of the kilns slammed into me. He pointed to a thick gray foam coating the inside of the door. "Soundproofing."

Heat pressed on us as we entered. Workers sat at gaffer's benches, some gathered molten slugs of glass, and another cracked a vase off a blowpipe and into an annealing oven. I smiled, remembering Opal's lessons on how to blow glass. That knowledge had saved my life and allowed me to leave the fire world.

I didn't recognize any of the workers, who glanced at us but didn't stop shaping the glass even when Leif said hello to a few.

A shriek pierced the kilns' roar. Leif and I grabbed our weapons, but a small girl with blond corkscrew curls dashed from between the equipment. Opal was hot on her adopted daughter's heels.

"Come on, Reema. You'll be late for school," she yelled as Reema hid behind Leif.

"Uncle Leif, protect me!" she cried.

"After you ditched me with an empty pie pan? No way." He sidestepped, exposing her.

She shrieked again and clutched my legs. "Aunt Yelena, don't let them take me away, please!" Reema implored with her big blue eyes.

Who could resist that? Not me. I picked her up. Technically, I wasn't her aunt by blood or marriage, but Opal insisted I was family. And Valek, too.

"Oh, for sand's sake," Opal said. "It's just school, Reema. You'll be home in time for dinner."

Reema smoothed her beautiful face into an innocent expression. "We have company. It would be rude of me to leave now."

What a con artist. I laughed.

Opal frowned. "Don't encourage her."

Devlen joined us. "There she is!" Most of his long black hair had escaped a leather tie and his shirt was rumpled. He nodded at us. "Come on." He took his daughter from my arms.

She shrieked. "No, Daddy, I want to stay and visit."

"We'll be in town for a couple days," I said. "If you go to school, I'll finish the story about the curious Valmur tonight."

"Promise?"

"Promise."

She pouted, but no longer assaulted our eardrums with that high-pitched squeal. Devlen carried her off.

"Let me down. I wanna walk," she said.

"So you can run off again? I think not," Devlen replied in a tired voice.

Opal gestured to her office. "Come in and let's have a proper hello."

We entered the room, and the kilns' noise and heat dulled. More of the gray foam had been sprayed on the glass walls, but a strip had been left clean. Probably so she could see the factory floor.

"I told you she was a scamp," Leif said, giving Opal a hug.

"And I never disagreed with you. Hello, Yelena." She hugged me next. "Nice to see you."

"What? No nice to see me?" Leif plopped into one of the chairs.

"Talk about a scamp," I said.

Opal laughed. After all of Opal's troubles, it was wonderful to hear the lighthearted sound and see the spark of amusement in her dark brown eyes. Her golden-brown hair had been pinned up in a knot, but strands hung down in a haphazard fashion.

"I'm sorry we came at a bad time," I said.

"Oh no. Don't worry. This is just our morning routine. Reema runs and hides and we search for her, drag her out from whatever hiding spot she's found and carry her to school. You actually helped by intercepting her."

"Ever think of homeschooling?" Leif teased.

"Yes. But she's never been to a school before, and if she wants to join her brother at the Magician's Keep, she needs to learn how to be with other kids her age."

"Do you think she'll be invited to the Keep?" I asked. At age ten, Reema was too young to show any magical potential, but her older brother, Teegan, had plenty to spare. Bain hoped he'd grow into master-level powers by the time he finished the five-year curriculum.

"Yes. She has an intuitive sense that is more than natural. It's hard to explain. She can be so mature and smart at times, acting older than ten, yet at other times, like in the mornings before school, she runs around like a spoiled five-year-old." Opal sank behind her desk. "While I'm happy to see you both, I sense it's not to discuss parenting methods. Unless you have some news about my sister, Leif?" She raised her eyebrows.

Leif blushed bright red. Now it was my turn to laugh. My brother, the prude.

"I'll take that as a no. Yelena?"

My mirth died in my throat. "Not even engaged."

"Too bad. Another wedding would be fun."

"Except we'd be targets. Better to elope like you and Devlen."

"Which worked until my mother found out about it."

I smiled, remembering the big gala Opal's mother had thrown for them.

"Best food, ever," Leif said.

"What about at your own wedding?" I asked.

"I was too nervous to eat."

"Wow, I didn't think that ever happened," Opal teased.

"Not funny."

After a pause in conversation, Opal asked, "Do you want to wait for Devlen to return before you tell me what's going on?"

"Probably a good idea," I said. Bad enough telling my story again. Best to avoid telling it twice.

"Then I'll fetch some tea." Opal left.

I scanned her office. Glass vases, bowls and sculptures decorated the tables and shelves. Stacks of orders had been arranged neatly on her desk.

Opal returned with a tray and poured four glasses. "Devlen's coming." She handed us each a steaming mug.

Devlen slipped into the room. He'd fixed his hair and changed his shirt. He said hello and stood behind Opal with one hand clutching his mug as if it would protect him and the other resting on Opal's shoulder. Leif stared at him as if scenting his intentions. When Opal had first married Devlen, the relationship between Leif and Devlen had been strained. Leif had dealt with Devlen when he'd been addicted to the blood magic, and hadn't witnessed Devlen's change firsthand, only heard about it through Valek.

I had seen Devlen's soul and knew him like no other. Probably why he acted embarrassed around me. Examining a person's soul was a ruthless and intimate experience, and I hadn't

MARIA V. SNYDER

shied away, stripping down the layers to see the good man underneath the childhood traumas and insatiable desire for magical power. He'd lost his way, but had been strong enough to find the right path. And Leif was learning to trust him, as well.

"Is this about the man who escaped Wirral?" Opal asked. "Devlen's been helping the authorities search for him, but the man's a magician and has just disappeared. Has the Council finally sent help?"

"That's one of the reasons we're here," Leif said. "But not at the Council's behest." He glanced at me.

I explained about my connection to Ben Moon and the attack in the woods. "Do you think he could have orchestrated it from Wirral?"

"No," Opal said. "That place is locked down tight. But he did have help, so one of his accomplices could have organized the attack to knock you out of the picture and ensure you didn't come searching for him. The prison break required a ton of planning and skill. Let's just say they'd never get a second chance."

"Do you know who his accomplices are?"

"Only two. A brother-and-sister team of magicians," Devlen said.

"Any clue as to where they are?"

"We tracked them for a couple days. They headed northwest from Fulgor before we lost them." Anger sparked in Devlen's blue eyes.

"Do you think they're hiding in Ixia?" I asked.

"We have searched most of Moon Clan's lands and still have not found them. It is the one place we cannot look."

True. I'd have to send Valek an update.

"You mentioned another reason?" Opal asked.

Here we go. I drew in a breath. You'd think the telling would get easier the more times I recited it, but no, it was even more difficult. At least I knew Opal and Devlen would understand better than anyone else. Each had lost their magic. However, Opal was immune to magic like Valek and Devlen was glad to be rid of the burden.

When I finished, Opal rushed over and embraced me.

"Oh, Yelena, how horrible!"

"I'm hoping it's temporary." I swallowed the fat fist in my throat. "And I'm hoping you might have some information."

"What type of info?" Opal asked.

"I suspect it's a poison, but there was a gap in time between the bolt's strike and my symptoms. What if someone siphoned my powers?"

Opal knotted her hands together. "Maybe Quinn learned—"

"It wasn't him. Unless he could do it from a hundred miles away?"

She relaxed slightly. "No. I needed to be close to the person."

Devlen squeezed her shoulder, giving her moral support.

"And Quinn's a good kid," Leif said. "He smells like the sea—fresh and honest."

"You mentioned being sick for a day. What were the symptoms?" Devlen asked.

I explained about my extreme swings in temperature.

Devlen almost sloshed his tea on Opal's head. "I know what it is!"

15

VALEK

Valek was pleased with the morning's matches. Ari and Janco once again proved why they were his seconds-in-command and Onora revealed quite a bit about herself. Gerik hadn't been lying when he claimed to be good at fighting. He hadn't won a match, but, then again, he'd been fighting the best in Valek's corps. And he'd picked the wrong weapons against those two. Next time, Valek would suggest Gerik choose the bo staff against Ari and hand to hand against Janco.

What impressed him the most about Gerik was the man kept his cool during both bouts. Something Onora struggled with. He'd also confirmed that the two of them at least knew each other. Ah, the plot thickened. And more reasons to take a trip to MD-2.

According to the Commander's detail, they'd followed security protocol to the letter the night Onora attacked and Gerik had not been on duty. Valek was certain the intel Gerik provided to Onora helped her avoid the sweeps.

No. The real problem lay in the protocol and why the security team hadn't noticed the gaps. Valek had read it that morning and spotted the lapses right away. Alarming, since Maren had written the new protocols while Valek had been in Sitia.

And he didn't like where his thoughts led. Perhaps Maren had done it on purpose because of the Commander's request. Perhaps this had all been a test, including Onora's timely arrival. All of which Valek had failed.

As for the reason for the test, the Commander might be feeling vulnerable. Maybe Onora sneaked into the Commander's suite before Valek had returned and they'd worked out a deal.

Regardless of why the Commander had tested him, Valek would not let anyone else write the protocols or assign members to the Commander's detail again. He'd start fresh with a new group. Although he'd still like to talk to Maren. Where was she?

He returned to his office to finish a few things before his trip north. Reviewing personnel files and writing instructions on how to patrol a castle failed to keep Valek's mind from wandering. There had been no clue as to what mission Maren had been given and that irked him. Was finding Maren another test?

Valek was very familiar with tests. When he had moved from hand-to-hand combat to dueling with weapons at Hedda's school, the older students and instructors had tested his new skills at random intervals. He'd learned to sleep with a weapon in each of his hands.

He'd learned how to fight with different types of swords, bo staffs and a number of other sharp implements and nasty-looking devices, but fighting with a knife was his favorite. He loved getting up close and personal with his opponent, despite the drawbacks, like finding out Arbon sprinkled too much garlic in his food. And he loved how the blade was a deadly extension of his hand. Soon no one could beat him in a knife fight.

Hedda's threat hadn't been serious. No way he could master all the weapons within ten days. That would have been impossible. It was closer to ten months, and during that time Valek had turned fourteen.

Near the end of the ten-month span and at the start of the heating season, Hedda led him into a room. Weapons hung on the walls and a mat covered the floor. An unarmed man stood in the center. He wore the same clothes as Hedda, a light green tunic and loose pants. No boots.

Valek turned to her. "Another test?"

She smiled. "Yes." Hedda gestured to the assortment of weapons. "Use as many as you like. The goal is simple. If you can draw Jorin's blood, you win."

Sounded easy enough. Valek pulled two knives from the wall and tucked a couple of daggers into his belt. He faced Jorin. The man remained relaxed with his arms at his sides. Still unarmed. Hedda watched from the doorway.

"Whenever you're ready, Valek," she said.

He suspected a trick and that he was about to get trounced by this man. A lesson in how weapons made you lazy and gave you false confidence. Or something like that.

Valek nodded to the man and assumed a fighting stance. He shuffled close and attacked, slashing at the man's throat with his left hand and stabbing at his stomach with his right. Jorin twisted, grabbed both Valek's wrists and yanked him forward, ramming Valek with his knee before tossing him aside.

Valek scrambled to his feet as pain radiated from his ribs. No doubt Jorin had more training and experience than Valek. Determined, Valek rushed him again and ended up on his back again.

New strategy. Valek flipped his knives over, grabbed the blades and threw one a second after the other. A stickiness brushed his skin as both knives veered, missing Jorin by inches.

Interesting. Valek yanked a sword from the wall. Best to keep away from this guy. He approached and encountered a heavy thickness as if he'd walked into an invisible spiderweb. Odd. But not as odd as the surprise on Jorin's face as Valek lunged with his sword. What else did he expect? It wasn't like Valek hid the weapon behind his back.

Jorin countered in time, but he scrambled to keep ahead of Valek's strikes, which had slowed because of that strange sticky pressure. Too bad his blade couldn't cut through the invisible strands.

Eventually, Valek nicked Jorin's arm and Hedda ended the oddest match Valek had ever fought.

"Jorin, I told you to use magic on him," Hedda said.

The man pressed a cloth to his bleeding cut. "I did."

"All of it?" she asked.

"I couldn't read his thoughts or manipulate them. He broke through the shield and I couldn't stop his charge. Nothing worked."

"Wait, magic?" Valek asked.

"Yes," Hedda snapped. "You need to learn how to fight a magician. How else can you…?" She gaped at him.

Confused, Valek glanced at Jorin. "You're a magician?"

"Yes."

"That's why the knives missed. You used magic."

"Yes."

"Is that why…?" Valek brushed his face. The feeling of cobwebs still tingled on his skin.

"Why what?" Jorin asked.

"Why the air was sticky?"

Jorin exchanged a look with Hedda.

"Try it again," she said.

Turning his brown-eyed gaze on Valek, Jorin's brow creased. A wave of thick air engulfed him, clinging to his clothes.

"Is this how magic feels?" he asked, moving his arms around.

MARIA V. SNYDER

"You shouldn't feel anything," Jorin said. "You should be frozen solid, unable to move a muscle."

The magic pressed on him, slowing him down but not stopping him. He walked toward the magician. The soupy syrup thickened, but he pressed on and reached Jorin.

Sweat beaded the man's forehead. He released a breath and the air returned to normal. "Nothing works on him."

"So that means..." Delight danced in her eyes. "He's immune to magic. And he might be the one to assassinate the King."

"I *will* assassinate the King," Valek corrected. While he was unsure what this immunity meant, there never was any doubt about the King.

"I've never heard of anyone being immune. How long have you had this?" Jorin asked him.

"I don't know. My grandfather was the only magician in my family, but he died years ago. Other than him, I really haven't been around any magicians."

"How about that sticky feeling? Have you felt it before?" Hedda asked.

Valek searched his memory. "Once when I waited on your stoop. During our talk, I felt a brief touch."

"Ah, that's why Colette couldn't get a read on you. We thought it was due to the trauma."

Trauma. What a nice concise word for such ugliness and pain.

Hedda shook her head as if she still couldn't believe it. "And here I thought this would be a surprise lesson for you and contain your cockiness. It was a surprise all right." She blew out a breath. "Well, now, King Killer, more good news. I'm going to personally see to your training."

Uncertain what it meant to be Hedda's student, Valek decided to focus on her inflection instead. Before when she called him King Killer, it was a tease, like calling a small man big. Now her tone implied a matter-of-factness. That he liked very much.

Hedda's training included the usual sparring matches and mind-numbing repetition until he could perform a move in his sleep. However, he finally was learning the art of being an assassin, reading body language, picking locks, studying poisons, climbing buildings and lying without giving himself away.

"Remind me not to play poker with you, King Killer," Hedda joked one night after he'd convinced the cook that Arbon had spilled the soup even though white cream spotted Valek's pants.

When Valek had been at the school for almost two years, Hedda declared he was ready. He was fifteen years old. A mix of pride and unease swirled in his chest as he entered her office. Would she assign him a mark? Hedda not only trained assassins, but she was the go-between for many of her former students, taking half the assassination fees for her services.

However, the bigger question was, could he kill a man who hadn't been a party to his brothers' murders?

"I've a job for you, King Killer," Hedda said. "Think you can handle it?"

He straightened. "Yes."

"Good. You're the new stable boy for the Icefaren Garrison."

Not quite what he'd been expecting. "Who's the mark?"

"No one."

Had he done something wrong? "Then why?"

"A huge part of this job is collecting information. You need to learn this aspect. The actual assassination is the least time-consuming task. First you spend months and months assembling information about your mark. Then you spend days

MARIA V. SNYDER

and days planning your attack. The attack itself might take hours at most."

"All right. What information do you need?"

"A precise account of the comings and goings of all the officers in the garrison."

"You could bribe one of the enlisted for a copy of the duty roster."

"I could."

He considered. "But that might tip them off."

"Right. It's always better to have someone trusted inside. And not just anyone, but a person who is invisible. And that would be…?"

Valek recalled his lessons. "Servants, housekeepers, low-ranking staff members and the homeless."

"Correct. No one pays attention to the stable boys. Make sure you act and dress appropriately. There will be a place for you to sleep. If you're arrested, you are on your own. You're to report at dawn. Better get going."

"Yes, sir."

"Oh, and King Killer."

He turned. "Yes?"

"You'll be paid. Not very much, but I expect half of your wages. The other half is yours."

It seemed a fair deal. Hedda had provided food, clothing and weapons for the past two years and had asked for nothing in return. He wondered just how much an assassin earned. From the size of her school, he guessed quite a bit. And in the past two years the local authorities hadn't bothered them once, which meant a large portion of that money had to go to bribing the officials.

Valek packed a couple of knives, a handful of the gray rocks and another set of clothes. Stable boys couldn't afford more than two sets. He changed into his oldest tunic and pants. The clothes he'd arrived at Hedda's in no longer fit. He'd grown taller and thicker. Not barrel-chested, bulging-biceps thick, but a ropy muscular. Valek worried about keeping in shape while mucking out stalls.

After walking for four hours, he arrived at the stable just after dawn. The Stable Master cuffed him on the ear for being late. The desire to stab the guy flared, but stable boys didn't stab their masters if they wanted to stay invisible. He swallowed instead, gazing at the ground.

"Git your ass in there and help Reedy," the Stable Master said.

Valek helped Reedy, a skinny kid barely twelve, groom, water and feed horses. He mucked out stalls, swept up horse hair and cleaned tack. All day. The Stable Master's leftovers were their meals—not enough for one let alone two. And the "place to sleep" was a pile of straw bales under a scratchy smelly horse blanket in an empty stall, unless all the stalls were filled—then it was on a pile in the aisle without a blanket. And since it was the start of the cold season, he needed that blanket.

He kept track of the officers and discovered their names from their companions and the Stable Master. Most went out in the morning and returned in the evening. But groups would leave and be gone for days, doing sweeps of the outer towns.

After adjusting to the hard labor and long hours, Valek used the cover of darkness to climb into the rafters and onto the stable's roof to keep in practice. He also scaled the garrison's main building. A four-story wooden structure with windows.

His pay was a pittance, but he saved half for Hedda. With the other half he bought a few carving tools and a blanket at the market on his day off—the first in a month.

He showed Reedy how to carve. The boy picked it up quick.

"Maybe you can apprentice to a wood-carver," Valek suggested. "It's better than here."

The boy shrugged. "I like it here. Better than starving on the street. And the horses like me."

True. They preferred Reedy's care over his. Even though he'd learned more about horses in the past month than he thought possible. At one point, he thought he had marked all the officers, but then a big group he hadn't seen leave arrived one night from a sweep. Guess one month wouldn't be enough time.

Boredom eventually drove him to attempt to open a window and slip inside the garrison, thinking he'd find a duty roster and copy it so he could return to Hedda's.

Late one night, he climbed up to the third story on the darkest side of the building. The window opened without trouble. He entered an office, but it was too dark to read anything and he hadn't brought a match for the lantern. Voices nearby spooked him and he left.

Some assassin. He'd gone in unprepared and without an inkling of who was around that office or knowing if a light would have tipped them off to his presence or not. Next time, he'd be ready.

"Hey, boy." A boot nudged him in the ribs later that night. "Wake up. Help the riders."

Half-asleep, Valek rolled off the straw and pulled saddles from sweaty horses as the men collected their saddlebags. They laughed and joked and ignored Valek and Reedy.

"There's Fester. What took you so long, Fester? Did you get lost?" The man chuckled as another rider entered the stable.

"Damn horse threw a shoe," Fester grumbled.

Valek froze as ice seized his heart. That voice. He turned as Fester dismounted. The stable's lanterns lit the officer with a pale yellow glow. Beady eyes, bulbous nose, cracked lips—

Valek would never forget this murderer's face. He reached for his knife and paused, closing his eyes for a moment.

Lose the anger. Hedda's words repeated in his mind.

When he opened his eyes, he noticed the details he'd missed before. How many other armed officers crowded the stable. How close the Stable Master stood to him. If he stabbed Fester, they'd be on him in seconds. And what about the two other murderers? They'd be from this garrison, as well. Kill one and it would alert the others. Better to wait.

As he groomed the horses, he had to give Hedda credit. This was more than a training exercise in patience. He'd been so focused on learning to kill, he hadn't spared a moment to consider how he would find the soldiers who'd murdered his brothers in the King's name. She'd been one step ahead of him.

Over the next season, he discovered the names of the other murderers. He learned their schedules, habits, vices, and virtues—none. After he collected enough information, the next stage, planning, loomed over him. Without any prior instruction on how to plan revenge, he returned to Hedda's school on his next day off.

"That's an impressive amount of intel you collected in three months," Hedda said. "You need to find the best way to kill all three without being caught."

"That's why I'm here."

"All right. How do you want to do it? Kill them when they're together or pick them off one by one?"

Valek mulled it over. He doubted he could pull off killing three men unless he poisoned their water. Too easy a death. Only a knife stabbed in their guts or slit across their throats would satisfy him. "One by one."

"It'll take time. Kill one and the garrison will beef up security while they search for the killer. Months might go by before they relax enough for you to get to another one."

"Unless I find a night when they are each alone. I could

MARIA V. SNYDER

kill them all, and by the time they're discovered in the morning, I'll be long gone."

"But what are the odds they'll be by themselves at the same time?"

"Slim. I could follow them when they're out collecting taxes."

"But what if they go in three different directions? That's a lot of ground to cover. And news spreads fast."

"I'm not going to get all three at once, am I?"

"I think you just figured that out."

"Best to get who I can, then wait. There's no rush. I know who they are."

"Now you're thinking like an assassin. And in between, you can earn money and experience doing *other* jobs," Hedda said.

Lieutenant Fester would be the first man Valek assassinated. As he waited for the perfect opportunity, he carved a statue, transforming the ugly gray rock into a black figure with sparks of silver. His chance came a week later. No squads were due to arrive that night and Fester had just returned from a long sweep.

After finishing his stable chores for the night, Valek lay on a stack of straw bales and waited for Reedy and the Stable Master to fall asleep.

The soon-to-be dead man had headed straight to the garrison and, Valek hoped, to bed. The lieutenant frequently complained about the uncomfortable travel shelters and run-down inns the soldiers overnighted in, and each time he returned home, he made a beeline for his own bed.

The ragged snores from the Stable Master's room at the far end of the stable soon joined the soft nighttime noises of the horses. Valek slipped out the window of the empty stall he shared with Reedy. The boy didn't move.

A half-moon provided enough light for him to navigate the compound even though he stayed hidden in the shadows. He wore all black, and once he was well away, he stopped to cover his face and hands with black greasepaint. The air held a chill. However, by the time he reached the main building, he'd sweated through his clothes.

Leaning against the wall below Fester's third-floor rooms, Valek pressed a hand to his chest, willing his heartbeat to slow. Emotions jumbled together, clouding his thoughts. Fear mixed with anger. Hate churned along with trepidation. One thing to think about killing a person, quite another to do the actual deed. Could he?

He focused on the image of his brother Vincent lying in a pool of his own blood and intestines. Vincent's expression frozen in surprised pain as he clutched his stomach. His skin as cold as the snow underneath him. The echo of Vincent's laugh thumped in Valek's heart as the memory of their mother chasing them after they'd knocked down her clothesline full of sheets. Neither one of them could resist the lure of fresh, clean sheets blowing in the breeze. Stealth tag had to be played despite stern warnings to keep away. And that time a rowdy collision led to a collapse. They'd bolted and hid behind the shed until their mother had cooled down.

Vincent had been fifteen when Fester's sword cut him down. Their mother had held Valek back as his brother staggered to the snow. Her fingernails had pierced his shoulders, drawing blood. Small half-moon-shaped scars still marked his skin.

Valek pulled in a breath.

Lose the emotions.

The man murdered his brothers. Justice would finally be done tonight. And experience gained for the ultimate goal—

MARIA V. SNYDER

the King. Pushing the fear, doubt, hate and anger away, Valek drew icy determination into his heart.

He scaled the wall to the third story, slid the window open and paused, listening. The creak of a bedspring and sleep mutterings sounded from the bedroom. Valek eased into the room. The dim moonlight outlined a bulky shape beneath a blanket. He grabbed his knife, advancing on Fester.

By the time Valek reached the bed, his heart rate had returned to normal. With one quick hop, Valek knelt on Fester's chest and pressed the blade against his fleshy throat.

"What the—"

"Shut up and listen," Valek said in a low voice. "Do you remember the tanner's sons? Three boys, Vincent, Viliam and Victor? Ages fifteen and seventeen-year-old twins?"

"Look—"

"Yes or no?" Valek cut into the skin. Blood oozed.

Fester hissed in pain. "Yes."

"You missed one. Sloppy."

"Orders." Panic sharpened his voice. "I was under orders."

"To murder?"

"To make an example out of them. The blizzards had been so bad…no one in Icefaren wanted to pay their taxes." The words tumbled from his lips in a rush. "Boss said the King needed his money and we had to show them what would happen if they didn't pay."

"He targeted my family?"

"No. Just said to pick—" Fester realized his mistake. "I didn't—"

"What's the boss's name?"

"Captain Aniol."

"You should have told your boss to go to hell." Valek sliced deep into the man's throat.

Blood sprayed, soaking Fester's shirt, sheets, blanket and

Valek's sleeves. A hot metallic smell filled the air along with the stink of excrement and body odor. The shine in Fester's eyes dulled as all color leaked from his skin.

Valek stared at the dead man. No regret pulsed inside him. Just a deep feeling of satisfaction.

He wiped his blade and hands on Fester's blanket. Then he removed the statue from his pocket. The figure resembled Vincent. He placed it on Fester's still chest before Valek climbed out the window. Sliding the pane back into place, Valek descended the wall. The compound remained empty at this time of night. The soldiers patrolled only the outer perimeter.

Before he had reached the stable, he had stripped off his shirt and thrown it into one of the still-smoldering burn barrels. Then he had washed the greasepaint from his hands and face. Slipping back into the stall, he had donned a clean shirt and reclaimed his spot on the hay bales.

No sense running away and tipping them off about the culprit. Better to stay and watch and learn all he could about Captain Aniol.

Hedda had called it hiding in plain sight.

A sudden notion jolted Valek from his memories. Maybe the reason he couldn't determine Maren's whereabouts was because she'd been hiding in plain sight all this time? No. Maren had a distinctive stride, and he'd have spotted her by now.

The reason must be because the Commander was up to something. And the only thing that he wouldn't inform Valek about or include him in was something big involving Sitia. Something that would ruin their diplomatic relationship if the Sitians found out.

Valek didn't know what was worse, the Commander not trusting him or the fact that more trouble between the two countries could lead to war.

MARIA V. SNYDER

16

JANCO

The Black Cat Tavern was everything a tavern should be—long bar with plenty of stools and bartenders, big tables for groups of rowdy soldiers, pretty servers who knew how to handle drunken customers, and little nooks around the edges for hosting private conversations. Plus the ale was to die for! Just the right blend of hops and barley and—

"Janco! Are you paying attention?" Ari asked.

"Sure, chief. Me and Little Miss Assassin are going to go undercover, and—"

"Not you—Gerik and Onora."

Janco shook his head. "Not happening."

"Why not?"

"'Cause we can't trust them together. And, as much as I'll miss you, Ari old boy, I'm gonna take one for the team."

Ari rubbed his face. They sat in their favorite nook—the farthest from the door and the deepest in shadow. Onora refused to order a drink. She'd leaned back in her chair with her arms crossed as if they were going to jump her. As if. The grunt sipped his ale, pretending to be relaxed. Except he gripped the glass hard enough for the muscles on his forearm to pop. Impressive pop, though.

"I know better than to ask, but...take one for the team?" Ari set his mug down.

"All your plans are swell, really they are, but they're not gonna work. The same people who recognize us are gonna spot Sergeant Grunt here right away. We need to come at this from a different direction."

Understanding lit Ari's eyes. "Sitia."

"Yup. I'll take the young pup south and you and the grunt do all the typical stuff we do to find information—interrogate the prisoners, follow the leads—so it looks like we're investigating."

"We have to determine a potential location of the smugglers first. The border's over a thousand miles long with lots of small Sitian towns nearby. And you'll need a good disguise. They know you in Sitia."

Janco pished. "The least of my worries."

"And what's your biggest worry?" Onora asked, speaking for the first time.

"My mother. I'm supposed to visit her. It's been forever and she's not gonna be happy."

She huffed in disbelief. "I can kill you in your sleep and you're worried about your mother?"

"You won't kill me."

"Why not?"

"'Cause Valek scares you. While my mother... Nobody scares her."

After their meeting, Ari and Janco returned to their office in the castle. Half the size of Valek's, it contained two of everything—desks, chairs, filing cabinets. One set was neat and organized, and the other set was Janco's. Valek had left a huge stack of reports from his spies in Sitia on Ari's desk. They scanned through the latest ones. Concentrating on the

MARIA V. SNYDER

information from the towns close to the Ixian border, they searched for anything out of the ordinary.

After a few hours, Janco's head ached with all the mind-numbing details. "Listen to this… Forty-three citizens attended the town meeting along with four officials. They voted to install a statue outside the town hall. Seriously? This is what our spies think is important?" He tossed the report on the messy pile with all the other useless data.

"This one dutifully records the entire conversation between two wives of two low-level aides in the Cloud Mist Clan. They talked about a woman named Melinda, who was in labor for three days and had triplets." Ari snapped his shut.

They worked for a while in silence. Janco's vision blurred as he skimmed an inventory list in a factory in the Moon Clan's lands—spare wagon wheels, hitches, nuts, bolts, drying racks, rollers, glass bottles, tubing… As he was about to close the file, an item jumped from the page. A barrel full of leaves.

Why would a factory need leaves? Maybe it was for a medical substance. Yelena's father created all types of medicines and healing salves from the plants he'd collect in the Illiais Jungle. Janco read the rest of the report.

The spies had targeted the place because there had been plenty of activity inside, but as far as they could determine, no products had been produced. They had sneaked in and still couldn't figure out what the factory was manufacturing.

If they'd been making medicine, then the spies would have spotted vials or pouches. What else could be made from leaves? "Cigars."

"What about them?" Ari asked.

Janco handed him the file. "I think this place might be producing them."

Ari flipped through the pages. "It's possible. But there's no way to know if they're manufacturing the illegal Greenblade cigars or regular cigars."

"The building is located in Lapeer near the Ixian border. It's an isolated area of the Moon Clan's lands and far away from the other factories down in Greenblade's forests. It's a place to start."

"We should talk to Valek. He might know what this is."

They found Valek outside his office. He unlocked his door and ushered them inside.

"Did you find something?" Valek asked.

Ari explained about the factory, handing the file to Valek.

He scanned the report, then tapped on a page. "This mentions an amber-colored liquid."

"Could be honey-tree sap used in the cigars," Janco suggested.

"Or real honey or resin or adhesive," Valek said. "There could be a number of different explanations."

"We should check it out since we're going to Sitia anyway."

"You are?"

"Uh…" Janco glanced at Ari for help.

Ari gave him a you-got-yourself-into-this-you-get-yourself-out-of-it smirk. Some partner. Janco told Valek about their meeting and conclusions. "It makes the most sense. We're not going to get far on this side of the border."

Valek studied him for a moment. "Finish reading through *all* the reports first."

Janco groaned. "That'll take days."

"Then I'd suggest you enlist the help of the rest of your team members," Valek said.

"But…"

"But what?" Valek used his flat warning tone.

Janco ignored it. "We don't trust them, do we?"

"I trust you to keep an eye on them." He accompanied

MARIA V. SNYDER

them out of his office. "I'm going to be leaving in a few days, as well."

"Where are you going?" Janco asked.

"North to MD–2."

"Investigating our new recruits?" Ari asked.

"Yes." Valek locked the door and headed in the opposite direction.

As they walked down the hallway, Janco scratched the scar where the lower half of his right ear used to be. "If he doesn't trust them, then why are they working with us?"

"No idea."

"What should we do?"

"We'll do what Valek said—keep them close." Ari shrugged. "Who knows, they might prove useful."

Stranger things had happened.

While Ari rounded up the grunt and Little Miss Assassin, Janco carried armloads of files over to a conference room. Over the course of multiple trips, he filled the long table. By the time the others arrived, Janco had finished writing the cheat sheet to help them decipher the code to read the reports.

Sergeant Grunt frowned at the piles, but Little Miss Assassin sat down and tucked her bare feet under her.

Ari explained what they sought from the reports. "…an oddity or something that doesn't belong. Anything that sticks out."

"Like your bare feet," Janco said to the young pup. "Don't your feet ever get cold?" He couldn't resist asking. Not many rugs covered the stone floors of the castle.

"No." She kept her gaze on Ari.

"Well, when we go undercover, you're gonna have to wear boots."

"Okay."

Janco deflated. He'd hoped for an argument, but she wouldn't rise to the bait. She wasn't the chattiest person, either. At least the grunt asked a few questions as they spent the rest of the afternoon and evening reading reports. How could a person keep quiet that long? Was it part of her assassin training? If so, he'd never pass the test.

When the words blurred together and his eyelids drooped as if they weighed a thousand pounds, Janco called it quits for the night.

The next morning after running laps and training with Ari, he returned to the dreaded task of going through the files. Little Miss Assassin had beaten them there and she had quite a stack of rejects piled on the floor near her seat.

"Have you been here all night?" Ari asked as he sat.

"No." She handed him a couple of files. "These meet your 'odd' criteria."

Janco peered over Ari's shoulder as he flipped through the pages. Most of the information she flagged could be explained.

"Sitians use magic all the time." Janco shuddered. "It is odd, strange, unnatural, weird, crazy—"

"It's a tool," Ari said. "You just don't like magic."

"For good reason! Remember the time—"

"Why did you tag this one from Ognap?" Ari handed her a report.

The pup scanned it and pointed to a passage. "The agent counted sixteen wagons going into the mines, but only thirteen leaving. Doesn't make sense. These mines produce coal and ore, so they'd need all those wagons to ship *out* the product."

"Maybe they were having a slow day," Janco said. "See? The next day they had sixteen in and then sixteen leave... Oh." What happened to those other three?

Ari reclaimed the file. "Looks like there's a pattern. Every three days, more wagons arrive than leave."

"Could this be the smuggling route?" Janco asked. "Through the mines?"

"You tell me. You're the one who spent a few weeks undercover at Vasko's ruby mines."

He scratched his scar. "There are a million miles of shafts under the Emerald Mountains. It's possible that there's a way to cross under the Ixian border and come out in the Soul Mountains. But..."

"But what?" Little Miss Assassin asked.

"The mine owners guard their maps with their lives. They don't let strangers into the mines. For one person to know how all those shafts connect..." He shook his head. "Impossible."

"They don't have to know all of them. Just the right ones," Ari said.

"And you said Sitians used their power all the time. Why couldn't they use magic to find a passage into Ixia?"

The young pup had a point. Unfortunately. A cold dread coated his stomach. Two things Janco despised more than anything—magic and being underground. And it appeared he might just get both at once. Oh joy.

17

YELENA

I gaped at Devlen as blood slammed through my heart. Did he just say…? "You know what the poison is?"

"I believe so. But I am not sure how it will help you."

Relaxing my grip on the teacup before it shattered, I calmed my out-of-control heart rate. "Please explain."

Devlen set his cup down and sat in the other chair opposite Opal's desk and between me and Leif. My brother perched on the edge of his seat and Opal leaned forward. All our attention focused on Devlen.

"Your symptoms of being hot and then cold sounds like the effects of a poison called Freeze Burn," he said. "It is made from the roots of the reedwither plant that grows in the Avibian Plains."

"How come I've never heard of this poison?" I asked.

"Only the Sandseeds know about it, and the plant is so rare, only one was found during my father's lifetime, but the Sandseed who discovered it refused to divulge the location. According to our stories, it is fatal, but before the victim dies, they suffer those extreme temperature swings you described for a full day."

Another near miss. The familiar ache of disappointment panged. "It can't be Freeze Burn. I didn't die."

"That's 'cause it's *you*," Leif said. "You said you expelled most of the poison from your shoulder. Combine that with your healing powers and...voilà! You survived."

Great. How did this information help me? "Is there a cure?"

Devlen shook his head. "Not that I know. In our stories, everyone died."

I considered. "If we can find the plant, then perhaps my father can find a cure. Do you know what it looks like and where it grows?"

"All I know is that it has long thin leaves, resembling blades of grass. In fact, it is often mistaken for a patch of crabgrass until you get closer and see that the blades are attached to a red stem. It is said that the Sandseed horses avoid those plants because the roots poison the water sources nearby."

"Who else knows about the reedwither plant?" Opal asked Devlen.

"The Sandseeds. Not many of them left, though."

"Less people to interrogate," Leif quipped.

No one smiled.

"I don't believe the Sandseeds would share this information with anyone or use the poison to attack Yelena," Opal said. "They view her as family."

"I agree," Devlen said.

My thoughts circled back to Ben Moon and his famous ancestor. Perhaps the knowledge of Freeze Burn had been passed down to Ben in Master Magician Ellis Moon's book. It wouldn't be the first time forgotten information had returned to cause major problems—blood magic and the Kirakawa ritual both sprang to mind. Unfortunately, it probably wouldn't be the last.

"Do you think you can envision the plant so Kiki can pick

up on the image?" I asked Devlen. Perhaps she could find it in the plains.

"I can try."

Devlen accompanied us to the Second Chance Inn. When we left, we promised Opal to return that evening for supper. On the way to the inn, we talked about Devlen's new family.

"It has been an adjustment," he admitted. "I am still in shock that Opal wishes to be with me and the fact she *married* me..." He spread his hands wide. "Plus taking care of two children is a bigger responsibility than I had thought. It is a bit overwhelming at times."

"And then you have to deal with the crazy in-laws." Leif smirked.

"Opal's parents and brother have been very supportive."

I laughed. "Notice he didn't defend *you*, big brother."

"Shut up."

"How is Teegan doing at the Keep?" I asked Devlen.

"I was hoping you could tell us. We have only gotten a few letters from him."

"I haven't seen him. I don't spend too much time at the Keep."

"I thought since Master Jewelrose has taken him on as her student, she would confide in you."

That I didn't know. "She hasn't said anything. Although, I've been focused on my own problems."

He gave me a wry smile. "I understand all too well. When Opal drained my powers from me, I could not think of anything else besides reclaiming my power."

"Do you miss it?"

"Not at all. But it took me a season to adjust to the loss and another to realize I was much better off without it. She freed me from the addiction—I had not realized just how much that craving controlled my actions. I had done nothing but bad things with my magic and have no wish to return to being that evil man. However, your loss goes beyond yourself. You have done nothing but good things, and if you do not recover your power, the entire world will suffer."

Leif huffed. "I think you're being melodramatic."

"Aren't you like the pot calling the kettle black or something?" I asked.

"Pardon me, oh great one. I forgot my place as a mere footnote in the history of Sitia."

Talk about being melodramatic.

"Is he—"

I cut Devlen off. "Annoying? Yes, all the time."

He studied Leif. "You are more…subdued at our house."

"That's 'cause I'm too busy keeping your daughter out of trouble."

"I take it Reema has Leif wrapped around her little finger?" I asked Devlen.

"Hey," Leif said.

"Yes. He needs a child of his own to learn how to *not* give in to her every demand."

I agreed. "That would certainly mature him. Unless it backfires and Leif regresses. Then poor Mara would have two children to deal with."

"I'm standing right here, ya know."

We ignored him. The late-morning sun warmed my back and I considered removing my cloak. The warming season would officially start in three days.

Arriving at the stable, we woke Kiki from a light doze. She nuzzled my pockets, searching for a treat. I explained to her what we hoped to do. "Can you help?"

She turned her blue-eyed gaze to Devlen and pricked her ears forward. He stared back. I glanced at Leif. Was it working? He shrugged. Leif had told me before he couldn't smell the horses' magic, but I hoped he sensed something.

Kiki snorted and returned to snuffling my pockets. I removed a small apple I had swiped at breakfast and fed it to her.

As she munched and slobbered apple juice on my palm, I asked Devlen about the search for Ben Moon. "Where was his last known location?"

"We had tracked him north to a town about two and a half days from Fulgor. A place called Red Oak. It is a small village—a handful of farms, houses and a couple factories along the Sunworth river. Their main industry is logging the surrounding forest and making parchment from the wood."

"And you lost him in a tiny town where strangers would stick out like a skinny pig in a hog house?" Leif asked.

"He left Red Oak in the middle of the night and disappeared without a trace. From there, he could have gone in any direction, but we circled the town and found no trail signs."

I mulled over the information. "The Sunworth river becomes the border between Ixia and Sitia for a few miles near the Emerald Mountains. Could he have traveled on the river going upstream to the mountains? Or perhaps downstream toward Featherstone lands?"

"We searched the banks for boot prints in the mud or evidence of a boat launch. Nothing for miles in either direction."

"Perhaps they used magic to erase their tracks," Leif suggested.

Logical. Ben was a powerful magician and he'd teamed up with at least a couple of others. "Does Ben have any other siblings?"

"One sister, who is taking care of their parents. They have not been in contact with Ben in years or his brother Owen's wife, who is still serving time at Dawnwood Prison."

Ah yes, Selene. I'd scared her by promising to take her soul

MARIA V. SNYDER

to the fire world if she didn't cooperate and release my brother and Valek. "Dawnwood? Not Wirral?"

Devlen nodded. "She is redeemable. Selene cooperated with the authorities. Wirral is for those who are beyond redemption."

Too bad. Everyone deserved a chance at redemption.

Leif and I sat in the inn's common room, eating dinner and discussing our next move.

"We'll leave in the morning for the plains," I said.

"What about visiting Pazia?" He filled his spoon with a huge mass of banana pudding. The portion wriggled on its way to his mouth.

"First we find the reedwither plant and deliver it to Father. If he can't help us, then we'll visit her." I swirled the yellow dessert around my bowl. Unless Bain learned something from one of his old books, Pazia represented my last hope for a solution.

Then what? Find and confront Ben? I shied away from those thoughts. I'd worry about it when the time came. Coward, who me?

Hale joined us and a server arrived to take his order. He studied our expressions for a moment after she left. "I'm guessing the news isn't good."

"It's mixed." I explained about the Freeze Burn poison.

"Not a very original name," Hale said.

"The Sandseeds aren't known for their creativity." Leif finished his dessert and snagged my full bowl. "They call it like it is. It's very refreshing."

"Unless they're doing their Story Weaver thing," I muttered. "Then it's all cryptic and annoying." And hard to describe. "What about you? Anything?"

Hale repeated most of Devlen's information. "The town guards believe there are five of them, including Ben."

Four unknowns. "Are any of the others magicians?" I asked.

"Yes." He scrunched up his face as if sniffing a bad odor. "All of them."

Leif choked, spitting out gobs of pudding. "You mean all five have magic?"

Hale snapped, "That's what 'all of them' means."

Ah. There was Hale's snooty side. But even more disturbing was the news that Ben traveled with four other magicians. Even if I had my magic, I had no chance against them.

Leif ignored Hale as he wiped his chin. "Then it's a good thing we're heading into the plains. Should we leave this afternoon?"

"Why? There's no danger. Besides, we can't. I promised Reema I'd finish the story tonight." I considered as the server returned with Hale's food. "Has anyone spotted them since Red Oak?"

"No." Hale pulled his dinner out of Leif's reach.

Smart man. "Devlen speculated that they're in Ixia. What do you think?"

"Even with uniforms and the proper papers, it's hard to hide in Ixia. If I were them, I'd head east to the Emerald Mountains. There are lots of hiding places in the foothills." Hale cut into his steaming meat pie.

True. But just in case, I would send a message to Valek after we finished. "Did you learn the names of the other magicians?" I asked Hale.

"Yes. Although I only recognize one of them, Tyen Cowan. He was Ben's best friend when they attended the Keep together. Tyen's power to move large and multiple objects is impressive."

"He's from Opal's clan. Do you think she knows him?" I asked Leif.

"It doesn't matter." Leif pulled his glass super messenger from his pack. "I'll ask Irys for more information. Who are the others?"

"Rika Bloodgood, Cilly and Loris Cloud Mist. I'm not sure if they're married or siblings," Hale said.

Leif stared into the messenger as Hale finished his meal. I considered what to do with the information we collected. Best thing would be to give it to Devlen. Perhaps it would help with the investigation.

"Irys said she'll gather information on the prison gang and get back to me later," Leif said. "What should we do in the meantime?"

"Can you talk to your friends in the Council Hall and see if they'll tell you how they broke Ben out of prison?"

"Will do." Leif leaned back. He'd scraped every morsel of pudding from the bowl.

"How will the details of a prison break help you?" Hale asked me.

"I don't know. But there might be something that might seem odd or irrelevant that might give us a clue as to what they're planning."

"Wouldn't the authorities have done that already?"

"Yes, but they haven't been trained by Valek. He taught me to look beyond the standard replies."

"Taught us," Leif said.

"Correct. And in looking beyond, take Hale with you to the Council Hall. He can overhear any conversations you spark."

"Spark?" Hale asked.

"Yeah. You know how sometimes people might not talk to you, but after you leave…"

"They discuss it with a colleague. I get it." Hale paused. "Are you coming along?"

"No. Too many people know me at the Council Hall. And if I'm spotted, the security officers will expect me to aid in the search for Ben Moon."

"But you are helping."

"Yes, *I* am." I tapped my chest. "But the *Soulfinder* is unavailable and they'd rather have her assisting them in capturing five magicians."

"Oh." After Hale finished his dinner, they left the inn and headed into downtown. I sent the message to Valek, warning him Ben might be in Ixia along with his powerful friends. Then I spent the next couple of hours grooming Kiki. The repetitive motion of the currycomb through her coat calmed my mind and centered my thoughts. Valek had his carving rocks, and I had my beautiful Kiki.

Leif and Hale returned a few hours later. They joined me in the stable. Kiki, Garnet and Rusalka gleamed.

"Did you learn anything at the hall?" I asked.

"No one would talk to us," Leif said. "So…" He pulled a thick folder from underneath his cloak. "We helped ourselves."

"You stole it?"

"We borrowed it. Big difference."

"How?"

"Hale put the whammy on one of the secretaries. When she dashed off convinced her boss needed her right away, we… er…appropriated the warden's file, detailing the escape."

"All right. Let's go inside and read through the file. Maybe something will pop."

We spread the pages on the table and each took a section to study, then swapped them when finished. In the late afternoon, Leif stopped to pull his messenger out. He frowned at the glass cube and wrote notes on a crumpled piece of parchment. When he finished, he met my gaze.

"That bad?" I asked.

"Worse. These are powerful magicians that had been operating on their own, but now have teamed up. The Ethical Code means nothing to them."

"Tell us what you learned from Irys."

Leif smoothed the paper flat. "Ben Moon is the most powerful of the group. He can produce a null shield, light fires, move small objects and influence others with his magic.

"Tyen Cowan can only move objects. Unlike Ben, he's not limited in the size and weight of the object. Tyen has been known to move boulders." Leif tapped the file with his index finger. "He's the one who slammed all those correctional officers into the stone walls, knocking them unconscious.

"Cilly and Loris Cloud Mist are siblings born a year apart. They have the strongest mental communication skills of the group. They're the ones who used their magic to force the correctional officers at Wirral to unlock the doors and guide them to Ben's cell.

"Rika Bloodgood's specialty is illusions. Strong illusions that can even fool other magicians. She also has the power to create what's known as mirror illusions that mimic the surrounding area and will remain intact even if you view it through a null shield."

"Will her illusions fool Valek, as well?" I asked.

"Yes, and Opal, too. During the escape, the Wirral officers not in the area of the attacks saw and heard nothing out of the ordinary until it was too late."

"Quite the crew," Hale said into the silence.

I considered the array of talents at Ben's disposal. "Devlen said they lost the gang in Red Oak. With Rika's ability to cast convincing illusions, perhaps they hid behind an illusion. They could still be there."

"Possible, but doubtful," Leif said. "The town's too small. Someone would have said something by now."

True.

"But they could have left clues or a trail to where they went," Hale said. "They'd be pretty confident at that point that they'd given the authorities the slip."

"Good point," Leif said, although he didn't appear happy about it.

I straightened the papers and tucked them back into the folder. "Leif and I will take this along with our information to Devlen. He can bring it all to Fulgor's security forces." I stood. "Hale, we'll be back later. We'll leave for the plains in the morning." Hale nodded and we left the inn. The sun had set while we'd been reading through the file. Leif insisted we stop at the Pig Pen to purchase a container of beef stew to take with us.

"We can't arrive empty-handed," Leif had said.

The savory smell of hot meat and spices teased me the rest of the way to the factory. My stomach growled in anticipation. But as we neared the entrance, Leif slowed.

"Something wrong?" I asked.

"I caught a whiff…" He sniffed the air as if trying to catch a scent. Leif handed me the bag of food. "Go on inside. I'll just do a loop around."

Unease replaced hunger. "We should have brought Hale."

Leif pished. "Nonsense. I'm sure it's nothing."

Devlen answered the door and frowned. "You should not be alone."

I explained about Leif's loop.

He gestured me inside. "Go upstairs. I will wait for Leif."

In the apartment upstairs, Opal helped Reema with her

MARIA V. SNYDER

homework, explaining fractions. But as soon as Reema spotted me, she abandoned her lesson, grabbed the bag and proceeded to unpack the food. By the time she'd ladled out five bowls, Leif and Devlen had joined us.

My appetite returned with a wave of relief.

"Told you it was nothing," Leif said.

"Really?" I cocked an eyebrow at him.

"Okay, it was a family of cats in the side alley." Leif gave Devlen an odd look. "Seems they are…friends and wished to enter the factory."

Opal laughed. "We're having a problem with rodents in the factory and those cats are happy to take care of them for us."

"And in exchange?" Leif asked.

"Food and a warm place to sleep the night," Devlen said. "That big black tomcat has earned his keep many times over. He has taken down rats that are almost as big as him. We named him Valek, the rat assassin."

I laughed. How fitting. "I'll save him a piece of beef, then."

Reema served the stew and quiet descended as we devoured the food. Between bites, Reema talked about school. "Today the class learned about percentages, but I already knew all about them, except I don't call it by that fancy name. It's a cut. No matter what you scored on the street, you always had to give a cut to the bullies or to the so-called landlords or to the officers to look the other way." She scoffed. "I'm not learning anything."

"You learned the word *percentage*," Opal said.

Reema didn't bother to reply. "And the other kids are so… so soft! Crybabies and whiners." She pitched her voice higher. "Teacher, I spilled my milk. Teacher, she pushed me. Teacher, I'm a blubbering baby."

Suppressing a laugh, I kept my expression neutral. Reema had grown up on the streets and survived by dodging the cruelties of that life and, in her mind, that was all she needed to know.

"Reema, that is enough," Devlen said. "School is important."

"For what? When is the history of Sitia *ever* going to be important?"

"I can answer that," I said. "I thought the same thing when I first started my studies at the Keep. Master Bloodgood gave me so many history books to read, I thought I'd be crushed under them. And while reading them, I wished they had crushed me so I didn't have to read anymore."

"This isn't helping, Yelena," Opal said.

"*But* when I was struggling to understand my powers and terrified I was a Soulstealer, it was the information provided in those history books which led me to realize I was a Soulfinder. Big difference. That *knowledge* saved me from execution."

Reema squinted at me as if not sure whether to believe me or not. Her dubious expression aged her and she looked years older than ten.

"It's true," Opal said. "I was there."

"Well, I'd rather learn how to be a spy like Uncle Valek," Reema said. "Do you think he'd take me on as his student?" she asked me.

Opal and Devlen held their breaths. Leif choked on his food.

"Only after you graduated from the Magician's Keep."

"You're lying," Reema said.

"Reema!" Opal and Devlen said at the same time.

I was unable to stop the laughter bubbling from my throat.

Once he caught his breath, Leif said, "Gotta love the honesty."

"Yelena, we are trying to teach Reema manners and respect," Devlen said.

"All right. Reema, you can be brutally honest with *me* and

Uncle Leif at any time. However, you can't accuse someone of lying. You first have to collect proof, and—"

"Yelena!"

This time Reema laughed as her adopted parents scolded me. Her humor died when Opal told her to get ready for bed.

"You'll finish the story, right?" Reema asked me.

"Yes. I'll give you a few minutes to get changed and I'll be in. Where were we?"

"The curious Valmur was hanging from a vine by only one claw and a jungle cat waited below for him to fall."

"Oh yes. Now go." I shooed her away.

Reema hurried down the hallway leading to the washroom and bedrooms. The apartment contained only six rooms, kitchen, living area, washroom and three bedrooms. The office had been converted so each kid would have a room.

Once Reema disappeared into the washroom, I asked, "May I make a suggestion?"

"Of course," Opal said.

"Perhaps Reema needs to be in a higher grade. That might challenge her."

"The problem for her is that no one grade fits," Opal said. "In some areas like math and street smarts, she's well above her peers, but in others like history and reading…she's well below. We thought it best to keep her with the other ten-year-olds."

It made sense.

"And this way she'll learn patience." Opal cleared the table.

"I'm ready!" Reema called from the hallway. "Come on, come on!" She dashed into her room.

"Patience, eh? Good luck with that." I ducked as Opal threw a dish towel at my head.

As I strode toward her room, I glanced at the intricate and beautiful stained-glass murals hanging on the walls. I had never appreciated the versatile aspects of glass until I met Opal. I lingered over one particular swirl of orange that curved into yellow, split into red and looped back, tracing the pattern with a finger. Lovely.

A dim light shone through the small gap between the door and jamb of Reema's room. I pushed it wider as I stepped inside. And froze.

Reema's bed was empty. The curtains billowed as a cold breeze blew in from the open window.

18

VALEK

Over the next two days, Valek read through all the files, discussed the smugglers with Ari's team and assigned a new squad to the Commander's personal security detail.

Happy with Ari and Janco's strategy, Valek watched them depart the castle complex that morning. Janco and Onora headed south while Ari and Gerik went east. Janco had been in high spirits, and by the crease in Onora's forehead, she would either kill him by the time they reached their destination or ditch him. If she was smart, she'd discover how useful he could be when he wasn't driving a person to distraction and when he was—Janco was talented like that.

Valek returned to his office to finish preparing for his mission to MD-2. A light knock on the door interrupted him an hour later.

"Come in," Valek said. He grasped the handle of his knife.

A young page entered. The boy held out a rolled parchment as if it was a shield. "Message for you, sir." His voice quavered.

Valek took the message. "Thank you."

The page nodded and bolted.

Amused, he broke the seal and unrolled the message. His grin widened when he realized the note was from Yelena.

But soon his humor faded as he translated the text. The Sitian Council should be assassinated. He wished Yelena hadn't talked him out of it when the Council had handed Sitia over to those Daviian Warpers. Why wouldn't they warn her about Ben? Valek's fingers twitched. A sharp knife pressed to a Councilor's jugular would certainly help loosen his tongue.

Fear replaced anger when he finished reading the message. Yelena, Leif and another magician were headed to Fulgor— probably there by now. Despite the fact he couldn't go, Valek calculated how fast he and Onyx could travel to Fulgor from here—about four and a half days. The Commander had ordered him to keep out of it, and besides…Yelena was more than capable of defending herself. Plus she had Leif and another magician. At least she was being smart and cautious for once.

Although the desire to assassinate the Council still pumped in his heart. It'd be so easy. He could kill every one of them in a single night. Valek already knew the location of all their apartments in the Citadel, thanks to his alter ego Adviser Ilom. While pretending to be Ambassador Signe's aide six years ago, Valek had had plenty of time and opportunity to explore the Citadel. Time he hadn't wasted.

Assassinating all the soldiers who'd murdered his brothers hadn't been easy. After Lieutenant Fester's body had been discovered, security had increased and an investigation had been launched. Valek had kept a low profile and continued to gather intelligence about the soldiers in the garrison while working as a stable boy.

It took a full season for the guards to relax and lapse back into old habits. Valek carved more statues as he waited another couple of weeks just to let them get comfortable. And when Second Lieutenant Dumin returned early from his patrol the day before Sergeant Edvard left for his sweep, Valek celebrated. His patience had been rewarded and killing those two murderers in one night would be sweet.

When the sounds of the garrison settled into the nighttime quiet, Valek slipped from the stable and crossed the complex. So familiar with the layout, he could have navigated the way to the officers' quarters blind.

As he scaled the outer wall, Valek remembered his brother Viliam, who had been the prankster of the family and the only one with gray eyes. The others had brown like their father and Valek's blue was inherited from their mother. Dad liked to joke that he would accuse the mechanic of improper behavior, except Viliam's twin, Victor, looked more like Dad. Of course, Dad wasn't laughing when Viliam had booby-trapped a container of leather dye. Their father walked around with black hands and arms for two seasons. Viliam wisely kept out their father's way during that time.

The image of Viliam's shocked and confused expression as a sword pierced his heart replaced Valek's fond memories. The weapon held by the soon-to-be deceased Second Lieutenant Dumin.

When he reached the fourth floor, Valek found Dumin's window and paid the man a visit. Just like he had with Fester, Valek woke him and informed him of the reason he was about to die. And just like Fester, Dumin pointed the finger at Captain Aniol.

"Not good enough," Valek said as he plunged his knife into Dumin's chest, angling the blade so it slid between the ribs and pierced the man's heart.

Cleaning the blood off his hands and blade on the blanket, Valek studied the dead man's face in the moonlight. A sense of rightness pulsed in his chest. Talk about the ultimate prank. Valek believed Viliam would agree. He placed the statue of Viliam on Dumin's chest.

Valek hurried to reach his second target. Sergeant Edvard stayed in the barracks and would be much harder to kill since he roomed with three other sergeants. Victor had shared a room with Viliam and, despite being twins, the two were opposites. Serious and thoughtful, Victor had been born first—a fact he never grew tired of reminding Viliam about every time the other wanted to include him in one of his schemes.

Of all his brothers, Valek had looked up to Victor. Even though his broad shoulders and thick muscles made others believe he'd be the bully of the family, Victor had a calming presence in tense situations. He also could be very protective if provoked, and when the soldiers had drawn their swords that horrible day, Victor had stepped in front of their father without hesitating.

Too bad Sergeant Edvard didn't pause before he sliced the edge of his blade along Victor's neck. Valek would never forget the angle of the blood as it sprayed from Victor's throat like a morbid waterfall.

The barracks consisted of four two-story buildings. The long structures lined the inside of the garrison's walls, one along each side. Edvard slept in a room in the west end of Barrack B on the second floor.

As Valek approached the barrack, he kept close to the shadows. A lesson he learned well—night and shadows were an assassin's best tools. Soldiers patrolled the top of the walls and had a good view of the courtyard if they turned around.

Unfortunately, Edvard's room lacked a window and the closest one opened into a large area full of bunks for the new recruits. Good thing this wasn't the first time Valek had entered the building. He'd been practicing while Edvard had been on patrol.

Grabbing the doorknob, Valek turned it in one smooth motion. Too slow and the damn thing would have squealed.

MARIA V. SNYDER

After Fester's murder all the doors in the complex had been locked at night, which gave Valek plenty of practice in using his lock picks. But their laziness had returned and now he didn't need to waste the time. He slipped inside the building and closed the door behind him.

He waited for his vision to adjust to the semidarkness. A few lanterns remained lit in hallways and the stairwells so if the soldiers were called for an emergency in the middle of the night, they wouldn't break their necks. Listening to the various soft sounds of many sleeping men, Valek ensured no one was awake before moving.

The old wooden steps to the second story needed to be climbed with care. His first attempt up these stairs resulted in a series of loud squeaks, which woke up a few soldiers who came out to investigate. With his heart hammering in his chest, Valek had scrambled up the wall and clung to the ceiling rafters like a large black spider. Too bad he didn't have the spider's eight limbs as his tired at an alarming rate and sweat slicked his grip. Just when he'd thought he'd fall on the men, they returned to bed.

This time, Valek knew where all the noisy spots lurked and he ascended to the second floor with nary a squeak. He ghosted down the hallway to the third door on the left. He pressed his ear to the door. Nothing. Turning the knob, Valek eased into the small room that contained two bunk beds and four trunks. He left the door ajar to let in some light. One of Edvard's roommates was out on patrol, so only three men slept inside. Two on the top bunks, and one on the bottom—Edvard.

Valek wished he could inform Edvard why he was about to die like he had the others, but that was impossible, so he crouched next to the bed and studied Edvard's body position.

He'd have only one chance, otherwise the noise would wake the man's roommates.

Edvard slept on his side, facing the wall. Valek pulled his knife. Stretching out both arms, Valek clamped his hand over Edvard's mouth while simultaneously slicing deep into the man's neck. Edvard jerked and a muted gargle came from his opened throat. Blood splashed against the wall and soaked into the pillow.

Valek pressed his hand to Edvard's mouth until the man stilled. His roommates didn't make a sound, but Valek had forgotten one important detail—the smell. Very soon the stench of blood, feces and urine would wake the sleeping men. Setting the statue of Victor on Edvard, Valek bolted.

He made it halfway down the stairs before the shout echoed on the wooden walls. No longer caring about being quiet, he raced down the steps, heading for the door.

Yanking it open, he dashed out just as another shout cried, "There he is."

Boots pounded, swords rang, voices yelled and called his position with heart-stopping accuracy. In his panic, he'd run right through the courtyard—visible to all. Rookie mistake. More soldiers poured from the other barracks.

Once he reached the far side, Valek slowed and glanced back. A swarm of soldiers followed a half dozen paces behind him. He wouldn't be able to outrun them, but perhaps he could outsmart them. Valek dived into the shadows along the next barracks, then scaled the wall to the roof and lay flat.

He drew in deep breaths in an effort to stifle the desire to gasp for air. As the bulk of the soldiers passed his hiding spot, Valek knew it would only be a matter of time until they found him. He needed to give them a target or a direction.

Valek rolled over and studied the activity on the wall. Soldiers rushed back and forth, trying to spot the intruder below.

MARIA V. SNYDER

They tended to cluster together as if more sets of eyes would improve their night vision. If Valek timed it just right…

Rolling along the roof, Valek traveled to the edge closest to the wall. He peeked over, searching for soldiers before sitting on the edge. Valek rubbed his damp palms along his pants and then reached across the two-foot gap. Running the tips of his fingers over the stones, Valek found small holes and ledges to grasp. Thank fate the garrison was one of the older bases. If it had been a new construction, the wall would have been too smooth to ascend. He stretched out his legs, seeking toeholds and locating secure positions. Well, as secure as this section of wall allowed.

Next was the hard part. Valek needed to transfer his weight to the wall without falling or alerting anyone to his presence. Either would result in his death. He mentally counted to ten, concentrating on steadying his jumpy heart. Valek had to be one hundred percent committed to the action. Any hesitation would result in failure.

Leaning forward, Valek launched. His fingers and arms strained to hold his body against the stones as he dug in his toes. One foot slipped, sending a rain of crumbling mortar to the ground, but he found another toehold before sliding any farther.

Valek pressed his hot forehead against the cold stones. He waited for a cry of discovery or for his abused muscles to give way. But he stayed strong. After he had struggled with clinging to the ceiling of the barrack's stairwell, Valek had worked on strengthening and endurance. Nice to see all those hours of lifting hay bales had paid off.

When no shout of alarm rose above the general noise of the chaos below, Valek climbed to the top edge of the wall. From this angle, only the shadows of the guards were visible. Once again, his next move required decisiveness and no mistakes.

He reviewed each step in his mind, envisioning the actions until he felt confident. Then he waited for the shadows right above him to clear.

His window of opportunity arrived a few minutes later. Valek scrambled onto the top of the wall, startling a cluster of guards five feet to his left. He saluted them, dived for the opposite edge, twisted so he went feetfirst over the wall and stopped his fall by grasping the edge with his hands. Once he found toeholds, he climbed down.

The yells and shouts sounded when he was halfway to the ground.

"Stop!"

"There! He's there!"

"To the left!"

With about ten feet remaining, Valek dropped the rest of the way, landing with a soft thud on the cold earth. An arrow slammed into the ground right next to him. Valek zigzagged as he dashed into the woods. More arrows whizzed past and one burned a line of fire along his thigh. But he didn't stop.

He reached the protection of the forest only to realize soldiers filled the woods. While he'd been clinging to the wall, they must have gone through the gate. And they were converging to block his escape route. Valek found a hiding spot to plot his next move.

What would be the last thing they'd expect him to do? He bit down on a groan. They'd never guess that he'd *return* to the garrison. All his survival instincts screamed at him to ignore that advice and to head for home right now. He wiped his forehead with his sleeve, but the fabric was wet. The thought of being caught soaked with Dumin's blood spurred Valek into action. They'd tear him apart.

Heading away from the guards, Valek neared the wall, but he stayed in the woods as he looped around the garrison. He searched for an empty section, but soon realized that would require a miracle, so he picked a spot with just a few soldiers. And when their attention was elsewhere, he crossed to the wall.

His abused muscles protested as he climbed. When he reached the top, he peered over the edge and waited until the guards were not looking in his direction. Pain throbbed in his leg as fatigue shook his limbs. When the prime opportunity arose, he stayed low as he traversed the wall, moving slowly so he wouldn't attract any attention.

The compound below appeared empty, but Valek eased down the wall and didn't relax until he reached the shadows at the base. He circled around. The bag with his clean stable-boy clothes remained hidden. Valek changed and stuffed the bloody ones into a burn barrel before he washed up.

Lanterns blazed in the stables and a couple of horses were missing. Reedy saddled a big mare while the Stable Master put a bridle on another.

"Where've you been?" Reedy demanded.

"At the latrine," Valek said and helped the boy with the girth straps.

"All this time?"

"Until all hell broke loose. Then a captain ordered me to stay in Barrack A until the ruckus died down. What happened?"

"The assassin struck again. I heard he got two men before they spotted him climbing over the wall." Reedy's voice held a combination of awe and fear.

They worked to saddle more horses as officers left to join the chase. When the flow of officers slowed, the Stable Master questioned Valek on his absence. He repeated his story.

The Stable Master backhanded him across the cheek, spinning Valek to the ground as pain exploded on the right side of his face.

He crouched next to Valek. "I'm your boss, not some captain. Next time you get your ass back here right away or I'll pound on you until you look like raw meat and then I'll feed you to the horses. Understand?"

"Yes, sir." Valek considered adding the Stable Master to his to-be-assassinated list.

Valek worked at the stable for another month. He viewed the effects of his double assassination with amusement. Twice the number of guards traversed the walls, extra locks were installed on all doors, patrols swept the woods surrounding the garrison every night and soldiers patrolled the compound, checking shadows.

Right now Captain Aniol was untouchable. On Valek's next day off, he left and never returned. He had spent a total of three and a half seasons as a stable boy and had learned so much more than he'd expected. Someday, he'd finish the job. No doubt.

He reported to Hedda's office when he reached the school.

"What the hell were you thinking when you killed Edvard?" she demanded. Two red splotches on her cheeks matched the color of her hair.

"I wasn't—"

"That's right, you weren't thinking!" She stood and jabbed a finger at him. "Never kill a target in front of witnesses."

"But they were…"

She waited.

"You're right. It was a disaster."

"You're lucky you weren't caught," Hedda said.

Valek couldn't resist. "Luck had nothing to do with it." He smirked.

A steely glint flattened her green eyes. "And what did?"

"Your excellent training."

She snorted, but she settled behind her desk. "And did my training include leaving clues?"

"Clues?"

"Those black statues. They're calling you the rock assassin."

"Not very original," he said.

"They can be traced back to you."

"How?"

"Asking around at the market, finding the person you bought them from."

He smiled. "I didn't buy them nor did anyone see me carve them."

If she was surprised, she hid it well. "You better make sure no one does. Now, where's my cut from your wages?"

He handed her a small pouch.

Hedda dumped the coins into her palm. "Not much. Talk about slave labor."

Valek shrugged. "I found the experience to be very valuable."

"Did you, now?"

"Yes."

"Are you ready to earn much more than this?" She shook the coins as she studied his expression.

He paused. It was one thing to kill the men who'd murdered his brothers, but to assassinate an innocent...

"They're far from innocent." She gestured to a chair. "Sit down and let me tell you about the people who are targeted for assassination. It's not because they're the pillars of the community or because they do good deeds for their neighbors. No, there is always a reason someone hires us to kill them. Corruption runs deep in this country. The royals are the worst of them. And then there're the drug lords and those exploiting children and forcing women to be prostitutes. Let's just say *no one* mourns their deaths."

"That would make it easier."

"And don't forget the experience alone would be..."

"Valuable." He'd made a big mistake with Edvard. And he still had much to learn. When he went after the King, there'd be no room for error.

"Are you ready for your first paid assassination?" Hedda asked.

"Yes."

Valek had then worked various jobs throughout the next two years. With each assassination, his skills improved and his heart rate steadied. Confidence had come with experience, and a high level of cockiness. Valek had started leaving his black statues for his targets to find, warning them of their impending assassination just to make the job harder. And it had, setting off a series of ruined plans, close calls and mistakes. However, his ability to quickly deal with complications had improved.

Dealing with problems had been a part of his life since he'd vowed revenge on his brother's murderers. And the message from Yelena that lay on his desk was one recent example. Valek tapped his fingers on the parchment, considering if the Commander's order not to get involved with Ben Moon's escape extended to Valek's corps. He could send a few trusted men to Fulgor just to keep an eye on Yelena. That wouldn't be disobeying the Commander's orders.

However, if Yelena found out...she'd probably be upset he didn't trust her ability to defend herself. Logic warred with his heart.

Hedda had trained him to lose his emotions, but Yelena had shown him that there was room for emotion. And he'd learned love trumped logic. He wondered what his life these past eight years would have been like if he hadn't met her. Lonely? Lackluster? Cold?

Truthfully, Valek had been content with his life before she

MARIA V. SNYDER

arrived. Would he have woken from his self-induced exile? He'd like to think so, but even though he'd had relationships with women before Yelena, they had always been part of a job he was working and not a true connection. Basically, he'd used them to reach his mark. Not the nicest thing to do, but the King's death had been all that mattered to him at that time. And after he'd assassinated the King, protecting the Commander and Ixia was all he'd cared about.

A sudden thought hit Valek hard. Perhaps it was time for him to be selfish. He should be with Yelena and not up here directing...traffic. The power twins and Maren could take over Ixia's security forces. He'd assumed he'd have plenty of time to retire and enjoy a life of leisure, but at any time, another assassin—one more skilled than Onora—could show up and kill him. Before Yelena, he hadn't cared about his own life, but now he did.

With those thoughts swirling around his head, Valek grabbed his travel pack and headed to the stables. He saddled Onyx in record time, hoping he'd reach a travel shelter before all the beds had been taken. Mounting Onyx, he huffed in amusement. In the past, he'd sleep anywhere—on the cold hard ground, on gravel, in the rafters, wedged under or behind various pieces of furniture. Now he preferred a bed.

The road north had few travelers, and those he encountered quickly moved to the side, giving Onyx a wide berth. Only officers and high-ranking advisers rode horses. All others walked. Valek would rather be on foot—better to spot trouble—and he'd rather be disguised as an ordinary citizen—better to gather useful information. But the travel time to and from the main military base in MD-2 would eat up four days of his allotted time.

The days of unlimited time were, unfortunately, in the past. He remembered spending three months just tracking Captain Aniol's movements. Aniol had ordered his men to kill a bunch of boys to make an example of them, and Valek hadn't been able to get close to the man until Aniol had been assigned a mission with four other soldiers. They'd camped for the night in a section of Icefaren province that was so remote there hadn't been any inns or travel shelters.

Valek waited for Aniol to take his turn for guard duty. After the man that Aniol had relieved fell asleep, Valek baited the captain by making slight noises. As Aniol moved farther and farther from camp to investigate, Valek looped around behind him and pressed his knife to his throat.

"Did you think you were safe, Captain?" Valek asked.

"Safe from what?" The captain's voice remained steady. "A thief in the woods?"

"From the rock assassin who killed Lieutenant Fester, Second Lieutenant Dumin and Sergeant Edvard last year?"

It took him a moment. "*You* killed those men? Why?"

Valek laughed. "I guess they couldn't tell you. I'd hoped the three statues would help you figure out the connection by now."

"I've no idea what you're talking about." His tone no longer held as much confidence.

"Then let me refresh your memory." Valek explained. "Your demonstration certainly worked for the King. No one else in Icefaren tried to ask for leniency or for extra time to pay their taxes. Did the King give you a medal or commendation for your excellent service?"

"No."

"Too bad. I'm sure your widow would have liked to display it during your funeral."

"I have kids," Aniol said.

"How many?" Valek asked even though he knew the answer.

"Two—a boy and a girl."

"My parents had four boys until your men slaughtered three

MARIA V. SNYDER

of them. You should have told them to make a clean sweep of it. Hmm...letting you live and killing your children would be a more appropriate punishment."

"No!"

"Don't worry, Captain. Unlike you, I don't murder innocent children." Valek had sliced his knife deep into the captain's throat. One of the benefits to being behind his victim—not as much blood on his clothes. He left a statue of six people holding hands—a family on the dead man's chest.

When Valek arrived in MD-2 two days later, he found a stable for Onyx a few miles away from the base, changed into a servant's uniform with MD-2's colors of black and tan and entered the compound without any trouble. He located Private Zoel, one of his agents assigned to keep an eye on the occupants of the base. Giving the young man the signal, Valek slipped behind the barracks to wait.

It didn't take long for Zoel to appear. He approached as if he faced a cobra ready to strike.

Valek didn't waste time on pleasantries. "Tell me about Captain Timmer."

"Captain Timmer's a hard-ass, sir, but his company makes all the others look like kids playing solider," Zoel said.

"No signs of him abusing his power?" Valek asked.

"No, sir. His company does train longer and harder than the others, but he doesn't push them past their limits, and if a soldier is unhappy, he can request a transfer." Zoel wiped a sweaty palm on his pants. "If I'd seen anything inappropriate, sir, I would have sent a report."

Valek studied the nervous youth. Zoel's average appearance and build helped him to blend in with the other soldiers. The young man's talent was the ability to make friends with anyone. He'd been a valuable resource, watching the various activities within the base and reporting anything suspicious.

"Why aren't you in Timmer's company?" Valek asked.

"Those extra training hours would limit the amount of time I have to perform my duties for you, sir."

"And in the course of those duties, have you heard anything about the captain?"

"The soldiers don't like him. He scares them in order to make them work hard." Zoel shrugged. "He's harsh and will scream and humiliate a soldier who isn't keeping up, but I haven't heard of any physical abuse."

Valek asked him about Onora and Gerik.

"Gerik wasn't here long," Zoel said. "Talented guy. Didn't cause any trouble. I suspect he'll advance pretty high in the ranks. I don't know an Onora. Is she new?"

"No. She would have been here two or three years ago."

"Doesn't ring a bell."

"Thank you, Zoel."

Zoel nodded and hurried away.

Valek spent the next couple of days observing Timmer's company. Professional and skilled, they performed their drills with uncanny precision. Impressive. The captain yelled and bullied a bit, but nothing that would cause Valek to be concerned. About to agree with Zoel's assessment of Timmer, Valek paused as he realized only a few women stood in the ranks. Not that their low numbers was a red flag, but their reaction to the captain when he neared set off Valek's internal warning bells.

One lady in particular—a tall blonde—flinched and her face set into a mask of fear when Timmer glanced at her. The captain's sly smile was all Valek needed. Timmer warranted a closer inspection.

That night, Valek sneaked into the base's record room to pe-

· MARIA V. SNYDER

ruse a few files. It took a bit of digging, but he located Onora's file. She had enlisted four years ago at age sixteen. Her instructors praised her skills and she gained a reputation for her lightning-fast attacks. The glowing reviews and comments stopped when she'd transferred to Timmer's company. After a year of service, she was noted as being absent without leave. Valek didn't need a good imagination to determine what had caused her to go AWOL.

Nothing in Gerik's file contradicted what Zoel had reported. In fact, there was a commendation from Gerik's commanding officer for going above and beyond the call of duty while battling a fire in the barracks. The only thing that caught Valek's interest was Gerik's hometown—Silver Falls. The town was also listed for Onora. Interesting.

Valek woke Zoel and sent him to Silver Falls to investigate and see if there was a connection between Onora and Gerik.

"What about my duties here?" Zoel asked.

"Give this to your commanding officer." Valek handed him a folded piece of parchment. "After you finish in Silver Falls, report back to me at the Commander's castle."

"Yes, sir."

After another day of investigation, Valek learned the blonde's name, Private Wilona, and her age, eighteen. Instead of living in the women's barracks, she had her own quarters. Anger simmered in his chest, but Valek needed to confirm his suspicions before he dealt with Timmer.

Valek followed Wilona to her quarters that evening. He knocked on her door. A faint "come in" sounded. Entering, he noticed her expression first—fear mixed with dread—and then how she'd hugged her arms to her chest, her posture rigid.

Not expecting a servant, she jerked in surprise. "Oh." She blinked as relief softened her pretty face. "Can I help you?" Wilona relaxed her arms, letting them hang by her sides.

"No. But I can help you."

She braced as if for a blow. "Who are you?"

He suppressed a sigh. What was the point of having an in-famous reputation if no one recognized him? Removing his cap, he introduced himself.

"Yeah, right, and I'm the Soulfinder. Who put you up to this? Cewen? You can tell her this isn't funny. In fact, it's quite cruel."

Curious. "It is?"

She balled her fists. "Oh come on! She pays you to pretend to be Valek because I… Oh, never mind. Just tell her to stop. She's going to make it worse."

"Cewen's worried about you." He guessed.

"Yeah, well. I can handle it. Goodbye." Wilona made shoo-ing motions.

Valek refused to move. "I disagree. You need my assistance. What time does Captain Timmer visit your room?"

She stepped toward him. "I'm gonna kill her."

"Cewen is not the one you should be concerned about." He laced his words with steel and met her gaze. "I'm not pre-tending, Wilona."

Whether it was his tone of voice or his expression that convinced her, Valek didn't care as long as she understood he meant business. A range of emotions from fear, disbelief, hope, to relief and back again flashed on her face.

"I'm sorry Timmer wasn't brought to my attention sooner," he said. "A mistake I will rectify tonight."

She sank onto the edge of her bed. "I should have reported him, but…"

"Men like him use fear to control their victims. You had the strength to confide in your friend. A step in the right di-rection. Did you think she was goading you into more action by sending a servant to pretend to be me?"

"Yes."

One mystery solved. "Would it have worked?"

"I...don't know. The captain is well connected. He has friends who are in charge of transfers, buddies working as messengers and is in tight with the Major. I doubt anyone here would have helped me."

He'd fix that later. For now... "Tell me everything."

Wilona glanced at the door.

"Will he be here soon?"

"He...visits at different times and not every night."

Typical predator behavior—keeping a victim guessing and off balance, Valek thought with disgust.

With some encouragement, Wilona told Valek her horror story. How she'd caught Timmer's eye and, at first, she enjoyed the attention until the flirting turned into threats, intimidation and forced physical contact. Valek wished Yelena was here. His heart mate had been through a similar experience and her magic could soothe Wilona's soul. All he could offer Wilona was the assurance that she'd be safe.

"Don't worry about Timmer anymore. The next time he comes to your room, *I'll* be waiting for him, and if he survives the encounter, he'll be rendered harmless and unable to sire children," Valek promised.

19

JANCO

A person could only listen to the forest sounds for so long before going insane. Janco sighed. Loudly. They'd been hiking southwest through the Snake Forest for hours and Little Miss Assassin had been as quiet as the grave. Her passage through the woods made no noise. Her bare feet padded on the cold hard ground with nary a whisper. Even her short black cape didn't dare flap.

They would stay on the Ixian side of the border until they neared the town of Lapeer, where they would cross over and investigate the suspicious factory before heading east to the Emerald Mountains.

He tried to fill the silence with comments on the case or on the scenery, but he gave up because after a while it sounded inane even to him. And he'd long since stopped asking her questions. Little Miss Assassin was a woman of few words.

This was going to be a long assignment. He sighed. Again.

"Will you stop doing that?" she asked. Annoyance colored her tone.

Janco perked up. "Doing what?"

"That huffing thing. Like you're leaking air."

"It's called sighing."

"Well, stop it."

A very childish "make me" pressed on the edge of his lips. He wisely kept those two words from escaping. Ari would be proud. Instead, he asked, "Why?"

"I can't hear if anyone is following us."

"No one is following us."

"How do you know?"

Good question. He'd known it just as he knew when to stop bugging Ari—by a feeling deep inside him. "The forest is...unperturbed."

"That's ridiculous."

"Do you think someone is following us?"

"I haven't heard any indicators—when I *could* hear." She shot him a sour look. "We need to remain vigilant."

"For what? It's not like they're planning an ambush. If someone is following us, that's good. It means we're on the right track. We're making people nervous. They want to see where we're going, what we're doing. In fact, we should be making *more* noise in order to lure them into coming closer."

Little Miss Assassin stared at him as if he had four eyes and a spike sticking out of his forehead. "How do you know they're not planning an ambush? With all your prattle masking any signs, we'll probably stumble right into a trap."

Janco hadn't realized just how much his friends trusted him until now. Ari would never question him about ambushes. Why not? It wasn't like he had magic. Perhaps years spent in the woods had given him a...forest vibe. If he told her that, she'd really think he was out of his mind. And why did he care what Little Miss Assassin thought? He didn't. Not at all.

"The real danger will come when we're in Sitia," Janco said. "Until then, it's just me, you and the birds."

"What about at the border? Do you expect trouble there?"

"Nope. We're going to slip into Sitia without a fuss."

"You mean without stopping to inform the border guards?"

"That's what I said."

"Sounds like a challenge." A gleam lit her pale gray eyes.

"It's easier than you'd think." Or was it? He'd always walked parallel to the border until he found a spot that was empty of guards. Then he simply crossed into Sitia.

When the Commander had taken over Ixia, he had closed the border to Sitia and had his men cut down all the trees and bushes, clearing a hundred-foot-wide space between the two nations. With the gap, the river and the scattered patrols it wasn't easy to cross the border.

"Now that I'm thinking about it," Janco said. "The crossing can be tricky, depending on who's on duty. I'm gonna let you take point on this one."

"All right," she said. "And just to let you know, I see what you're doing."

"Me?" He attempted to look innocent—a hard expression for him to pull off. Janco hadn't been guiltless since he'd been a baby. Then again…his mother had claimed he'd come into the world feetfirst just to be difficult.

"Save it for someone who has poor vision."

"Ouch." But Janco smiled. She had joked, which meant there might be hope for her yet.

When they stopped for the night, Janco tried asking her questions again, but this time he stayed away from the more sensitive topics. She had donned a pair of well-worn, black fur-lined boots.

He gestured to them. "Looks like Black Angus leather. I hear the people who live near the ice sheet will only wear those boots. Is that why you're not cold? It must feel like the warm season to you down here."

"Yeah. I only brought this cape along for the nighttime. Is Sitia really hotter?"

"Oh yes. During the hot season, it's like swimming in the White Mist Springs up in MD-2. Do you know about them?"

"They're near the place I grew up," she said.

Aha! "Sweet. Did you go there all the time? I would!"

"No. Half the year the snow cats gather around them. And in the warmer weather, it's not as much fun."

"For you." He shivered, remembering being on the ice sheet during a blizzard. Hands down, it was the coldest he'd ever been in his entire life.

She smiled and he marveled at the change. The harsh lines of her face softened, and for the first time since meeting her, he thought of her as truly pretty. Her nose crinkled and two tiny dimples marked her cheeks.

"I guess you didn't grow up in the north?" she asked.

"Nope. I lived on the coast in MD-7. I could have been a beach bum, but I hate sand. Nasty stuff. Gets everywhere. And I mean *everywhere*. My dad tried to make me a fisherman, but I got seasick. Even now the smell of fish makes me gag."

"What does he think of your job?" she asked in a quiet voice.

"Don't know. He was out on his boat when a big storm came through. I was eleven. We never saw him again."

"Too bad. Do you have any siblings?"

Janco laughed. "After I was born, my mother swore off kids. When my dad disappeared, we moved to my uncle's farm and I had to deal with all these annoying cousins! What about you?"

"An older brother. He raised me until he couldn't."

A million questions shoved their way up his throat, but Ari's voice sounded in his head. *Don't scare her off, you idiot.* He swallowed them down. Instead, he asked, "Do you want to take first shift?"

"Won't the forest wake you if someone comes close?" Onora teased.

"Ha-ha. There's no one around. But that can change. Besides, I thought you'd feel more…comfortable if we took turns on guard duty."

She gazed at him a moment. A crease puckered the skin between her eyes as if she couldn't quite figure him out. Janco repeated his comments in his mind, trying to determine what he'd said to cause such puzzlement.

"I'll take the first shift." Onora stood, removed her short cape and boots and tucked them into her pack.

"Won't you be cold?"

"I'm used to it. Besides, the cape's extra fabric can snag on the branches, and it's hard to climb a tree with boots on. Don't you do the same thing when on duty?"

"No. I find a good spot and hunker down."

Alarmed, she asked, "How do you stay awake?"

"If I tell you, do you promise not to tell anyone?"

Instantly wary, Onora bit her lip before nodding.

"That's when I compose my rhymes. Everyone thinks I make them up as I fight, but I have a whole bunch of them ready for my next match." He tapped his temple.

"Oh. Okay." She pinched her thumb and index finger together, touched them to her lips and twisted as if locking her mouth shut. "I won't say a word."

Grinning, Janco set up his bedroll and blankets by the small fire. He squirmed until comfortable. Each year, it seemed to take longer for him to find a position where his muscles and/or joints didn't ache when lying on the hard ground.

Before closing his eyes, he scanned their campsite. Onora had disappeared into the forest. Probably climbing a tree. And then he wondered when he'd stopped thinking of her as Little Miss Assassin.

After a couple of days of hiking, they were close to the Sitian border. Instead of crossing into the Featherstone lands, they headed east, paralleling the edge of the Snake Forest. Janco thought it best to enter Sitia near the west side of Lapeer. He remembered a river that flowed nearby that would be hard to forge this time of year. Not to mention freezing cold. Brrr. Much better, and smarter, to use the bridge.

They traveled east for another five days and dodged the border patrols performing their sweeps of the forest. When the first squad had drawn near, Onora had grabbed Janco's arm at the same time as he put a finger to his lips to warn her. Without a word, she'd melted into the surroundings, while he'd scouted the patrol's position, tracking them and ensuring he and Onora wouldn't cross paths with the guards.

And soon dodging patrols became routine. His forest vibe would trigger when her assassin senses tingled. She melted while he scouted.

Janco squeezed a few more personal facts from her. The most interesting tidbit was she'd had to join the military when she turned sixteen or she would have starved.

Early in the morning on the eleventh day, pain radiated from Janco's right ear. He pressed his fingers to the scar that had formed after the lower half of his ear had been hacked off. The burning pain spread to his jaw and drilled a hole into his brain. Janco scanned the surroundings while Onora waited.

"Strong magic," he puffed. "Close by."

She drew her knives. He didn't have the energy to tell her the weapons would be useless against a magical attack. She'd discover that lovely little surprise soon enough.

20

YELENA

I raced to Reema's window. A grappling hook bit into the wood underneath the ledge. A rope with knots tied every couple of feet hung to the ground. I looked out in time to see a man hurrying away with a large sack slung over his shoulder. Reema!

Without thought, I swung my legs over the ledge, grasped the rope and scrambled down. Catching sight of his cloak disappearing around a corner, I followed him through Fulgor's alleys and side streets, staying far enough back so he wouldn't see me. There was just enough light from the lanterns to discern his form as he navigated the city.

I debated my next move. Should I rush him before he reached his destination? All I had was my switchblade, which I palmed. I'd left my cloak with its hidden darts and my bo staff at Opal's. Perhaps I should wait until he arrived, then attack? What if he had friends? Maybe I should learn his destination and then fetch help. But what if he left after I did? Argh.

Unable to decide, I trailed him, encountering no one. No security officers. Not even a mugger. After about an hour, he cut down a narrow, dank, foul-smelling alley. Ari's shoulders would never have fit.

He stopped at the halfway point and raised a fist as if to knock on a door.

If he disappeared inside, I might never see Reema again. I yelled, "Hey." Then rushed him.

The kidnapper turned his head and reached for his sword. But I collided with him before he could draw it. We slammed into the ground, landing with me on top and him facing the wall. The sack was wedged behind him.

I pressed my knife to his throat. "Release the girl. Now."

He let go and held both his hands up. "Take it," he said.

"Reema, are you all right? It's me." I pulled open the top, peered inside and stopped as my heart lurched.

The man laughed. "Followed me all this way for a fifty-pound bag of potatoes."

"Where—"

The door swung open. Bright light spilled into the alley, blinding me. The kidnapper grabbed my switchblade as shadows converged and multiple hands yanked me to my feet and dragged me inside. The door banged shut.

A familiar male voice said, "Don't worry. She won't bite. There's a null shield around her."

I won't bite? My eyes adjusted and I counted five people. The man I followed plus another I didn't recognize held my arms. Ben Moon stood in front, gloating with two women beside him.

"Hello, Yelena," Ben said. "So *good* to see you again."

Paler than I remembered, he'd also lost weight. His clothes hung on his tall frame and his sunken cheeks made his face appear skeletal. More gray stubble than black covered his scalp—the officers in Wirral must have shaved his head—but intelligence still shone from his brown eyes along with a gleam of…insanity? Cruelty? Evil? Perhaps all three. Not like the knowledge would improve my situation. Nothing would.

"What? No hello back?" Ben smirked.

"Where's Reema?" I demanded.

"Asleep in her bed. Well, *under* her bed as we didn't want to tip you off. But she's safe and sound."

"You— Oh." Her "kidnapping" had been a ruse to get me here. It worked, except... "Why should I believe you?"

"Because *I'm* not after her. *She's* not the one who is responsible for my brother's execution. *She's* not the one who sent me to Wirral," Ben said.

"Owen is liable for his own execution. He knew the consequences of getting caught in Ixia. And you—"

"Shut up. No one deserves to be in that horrid place. And I'm not going back. You didn't do me any favors by letting me live." A crazed expression flitted over his face before an icy calm replaced it.

"I can rectify that right now." I glanced around. "Where's my switchblade?"

"Are you sure you've got a shield on her?" the man on my right asked. "She's not scared."

Now I was. His comment terrified me. If Ben had a null shield around me, that meant he didn't know about my lack of magical powers. The assurance that I wouldn't bite now made sense, yet I wasn't any closer to an answer. If he didn't send the assassin, who did?

"I'm not going to play around anymore," Ben said. He drew a long dagger. "Hold her still."

Years of self-defense training kicked in and I broke their hold on me, ducked out of reach and ran about two paces before being tackled to the ground. I landed hard and twisted. But the others were on me, trapping my arms and sitting on my legs.

Ben knelt next to me. He raised his knife.

MARIA V. SNYDER

"Ben, stop," a deep male voice ordered from the other side of the room.

"The Boss," the man pressing down on my shoulders said. Fear laced his voice.

Instead of listening, Ben pressed his lips together and brought his arm down. I braced for the explosion of pain, but the blade halted mere inches from my stomach. Ben grunted with effort and his muscles trembled. However, he didn't move.

A hooded figure loomed behind him. "What part of 'stop' don't you understand?"

"She deserves to die." Ben forced the words out as if his vocal cords were pinched tight.

Perhaps they were. No doubt magic was involved in preventing Ben's knife from plunging into my body. A good thing, but the Boss's arrival might just delay the inevitable.

"Yes, she does deserve to die. But what happens when the Council, the Master Magicians, the Commander and Valek find out she's been murdered?"

Ben hissed in frustration. "They'll come after us."

"And your rescue has drawn too much attention already. Besides, Valek won't stop until we're all dead," the Boss said.

"But now she knows where we are."

"Thanks to you." The Boss sighed. "And once again, I'll have to take care of it."

Ben flashed me a look of pure venom. He relaxed back on his heels and lowered his knife. "We're not done," he said to me. "I might not be allowed to kill you, but I can hurt you. Bad."

"That's enough. Ben, go fetch the Theobroma."

"But she's—"

"Go now," the Boss ordered.

Ben left, but my heart rate kept its frantic pace. Theobroma reduced a person's resistance to magic. The Boss believed I still had my magic, and if I ingested the Theobroma, then I wouldn't be able to defend against his power. He had no idea he didn't need the substance.

I scanned the room, searching for a way to escape. Small with only a few benches. A couple of lanterns sat on a table near the door. The unlocked door.

"Not yet," the Boss said, correctly reading my intentions.

"You'll let me go? Yeah, right."

"I plan to, and do you want to know why?"

"Because you're afraid of Valek?"

"For now."

Ben returned. He held a brown lump in his palm.

"Give it to her," the Boss ordered.

I struggled, but the four people holding me down didn't budge. Clamping my mouth shut, I was determined not to open it, but Ben pinched my nose closed until I had to either part my lips or pass out. He shoved the Theobroma into my mouth, then held my jaw tight.

The nutty sweet substance melted on my tongue. I resisted swallowing, but due to my prone position, it dripped down my throat and I instinctively gulped.

The Boss said, "Ben, lift your null shield now."

"Okay."

A pause. Then the Boss turned to Ben. "What are you waiting for?"

"It's off, I swear."

Silence stretched and I braced, but nothing happened.

"A shield remains. Take her clothes off," the Boss ordered.

Renewing my efforts to free my limbs, I bucked as hands grasped my shirt and yanked. Buttons flew into the air, exposing my undershirt and the glass octopus pendant.

"Stop." The Boss held a hand up. He knelt next to me and picked up the octopus. "Interesting. No doubt the work of

MARIA V. SNYDER

the Keep's new glass magician." Tugging the chain over my head, he removed my last defense. "But the real question is why *you* are wearing it."

I kept quiet.

"No matter. I will find out soon enough." He pulled his hood down.

Recognition shot through me an instant before his voice invaded my mind. Without my magic or a natural resistance to his power, I couldn't stop him from delving into my memories. A horrified revulsion flushed through me, but he probed deeper and deeper until I split and shattered, exposing everything.

I stood on the street, blinking at the row of lanterns. How did I get here? It took a few moments for me to recognize the town. Fulgor. And another couple of minutes to remember I'd been on my way to Opal's to read a story to Reema.

Reema. My stomach knotted. I needed to leave Fulgor or an assassin would target her. In fact, if I didn't go now my family and friends would all be in grave danger.

I ran to Opal's glass factory. The place was surrounded by Fulgor's security officers. Their presence increased my panic. I'd been too slow to leave and everyone was dead!

The sergeant at the door smiled when he spotted me. "They've been searching the city for you. You better report in to HQ."

"Reema?" I asked, breathless.

"She's upstairs sleeping."

"Are Opal and Devlen with her?"

"No. They joined the search parties along with your brother. A couple of our officers are watching her."

Search parties? That was the second time he'd mentioned that. Had they been looking for me? It didn't matter. All that concerned me was leaving town to keep them safe. "I'll…just check on Reema and…report in."

He stepped aside and I raced up the steps. The two standing guard relaxed when they recognized me. I waved to them as I confirmed Reema was unharmed. She slept on the couch.

She looked so innocent. No lines of worry or cunning creased her face and her pure beauty shone through. The instinct to protect her burned through me like a sudden fever. Move. Now. Or she'd die.

I gathered my pack, bo staff and cloak and dashed from the factory, heading to the stables at the Second Chance Inn. The knowledge that *they* watched me to ensure I left pressed on my back. No time to waste. Kiki nickered a greeting when I entered. I waved off the sleepy stable boy who appeared while I saddled her in record time. Rusalka poked her head over the wall. Her ears cocked forward.

"Please tell Rusalka not to worry," I said to Kiki. "Tell her we're going…" Where? The urgency to leave didn't specify a direction. I strained to recall elusive details. There had been something about a plant in the Avibian Plains and it had been important…Freeze Burn! "Tell her we're going to the plains and ask her to keep Leif from chasing after us. He needs to stay away from me. It's too dangerous."

Kiki stared at me for a moment. Then turned her head toward Rusalka, doing her silent horse communication thing. Rusalka snorted in either agreement or disagreement. It was hard to tell.

When I mounted Kiki, she twisted one ear back. "We're going to search for that plant Devlen…er…Changed Man showed you. Do you remember it?"

She flicked me with her tail as if insulted that I'd question her memory.

"Good. I'd like to get to the plains as fast as possible." This

MARIA V. SNYDER

earned me another long gaze. "I have to leave to keep Reema safe. Okay?"

Just when I started wondering what I'd do if Kiki refused to take me, she trotted from the stables. I let her pick a path through the empty streets. Scanning the surrounding area for potential problems or for anyone following us, I stayed alert until we reached the plains two hours after dawn.

The panic released its vise grip on my heart and I drew a deep breath when we entered the vast grasslands of the plains. My family and friends would be safe. And as long as I stayed away, they'd live. The reason for my conviction eluded me, but just the thought of returning to Fulgor sent waves of fear along my spine. Sorrow weighed heavily on me. I already missed them so much it burned inside me. I imagined it would consume every part of me, leaving behind a hollow husk. And I couldn't even think of Valek right now or I'd collapse in a puddle of misery and never move again.

Kiki broke into her gust-of-wind gait. We sailed on a river of air. I closed my eyes, enjoying the rush of the wind on my face. It banished the sadness if only for a moment. After being up all night, it didn't take long for me to doze in the saddle.

Kiki woke me when she stopped for a rest. The plains stretched in all directions. Clumps of small scrub trees dotted the land-scape. A few rocks littered the sandy soil. Kiki sipped water from a narrow depression—all that was left of a streambed.

Despite the desolation, I felt safe. Or was that because of it? When she finished drinking, I fed Kiki grain and then I groomed her. In two days, the warming season would officially start and, halfway through, shedding season would begin. The amount of hair raining to the ground would triple in another month's time. Every year I'd been amazed that Kiki didn't turn bald by the warm season.

After I washed the horse hair from my hands, I ate a quick

meal. Quick because I didn't have much food with me and it would soon be gone. My bo staff and switchblade were useless for hunting, but I might be able to use my Curare darts. Or could I? If I ate the meat of an animal frozen by Curare, would I also be affected? Perhaps I should stick to edible plants and roots. If I found them.

While I waited for Kiki to reenergize, I searched for recognizable vegetation. My thoughts drifted, wondering how Leif and the others had reacted to my sudden exit. Were Leif and Hale chasing after me? I hoped not. Just being near me would endanger their lives. And while my heart ached to see them, I refused to give in to such selfish desires.

I poked around the sparse clusters of greenery. Nothing matched my limited list of safe plants. Perhaps I'd find some at the next stop. Wrapping my cloak tight around me, I lay on the ground near Kiki. The sun warmed the dark fabric, lulling me to sleep.

Kiki nudged me awake a few hours later and we resumed our journey. Did she know where the reedwither plant grew or was she searching for it? For the thousandth time, I longed for my mental link with her. Finding souls and guiding them to their final destination had been satisfying, healing others had been rewarding and even examining a person's soul served a purpose. But my ability to communicate with Kiki, Irys, Bain, Leif and even Valek had been such a deep part of me for so long, I felt disconnected. Adrift. Lost.

Recovering my magic, however, didn't elate me as much when I realized I still wouldn't be able to see them or they'd die. At least I'd have Kiki and I could resume helping souls and others in need. The hardest part would be avoiding Valek. No doubt he'd hunt for me. No doubt he'd find me eventually. I dreaded that time.

We stopped two more times before I located a few edible

MARIA V. SNYDER

berries and roots. At our fifth rest break on the second day, instead of moving away to find water to drink, Kiki pawed at a patch of crabgrass. Odd. I moved closer. Long thin leaves grew from red stems. The reedwither plant.

"Kiki, you're brilliant!" I hugged her and fed her a peppermint. Then I knelt next to the cluster and considered. Should I dig around the plant to harvest the roots or pull it out like a weed?

Perhaps I shouldn't touch the leaves or roots. I dug into my pack for a pair of gloves and returned. I would try yanking out a small section first, and if that didn't work, I'd dig around the base.

I grasped a handful.

"Stop," a male voice commanded behind me. "Let go of the reedwither."

I hesitated. A dagger slammed into the ground near me.

"Let go or my next knife will not miss."

21

VALEK

With Wilona safely tucked into a bunk next to her friend Cewen in the women's barracks, Valek returned to the private's room. Not wishing to alert anyone to his presence just yet, he'd had Wilona tell her friend that she'd decided to take action on her own.

Extinguishing the lantern, Valek stretched out on Wilona's bed. He longed for a blond wig. It would add to Timmer's confusion. However, the captain failed to visit her room that night.

In the morning, Wilona reported to training, acting as if nothing had happened, and Valek spent the day investigating Timmer's network of supporters. The layout of the base matched all the other military complexes in the Territory of Ixia—the Commander insisted the bases and the General's manors be identical, which aided Valek and his corps.

It didn't take long to spot the officers who were truly corrupt, like the captain in charge of personnel transfers, and those that had been bullied by Timmer, like the lieutenant overseeing all outgoing messages. Valek noted each of their names. After he dealt with Timmer, Valek planned to make major changes for the command structure of the base. And he'd retrain the soldiers in spotting intruders. Even dressed as a servant, Valek shouldn't be able to move around the base with such ease.

Before settling in Wilona's room for the evening, Valek changed back into his adviser's uniform and prepared for a late-night visitor. He lounged on her bed in the dark, considering what he'd learned that day. It had been a couple of years since he'd organized surprise inspections of the bases, and his agents here had missed a number of illegal activities, which probably meant the same lackluster reporting must be going on for the other bases, as well. It was well past time for another shake-up, but the idea failed to excite Valek. He had more important things he'd rather do. Like discover who had targeted Yelena.

A creak of metal interrupted his musings. Lantern light from the hallway outlined the door as it swung inward. A dark figure entered the room and shut the door. Valek smiled as the man banged his shin on a chair.

"Damn it, Wilona, I told you to leave your light on," a gruff voice said.

Valek pulled the metal slide of the bull's-eye lantern open an inch. A beam of light illuminated Captain Timmer. The tall muscular man cut an impressive figure even in his robe. Clean-shaven with short black hair and brown eyes, Timmer held up a meaty hand to block the light.

"That's not funny, Wilona." Menace rumbled deep in his throat. Timmer stepped closer. "Move the light or I'll—"

Valek stood. "Careful, Timmer. You don't want to get into any more trouble." He yanked the slide all the way open, flooding the rest of the room with light.

Timmer grunted in surprise, pulled a knife from the pocket of his robe and froze when he met Valek's gaze. Recognition flashed. He straightened, but didn't put his weapon away. "Sorry, sir. I thought you were an intruder."

Smooth recovery. Impressive. "Since these aren't your quarters, Captain, I could say the same about you."

"I…was invited. Wilona and I have been dating for a couple months."

"You're dating a soldier in *your* company? That's unethical."

"Her transfer—"

"Has been denied by your buddy Captain Maitol twice. Don't lie. I already have enough reasons to kill you, Timmer."

Timmer's grip on the knife tightened along with the muscles in his jaw, but he wisely kept his mouth shut. Good.

"You're going to cooperate," Valek said. His matter-of-fact tone warned there wouldn't be any arguments. "Give me your knife." He held his hand out.

Timmer hesitated.

Valek waited. A part of him hoped Timmer would attack. The feel of his fist ramming into the man's gut would be sweet. Too bad the captain handed his knife to Valek.

"It's her word against mine," Timmer said.

"I believe her. Case closed. Now you're going to tell me about another private who came through here about four years ago. Private Onora. Do you remember her?"

"I've hundreds of privates come through my company." Timmer shrugged, trying to act casual.

"Yet according to the base records, very few who transfer into your company are women. In fact, I memorized all their names and plan to interrogate all of them. Well, the ones who didn't go AWOL on your watch."

"There's not much to tell." Timmer almost growled the words. "Onora showed such promise, but she couldn't keep up with my rigorous training schedule and she left."

"Were you *dating* her?"

MARIA V. SNYDER

Timmer clamped his mouth shut, but his gaze darted to the bed. And that would be a yes. Valek twirled the knife, deciding if this man deserved to walk out of here with his balls still attached or not.

"Do you know where she went after she left?" Valek asked.

"No. We sent the military police to search for her, but they lost her trail in MD-1. Why are you so interested in her?"

"She has reappeared. And she has honed that potential into a new occupation."

"Oh?"

"An assassin."

"Oh." Timmer swallowed. "Is she any good?"

"She managed to reach the Commander's suite. Unprecedented."

The captain relaxed. "You took care of her."

"I did more than that."

"Good. She was willful, disrespectful and unable to follow orders. No one will mourn her."

Valek raised an eyebrow at his outburst and waited.

The captain finally put it together. "You didn't kill her?"

"I recruited her."

"Oh."

"It should be a fun reunion between you two."

"You can't—"

"I can."

Valek escorted Timmer to the base's MPs and gave them strict instructions to transport the captain to the Commander's castle. He reported the lax security and other infractions to the colonel in charge of the base. Valek wished to stay longer, but he had only two days left to return home.

The two-day trip to the castle was uneventful. After Valek unsaddled Onyx and groomed the horse, he washed up and changed into clean clothes. Then he swung by his office and paused.

The door stood ajar. He grabbed his knife and pressed against the wall to the side of the entrance. It'd be stupid to rush inside. The intruder could be armed with a crossbow. Valek slid his small mirror from his pocket. It resembled a lock pick, but with a round reflective surface on the end. Careful not to catch the light from the lanterns, Valek angled the mirror to look inside. A dark-haired man sat at his desk.

"Come on in, King Killer." The man waved.

Valek kept his weapon in hand as he entered. Only a few people could breach the castle's security and then be brazen about it. "What are you doing here, Arbon?"

"I heard you were looking for me." He spread his arms wide. "So here I am."

Keeping a firm grip on his knife, Valek approached his desk.

Arbon grinned and gestured at Valek's hand. "I see you're still skittish."

"Cautious," Valek corrected. "You don't live long in this business without it."

"Ah yes. I've heard about the young chicky who almost took you out."

Leaning back in Valek's chair, Arbon appeared relaxed. Patches of silver painted his black hair, he had filled out a bit in the middle, and wrinkles creased his tan skin, yet he still resembled the young boy who'd trained with Valek at Hedda's school. He wore a servant's uniform with the Commander's colors of red and black.

"You've been hearing lots of things. Does this mean you've been in town for a while?"

Arbon's booming laugh echoed on the stone walls. "I'm surprised you don't know. Or is it in one of these reports?"

MARIA V. SNYDER

Arbon ran his fingers over the stacks of files. "I'd never pegged you for a desk jockey. No wonder you're losing your touch."

Valek stepped closer and brandished his knife. "Care to test your theory?"

"Love to, but this is a *friendly* visit. What did you want to talk to me about?"

He sheathed his weapon. "My chair."

A smile played on Arbon's lips. "You wanted to talk to me about a chair?"

Valek waited.

With a huff of amusement, Arbon stood and made a grand sweeping bow before relocating to the visitor's chair.

Valek settled behind his desk. He pulled one of the files from a stack and opened it. "I'm looking for information about an assassination attempt on Liaison Yelena Zaltana. According to my records, you've been living and working in Sitia."

"Thanks to you and the Commander, that's where the jobs are. The market in Ixia dried up after the takeover."

Ignoring Arbon's jab, he asked, "Did anyone contact you about this job?"

"Of course they did. I'm the best in Sitia. But once I learned who the mark was, I told them to find someone else. Going after your girl would be suicide. I'm not suicidal."

"Do you know who tried to hire you?"

"You know better than to ask that."

Hedda had never shared the names of her clients with her assassins. It had provided protection for both of them. And Valek had been content with that arrangement until he'd met Ambrose.

"Do you know who agreed to take the job?" Valek asked.

"I'm not ratting out my fellow assassins."

"I didn't ask for a name."

Arbon stared at him a moment. "I know a few others who

might have taken the assignment despite the risks, but I don't know which one."

"I'm looking for a male magician. Know anyone like that?"

"Why a magician?"

"He hid behind a null shield."

"Hell, Valek, that could be anyone. These days it's easy to purchase a cloak or even undergarments that have null shields woven into the fabric. What weapon did he use?"

"Bow and arrow."

Arbon laced his fingers together and rested them on his stomach. "That narrows it down to three or four. When did it happen?"

"Seventeen days ago."

"That rules out the Hunter."

"The Hunter?"

"Yeah, the Sitian assassins all have monikers to keep their real identities a secret." Arbon didn't sound impressed.

Valek couldn't resist asking, "What's yours?"

"The Ixian. Original, eh?"

"Accurate. What about the other possible assassins?"

"Sorry, can't do it. I'm planning on retiring soon and don't need some guy with a grudge tracking me down."

"Fine. How about *you* find out who took the job and ask him who hired him? Get me the name of the patron and I won't go after the assassin."

"And why would I do that?"

Time for the ace. "Because you owe me a favor and I'm collecting."

Arbon shook his head. "I waited all these years for you to ask for that favor. I figured after the takeover, you'd forgotten or you didn't want help from me."

"I offered you a position on my staff."

"Yeah, well, I like my freedom."

MARIA V. SNYDER

"I have freedom."

"Do you?"

"Yes." Valek's tone turned icy.

"It doesn't look like it from where I'm standing. From what I've seen and heard, the Commander holds your leash and has since you first met him."

"You know nothing about it. Now, can you get me that name or not?"

"I can, but I'm going to need lots of gold. That information doesn't come cheap. And once I do then we're even."

"As long as the information is accurate. If not—"

"Save it for one of your green recruits. Give me some credit. I've known you longer than anyone else. Do you really think I'd double-cross you?"

"Not if you value your life."

"Exactly. Now, where's that gold?"

"How much do you need?"

"Forty pieces."

Valek waited.

"All right, gimme thirty-five. That should be enough."

"Thirty. I don't think we need to help fund your retirement."

"Too bad. I've a sweet little place picked out on the coast."

"Ixia?"

"No way." He shivered. "Too cold."

"I like the cold."

Arbon laughed. "No surprise. You spent more time hanging out on that freezing-cold rock than in your room at Hedda's."

Valek sobered. "Have you heard about Hedda?"

All humor dropped from Arbon's round face. "No. What happened?"

Surprised Arbon didn't already know, Valek broke the news.

"And you let this chicky live?" Outrage colored his voice. "I would have sliced her into three pieces."

"I need to learn more about her and the situation before I decide on her future."

"What else do you need to know? Hedda took us in, she taught us, she—"

"I'm well aware of Hedda's generosity. However, the girl has made an impression on the Commander."

"So what?"

Valek met his gaze.

"Oh yeah, I forgot." Arbon put his fist up near his neck and pretended to yank on an invisible leash. "He's your master. But he's not mine. If I just happen to run into this chicky, I'll ensure she gets what she deserves."

"Better brush up on your knife-fighting skills, Arbon. She's younger, faster and more skilled than you. In fact, if you do go after her, make sure you get me that name first." Valek unlocked the lower drawer of his desk. He filled a pouch with thirty gold coins and tossed it at Arbon, who caught it in midair.

"That good, eh?" He jiggled the pouch. The coins rattled. "I'll think about it." Arbon stood to leave.

"Would you like an escort, or would you rather sneak out the way you came in?" Valek asked.

"I'll find my own way out." Arbon waved and left.

Valek counted to two then raced to the door. He caught sight of Arbon's back as the man turned the corner. Curious to see how Arbon had reached his office without calling attention to himself, Valek followed. However, the assassin didn't duck down a secret passage or climb out a window or bribe one of the guards. He simply sauntered through the corridors as if he owned the place. Arbon nodded and said good afternoon to the people he passed. No one questioned him or glanced at him in suspicion. He exited the castle complex without trouble. And when Arbon reached the other side of the gate, he turned and saluted Valek.

No wonder Onora had reached the Commander with ease. Not only had his security detail been compromised, but everyone in the entire castle had relaxed just like at MD-2's military base. Valek had assumed Onora scaled the outer wall and climbed up the castle, but after this little demonstration, she could have waltzed right in the main gate.

Valek pulled the guard who had let Arbon through aside. "Who is that man who just left?" he asked.

"One of the servants," the guard said.

"What's his name?"

"Uh…" The man glanced at his colleague, who pretended to be engrossed in another task.

"Here's an easier question. Where does he work?"

"Um…"

"You've no idea, do you?" Valek demanded.

"He's wearing—"

"A basic uniform that could have easily been stolen. Have you seen him before today? Did he have the proper papers?"

Fear replaced the man's confused expression. "I—"

"You are relieved of duty, Sergeant. Collect your things and come to my office in one hour for your transfer papers."

"Yes, sir." The man hurried away.

Valek turned to the other three guards. White-faced, they braced for his anger.

"Do not let anyone into or out of this complex without checking their papers and making sure their name and position are on the approved list. Do you understand?"

"Yes, sir," they chorused.

"Make sure all of the shifts are following the proper procedures. You will be tested *frequently*. Failure to catch one of my agents will result in immediate reassignment. They're always looking for more workers in the mines."

They blanched. "Yes, sir."

Fuming, Valek strode to the castle. Something had happened to his security measures while he'd been gone. He'd trusted Maren to be in charge, but it seemed as if she'd left long ago and not the few weeks the Commander claimed. Unless she'd been overwhelmed by the job, which allowed the guards to be lazy. Either way, he had to test all the security for the entire castle to discover what else had changed.

Again he wondered if the Commander had orchestrated all this to test Valek. Although he couldn't fathom why Ambrose would put himself at risk. The man had a strong sense of self-preservation. Always had.

Valek remembered when Hedda assigned him what had seemed at the time an easy job.

"It should take a couple weeks at most," she had said. "This young man's been making people nervous with his speeches, and we've been paid a whole pile of gold to make him disappear for good."

"What's the mark's name?" Valek asked.

"Ambrose Diamond. He has all the miners agitated and has amassed quite the following. According to our patron, he has based his operations in Pinchot."

That was on the other side of Ixia near the Soul Mountains. "What's he look like?"

"Black hair, average build, your height, but he's about seven years older than you, around twenty-four. I'm told his eyes are distinctive—almond-shaped and gold in color."

"Does our client want me to give Ambrose a message before I kill him?"

"No."

So this wasn't personal. Probably political. "Anything else?"

MARIA V. SNYDER

"No. This job shouldn't be too difficult. He's been making public speeches. You could probably blend in with the crowd and put a bolt in his heart."

Valek scoffed. "Where's the fun in that?"

"Careful, King Killer. I lose more assassins to overconfidence than to the authorities."

He grinned. "That's sweet. I didn't know you cared."

"Only until you kill the King. That's the only reason I've kept you around."

His humor faded. He'd been working as an assassin for two years, but Hedda kept insisting he get more experience before he went after the King. More like accumulate more money. While he was grateful for the gold he'd earned, he suspected Hedda wasn't ready to give up her best source of income.

"If I kill this guy in public, he might turn into a martyr, and I'm sure our client wouldn't want his successor to gain sympathy and supporters because of the assassination."

"Good point. Just get in and get out. I've more jobs waiting for you."

"Assign them to another. Isn't T-quin back from his southern jaunt?"

She stared at him. "T-quin takes too long."

"Arbon?"

"Is lying low. His last job was a fiasco and he's too hot."

"Sounds like this would be a good time for me to ask for a raise."

"You would think that, but you'd be wrong."

"I see. How about a timeline, then?"

Hedda rested her elbows on her desk. "What do you mean?"

"Don't play dumb. How many more jobs must I complete for you before I can go after the King?"

"It will take a couple years for you to get close enough to him. You're one of my best assassins and, at seventeen, you haven't even hit your prime. You've plenty of time to go after the King. Right now you can earn heaps of gold for your… retirement. Plus once you kill him, you're done. His guards will either kill you or you'll be too hot to stay in Ixia or work as an assassin for a decade."

"In other words, I would no longer be an asset for you."

"Of course. Wasn't that your sole desire? Kill the King? Have you thought about what happens afterward? If you live, that is."

No, he hadn't. Back when he was thirteen, he'd assumed he wouldn't survive. However, he'd gotten quite skilled at this business and he might have a future after all. Hedda had given him much to think about on his trip west to Pinchot.

When he arrived in the city, it didn't take him long to locate his mark. Ambrose made nightly speeches at various taverns around town. Valek kept to the edges of the crowd, listening to the man's propaganda.

"…own a diamond mine, but are we rich? No!" Ambrose sat at the bar, drinking from a mug of ale. "The King confiscates all our product, paying us only enough to keep the equipment running. The King of Ixia claims our taxes go to improve our lives, yet when the south section of the mines collapsed, he refused to send his soldiers to help clear the debris. Twenty-nine miners died, not from the collapse, but from being trapped underground."

Each evening, more people showed up to hear Ambrose speak. Valek recognized many faces from before and it appeared they'd dragged their friends along to listen. He had to admit the man was worth listening to. Valek agreed with him. In fact, the more he learned about the King's crimes in this region of Ixia, the greater his desire to assassinate the King.

Hedda's comments about what happened after the King's death had been in reference to Valek's life. But what about

Ixia? Who would take the King's place? Another corrupt royal? One of his spoiled princelings? Would anything change? Probably not. Yet Ambrose spoke of a new government with clear laws that applied to all. He argued for a fair system where everyone worked and basic needs were provided for by the government.

Too bad Valek had to assassinate Ambrose. The man had good ideas and appeared to be very organized. Valek spotted evidence that this was more than grandstanding at the local bar. Ambrose's loyal inner circle acted more like a military squad, and Pinchot was the sixth major city in his campaign.

After a couple of weeks, Valek pinpointed the ideal location for the assassination. Ambrose always left the taverns by the back entrance with a couple of brutes on his heels. He'd slip through the back alleys to the inn where he stayed.

Valek debated between ambushing him in the alley or in his room and decided on the alley. It seemed more dramatic and those two brutes would be easy to take down in the open versus in the tight hallway. Plus Ambrose had been smart enough to rent an interior room and hire a man to stay inside while he was out campaigning. It made it difficult for Valek to place a sculpted black diamond on Ambrose's bed, but not impossible.

On the big night, Valek followed Ambrose to the Pewter Tavern. He sat in the back until Ambrose hit his stride. Then Valek slipped out and found a dark shadow along Ambrose's route home in which to hide. Pulling on black gloves and a hood with a full face mask, he readied two darts. The hood worked much better than greasepaint. Easier to just yank it off when in a hurry than to stop and wash the incriminating black off his face. Plus it kept his face warm during these cold-season nights.

As Valek waited for his target, he envisioned the sequence of actions he'd need to perform to complete this mission. A slight pang of regret touched him. All of his targets deserved to die, but Ambrose might make an actual difference. He banished the sentiment. Hesitation was lethal in his line of work.

A few hours later, voices echoed off the stone walls of the alley. Three men approached—Ambrose and his bodyguards. As soon as they passed his hiding spot, Valek stepped out and threw the darts. One in each man's thick neck. He silently counted to ten as he followed the group. When the men wobbled on their feet, Valek drew his knife.

Valek slid between them as they thudded to the ground. Ambrose turned to see what had happened. Valek thrust his blade at Ambrose's stomach, expecting to pierce flesh while he met the man's shocked gaze. However, Ambrose shuffled back and a long dagger flashed in his hand.

"Nice," Valek said before engaging him in a knife fight.

Ambrose blocked his first series of strikes with ease. A couple of combinations later, Ambrose went on the offensive. Wow. The man was skilled with the blade. Valek backpedaled long enough to grab another dagger. Now armed with two, he attacked both high and low.

"Feeling more confident?" Ambrose asked.

"Oh yes."

"You won't for long." Ambrose increased the pace. His weapon snaked passed Valek's defenses and slashed his arm. "First blood." He grinned.

Unease stirred. Ignoring the unfamiliar feeling, he switched his strategy, using a more sophisticated series of strikes and blocks that he'd tested against his fellow assassins. Ambrose gave ground, inching toward the wall. Then he quickly stepped to the side and yanked another knife.

It didn't take long for Valek to realize he was outmatched. For the first time in years, fear unfurled and wrapped tentacles around his heart.

MARIA V. SNYDER

"Who hired you?" Ambrose asked.

And this was a great example why Hedda kept that information a secret. Valek's answer was a double thrust to Ambrose's throat, which missed by a hair because the man leaned back, all the while keeping his arms outstretched and dangerously close to Valek's chest. Twin slashes seared into his skin.

Valek shuffled away as Ambrose advanced. He no longer considered this an assassination, but a fight for his life. One that he was losing.

"Did the King send you?" Ambrose asked.

The question took him by complete surprise. Could he be working for the King? It was possible. Distracted by these thoughts, Valek made a critical error. In a blur of motion, Ambrose unarmed him and slammed him into the wall, pressing his blade to Valek's throat. The cold steel burned his hot skin as pain radiated through his skull. Fear squeezed his heart along with outrage—the King would live while he died.

"Who hired you?" Ambrose asked.

"I don't know."

Ambrose ripped off Valek's mask. Cool air fanned his sweaty face.

"Ah hell. You're just a kid."

Valek bit down on a protest. It might work in his favor.

"Just tell me if it was the King or not and I'll let you live."

He considered lying. After all, his life was at stake. But that golden gaze seared right into his soul. "I don't know. I hope not."

"Why?"

"The thought of working for the King makes me ill."

"No love for your King, eh?"

"He's not my King. All he is to me is another target."

"You plan to assassinate him?"

Valek gave him a bitter smile. "I did."

Ambrose laughed at his tone, but then turned contemplative. "*Can* you kill him?"

"Yes."

"He's a powerful magician."

"Doesn't matter."

"Why not?"

A lie sprang to his lips, but he sensed Ambrose would know. "I'm immune to magic."

Surprise and shrewd calculation flashed. Valek expected to be questioned for the details of his immunity.

Instead Ambrose asked, "Can you discover who hired you?"

Strange switch in topic. "I can."

"Would you?"

Ah, there was the right question. "And in exchange?"

"Your life."

"You'd let me go for a name? Just like that?"

"Oh no, not that easy. You see, you're mine now. Live or die, I decide." He slashed his other dagger along Valek's sternum, ripping the fabric of his tunic. Ambrose then carved a half circle into Valek's flesh.

Valek grunted as an intense pain coursed through him.

"It's a *C*. It stands for *Commander*. Meaning, I'm *your* commander. Pledge your loyalty to me and I'll help you reach the King. After all, I want the son of a bitch dead, too."

"And if I don't?"

"I'll slit your throat and leave you here."

Not much of a choice. Valek met his gaze. Deep down, he trusted that this man would keep his promises. Odd. He hadn't felt that way about anyone since he'd witnessed his brothers' murders.

"How soon can I go after the King?" he asked.

"Within the year."

Ambitious. "And when the King's dead?"

"I become the Commander of Ixia, and you can have a position on my staff. But first you need to find out who hired you and then kill him or her."

"What if it was the King?"

"Then assassinate his go-between. A warning to the King not to underestimate me."

"All right. I'm in."

Ambrose stepped back. "Do it right."

A different type of fear gripped him. Dying was a known state—he'd cease to exist—but giving his loyalty to another... one he barely knew...was a new form of terror. Yet his curiosity nudged the uncertainties aside, and his desire to plunge his knife into the King's heart trumped all fear.

Valek knelt on one knee. "I pledge my loyalty to you."

"What's your name?"

"Valek."

Ambrose cut his right palm and held his hand out. Valek swiped his fingers along his bleeding chest before clasping the man's strong grip.

"I accept your pledge, Valek."

They shook hands, linking their fates together.

Valek returned to Hedda's school and reported success. She'd never reveal her client's name, so he followed her when she left to collect the rest of the assassination fee. The man who paid her wore tailored silk clothes and had a half dozen bodyguards around him. Valek recognized him as Prince Theoin, one of the King's four nephews.

Fury burned in his chest. Hedda was well aware of Valek's hatred for the King. To send him on a mission that would benefit the man... He clenched his hands, digging his fingernails into the flesh of his palms in order to calm down. Valek needed to remain emotionless and view the situation with logic.

The King had sent a trusted family member to hire an assassin, which meant he must be terrified of Ambrose. As he should be. Valek looked forward to killing Theoin. It would remove one more corrupt royal.

Valek waited for Hedda in her hidden windowless apartment. The one she thought no one could find. The one where she kept her safe, her personal files, her belongings and her bedroom. It made sense for her to be so well protected. It had to be hard to fall asleep knowing you were surrounded by assassins.

He scratched his chest. Ambrose's cut had scabbed over and the throbbing had been replaced by an annoying itch. Valek decided he'd rather have the pain until his fingernail ripped a scab off. Ouch.

When Hedda arrived, she didn't react to Valek's presence. No surprise she had a warning system in place for when someone breached her private rooms.

Valek lounged in a chair in her living area, giving the impression he was relaxed even though he was far from it.

Hedda held up a pouch. It jingled. "Couldn't wait for your half?"

"Keep it," he said. "In fact…" He tossed a large sack onto the end table. It slapped the wood with a hard rattle. "Here's all my halves, minus living and travel expenses."

"Why?"

"I was never in this for the money."

"But—"

"Consider it payment for all the food, shelter and training you provided. I'm grateful for that." He stood.

"You don't need—"

"Yes, I do, because I quit."

Understanding flashed. She stepped back. Her hand reached for her dagger.

"Relax, Hedda. I'm not going to kill you even though you

MARIA V. SNYDER

knew the King ordered Ambrose's assassination. Have I done his dirty work before?" he demanded.

As expected, she refused to answer. At least she was consistent.

"You'll never get close enough to the King without help," Hedda said.

Nausea swelled as her words sank in. "And you never intended to help me since he's probably your best customer."

Again she kept quiet. Smart.

He clamped down on the anger boiling in his stomach. "Better not spend the fee you collected on Ambrose's assassination. Your King will soon be asking for a refund."

"You didn't—"

"Nope. He's alive and well. And I advise you not to send anyone else after him."

"Why? Are you planning to protect him?"

"I don't need to." Valek left her rooms and hurried from the school's grounds. If Hedda sounded the alarm, he'd be outnumbered and thrown off the cliffs.

Besides, he had a prince to kill.

Valek was jolted from his memories by two border soldiers bookending a young man. The three of them waited for him in front of his office door. The guards' grim expressions warned him to expect trouble. Valek studied the scared man trapped between them. He wore Sitian garb. Ah.

"Report, Sergeant," Valek said to the man on the right.

"This man claims to be a messenger from Sitia, but he wouldn't relinquish his message at the border as required."

"Why not?"

"I've been ordered to deliver it to you directly," the young man piped up.

Interesting. "By who?"

The messenger glanced at the guards. "It's confidential. For your ears only."

"All right." Valek unlocked his office door.

"Sir, he may be a Sitian spy or an assassin," the sergeant said.

Valek stared at him. "And what are you basing this...assessment on?"

"Uh...his insistence on seeing you."

How did this man get promoted to sergeant? "Let me give you a quick lesson on assassins, Sergeant. They don't walk up to the border and announce their plans. Nor do they wear conspicuous clothing. You're both dismissed."

"But our captain told us to stay with the Sitian at all times."

"I outrank your captain. Wait out by the castle's gate."

The messenger wrung his hands as Valek escorted him inside his office. Bad news, or was he just nervous about being alone with the infamous Valek?

Valek leaned against his desk. "What's so important?"

"I'm...er... Second Magician Irys Jewelrose sent me."

His first thought was something had happened to Yelena. It took all of Valek's considerable willpower to keep from shaking the rest of the information from the messenger. "Go on."

"She's very concerned about Liaison Yelena. There's been..."

He straightened. "What happened?"

"The Master Magicians have uncovered a plot to harm the Liaison."

"I already know about the assassination attempt in the woods."

"They're uncertain if this is related to that attack or a new one. And since the Liaison is vulnerable, Master Jewelrose thought you should be informed right away."

"Vulnerable?" Ice rushed through his body. He gripped the edge of his desk. "What do you mean by vulnerable?"

MARIA V. SNYDER

22

JANCO

As the pain in Janco's head increased, Onora prepared for a magical attack. After a few minutes, nothing happened. No one attacked. Yet the agony continued. Janco's vision blurred, and from the corner of his eye he spotted the reason. An illusion. Or rather, a magical illusion right in the middle of the freaking forest.

The pain in his right ear intensified as Janco drew closer to the magical illusion. Onora followed him with her knives drawn. As far as illusions went, this one was rather lame. It matched the forest exactly. Bare trees, bushes, piles of dead leaves—all normal for being in the middle of the Snake Forest.

That meant it hid something important. Janco held his hands straight out as he walked toward the illusion. He grimaced as his head pounded.

"Uh, Janco, there's a tree right— Oh!"

He pierced the illusion and a strange burning sensation flashed through his body. At least the agony in his ear dulled.

"Janco, are you all right?" Onora asked. "Where are—"

He reached through the magical border and yanked her inside. She yelped in surprise, but recovered quickly.

As he caught his breath, he scanned their surroundings.

Wagon-wheel grooves marked the forest floor and led to a mouth of a cave a few feet away. The illusion camouflaged the cave's entrance so the border patrols would walk right by it.

Onora peered inside then entered. She returned with an unlit torch. "Looks like the cave's in use. Could this be a hideout?"

"Was there any evidence that someone is living in there?"

"It's narrow and I couldn't see far. There might be a bigger cavern farther in."

"Then light the torch and we'll go have a look."

"Are you crazy?"

"Define *crazy*."

"Walking right into a trap." She stabbed the tip of her dagger at the cave.

Janco crouched on the ground. "The wagon marks are a few days old. No fresh boot prints. I don't think the cave is occupied at the moment."

"So now you have a cave vibe, too?"

"Okay, Little Miss Assassin, what do you suggest we do?"

"Hide and wait. See who comes out or goes in."

Oh. Actually, that was a pretty good plan. Annoyed he hadn't thought of it, Janco crossed his arms. "For how long?"

"For as long as it takes."

"What about our mission?" And then it hit him. "This could be what we're searching for—a way for the smugglers to cross the border without being seen."

"*If* it tunnels under the border into Sitia, and *if* it isn't just a hideout."

"Killjoy."

"If I was going to kill, it wouldn't be *joy*." Onora gave him a pointed look.

He laughed. "You wouldn't be the first person who wished me dead, sweetheart."

MARIA V. SNYDER

She flinched at the endearment and shoved her weapons into their holders to cover her...anger? No. Fear? Not quite. More like an old nightmare that hadn't faded. He waited for her to threaten him with bodily harm if he used "sweetheart" again, but Onora kept quiet. Smart. If she'd fussed, he'd use it all the time just to goad her. Ari had called it childish, but Janco used it as a tool. He needed to discover just how much tolerance she had and where her breaking point was.

"How did you see through the illusion?" she asked. "Do you have magic?"

"Oh no. Not at all. I'm allergic to magic." He explained about the warning pain. "I had no idea what it hid."

"Since you can sense it, you should find a position outside the illusion, and I'll stay inside," she said.

He glanced around. There wasn't much room. "Where—"

"Not many people look up." She shoved her boots and cape inside her pack, then stashed it out of sight. Onora climbed the rough stone wall next to the cave's mouth until she reached the apex. Settling into a comfortable position, she shooed Janco.

He paused. She appeared to blend in with the gray stones and brown earth that had collected in the nooks of the rock face. Janco glanced away and rubbed the back of his neck. Lack of sleep could do strange things to a guy. He turned to assess her line of vision so he didn't watch the same patch of forest. Except she'd disappeared.

"Get going before someone shows up." Her voice sounded above his head.

Holy snow cats! Did she...? Was she...? He stepped closer to the cave's entrance, expecting his scar to burn. It didn't. Maybe the illusion's magic covered her power. He rubbed the spot as he considered.

"What are you doing?" she asked.

"Uh, just checking something." Janco poked his head into the cave as if it contained all the answers. It didn't. Unless darkness had something to do with the mystery of Onora. Perhaps it did. Perhaps—

"Janco."

Her irritation snapped him from his thoughts. "All right, I'm going." He braced for the pain as he crossed the illusion. It flared to life, stabbing into his head. Janco kept walking until the intense stinging dulled to a tolerable level. Then he found a place to hide.

His thoughts circled back to Onora. In all their time together, Janco had never felt that creepy crawly sensation along his skin, which he'd learned meant magic was in use but not directed at him. Hard to describe. It was like hearing an echo.

She could be one of those One-Trick Wonders who had enough magic to do only one single thing like light a fire or spot a liar. Hey, that rhymed—he'd have to remember that for later. Perhaps her power was blending in with her surroundings like a chameleon. No wonder she'd reached the Commander and escaped the dungeon. For an assassin to have that ability...was pretty sweet! Of course, he could be way off base. The pain from the illusion might have screwed with his vision.

But as he waited for...well, anything at this point. Talk about bored. Janco remembered the times he and Onora had encountered a patrol and she'd melted into the forest. The creepy crawlies hadn't attacked him then, but her ability to disappear seemed...off. He decided to not jump to conclusions— Ari would be proud—and keep an eye on Little Miss Assassin, see if she had any more tricks.

The day dragged, limping toward twilight. Janco's stiff muscles complained about the inactivity. His stomach growled. Wonderful. He'd wait until full dark and then take a break. After all, a man had to eat and sleep and pee.

MARIA V. SNYDER

★ ★ ★

A rumbling creak woke him from a light doze. Darkness surrounded him. It took him a moment to orient himself—Snake Forest—on lookout—with Onora. Check.

A harness jingled and the thud of horse hooves on the ground vibrated under him. Soon two wagon teams rolled into view. The figures sitting on the benches didn't have a lantern, but there was enough moonlight to discern big obstacles like trees. Besides, most horses just needed to be pointed down a trail. They instinctively followed the cleared path.

As they passed his hiding spot, Janco noticed a burlap blanket covering the lumpy contents of the wagon. Intrigued, he followed the wagons as they neared the illusion then slowed.

"Where's that damn cave?" one man asked. "Did we miss it?"

"No, it's a little further," his companion said.

"Just stop here," a woman called from the second wagon. "The horses get too skittish if we get closer. Mattison will meet us."

They unhitched the horses and fed and watered them. They appeared to be waiting for this Mattison. Too curious to stay put, Janco crept up behind the second wagon, noting the long and narrow bed. He lifted the blanket, revealing barrels. Words had been burned into the oak, but it was too dark to read them.

A bright yellow glow pierced the illusion, momentarily blinding him. Three huge men carried torches and pulled a small cart. Another set of three big brutes emerged, but they didn't tow anything. All six men wore some type of leather harness.

The two groups merged. Janco slipped back into the forest while they were distracted.

"Anyone follow you?" one of the big brutes asked.

"You kidding? No one's around for miles," the wagon leader said. "How much did you get?"

"Six golds a barrel."

"Next time ask for eight. It's getting harder to smuggle this stuff out. Valek's got his dogs sniffing around."

An indignant huff sounded next to Janco. He jumped and clamped down on a cry.

"Don't sneak up on me like that," he whispered to Onora.

"Assassin, remember?"

"But I'm on your side."

She shrugged. "Habit."

"Did you see what's in the cart from the cave?" he asked.

"Yes. A few small barrels."

They watched the smugglers as they hitched one wagon to the three big men, attaching the chains to their harnesses, and then they hooked up the other three with the other wagon. Odd. Why not use the horses?

"I'm going to crawl under the burlap on that second wagon," Onora whispered. "You track the cart and see where it goes. We'll meet back here once we learn what's going on."

He opened his mouth to protest, but she disappeared. While the others were distracted hooking up the men and horses, the blanket rippled and the wagon creaked under the additional weight. No one but Janco noticed.

After they finished, the smugglers made arrangements for another meeting, then headed in opposite directions. The horses pulled the cart from the cave back into the forest, and the men lugged the two wagons toward the cave.

Ah. The horses either couldn't fit inside the tunnel or were too scared to go underground. Onora's plan had merit, but Janco still didn't trust her. And Valek had ordered him to keep an eye on her.

Janco waited a few minutes before dashing through the

illusion. A brief surge of fire ringed his head before dying down. The circle of torchlight retreated deeper into the cave. He summoned the courage to follow. Janco hoped it was a short tunnel.

After all, he hadn't had time to eat or pee.

23

YELENA

I released the reedwither plant and spread my hands wide. "Good. Now stand and turn around slowly," the man behind me ordered.

Wondering why Kiki hadn't warned me of his presence, I straightened and faced him. A tall and muscular Sandseed warrior watched me. I didn't recognize him. He held a scimitar in his left hand and another dagger in his right. His skin was the color of shadows and he had a green-and-brown-patterned cloth wrapped around his waist. It must be for modesty because the rest of his body was bare despite the cold.

Unconcerned, Kiki grazed nearby.

"You must continue on your journey," he said.

Not a chance. "I need to collect—"

"It is forbidden to harvest the reedwither."

"Why?"

"It is a powerful poison."

"I know. I may have been injected with it."

"Not possible. You are alive."

I stifled a sarcastic retort. No need to upset the well-armed man. "I have healing abilities. I may have stopped the poison from killing me."

He stepped closer. "I sense no magic from you."

All right, time to try another tactic. "I'm friends with al-most all of the surviving Sandseeds, but I've never seen you before. Who are you?"

The Sandseed puffed out his broad chest. "I am the guard-ian of the reedwither plants."

Plants. As in plural. At least there were more.

"Do not think you can steal from another patch," he said. "I watch all."

And that would only be possible if... "There's a magical shield over the plants, and when it's broken, you appear."

"Yes." His eyebrows pinched together, rippling his bald head.

"And you wait in the shadow world."

"How do you know this?" he demanded.

"I've been to the shadow world."

"Not possible. You are not a Sandseed Story Weaver."

"I was the Soulfinder."

"Was?" Confusion gripped his expression. "You cannot undo what is done."

"I wish that was true, but someone poisoned me with reed-wither and now my Soulfinding days are over. That's why I need a sample so I can take it to my father and have him pro-duce an antidote."

"Who is your father?"

"Esau Liana Zaltana." Although I had no idea how his name would help.

"I know this Esau."

Then again... Hope rose.

"He will not be able to aid you. This plant cannot do what you claim."

"How can you be so sure? No one has used it on a Soul-finder before."

"True." He tucked his weapons into the cloth around his waist. "But I know I have not been called from the shadow world to protect the plant for many years."

I considered. Some substances remained potent for years. "Did they succeed?"

"No one has since I have been on duty. Before I died, my life threads were woven into the reedwither plant so I could protect it while in the shadow world."

"How long ago?"

"Back when your father, Esau, was a curious young boy, visiting the plains for the first time. Esau asked so many questions, I thought our elders would send him home early."

Sounded like my father. A mix of emotions rolled through me. If the poison wasn't from the reedwither plant, then what had caused my magic to disappear?

The Sandseed moved closer and spread his hands. "May I?"

"May you what?"

"Read the threads of your life."

"You're a Story Weaver?"

"Yes."

Sifting through the logic, I couldn't think of a reason not to let him. Perhaps a ghost Story Weaver would be able to discover what happened to my magic. "All right. What's your name?"

"Midnight Son." He grasped my hand. "There is a...barrier."

I'd forgotten about the null shields. Releasing his grip, I removed my cloak and pulled the octopus pendant from around my neck, setting it down with care. A cold breeze caressed my skin and I shivered.

Midnight Son took my hand in both of his. Heat enveloped my skin and I panicked for a moment, remembering the Fire Warper. Stupid of me to trust so easily. Midnight Son could be from the fire world. And now I was unprotected.

MARIA V. SNYDER

"You do need to be more careful," Midnight Son said, holding tight. "You are very vulnerable." His gaze grew distant. "Your story threads are complex and woven into an intricate pattern." He chuckled to himself. "No wonder my son struggled at times. And why the elders believed he was the only Story Weaver up to the challenge."

"Your son?"

"Moon Man."

I relaxed and wondered why I hadn't noticed the resemblance. The weapons must have distracted me.

"Are you ready?" he asked.

"Yes." My voice squeaked.

"Let us go back."

With a dizzying swirl of color the Avibian Plains spun around us like sand grains caught in a whirlwind. The daylight turned to night and trees erupted from the ground, turning the flat landscape into a forest.

Movement underneath me jerked to the side as pain pierced my shoulder. I relived the events of the night of the ambush in quick succession. My time with Valek and enduring the hot and cold fever sped by along with the trip to the Magician's Keep. Everything I'd done and everyone I'd talked to flashed in front of me. A span of blackness arose after Ben's smug face jumped into view. I flinched as fear pushed me to run and hide, but I had no control over my body or the images.

Midnight Son didn't release me until we reached the present. I sank to the ground exhausted, which seemed strange since I hadn't done anything.

"You did all the work," he said.

Looping the octopus around my neck, I pulled my cloak around my shoulders. The air had turned icy. So much for this being the last day of the cold season.

"Then what did you do?" I asked.

"I watched and learned."

I clutched the fabric of my cloak tight. "And?"

"It confirmed that the reedwither plant is not the culprit."

Another dead end.

"It also confirmed that you did not die."

"What?"

"You are the Soulfinder. You have the ability to bring a person back to life by healing the body and returning the person's soul. You could have kept your soul inside your body after it died, then healed yourself."

I'd returned two souls—Stono's and Gelsi's. Both killed themselves within a year of being saved, and I'd vowed never to do it again. Good to know that, in my panic, I hadn't re-animated myself. A shudder ripped through me.

"If I had done that, would that have caused my problem?" Stono hadn't had magic, but Gelsi had. However, I couldn't remember if she'd still had access to her powers after I brought her back to life.

"That is an interesting question."

"And do you have an interesting answer?"

"No. But it does not matter." His eyes gleamed.

Energized, I shot to my feet. "Do you know what happened to my magic?"

"Yes."

"And?"

"It is blocked."

"Like a null shield?"

"No."

Frustration rose and I tightened my grip on my cloak's rough fabric until my fingernails pressed into my palms. I drew in a calming breath. If Moon Man had learned how to be cryptic and annoying from his father, I needed to choose my words with care. "How is my magic blocked?"

MARIA V. SNYDER

"It just is."

I clamped down on a growl. "You said it was unlike a null shield. Can you explain?"

"A null shield blocks magic from both directions, while this only prevents *you* from using magic. However, you are vulnerable to magic. For now."

Old news. "What is 'this'? A poison? Magic? A virus? A one-way null shield?"

He didn't respond.

I searched his expression. "You don't know!"

No reaction.

Groaning, I plopped back onto the ground, lying back with my arm over my eyes. "You're not going to tell me. Are you?" My throat closed as a hot pressure built. Sheer force of will kept tears from spilling.

"I can tell you this."

I peeked at him.

"You will figure this out, Soulfinder."

"When?"

"When the time is right."

Midnight Son sounded just like Moon Man.

"Did you teach your son how to be cryptic or is it an in-born trait for Story Weavers?" I asked.

"Inborn. We guide, but we do not provide easy answers."

"I'm very familiar with that annoying aspect of your personality." Sarcasm sharpened my tone. I sat up. "Sorry, this has all been…"

"Overwhelming."

"Yes. Can you tell me if my magic returns?"

"No." He held out a hand. "Your future story threads do not reveal the answer. Both futures are equally possible."

That meant I'd have a fifty-percent chance of regaining my magic. Better than zero chance. The black despair that had stained my thoughts since I'd woken without magic receded a fraction.

"What should I do next?" I asked, not expecting an answer.

"You should return and finish what you started."

Ah. "I can't. They'll die."

"How do you know this?"

I searched my memories. A vague image of Ben accompanied the red-hot knowledge that my presence would result in death. "I just…know."

"A powerful magician has altered your memories, planting this fear inside you."

"Ben Moon or maybe Cilly and Loris Cloud Mist?" They might have the talent.

"I do not know."

"Can you fix it?"

"No. You must learn to ignore this fear."

Easier said than done. I huffed. "You know, the longer I spend with you, the less I miss Moon Man."

"Thank you."

Curiosity replaced my apprehension. "Why did you name him Moon Man?"

Midnight Son smiled, revealing big white teeth. "He was conceived during a full moon and born on the night of a full moon, so we named him Moon. Fitting, since the boy never liked to wear clothing. The Man came after his Story Weaver powers manifested. He thought Moon was not…impressive enough." Midnight Son laughed.

I soaked in the sound of his laughter, closing my eyes and imagining Moon Man standing there scowling at his father for embarrassing him. Then again, Moon Man wouldn't be embarrassed. He'd be scolding me for running away without thinking it through.

But what could I do without my magic?

MARIA V. SNYDER

"It is a shame that people without access to the power blanket are so helpless. It is a wonder they do not die at an early age." Midnight Son tsked.

"Don't start that mind-reading stuff."

"I am sorry. You wish to wallow in self-pity. I will leave you to your brooding. But I will say this… You should not feel disconnected from your family and friends nor should you fear for their lives. Their story threads are woven with yours. Even without the strand of magic twisted around your story, the rest of your threads remain strong."

"In other words, I'm not going to unravel."

"Exactly." He grinned and bowed. "A pleasure to meet you, Soulfinder. If you need further assistance, you know how to find me. I will admit, chasing intruders away from a plant is not nearly as exciting as talking to you."

"Glad I could provide some entertainment."

Midnight Son flashed me another toothy smile and stepped into a shadow. He disappeared as he returned to the shadow world. I stared at his boot prints in the sand. His comments spun in my mind. Three main things snagged. Midnight Son had claimed I'd figure out how I lost my magic and he'd given me a fifty-percent chance of regaining my powers. Plus he'd called me Soulfinder, which could have been a slip of the tongue due to something he'd seen in my story threads.

I needed to keep trying to solve the puzzle. What options did I have left? Pazia Cloud Mist might have some answers. She lived in Ognap, which I guessed was northeast of here. Although I'd no real idea where in the Avibian Plains we were. My other choice was going south to the Illiais Jungle to visit my father. He might know about or have heard about a magic-blocking substance. I chewed on my lip, deciding.

Kiki nudged my arm, surprising me. Glancing at her saddle, she turned her blue-eyed gaze back to me.

"Ready to go?" I asked.

Another nudge.

"Okay." Securing my cloak and shouldering my pack, I mounted Kiki. In that instant, I knew the right thing to do despite the terror clamping down on my guts. "Back to Fulgor please, Kiki."

I wasn't surprised by the extra security measures that had been installed around Opal's glass factory. In fact, I approved despite the fact they wouldn't be enough to protect Reema from a determined assassin. One of the many things I'd learned from Valek was that an assassin would sit and wait for days, weeks or even months to find the perfect time to kill.

Looping Kiki's reins around a nearby post, I shouldered my pack and approached the entrance. I tried to ignore the certainty that watchers followed my every move, and the creepy crawly sensation of invisible gazes pressing on my back. The afternoon sunlight had done nothing to dispel the chill in the air, and now that the sun balanced on the horizon, the cold intensified. Or was it the icy glares the guards outside the factory turned on me?

While I waited outside, one man went to verify my claims. He returned with Devlen in tow.

"Have you found the plant?" he asked in a flat tone.

He was probably angry at me. I didn't blame him. I tilted my head toward the guard hovering over me. "Can we talk inside?"

"Opal's not here."

"Opal's not the one I'm worried about. How's Reema?"

Ire flared in his gaze, but he gestured for me to follow him into the factory. Then he stopped. Workers buzzed around the kilns. The heat rolling off the four enveloped me. My numb fingers thawed.

MARIA V. SNYDER

"Reema is driving me crazy." Devlen crossed his arms. He wore short sleeves and pants. "Being cooped up inside is not...ideal for her."

Alarmed, I asked, "Is she upstairs alone?"

"No. Two more guards watch her. Are you going to tell me what happened that night?"

"Where's Opal?"

"In the city, searching for Ben."

"Have they found him?"

"No. You did not answer my question."

"I've no idea what happened that night. They must have lured me away and changed my memories. All I know is if I remained in Fulgor, Reema would be assassinated and the rest of my friends and family would be killed, as well." I held up a hand, stopping his questions. "Even though I think it's just a planted threat, we have to send Reema away or I won't be able to function. She's not safe here."

"She sleeps with us and we have four guards from Fulgor's security forces here at all times."

"Not enough. An assassin might be coming after her."

Fear replaced his anger. "How do you know this?"

I met his gaze. "I don't know, but we can't take the chance that it's one of my fake memories. If Ben thinks his..." I tapped a finger on my temple. "Plan didn't work, he might go after her out of spite."

He nodded. "All right. What do we do?"

"Get Reema. Tell her to pack a bag and don her warmest cloak. You're going with her, so grab your travel kit."

While he rushed off to collect Reema, I pulled my new purchases from my pack and set them aside. They had rested atop my cooking paraphernalia, flint, Esau's field manual and other travel essentials that had all jumbled together. I also kept my valuables in my backpack and I'd tied my bedroll to the bottom.

The heat finally soaked into my bones. I removed my cloak and most of the hidden weapons inside the fabric.

Devlen returned with Reema. They both carried small rucksacks.

Reema raced over to me. "I knew you didn't run away. I told them you were chasing the bad guys, but they didn't believe me. Did you catch them?"

I smiled at her utter confidence in me. "Not yet. I need you to go on a secret mission with your dad. Do you think you can handle it?"

Her cheeks blushed with excitement. "Yes!"

"Good. Do you know how to ride a horse?"

"Yes."

"She's only been on Quartz with Opal," Devlen said.

She shot her father a withering look. He ignored her.

"Can you mount without help?" I asked her.

"Of course."

"That's all you need. Just hold on and Kiki will do the rest."

"Kiki!" she squealed.

"Reema, this is very serious," Devlen admonished.

She settled down, but pure impish delight danced in her gaze. Oh boy, this was going to be…interesting.

"Let's go into Opal's office. Bring your packs." I hefted mine along with the new package.

Once inside the somewhat private space, I showed them the two wigs—one with straight black hair and the other with blond corkscrew curls.

I held up the black one. "Reema, you're going to pretend to be me. If you wear this wig, my cloak, and pull the hood down low, no one should suspect anything. Kiki will take you northeast."

MARIA V. SNYDER

"That's all?" Disappointment laced her tone.

"It is very important. You can't show your face. You need to be serious and stay on Kiki until your dad meets up with you. Kiki will protect you. Okay?"

She nodded. "I won't mess up."

"Good."

Reema exchanged her cloak for mine. The hem dragged on the ground, but not enough to be noticeable in the dark. I hoped. I wrapped her hair into a bun and set the wig on her head.

I showed her where the darts were hidden in the fabric. "These have Curare, and these have sleeping potion. Only use them in an emergency. Don't try to throw them. Just jab into skin if you can."

We walked her to the front door.

"Ready?" Devlen asked, drawing her into a brief hug.

"Where are we going?" she asked.

"It's a surprise. Your dad will tell you when he sees you later. Don't worry. Kiki knows the way."

Reema pulled the hood down low over her face and without looking back strode from the factory as if on an important mission. Which she was. I raced upstairs to a front-facing window and peeked out just in time to see her spur Kiki down the road. Two heartbeats later a couple of shadows detached from the building across the street and followed, proving that not all my memories were false.

Now for part two. I joined Devlen in Opal's office.

He played with one of the blond curls. "I hope you are not endangering her."

"Kiki is going to head straight northeast, pass the town limits, and that should make them happy. And Kiki will not let anyone harm her."

"And this?"

I braided my hair and wound it around my head before taking the wig from him and securing it to my head. "This is to show the other two watchers that Reema is still here." I tied her cloak around my shoulders. It fell to my knees, shorter than I liked, but with my black boots and dark pants no one should notice. Letting a couple of curls escape the hood, I drew the fabric low. "Let's go."

"Where?"

"Where would you take Reema?"

"There's a taffy shop a few blocks away."

"Perfect. Leave your bag. You can catch up with her and Kiki later."

We left the factory. The two guards at the entrance accompanied us as we walked to the taffy shop. The other watchers followed us at a discreet distance. They were professionals. If I hadn't been searching for them, I would have missed them. My heart skittered and urged me to run away. It pulsed a warning that death would befall all if I stayed in Fulgor.

"Where am I meeting Reema?" Devlen asked.

"Just head north. Kiki will find you."

"And then where?"

I twirled one of the curls around my finger. "Kiki can carry you both."

"Yelena."

"You're going to the only place Reema'll be safe from an assassin."

"The Magician's Keep?"

"No. The Commander's castle. Valek will protect her."

He opened his mouth. Probably to protest. Then he sighed. "You are right. As much as I would like to believe I can keep her safe, I cannot."

"Once this mess is settled, you can return home."

We reached the taffy shop. The owner was about to lock up,

but she let us in. Devlen bought a pound of Reema's favorite—peppermint mixed with vanilla. We shared a portion of the confection as we returned to the factory.

"How long should I wait?" Devlen asked.

"When is Opal due back?"

"It depends. Some nights not until late, others..."

"Wait for her and explain what's going on."

"What about Reema?"

"Ben's men should stop following her once they've determined she isn't looping back into the city. Kiki will know and turn west to rendezvous with you. Do you have another way out of the factory?" I peeled off the blond wig.

He smiled. "Of course. Opal insisted we have a few options. Not many people know we purchased the building next door."

"Wonderful." I hefted my pack. "Where's the hidden exit?"

"Where are you going?"

"To find out what really happened that night."

24

VALEK

The poor messenger shrank back.

Valek eased his death grip on his desk and asked again, "How is Liaison Zaltana vulnerable?"

"I…I…don't know, sir. Master Jewelrose said you would know."

Could Irys mean Yelena was vulnerable because of Ben's escape? Looking at the situation from Ben's point of view, Valek would also target Yelena. She posed a dangerous threat to his continued freedom. Plus Ben had to have help in his escape, which meant she was up against more than one magician with a grudge.

"Do you have more details regarding this endeavor to harm her?" he asked the messenger.

"There's been anti-magician rumblings and Master Jewelrose believes someone wishes to make an example of the Liaison as to why the Council shouldn't rely on magicians anymore. Proof to all that magicians can be easily compromised."

Valek wouldn't have used the word *easily*. Curare wasn't available to just anyone and null shields… They might have a point about those. Arbon had said cloaks with null shields were available for sale. Plus Opal's magic detectors had made it

difficult for a magician to be subtle. However, he doubted the
Council would interfere with the production of the super messengers. They were too vital to Sitia. Valek wondered how they
justified the super messengers' existence, but not magicians.

"Does Master Jewelrose know who this *someone* is?" Valek
asked.

"Not yet. She just wanted to inform you of the situation."

Remembering the Council had kept the news about Ben
from Yelena, Valek asked, "Has she warned the Liaison?"

"I don't know."

Not good. Once again Valek's heart wished to hop onto
Onyx and ride straight for Fulgor, but the Commander's order
that he remain uninvolved kept him from racing to the stables. Arbon's comment about the Commander holding Valek's
leash repeated in his mind. Valek squashed it. Besides, she,
Leif, Devlen, Opal and that other magician she mentioned in
her message had plenty of protection.

Valek flagged down a servant to escort the messenger to
the gate. He returned to his office, but couldn't sit and read
reports. Despite all the logic, worry for Yelena churned in his
stomach. He changed into his sneak suit and under cover of
darkness tested the security measures inside the castle complex.

After a few hours of creeping, crawling, climbing and ghosting, his agitation had diminished. The security wasn't horrible, but the protection in certain areas had gotten lax. Valek
understood why as most of the guards probably assumed that
a threat from those areas was slim. But it was precisely those
particular weaknesses that a shrewd assassin would exploit.

That was how he'd gotten to the King—by discovering
that single lapse in security. It had taken Valek months to find.
After working for the Commander for a couple of seasons,
Ambrose led him to a back corner of the tavern. He carried
two mugs of ale and handed one to Valek.

"My supporters are moving faster than expected. We should be closing in on the castle in three seasons. Is that enough time for you to assassinate the King?" Ambrose asked.

Finally! Valek kept his excitement from showing on his face. "Depends if I can identify a way inside. The King—"

"Is well protected. Don't waste time looking for a hole in the security around him. Go through someone else who is close to him. That will be your best shot."

"Like the Queen?"

"Exactly."

Valek sipped his ale. "How will I know when you're ready to attack?"

"By the end of the warm season, I will be in Jewelstown, making my speeches in the taverns. Find me and we'll set a time to strike."

"You're not worried the King will send his soldiers to arrest you?" Valek asked.

Ambrose smiled. "No. By then, he won't have many loyal soldiers. You'd be surprised what the promise of double wages does to loyalty."

"And can you keep that promise?"

"You don't think we gave the King all the diamonds we mined, do you?"

"Ah."

"When the bastard refused to send help to dig out those trapped miners, we decided we weren't going to play nice anymore."

"What happens when the money runs out?"

"The King's coffers are quite full and I plan to close the border to Sitia. Our money has been flowing south, buying imports and making the Sitians rich while our people beg on the streets. Stop the imports and we'll have to manufacture

MARIA V. SNYDER

our own supplies, generating plenty of jobs for everyone and keeping our money here in Ixia."

Valek wondered if it would be as easy as the Commander made it sound. He hoped so. "Speaking of money, I need a handful of gold for expenses."

Ambrose filled a pouch. "I included a few diamonds. They're perfect for big bribes. Ladies find them irresistible." He tossed it to Valek. "Buy yourself a new dagger. That one you carry is—"

"My favorite blade and I plan to sink it deep into the King's heart."

"You do that and you'll become my chief of security. Who better to protect me than one who can get through the tightest security?"

"No one."

Ambrose grinned. "Right."

Valek stood, saluted Ambrose with his mug, downed the contents in one gulp and set it on the table.

"Valek," Ambrose said.

He turned back. The humor was gone from Ambrose's gaze. In its place was a cold hardness like a dagger made of ice.

"Kill them all," the Commander said.

"All?"

"All the royals. King, Queen, princes…everyone with royal blood."

Valek stared at him.

"They're a weed. If we don't get all the roots, they'll grow back. Do you understand?"

He did. It just seemed…heartless despite the logic. "Yes, sir."

The countdown had begun. Six months to assassinate the King and his entire family. Valek traveled to Jewelstown, which was located near the castle's complex. The town had been renamed after Queen Jewel—a wedding gift from the King. Valek spent every night the first week searching for a way inside the complex. The steep and smooth outer walls were not only difficult to climb, but too exposed.

He dressed as a servant and was able to enter the main gates without trouble. However, he soon discovered the servants were restricted to their corridors and quarters and rarely saw the royals let alone interacted with them. Only the trusted servants, who'd worked in the castle for years, were allowed into the royal apartments and kitchen. Smart.

One thing he'd learned at Hedda's was patience. Hired as an errand boy, Valek gathered information about the daily activities of the staff for a few weeks before discovering one way to get inside the royal apartments.

"Where's Darrick?" one of the housekeeping servants asked. "He was supposed to clean the chamber pots hours ago." She twisted her apron.

"He's sick," Valek said. "I heard him in the outhouse." He lowered his voice. "It sounded bad." Thanks to the dose of White Fright Valek had slipped him yesterday morning. "I'm between jobs, ma'am. I could dump them for you."

She chewed on her lip.

"Unless you want to?"

"Heavens no. Follow me." She set off.

Valek hurried to keep up. She led him to a wash station.

"You dump the contents into that bucket." She pointed to a grungy, smelly metal pail. "Then you wash the pot in the soapy water, dry it and return it. When you're done, take the bucket down to the outhouses and dump it. Understand?"

Ah, the glamorous life of an assassin. "Yes, ma'am."

"Good." She escorted him through the royal suites and guest rooms, showing him the location of all the pots. The

MARIA V. SNYDER

housekeeper watched him for a while, but soon another ser-vant caught her attention and she hurried off.

As Valek continued cleaning pots, he noted the room lo-cations, guards and who the other servants were. The next day, poor Darrick wasn't any better and Valek filled in for him again. By the time Darrick was well enough to return to work, the housekeeper had assigned the boy to other duties. Darrick didn't complain at all.

Valek learned as much as he could during his twice-daily forays into the royal apartments. Within a couple of weeks, he determined that he wouldn't get close to the Queen or the King by cleaning chamber pots. However, he noticed one of the Queen's women wasn't a lady-in-waiting or a servant. She arrived in the morning and styled the Queen's hair, picked out her gown for the day and applied makeup to Queen Jewel's face. She would return again before dinner and help the Queen get ready for the evening meal. They spent much of the time alone in the Queen's quarters. Her guards were banished to the outer rooms while she dressed.

He made a few discreet inquiries about this woman.

"Oh, that's Parveen," one of the biggest castle gossips said. "She has a little beauty shop in Jewelstown she won't give up. The Queen indulges her because she's supposedly the best." The woman lowered her voice and leaned close. "I personally think the Queen can do better. Did you see her hair yester-day? It looked like a bird's nest." She tsked.

After he cleaned the pots in the morning, he followed Parveen into Jewelstown. Sure enough, she entered a shop along Lowell Street. Valek wouldn't describe it as "little." The place spanned almost a full block. Mirrors covered the walls, and chairs ringed the interior.

Customers filled those chairs as an army of beauticians worked on cutting and styling hair. A few barbers attended male customers. Parveen smiled brightly, calling to her associates. Soon she was braiding a young woman's long copper hair.

Within a few hours, Valek understood why Parveen kept her shop. The women treated her with respect and kindness, unlike the Queen, and Parveen thrived in the homey atmosphere. As soon as Parveen left to return to the castle, her warm smile disappeared.

An idea sparked. This woman may be the key to getting to the King. He just had to figure out the best way to use her. Valek considered romancing her, but there'd be no reason for her to take him to her appointments with the Queen. He could disguise himself as Parveen. Except he didn't have the hairstyling skills to convince the Queen. And while he could kill the Queen before having to fix her hair, he'd no idea how he'd reach the rest of the royals. No. He needed to be working inside the castle for a season at least.

After watching her and the shop for a few days, Valek formulated a plan. He ran his fingers through his hair. Good thing he hadn't cut it in seasons. The black strands fell past his shoulders. Valek bought a long skirt, blouse, female undergarments, socks and a heavy shawl from a used clothing store.

As he worked to hide weapons, money and the diamonds in the skirt's fabric, Valek smiled, remembering the teasing he'd gotten from the other students at Hedda's school when he learned how to sew from the seamstress. He ignored the taunts of "King Knitter" because, unlike them, he understood how useful having skill with a needle and thread would be. Hedda taught them how to apply makeup and create disguises, but didn't see the benefit in sewing.

With a small pack slung over his shoulder, Valek emerged from the inn where he'd been staying to live on the streets as Valma. After a week of scavenged food, sleeping in alleys and no bathing except to shave, he resembled a homeless teen girl.

MARIA V. SNYDER

Valek avoided the dangerous crowd, but befriended a fringer to help him with the next part of his plan.

"Wait, you want me to *pretend* to rob the lady?" Bug asked.

The skinny boy was around thirteen, but he was tall for his age. His light green eyes were the only spots of color on him. His clothing, skin and greasy hair had been coated by multiple layers of gray street grime.

"Yes. Do you have a weapon?" Valek asked, pitching his voice higher so he sounded feminine.

Bug flicked open a shank made from an old razor blade, wood and wires. "I don't know about this, Valma. What if the watchers show up?"

"They won't." Valek had already bribed a few town watchmen to avoid patrolling the area that night.

Bug scratched his neck. "So I jump the lady, demand money, and you come to the rescue, chasing me off?"

"Yes."

"What for?"

"It's better you don't know."

"Yeah? What's in it for me?"

"A couple silvers."

"How about I keep the lady's purse? Gotta be more than two silvers in there," Bug said.

"Do you want the town watch hunting for you?"

"No. All right, but I want four silvers."

"Three or else I'll ask Hoot."

Bug scoffed. "Hoot won't do it."

"He will for three silvers."

"Okay, but if I smell a watcher, I'm outta there."

By this time, Valek knew Parveen's routine by heart. She traveled the same streets to and from the castle unless she was running late. Tonight, the Queen kept her longer than normal, so instead of walking her typical route home, Parveen took a shortcut through a narrow street without lanterns. It saved her a few blocks and allowed Valek to put his plan into motion. Bug blended in with the dark factories facing the street.

When Parveen reached the halfway mark, Bug leaped from his hiding spot and pressed his blade to her neck. "Gimme all your money or I'll slit your throat!"

She stared at him in shock. Her mouth opened and closed, but no sound escaped. Parveen clutched her purse tight to her stomach.

A freezer, Valek thought as he slipped from his place and shouted, "Hey!"

Bug turned his head and cursed right before Valek slammed into him, knocking him down. The shank flew from his hand. Then Bug and Valek grappled for a bit before Bug scrambled to his feet and bolted.

During the entire encounter, Parveen stood blinking at them as if she couldn't quite comprehend what had just happened.

"Are you all right?" Valek asked in a falsetto. "There's no blood."

At the word *blood*, Parveen gasped and touched her neck. "Oh my...he wanted my money... I'd never..."

"He's gone now. You're safe."

"I am..." And then with more animation, "I am, thanks to you!"

Valek shrugged. "Are you going to report this to the town watch?"

"I... Did you get a good look at him?"

"A street rat like me."

"Oh." She peered at him as if seeing him for the first time. "I...don't think so. No harm done and I'm late for..." Parveen

MARIA V. SNYDER

drew in a breath as if to steady her nerves. She opened her purse. "Here, let me give you—"

"No, thanks. That's not why I helped you."

"Surely you could use some money for food?"

"Yeah, but it's…" He glanced at the ground. "You wouldn't understand."

"Try me."

Gotcha. He met her gaze. "I'd rather earn a living then beg for it."

"Then why don't you apply for a job?"

Valek gestured to his shabby and stained clothes—street living was hard on a skirt. "Most people won't let me into their place of business let alone hire me."

"Oh. Well, in that case, you can work for me."

He acted surprised. "Really?"

"Yes. As long as you don't mind cleaning up hair and washing towels?"

"I don't mind."

"All right, then. What's your name?"

"Valma."

"Valma, I'm Parveen. Let's go and I'll introduce you to my staff."

Parveen not only hired him, but let him stay in a small room above the beauty shop and gave him an advance payment so he could buy clean clothes. All in all, a lovely woman. He hoped he wouldn't have to kill her.

Valek worked hard in the beauty shop. Leery at first, the staff welcomed him once Parveen explained how he'd saved her life. He paid attention to the stylists and after two weeks they showed him a few basics. His finger dexterity proved to be useful for braiding hair and soon he learned how to weave the strands into intricate patterns. Then it was only a matter of time before he had his own clients.

"You're a natural," Parveen said one day as she admired his work.

Valek discovered that cutting and styling hair was similar to carving a stone. You started with a formless mass and then you shaped it into a thing of beauty.

After a season of working in the shop, Valek felt confident not only in his ability to blend in as a female, but in his ability to set the next phase of his plan in motion. Getting to this point had taken almost two seasons. He had only about ten weeks left until the Commander arrived.

One morning near the end of the warming season, Parveen arrived to open the shop. Sweat beaded her pale face and she moved as if she walked on the deck of a boat in storm-tossed seas. She pressed a hand to her mouth while her other groped for a chair.

Valek rushed to her side and helped her sit down. "You look awful."

"I feel awful." She hunched forward, resting her forehead in her hands.

"Let me take you home. You should sleep."

"I can't. The Queen—"

"Wouldn't want to get sick."

"She thinks she's immune. That illness only strikes commoners." Parveen pushed to her feet. "I'd better leave now. It'll take me…" She wobbled. "Longer."

"I'm coming with you," Valek said.

"But—"

"Do you want to be alone when you pass out in the street? If that's the case, leave your purse here."

"All right."

It took forever to get Parveen to the castle and up to Queen

MARIA V. SNYDER

Jewel's rooms. Before Parveen collapsed into a chair to catch her breath, Valek pricked her with a sleeping potion.

"Why are you here?" the Queen demanded. "What's wrong with her?"

This was the first time Valek had seen the Queen in person. Known for bewitching the King with her exquisiteness, her emerald eyes, long eyelashes, full lips, high cheekbones, curvy figure and flawless skin were legendary, yet he found no beauty within her. He curtsied and explained.

"Help her stand, then. I need my hair done."

But Parveen had passed out. He made a show of trying to wake her.

Impatient, Queen Jewel strode over and slapped her cheek. Hard. "Wake up, Parveen. I will not be late for my appointments." She reached back to deliver another blow.

Valek stepped close and the Queen's hand slammed into his back instead. It stung. The lady had an arm. He ignored the pain. "If I may, your majesty. I can style your hair for you."

"You?" Her cold gaze swept over him.

"I've been working with Parveen for seasons."

She glanced back at the unconscious woman and sighed. "All right, but if I look hideous I'm sending you to the gallows."

Nice lady. The idea of killing her no longer seemed so heartless.

The Queen settled into an overstuffed chair facing a mirror. Valek gathered her long thick auburn hair in his hands. It reached halfway down her back and flowed like silk. He studied her oval-shaped face and slightly pointed chin, deciding on a style that would enhance her features.

With quick, sure motions, he pinned her hair up, creating rows of curls that gathered into an intricate knot at the back of her head. Then he pulled a few tendrils down to drape over her shoulders. Without being asked, he sorted through her gowns and selected a pale green one trimmed with cream lace. Then he matched her makeup to the colors of the gown and sewed an extra piece of lace onto a barrette, clipping it into her hair. He fished a long pearl necklace from her overflowing jewelry box. It was so long that he looped it three times around her neck to create a cascading effect over her décolletage.

When finished, she surveyed herself in the ring of full-length mirrors for a long time. "Quiet, quick and efficient. What's your name?"

"Valma, your majesty."

"All right, Valma, you can fill in until Parveen is better."

"Thank you. I'll take her home and be right back."

"Back?"

"Just in case you need your makeup fixed or would like a new hairstyle for the afternoon."

"What about your clients?" she asked.

He gave her a puzzled expression. "No one is more important than you. I'll cancel all my appointments."

Her expression grew distant and he saw the wheels turning. Had he hooked her?

"Can you stay overnight, as well?" she asked.

Yes. "If it pleases your majesty."

"It does." She returned to gazing at herself in the mirror.

By the time Parveen felt better, Valek had usurped her. Parveen took the news well. Actually, she seemed relieved and was thrilled with the diamond thank-you gift for her years of service that was supposedly from the Queen. Happy that he didn't have to kill Parveen, Valek settled into his new position. The Queen assigned him a small two-room apartment between the guest wing and her suite.

Between grooming sessions with the Queen, he explored

every inch of the castle. He marked the location of every member of the royal family's sleeping quarters except the King's. Valek avoided encountering the King. He'd seen paintings of the man—tall, broad-shouldered, with graying black hair and rugged good looks, but Valek worried if he saw the King in person, he'd kill him right there.

No. Valek planned to strike in the middle of the night—an assassin's best friend. And the only time the King spent without his entourage of guards was when he visited the Queen's bedroom at night, which wasn't often or predictable. And with the rumblings of revolt in the air, his visits became more infrequent. At least when the King planned to visit her, she received word in the early evening and she'd call Valek to style her hair the way the King liked it.

When the warm season drew to a close, Valek took an evening off to go into Jewelstown. He changed before meeting the Commander. The fabric of his pants chafed against his thighs and calves. He'd been wearing a skirt so long, pants now seemed to restrict his movements—odd and amusing at the same time.

Valek looped around the Black Cat Tavern. A clash of voices and clangs of dishes and mugs poured from the open windows—normal tavern sounds. Too bad the four goons hiding in the shadows around the building were not standard. Assassins? No. They were too easy to spot. Valek waited until a group of people entered and he slipped inside with them.

A mix of patrons filled the bar and occupied the tables. Even without spotting the subtle differences in clothing, the body language marked the soldiers from the civilians. The Commander sat in the darkest corner of the room. Valek wondered how close he'd get before someone tried to stop him. Not many of the Commander's followers knew about Valek.

Sure enough, a wall of muscles inserted themselves between him and the Commander about two tables out.

Valek showed them his empty hands. "I'm just looking to sign up, boys."

"Let him through," Ambrose said.

They parted. He squeezed in between them and sat across from the Commander.

Valek hooked a thumb at the brutes. "Are they here in response to those four waiting for you outside?"

"Four? Hell, Lenny said there were two." He waved a man over and told him about the others. "Do another sweep right before we leave and make sure no more have joined their friends."

"Yes, sir." The man glanced at Valek before moving away.

"They're not the King's men or assassins. Mercenaries?" Valek asked.

Ambrose gave him a tired smile. "Close. They're bounty hunters. Once the King figured out he couldn't reach me with the professionals, he thought if he offered enough gold some untrained hack would get lucky. They're more annoying than dangerous." He swigged his ale. Dark smudges lined his eyes. "How's your pet project going?"

"I'm in."

He straightened. "How soon?"

"The next time the King is feeling amorous."

Ambrose laughed. "And how will we know that?"

Good question. "Do you have anyone else inside the castle?"

"Half the servants and more than half the soldiers."

Impressive. "I'll give a message to one of them to deliver to you. You'll have about five hours' notice. Will that be enough?"

"Plenty. Give the message to a housekeeper named Margg. Do you know her?"

"I've seen her around. Is she trustworthy?"

MARIA V. SNYDER

"Yes. She's from my town. I sent her to work undercover at the castle years ago."

"All right. Do you want me to take care of those annoying bounty hunters lying in wait for you?"

"No. They're potential recruits."

"And if they refuse to join the cause?"

"I haven't encountered that problem yet."

"You certainly present a convincing argument," Valek said. He rubbed his chest as he remembered their first encounter. "Does everyone get a *C* carved into their skin?"

"Only you."

That surprised him. "Why?"

"You're the only one who managed to get close."

"Even the other assassins?"

"Yes. I can sense them coming, while you were a complete surprise."

Funny, it didn't seem that way to Valek. Perhaps the Commander was a magician. "Sense them with your magic?"

Horror creased Ambrose's face. "No. Magicians are vile creatures and we will cleanse our society of them, starting with the King."

We, meaning Valek. He had no love for magicians, but to kill them all...seemed a waste of resources. "They could be an asset to your rule."

"No. They're not trustworthy."

This was the first time Valek hadn't agreed with the Commander. Not that it changed anything. He'd sworn his loyalty to the man.

Valek left the tavern and changed back into female clothing. He rubbed a hand along his jaw, testing for stubble. Sometimes he needed to shave twice a day. Returning to the castle, he checked in with the Queen in case she required anything. She didn't.

Three more nights passed without a visit from the King, but on the fourth night the Queen received a message. Anticipation curled in Valek's stomach. He handed a note to Margg to deliver to the Commander.

That night as he arranged the Queen's thick hair so it fell in waves over her shoulders, he handed her a drink.

"This is called My Love. It's supposed to…ah…greatly enhance the mood," he said. "The cook swears by it and she has six children."

The Queen blushed, but downed the drink pretty quick. Soon after, she complained of being dizzy and he helped her into bed. As Valek fluffed pillows, she died from the poison. A quick death—more than she deserved for being a nasty person.

He closed her eyes and turned the lantern down low. The biggest problem tonight would be the King's guards. Six of them would escort the King to Jewel's suite and they would then wait in her receiving room until morning. Her guards had the night off. Valek had to take the King's men out before the King realized Jewel was dead and raised the alarm.

Valek changed into his black sneak suit and scanned the receiving room, searching for a good place to hide. Dark corner? No. Behind the curtains? No. Under the couch? Not if he wanted to live. He glanced up. The ceiling had shallow wooden rafters. He climbed up the wall and wedged his body between the stone ceiling and the beams that crossed above the room. It wasn't ideal. If the soldiers spotted him, he'd be an easy target. He readied his blowpipe and darts as he waited for the King's entourage. Hesitation wasn't an option.

"…sir? Sir?" One of the Commander's security officers poked his head into Valek's office.

Valek waved him closer. "Yes?"

"The Commander has retired for the evening, sir."

MARIA V. SNYDER

Already? He glanced at the array of candles on his desk. They had burned down a few inches. Absorbed in his memories, Valek had lost track of the time. "Thank you, Lieutenant."

The man retreated. Valek finished writing the notes on the security weaknesses he'd seen earlier. He'd address the issues with the soldiers in the morning. Extinguishing the candles, Valek locked up and joined the Commander.

"Anything to report?" Ambrose asked, handing Valek a glass filled with a dark red liquid.

Valek sat in the soft armchair. He swirled the contents of the glass and sniffed. General Dinno's homemade cherry brandy. Swallowing a mouthful, he savored the sweet taste as it burned down his throat. Then he informed the Commander about the messages from Yelena and Irys, Janco's mission and Arbon's visit.

"I'd like to send a couple agents to keep an eye on Yelena," Valek said.

"Do you really think she needs the help or is sending them a way to make you feel better about the situation?" The Commander studied Valek over his brandy.

"I'll admit, after the first message I wanted to go myself. That was my knee-jerk reaction. But after learning about this new threat from Irys, I'm thinking she'll need added protection."

"From an *unidentified* threat. Could Sitia be trying to get you to do their dirty work for them?"

"I wouldn't put it past the Council, but I think the Master Magicians are sincere."

"We could invade, take over Sitia, and then your loyalties wouldn't be divided."

Valek paused, letting the Commander's comment sink in. Ambrose had put that bit in there about invading Sitia to throw Valek off.

"You believe my loyalties are divided between you and Sitia?" Valek asked.

"Perhaps not Sitia, but between me and Yelena. Am I right?"

Ah. Valek considered.

"Let me put it this way. If she was in mortal danger and I ordered you to stay here and write reports, what would you do?" Ambrose leaned forward. "No need to answer. Your expression gives you away. You'd bolt for the border."

The Commander was right. Valek would. When had his feelings changed? He'd been prepared to kill Yelena for the Commander eight years ago.

"I'm sorry."

"No need to be. You've served me faithfully for twenty-four years. And what I've learned in your absence is that I need someone here who is as committed as you once were."

"I've been trying to train Maren, Ari and Janco."

"Won't work. Maren isn't organized and the boys would rather be playing spy."

Valek had to agree. "You think Onora could do my job? She's pretty inexperienced."

"I hate to disappoint you, Valek, but I'm looking a few years, not a few days, into the future."

"You don't know much about her."

"And I knew nothing about you when I accepted your pledge in that alley twenty-four years ago."

True. "Why did you? You had no idea if my word meant anything."

"You had a hungry determination in your eyes. The same look Onora has now."

"I wanted the King's blood. Whose blood does she want?" Valek asked.

"Perhaps that captain in MD-2?"

MARIA V. SNYDER

"Perhaps." But Valek wasn't convinced. And if he was going to relinquish his job to her, he would make sure she had more to her than a hungry look in her eyes.

25

JANCO

The clatter of the wagon's wheels echoed off the tunnel's stone walls. Janco followed the glow of the torches while remaining far enough back to avoid being noticed. Not that the six guys would have the energy to look behind them. Each set of three men pulled a heavy wagon through the narrow cave that was too tight for horses.

They had been going downhill, but now the ground slanted up. He wondered if they noticed the extra weight in the second wagon. Onora had sneaked under the burlap. She'd ordered him to follow the cart heading into Ixia, but that was Ari and Gerik's territory. Besides, he didn't completely trust Little Miss Assassin yet.

Janco hoped the incline meant they neared the end. The air seemed thicker in here and harder to draw into his lungs. He'd inspected the walls of the tunnel as he traveled through. The natural cave formation had narrowed then ended. At that point, the smugglers had carved a hole and dug out a mix of dirt and rocks. Shovel marks scored the walls. Janco wondered how long it'd taken them and where all the dirt had gone.

He hunched a bit, half expecting the ceiling to collapse on top of him at any minute. The cool air smelled earthy and a dampness clung to him. Or was that sweat? Being down here was almost as bad as being in the Creepy Keepy.

Finally a fresh breeze fanned his face. The tightness around his chest eased. The tunnel emptied into a forest. It resembled the Snake Forest, which meant they hadn't gone too far into Sitia. And from the location of the entrance in Ixia, Janco guessed they were in the Moon Clan's lands.

A team of horses and four people waited in the forest outside the cave. Janco stayed in the darkness of the tunnel as the men transferred the wagons to the horses. Once they finished, everyone jumped on the wagons. Janco hoped no one discovered Onora. He wondered if she blended in and resembled one of the barrels like she had matched the colors of the rocks earlier.

When the wagons trundled out of sight, Janco followed. Pain pierced his skull as he exited the cave. When it dulled, he turned around. The cave's entrance was no longer visible. Another magical illusion hid it.

Keeping well back from the wagons, he wasn't too worried about losing them. The heavy wagons made deep impressions into the ground. Plus the moon cast enough light to illuminate the wheels' tracks, and dawn was still a few hours away. Janco yawned. Guess it'd be another night without sleep.

He increased his pace when he noticed a faint glow in the distance. There could be a city ahead, and it would be difficult to track the wagons over cobblestones. The smugglers headed toward a town and crossed a bridge. Only one street had been lined with lanterns, which meant calling the place a town was being generous.

The rush and gurgle of water sounded loud in the quiet night. A cold mist hovered over the banks of the river. The temperature dropped as he ghosted over the bridge, keeping low to avoid being seen. The smugglers entered a warehouse on the edge of town.

After the wagons disappeared into the darkness, a big metal door rolled silently down. Someone kept that door well oiled. Considering the moisture in the air, that sucker would have squealed without proper care. The air also held a familiar scent, but Janco couldn't put a name to it.

Janco scanned the streets, but no one was in sight. He cased the building—two stories, flat roof, brick construction and easy-to-break-in windows—his favorite type. Debating if he should sneak in or wait for Onora, he decided to wait—for now. Janco found a perfect spot to watch for signs of activity like lantern light in the windows, which would mean they planned to stay awhile. Noises would also tip him off. Even if she knew he was here, Janco doubted Onora would be the type to yell or scream for help. His spot also gave him a view of all the exit points. Bonus!

When no one left after an hour, Janco figured the windows might be blacked out. And they could have soundproofed the building. It depended on how smart they were. Considering the magical illusion and tunnel, Janco guessed they had a certain level of sophistication. Adding that to the fact that once the sun rose, he'd be stuck until nightfall, he left his hiding spot and climbed to a second-floor window.

Thick curtains had been drawn across it. He eased open the lower pane, listening for…well, anything. Nothing. So far. Counting to ten, he widened the gap and waited. It remained quiet. Janco parted the curtain, peeking inside. Blackness. He pushed the fabric aside, letting in the faint street light to reveal the contents of the room.

Janco relaxed. Crates had been piled in a haphazard fashion, suggesting this was a storage room. He clambered onto a pile, careful to transfer his weight slowly so the wood wouldn't creak. Then he tied the curtain back. He planned to leave before dawn and he'd need the light to find the exit—especially if he was in a hurry.

MARIA V. SNYDER

After navigating over the crates and boxes, he reached the door. The knob turned without trouble. A brief thought—this seemed too easy—flashed, but he ignored it as he opened the door. Peeking out, Janco confirmed that the dark hallway was unoccupied. No light shone under any of the doors, so he kept moving. It didn't take him long to find a stairwell on the far end of the building. Darkness swallowed the bottom of the stairs.

Janco trailed his hand along the railing and descended. When he reached the last step, he groped for the door and encountered a number of spiderwebs—yuck—before finding a handle. He sucked in a breath and pushed it open.

More blackness greeted him, but a slight lightening of his surroundings crept in as his eyes adjusted. That familiar scent overpowered his senses and he stifled a cough. He covered his nose with his sleeve.

Large dark shapes of machinery filled the area around him. They appeared to be big vats of liquid with pipes snaking between them along with mixing tools. Distant light called like a beacon. He avoided the equipment as he crossed the factory, aiming for an oversize entrance. Beyond that, light flickered.

He peered into the other room—a storage area. A bunch of people grouped around a stack of barrels, drinking, talking and laughing. The two wagons and four sweating horses stood nearby. Janco half expected Onora to sneak up to him and demand why he was there, but she didn't.

Moving a little closer, Janco squinted at the words burned into the barrels. Ixian white brandy. Ah, the Commander's special brew, which was illegal to sell to Sitia. That solved that puzzle.

Janco then scanned faces, counting the six muscular men who'd towed the wagons through the tunnel and the four who'd met them on the Sitian side.

And one extra. Maren.

26

YELENA

I slipped through the building next door to Opal's glass factory, exiting into an alley. Letting my eyes adjust to the darkness, I paused. The acrid odor of rotting garbage filled the air. Distant sounds from the street reached me, but the narrow alley remained quiet.

Still wearing Reema's cloak and the blond wig, I walked to the south end and turned right. Then I pressed next to the building, waiting. If anyone had been hidden in the alley, he would have to hustle to catch up and I'd spot him.

No one emerged. After a few more minutes, I continued down the street. Valek had taught me that trick and a few others. Without my powers, I'd need to rely on them and the null-shield pendant. Since Reema had my cloak, only the octopus remained to protect me from magic.

I kept to the shadows and let my fear guide me. When I turned west, my heart rate increased. Keeping to side streets, I traveled toward the heart of my terror. I reached a tight alley and every fiber of my being pressed on me to turn around and bolt. Death waited for me down this path. This alley must lead to Ben's hiding place. Before entering, I opened my cloak and draped the fabric over my shoulders to free my arms. I palmed a couple of Curare darts in my left hand and my switchblade in my right with my thumb near the button. My hands shook as my heart skittered.

Summoning my courage, I strode down the alley to a door that pulsed with malevolence. I waited for Ben's magic to alert them. But when nothing happened, I returned my weapons to their hidden locations and grabbed my diamond pick and tension wrench.

I knelt next to the door and worked on popping the lock. Good thing light wasn't a requirement for picking a lock. As I lifted each pin, a distinctive click sounded along with a slight vibration through the metal pick. When all the pins were aligned, the tumbler turned, unlocking the door. It swung inward with a creak. I froze as fear burned in my guts.

No other sounds pierced the darkness. Returning my picks, I pulled my switchblade, stood and entered the building. If Ben and his gang had moved on, perhaps they'd left a clue as to where they were headed.

A faint memory of lanterns sitting on a table near the door stirred and drew me deeper inside. I held a hand out, but it failed to warn me as my legs crashed into...something. Sweeping my hand lower, I found a lantern, but before I could dig in my pack for my flint, the scrape of metal sliding along metal rang.

A beam of light from a bull's-eye lantern speared the blackness, blinding me.

Voices shouted. I'd walked right into an ambush. Stupid.

I moved into a defensive stance, but a dark shape tackled me. We hit the ground hard. I landed on my stomach. The impact robbed me of breath. More shouts sounded and someone kicked my switchblade from my hand. Light reflected off the knife as the weapon spun away. Funny, I didn't remember triggering the blade.

I struggled to knock off the person on top of me, but a knee jammed into the small of my back as my arms were wrenched behind. Metal cuffs bit into my wrists. Two sets of hands grabbed me under the arms and yanked me to my feet. The motion knocked my wig to the ground, inciting a gasp, a groan and a couple of curses.

"Yelena, what are you doing here?" Leif demanded.

"Uh…looking for Ben. Did you find him?"

Another lantern glowed to life. I blinked. Hale held up the light. He stood next to Opal. Both frowned. In fact, no one looked happy. Tired, dirty and angry, but not happy.

"Did I ruin your ambush?" I asked.

"Yes," Leif said.

"No," Opal said.

I waited, sensing I trod on very thin ice.

"We're not telling you anything until you explain what the hell you're doing here," Leif said. "And why you ran away."

I'd hoped to avoid all this right now, but they deserved answers. I explained about my memory laspe, my fear, my trip to the plains and my return. "Don't worry," I said to Opal. "Reema's with Kiki and they're on the way to safety as we speak."

"Where?" she asked.

I glanced at the others. "Devlen is waiting for you at the factory. He'll tell you before he leaves to catch up with her."

"All right." Opal turned to Leif. "I'll meet you at HQ."

He nodded and she moved to leave, but paused next to me. "Thanks for protecting her, Yelena."

"Don't thank me. I'm the reason she's in danger."

"This time." Opal gave me a tired smile. "Next time it'll be me or Devlen or her brother."

"Then why not stay far away from those situations?"

"Because we can help and it wouldn't be right not to." She squeezed my shoulder and left.

"Be careful," I called after her, unable to stifle that little voice that threatened all my loved ones.

Hale stared at me with a sullen expression.

"Uh…can you unlock these manacles now?" I asked.

Leif tightened his grip on my arms as if he expected me to make a break for it. A bad sign.

Leif shook his head. "You planned to find Ben by yourself. Don't you think that's really…?"

"Dangerous," Hale supplied.

"And incredibly stupid."

"I wasn't going to attack. I just wanted to locate him for the authorities. I want my memories back," I said. "Besides, Midnight Son—"

"I don't think citing a dead Story Weaver will help you," Leif said.

"Okay, Leif. I get it. I'm sorry for running off, but at the time, I thought I was saving your life and protecting Reema. He might be a dead Story Weaver, but he helped me figure it out and I came back. Doesn't that count?"

"How about a promise to remain uninvolved?" Leif asked.

My stomach squeezed just thinking about it. "I can't. It's just like Opal said. It's—"

"All right, then. Protective custody it is," Leif said.

"What? You can't!"

"I can. I've orders from Second Magician Irys Jewelrose to place you in protective custody if you're too stubborn to see reason—her words, not mine." Leif pulled me from the building. Hale followed with the lantern.

"You can't be serious!" I protested.

Leif lowered his voice. "Irys discovered another plot to harm you, Yelena. The attack in the forest might be connected or this could be a new threat. Either way, she says word is out about you and you're too vulnerable."

"I'll be careful and—"

"Like chasing after Ben on your own?"

I opened my mouth to reply that I'd acted on pure instinct, but that wouldn't go well in my defense. Leif towed me to Fulgor's security headquarters. Nothing I said changed his mind. Citing orders from the Second Magician, Leif explained to the officers on duty that I was under protective custody until the danger had passed. Only orders from him or the Master Magicians should be obeyed.

After transferring me to the soldiers in charge of the jail cells, Leif and Hale left without saying a word. The guards confiscated my cloak, pack and weapons before locking me in a cell with a blanket.

The evening had not gone as expected. Not at all. I prowled around the small cell. Frustration, anger, exasperation, amusement and disbelief churned in my chest. It was one thing for them to be upset with me. But protective custody? This had to be a joke. Or temporary. They'd made their point. Lesson learned. They were bound to be back soon to release me and we'd discuss plans. Right? Right.

Minutes turned into hours and my certainty slowly diminished. I inspected the locking mechanism on the cell's door—all my clothes had lock picks sewn into the hems. But the complex bolt couldn't be opened with standard tools. Only the front side of the cell had bars. The rest of the walls were made of stone. Actually, it appeared as if the builders had dug rough square cubes into the bedrock underneath the headquarters. Dim light shone from the two lanterns hanging on the wall opposite the cells. And from the utter quiet, I guessed I was the only occupant. Lovely.

MARIA V. SNYDER

Hours turned into a day. I pestered the guards with questions when they brought me food, but they refused to answer. Nor did they agree to deliver a message to Irys for me. I pouted. However, with no one there to see me pout, I felt silly. Perhaps I'd get more attention with a hunger strike.

I considered my options for an escape. Inventorying the contents of my hidden pockets, I had two sets of picks and three darts filled with... I wasn't sure. I sniffed the liquid contents. Curare in two of them and goo-goo juice in the other. Too bad. I'd rather use sleeping potion on the guards. Curare seemed harsh for a couple of guys just doing their job. Of course, I needed to get close enough. My aim without a blowpipe was horrible.

During the next few meals, I watched the guards. Only one approached the bars. He slid the full tray through the slot near the floor, while his partner—the one with the keys—stood well away from the cell. Shoot. I'd have to get the second guy to either open the door or stand right by the bars.

One day turned into two as I searched my memory for a way to trick the guards. All my ideas—fake an illness, fake death, fake a swoon—were all unoriginal and I doubted anyone would fall for them.

Huddled under the blanket on the hard metal slab they called a bed for the third night of my incarceration, I stared at the ceiling, plotting revenge on my brother. Just the thought of wrapping my fingers around his thick neck helped ease my frustration and anger. Other more creative tortures came to mind and I almost smiled until the clang of a metal door signaled the first of many nightly bed checks.

Only one guard entered the jail tonight. He peeked in through the bars, confirmed I remained locked inside and retreated. Just then, an idea sparked for a way to escape. I mulled it over. With just one guard, I had a better chance of escaping. A few problems like how I would get past the soldiers in the processing area and the people working the night shift in headquarters might make it difficult. Aside from that, my plan just might work. After all, I had to do something, and getting caught would just land me right back here. Maybe my escape attempt would bring Leif so I could strangle him in person. One could hope.

I decided to wait until the third bed check to spring my surprise, but a ruckus woke me from a light doze. Standing close to the bars, I watched two unfamiliar guards struggle with a prisoner. As he resisted, he shouted slurred curses. The reek of bourbon reached me, and a couple of bleeding cuts marked his face. All the evidence pointed to a bar fight.

They tossed him into a cell and locked it. He rattled the bars, yelling about injustice and how the other guy started it.

"You're wasting your breath," I said. "They don't care."

"Huh? Who's there?"

I hesitated. He might recognize my name, so I used my middle name. "Liana. I'm in the cell next to yours."

"Oh. Whadda ya in for?"

"Nothing. I was framed."

He laughed. "Me, too. Name's Kynan. Anyone else in this rat hole?"

"I don't think so."

He huffed. "No wonder they busted me. It's a slow night. Just my luck." Then he launched into a drunken rambling explanation of his terrible luck.

Eventually, he ran out of story, and from the thump, I guessed he found the metal bed. Soon light snores filled the silence. I returned to my bed and lay down, debating if I should attempt an escape tonight or wait until tomorrow, when Kynan would most likely be gone.

The snap of a lock signaled a bed check. The guard's foot-

MARIA V. SNYDER

steps paused and he snorted and muttered, "Passed out already." Then he peered in at me before leaving.

I decided to put my plan into action during the next check. First, I flapped the blanket a couple of times, hard, sending a gush of air to blow out one of the lanterns. The shadows in the cell deepened. Then I smoothed the blanket over the bed, letting the edge hang to the floor. From the doorway, it would appear as if I hid underneath.

Second, I needed to test a theory. I kicked off my boots, stashed them under the bed and climbed the bars to the ceiling. The uneven surface had a number of finger- and toeholds. Except I didn't have the arm strength to cling to the ceiling. How did Valek do it? Perhaps if I held on to the bars and tucked my legs up, curling into a small ball. It worked, but it'd be better with my boots on. The rubber soles would grip the metal bars. I slid back to the floor, laced up my boots and waited.

After an hour or so, a metallic clicking sounded. It felt too soon for a check. Regardless, I climbed the bars as the noise continued. Once in position, I peered down the hall. Kynan's cell door creaked open. What was he doing? Was he escaping? He approached my cell and stared at the blanket for a moment. Kneeling, he inserted a strange hooked tool and, after a series of ticks, the lock released.

My heart pulsed a warning and I stayed in place despite my burning arm muscles. Kynan exchanged the tool for a long metal shaft—not quite a blade but an...ice pick? Now would be an ideal time for the guard to return. Should I scream for help? So much for *protective* custody.

Kynan crept toward my bed. He probably believed I slept below. My arms shook. I wouldn't last much longer. Sliding down without making a sound, I palmed a dart.

"Wake up, Yelena," Kynan said. "I've a message for you."

I didn't wait for the message. Charging him, I jabbed the

dart into his neck. He spun and lunged, aiming his weapon at my throat. I backpedaled. The goo-goo juice worked fast and he stumbled forward.

Kynan giggled. "Surprise!" His second lunge went wide.

I stepped in close, trapping his arm. Wrapping my hands around his wrist, I controlled his weapon as I hooked my heel behind his ankle and tripped him. He fell back and I landed on his chest. The pick clattered to the floor, but he made no move to reclaim it.

"Ah, darlin', you just had to ask. I always grant last requests for a quick tumble."

"You have a high opinion of yourself, don't you?" I sat on his stomach and checked him for more weapons.

He grinned. "The ladies love me."

"And your clients?"

"Happy. Happy. The Mosquito never fails."

"Except this time."

Kynan rubbed my arms. "The night is still young, darlin'."

I knocked his hands away. "And you missed me the last time."

"I never miss!"

"Is this your first attempt on my life?"

"Yup. Won't be the last neither."

So this was a separate attack from the one in the woods. Lovely. A number of questions bubbled, but I concentrated on the most important ones first.

"Who hired you?" I asked.

"Can't tell. Big no-no."

The question was too direct. I tried another tactic. "What was the message?"

He perked up. "How's it feel to be at someone else's mercy?"

Gesturing to my position on top of him, I said, "I'm not at your mercy."

Kynan waved a hand. "Details. You're like the rest of us now—slaves to the magicians."

While it was a harsh view of Sitian society, I suspected he knew my secret. "Who told you this?"

"Client. He says you're regular. Unremarkable. An easy mark. No—"

"I get it." Just how far had the news about me spread? If it was common knowledge… Fear tingled along my skin. I drew in a breath. Kynan's client must have learned it a while ago in order to send the assassin. He had to be close to the Sitian Council. "Did the Councilman learn about me from the Council?" I guessed.

"Yep. He gets a pile of gold for nuggets."

I considered. "The Councilman isn't your client."

"Nope."

But his client was bribing a Councilman. I took another guess. "Your client is a wealthy man who is very unhappy with the Sitian Council for not taking control of the magicians. After all, the magicians should work for us and not be setting the rules."

Kynan's mouth gaped open. "How did you know?"

"I had dinner with him last season." I tsked. "He never gave me any indication he'd use such drastic measures to change things."

"Yeah, that's Bruns. He keeps his emotions in check."

Bingo. And now for the clan name. "Which is a good thing. That's how he made all his money."

"Yeah, can't go blabbing about your radical views when you're a respected businessman."

"And he has lots of clients. They all love his…"

"Designs! Man is a wizard with a gemstone."

Aha. Bruns Jewelrose. I didn't recognize the name, but I planned to make his acquaintance. Kynan stared at me in suspicion. The goo-goo juice must be wearing off and I doubted my hand-to-hand fighting techniques would be effective against a trained assassin. I pulled another dart and pricked him with Curare.

While under the influence of the drug, he could breathe and hear, but not move or speak. I emptied his pockets and picked up his weapon. It was shaped like an ice pick, but the metal shaft was hollow. He'd been aiming at my throat. If he'd pierced my jugular, would the shaft speed up the rate my blood would have gushed out? I'd have to ask Valek. I grabbed the device that opened the cell door.

Then I yanked my blanket off the bed and wrestled him up onto the metal so he lay on his side, facing the back wall. I drew up his legs so he looked shorter and closed his eyes before covering him with the blanket.

"Thanks for helping me escape," I said.

Leaving my cell, I pulled the door shut. It locked with a click. Good. I entered Kynan's cell and arranged his blanket like I'd done to mine earlier—smooth on top and hanging over the edge. I left, closing the door. Then I switched the lanterns, so the lit one was farther from the door into the jail.

I stood in a shadow right next to the jail's entrance and waited. The fluttering in my stomach distracted me from my loud heartbeat. To pass the time, I thought about Bruns Jewelrose. I didn't remember crossing paths with him. It sounded like Bruns paid Councilor Jewelrose for information, and Bruns wasn't a magician. Many rich and powerful men in Sitia believed they should control the use of magic like they controlled other resources.

The clang and snap of metal broke through my thoughts. I sucked in a breath. If two guards entered, success was unlikely. One man stepped down, heading to Kynan's cell. He left the door open.

Slipping out, I didn't wait for the inevitable cry of alarm.

MARIA V. SNYDER

No one else was in the processing area, which explained why a single guard performed the bed checks. Instead of crossing through the bull pen to the exit, I headed down a hallway and toward the captain's office. I'd wait for him to arrive and I'd plead my case or I'd threaten to send his soul to the fire world, depending on his response.

His office door was locked. I yanked my lock picks from my pocket and set to work, popping the complex mechanism just as the guard raised the alarm. Dashing inside, I closed and relocked the door. Once my eyes adjusted to the darkness, I spotted a window. Except for the bars, it would have been a perfect escape route. I settled into the captain's chair and, once again, waited.

Muted shouts and pounding boots sounded through the door. A few times, someone tested the knob, ensuring it remained locked. Not much I could do if they checked the captain's office. After an hour, exhaustion caught up to me and I crossed my arms, resting them on the desk, then laid my head down.

An angry male voice boomed, waking me. I straightened. Weak sunlight flooded the room, and streaks of color painted the sky. Keys jangled, metal scraped on metal and the door swung open.

Captain Alden stepped into his office and jerked to a stop. "Yelena! I—"

I put my finger to my lips. "Close the door, please."

He complied, then turned to me. "I'm very sorry about the assassin. It appears we were overconfident in our ability to keep you safe."

"He's a professional. And as you can see, I'm quite capable of handling myself."

"Yes, I know. But I have orders from the Second Magician."

"What happens when the next assassin doesn't fail? How would you explain my death to Second Magician?"

Alden sighed. "This is a no-win situation."

I stood and offered him the seat. "Then tell the Master Magician I escaped. You know I'm safer on my own."

Alden wilted. He removed his cape and hung it on the rack before sitting down. "Can you answer a few questions first?"

"As long as you're willing to reciprocate."

"All right. What happened last night?"

I filled him in on everything except the part where I climbed the bars. No need to give away all my tricks. Besides, there was always a chance I might need it again.

"Do you know who hired him?"

"No, but he called himself The Mosquito." I lied for a good reason. No sense alerting Bruns that I was onto him. Kynan shouldn't remember too much from when he was under the influence of the goo-goo juice.

"How long until he wakes?"

"Curare lasts about a day."

"Okay. Your turn."

"I need an update on the investigation into Ben Moon's whereabouts."

"There's not much to tell. We scoured Fulgor, searching every factory, warehouse, empty building, and found nothing. They suspected you purposely misled them into believing he was in Fulgor."

Which explained some of the hostility from Devlen and the others. "Yet they'd found his hideout."

"Opal walked through every single alley, seeking magic. She discovered an illusion that hid a door. The place appeared to be occupied, so they set an ambush and that's where you came in."

Lucky me. "Did anyone go to Red Oak?"

MARIA V. SNYDER

"No. They concentrated their efforts here. None of Ben's men have returned to the warehouse since our people have found it, but evidence at the scene suggests Ben and his gang are headed west toward Owl's Hill. The task force left for Owl's Hill yesterday."

Too easy. Ben would never leave real clues. He was probably sending them on a wild-Valmur chase. My gut instinct said Ben was in Red Oak or in a town nearby. No logical reason for it, but I'd learned to trust my instincts.

"Task force?"

"A fancy name for Leif, Hale and Opal."

So they planned to keep me in protective custody until they returned. Anger burned, but I kept my voice even. "Can you return my effects and escort me from the building?"

"I can't convince you to stay?" He had a hopeful tone.

"No."

All activity ceased when Alden and I stepped into the bull pen. He glared at his men and ordered them to fetch my cloak and pack. One guard rushed to comply, and in a matter of minutes, I was free.

First stop, a decent meal. I walked to the Second Chance Inn and feasted on sweet cakes. Then I inquired about renting a horse. Red Oak was too far to travel by foot.

"There's a stable a few miles north of here called the Clever Fox," the waitress said. "They lease horses, but they require a pretty hefty deposit."

That wouldn't be a problem. No, the biggest problem I foresaw was what I would do if I found Ben in Red Oak. And I couldn't shake the feeling that Ben and his friends were the least of my worries, but when I focused on it, the memory faded. At least I had a couple of days to think about it. I thanked the waitress and left a big tip.

Before visiting the stable, I shopped for supplies. I'd need the standard travel fare—beef jerky, bread, cheese and tea. Not the most appetizing. I laughed. Leif had rubbed off on me. Traveling with him certainly had its perks. Too bad I still wanted to strangle him.

Once I left Fulgor, no one would know my whereabouts. While desirable for avoiding assassins, Ben's spies and annoying brothers, I thought it best to send a message to Valek just in case I ran into trouble.

The Clever Fox stables offered a number of horses for loan. The tidy barns, neat tack room and the clean earthy smell all pointed to a well-run, well-cared-for place of business. The owner, a man named Ellard, peered at me as if I was crazy when I inquired about Sandseed horses.

"I wish, missy," Ellard said. "Sandseeds won't tolerate multiple riders, but I had one as a boarder here a couple years ago. Ah...she was a thing of beauty she was." His brown-eyed gaze grew distant. "But I might have a good match for you. She's a bit older, but smart like those Sandseeds. Come on."

He led me to a stall in the back of the barn. A gray dappled mare poked her head over the door. Curiosity and intelligence shone in her light gray eyes.

"This here's The Madam. She's strong and steady, unflappable in most cases."

"And what upsets her?"

"Picket fences. Not sure why, but I suspect that scar on her chest might be the reason. It's just a guess, mind you. But if you keep her away from them, you'll be fine."

Good to know. "How much?"

We haggled over a price that included a saddle and tack. When we settled on a price, he saddled The Madam. Then I transferred my supplies, filling the saddlebags with my pur-

MARIA V. SNYDER

chases. The Madam watched me instead of grazing on the grass under her hooves.

I thanked Ellard and mounted. "Let's go," I said to The Madam.

She didn't move.

"Are you sure you have riding experience?" Ellard asked.

"Yes." Just not with a regular horse. I thought back to my riding lessons six years ago.

I tapped my heels against The Madam's flanks and clicked my tongue. She lurched forward into a walk. Ellard waved goodbye as we exited his stables. Once we reached the north-eastern road, I spurred her into a trot.

As we passed farm fields, tiny villages and forests, I altered The Madam's gait between trotting, cantering and walking so I wouldn't exhaust her. At least, that was my intention. Kiki always picked her pace and stopped when she was tired.

A few hours after sunset, I searched for a safe place to rest for the night. This route was too remote for travel shelters, and none of the towns had inns. I needed to find a camping site hidden from view.

An hour later, I discovered a small clearing behind a rock pile, which would block us from other travelers. Since we hadn't encountered anyone so far, I risked lighting a minia-ture fire to heat water for my tea.

While waiting for the water to boil, I removed The Mad-am's saddle, fed her and groomed her. She stretched her neck and leaned into the currycomb, encouraging me to rub harder. Then she moved around, presenting me with various body parts to comb. The behavior seemed odd to me, but when I thought about it, it made sense. After all, she knew the itchy places on her hide and I didn't.

I returned to the fire and ate a bland supper of jerky and cheese. At least my cinnamon tea tasted spicy. Memories of past campfires swirled—Ari and Janco arguing over the definition of the word *suspect*, Leif cooking up one of his delicious road stews, Valek's gaze meeting mine over the flames as a warmth spread through my body that had nothing to do with the campfire and everything to do with Valek.

Ah, the good old days. As long as I ignored the reasons that sent us on the road and all those miserable nights freezing or being drenched by the pouring rain or experiencing both. Selective recall suited me better—especially when I sat by myself, feeling lonely and skittish.

Plus the alternative, contemplating Ben's reasons for being near the Ixian border, was unpalatable. Except I should develop a plan of action. He might not be in the area now, but he had to have a purpose for going there. Other than leading the posse away from Fulgor.

I decided to snoop around, following the Sunworth river east. If I found him then I'd... What? Deliver a message to Fulgor, reporting Ben's whereabouts.

Report him to whom? Part of me was tempted to send a message to Valek. If he'd had his way three years ago, Ben would be dead and all these problems wouldn't be. Of course, there'd be a whole new set of problems. It never ended. Perhaps I should just travel to Ixia and let Alden and the others deal with Ben and this mystery threat. It was tempting. Very tempting.

But Opal's comment, "Because we can help and it wouldn't be right not to," replayed in my mind. And while I might have lost my magic, I hadn't lost the past eight years of experience in outsmarting the criminal element. At least I could determine Ben's location and possible schemes and then send the information to Captain Alden.

Now that I had a plan of action, I doused the fire and tried to sleep. *Tried* being the key word. Every noise jerked me awake despite The Madam snoozing unperturbed nearby.

There was a downside to unflappable. I worried she wouldn't alert me to danger.

Giving up a few hours after midnight, I packed up the camp and woke The Madam. We'd take our time so we'd reach Red Oak after dark.

It didn't take long to determine the two main sources of income for Red Oak. Between the floating logs and barges, it was easy to guess. The place had a sawmill that misted the air with the fragrance of freshly cut wood and clouds of sawdust. Stacks of lumber filled the wagons trundling south to make deliveries.

Barges loaded with coal bobbed dockside. Men shoveled the black rocks into wagons, emptying the metal boats and paying the tender. Then the barge was tied to a team of horses and pulled back upstream to the foothills of the Emerald Mountains to be reloaded.

By the amount of inns and taverns, I guessed the town benefited just as much from the influx of tenders and merchants as it did from the goods.

I kept to the shadows until I felt safe. A new face probably wouldn't attract attention, but a female one might. The majority of the laborers were men. No surprise, considering the backbreaking labor and strength needed to muscle the logs and shovel the coal.

After searching the entire town, I found no signs or clues that Ben had been here. None of the waitresses in the local taverns remembered serving them. Disappointed, I continued upstream, scouting two or three small towns each night, depending on the size.

Once I determined Ben and his gang weren't in town, I moved on. I had no real strategy for figuring this out. It was a gut instinct based on odd or furtive behavior or unusual interest in my presence. I doubted Ben's men would be working in a mill. After the place settled for the night, I'd visit the tavern for a meal and listen to the town's gossip. Strangers setting up shop or buying abandoned buildings always caused the locals much concern, which they discussed at length.

When it grew too late, I rented a room and pumped the innkeeper for any news. Then I'd be on the road before dawn.

After three nights of finding and learning nothing besides the general grumbling over the price drop of black coal, I approached Lapeer without any expectations. The place matched all the other river towns. But once I neared, a familiar scent jolted me as if I'd been struck by lightning.

Curare.

27

VALEK

"We traced the smugglers to the foothills of the Soul Mountains," Ari said, plopping into the chair in front of Valek's desk. The wood creaked in protest.

"And?" Valek asked.

"We lost them," Gerik said. He stood behind Ari, his posture rigid as if expecting a blow for reporting bad news.

It had been eleven days since Ari and Janco had left for their respective missions.

"Lost them how?" he asked.

"They either vanished over the mountain or under the mountain," Ari said. "The trail signs just stopped, and we suspect magic is the reason for the disappearance, but we can't be certain." Ari shook his head. "I can't believe I'm saying this, but…we need Janco. He's the only one besides you who could see through the illusion."

Valek considered. "It makes sense for them to use the tunnels to enter Ixia and for them to conceal the entrance with magic." Technically, no one in Ixia could sense it except Valek.

"Did Janco report in?" Ari asked.

"Not yet."

"Should we be worried?" Gerik asked.

Valek exchanged a glance with Ari.

Ari shrugged. "Depends. If he's found nothing, he won't bother to send a message, and if he's hot, then he won't have time. I think it's too soon to worry." He turned to address Gerik. "Besides, your girl is quite capable of handling herself."

"She's not mine," Gerik said in a gruff tone.

"So you say." Ari smirked as he leaned back in the chair.

Interesting. "Anything else to report?"

"We did uncover where they're distributing all the black-market goods," Ari said. "There's a warehouse in the factory district of MD-5, a few miles south of the General's manor house."

"Do you think General Ute is involved?"

"Not sure. We didn't do a full investigation, just watched long enough to confirm the transfer of illegal goods."

He mulled over the information. Getting inside the warehouse wasn't as critical as finding the smuggling route into Ixia. Neither Ari nor Gerik had the skills or the size to stow away in one of the wagons heading to the Soul Mountains, and all his best people had been assigned to other missions. Plus if there was magic involved, only he would be able to detect it. Valek would have to go.

After Ari and Gerik left, Valek contemplated the best way to present this new information to the Commander. He outlined a plan, then worked on reports. When the sun set, he lit the lanterns and candles scattered around. He liked plenty of light.

Just as he returned to his desk, the window behind him creaked. In an instant, he was on his feet with his knives in hand. Valek turned. Arbon climbed through the window.

"That's a quick way to get yourself killed," Valek said.

"How else was I supposed to get in here? You've tightened security." Arbon jumped down, landing lightly.

"Apparently not tight enough. You could have sent me a message."

"Where's the fun in that? Besides, I gotta keep my skills sharp." Arbon grinned and made himself comfortable.

Valek remained standing. "How did you get in?"

"Come on, King Killer. You know better than that. How about a pat on the back? It wasn't easy, ya know."

Valek admitted he was impressed. And Arbon had done him a favor by testing his security. Obviously more measures needed to be implemented.

"Do you have the name of the person who put the hit on Yelena?" Valek asked.

"You know how tight-lipped assassins are about their clients, and—"

"Yes or no, Arbon. It's not a difficult question."

"All he would tell me is the client is wealthy and has ties to Councilor Jewelrose."

Valek considered. That narrowed it down to one clan. "Do you know why this person hired the assassin?"

"No. But I will tell you the assassin is called The Mosquito because he keeps a vial of the victim's blood as a souvenir. He also won't quit until he finishes the job. Even if it takes years."

Not good. "Do you know his real name?"

"No. And I don't want to. I plan on retiring soon."

"Anything else?"

"The Mosquito wasn't hired until after that attack on your girl."

Valek sat down. "There's another assassin."

"It's possible, but no one contacted any of the Sitian assassins for hire. Either there's a brand-new player, or it's someone from Ixia."

Or both. Valek thought about Onora. She had the skills

and the intelligence to wear boots sized for a man to throw him off. But why would she?

"Last thing," Arbon said. "The Mosquito mentioned that the only reason he took the job was because his client assured him she is vulnerable." He shook his head. "No. He didn't elaborate."

Valek's stomach pinched with worry. If the rumors about Yelena being weak spread, she'd have more than two assassins after her. "Thanks, Arbon."

"Are we square?"

"Yep."

Arbon left the same way he'd arrived. Valek brooded in his chair, mulling over everything Arbon had said. Onora's arrival the very night he returned from Sitia had seemed rather convenient. Was the attack on Yelena a test to see if Valek would remain with Yelena instead of returning to Ixia? Something had happened to the Commander while Valek was gone. Perhaps Onora had sneaked into his suite prior to Valek's return and surprised him.

Guessing would get Valek nowhere. He needed to find the right time and place to talk to the Commander—maybe after they'd stopped the smugglers. And while Valek's heart urged him to abandon his duties in Ixia and race to protect Yelena, his mind reminded him she was traveling with Leif and another magician, and that many others had underestimated her in the past and all had regretted it.

Valek decided that he'd discover the smugglers' new route and then make a detour to find Yelena.

"You just returned," the Commander said. He swirled pear brandy around his glass, staring at the pale yellow liquid.

"There's evidence that magic is involved with the smuggling operation and only I can sense it," Valek said.

"All right. Go and shut them down. If you find a tunnel, collapse it. If you find a hole in our border defense, plug it. If you find a warehouse full of illegal goods, burn it down. If you encounter anyone who doesn't have permission to be in Ixia, arrest them. If you discover a magician within our borders, kill him."

Oh boy. Valek drank a mouthful of brandy to give him time to absorb the Commander's intent. "You wish to send a message to the smugglers." A *big* message.

"Yes."

"Pull the weed and all its roots so it doesn't grow back?"

The Commander smiled. "Exactly. Take as many soldiers as you need."

"All right, but I'll leave Ari in charge of security."

"Are you worried I'll be targeted again?"

"No. I'm concerned our security forces will revert back to their old ways while I'm gone. Ari will ensure the castle guards and your detail follow the new procedures I've implemented."

"And save yourself some work."

"Exactly."

"When do you plan to leave?" the Commander asked.

"I'll need time to organize my people, brief them and collect supplies. I expect small teams to leave the complex after sunset. Better to travel at night just in case anyone's watching the castle for unusual activity."

"Keep me updated if possible."

"Yes, sir." Valek finished his drink and left.

He crossed the hall to his apartment. Margg had lit the lanterns in his living room. And even though a warm yellow glow coated the furniture, his piles of books and his heaps of carving rocks, an emptiness hung in the air. The challenge and thrill of the hunt had dulled somewhat. Valek paused at the door to Yelena's old bedroom. Maybe if he wished hard enough, she'd appear in the threshold. And probably admonish him for being so maudlin. At least with shutting down the smuggling operation, he'd have an excuse to travel to Sitia and see her.

Before going to bed, he sat at his desk and wrote a list of people for the mission. Then he outlined a few ideas on how to optimize their strike, using the three key ingredients for success—surprise, speed and intensity.

Valek glanced at his collection of weapons hanging on the wall. His favorite knife hung in the center. Those three elements had been vital in assassinating the King.

That night remained crystal clear in his memories. Once he was in position—wedged between the ceiling and wooden rafters of the Queen's receiving room—Valek waited. It wasn't long before the King arrived with his six guards. When the King entered her bedroom, Valek would have mere seconds to disable the guards before the King realized the Queen had been poisoned.

The guards fanned out. Two by the Queen's bedroom, two near the entrance and two by the windows. Valek pressed his blowpipe to his lips. His left hand clutched the other darts. He had a clear shot at four of the guards. The ones by the window would be harder.

As soon as the Queen's bedroom door clicked shut, he targeted the guards by the entrance, hitting them in their throats. Then he hit the two by the door. The guy on the left swatted at his neck as if he'd been bitten.

"What the...?" The first guard held a dart between his finger and thumb, showing it to his partner.

The gig was up. Valek dropped to the ground and spun. He threw his last two darts at the men by the window.

"Hey!" one of them yelled, pointing to Valek.

The others drew their swords and advanced. Valek stood

MARIA V. SNYDER

in the middle of a tightening circle, hoping the sleeping potion would kick in before they skewered him.

The King rushed into the room, his face ashen. "Help me! The Queen is..." He stopped, taking in the situation.

The guards paused. "Orders, my lord?"

"Did you kill my Queen?"

"Yes," Valek said.

"Kill him," the King ordered.

Only one tactic worked when encircled. Valek lunged at the weakest point—the first man he'd hit. The blasted potion finally started to affect the big brute. Valek knocked him down and grabbed the man's sword.

Deflecting the other blades, Valek remained on the defensive while he waited for them to be overcome. The King urged them on. Valek ducked and dodged, earning more than a few cuts before they all collapsed to the ground.

"Are they all dead, too?" the King asked in an icy monotone.

"No. They don't deserve to die." Valek wiped blood from his eyes. A cut on his forehead stung.

"And I deserve to die? You're not the first to think this, nor will you be the last. Who sent you? That young brat from the diamond mines?"

"You sent me." Keeping a firm grip on the sword, Valek stepped over one of the fallen guards.

He laughed. It was a harsh sound. "In that case, you're fired."

"Nice try, but *you* set me on this path. *You* are responsible for your own death." He moved closer.

"I'm sure you have a sob story, but I don't care. And unless you're a master-level magician, you soon won't care, either. Death has a way of eliminating all your problems just like that." The King snapped his fingers.

A bubble of stickiness enveloped Valek. It pressed on his face as if trying to suffocate him. Probably was—the King was known to strangle his enemies with his power because he didn't wish to get his hands dirty. Valek pushed through the magic, advancing on the King.

The King of Ixia frowned. The air around Valek turned to sludge. Drawing a breath took effort; stepping forward was like wading through thick syrup. It was difficult to move, but not impossible. Two more strides and the King would be within striking distance of his sword.

The first gleam of fear shone in the King's eyes as he bent to retrieve a sword from one of his men. If the King had any skills with the weapon, Valek might be in trouble. Hard enough to walk through the magical mire... He couldn't imagine fighting in it.

Another push forward and Valek reached the strike zone. The King of Ixia slid into a defensive position and raised his sword. Not good. However, Valek would not let *this man* walk away from *this fight*. As he had said to Hedda five years ago, if his last breath was one second after the King's he'd die a happy man.

Determined, Valek summoned all his energy and attacked. The King blocked and they launched into a back-and-forth exchange of strikes and blocks. The thin metal rapiers sang with the contact. The monarch knew how to handle a blade and Valek had trained with mostly thicker, heavier swords, which required more muscle than speed. Valek's parries went too wide, leaving his middle exposed. Plus the sticky air dragged at his arms and legs.

The King of Ixia took full advantage of Valek's clunky style. With a flick of his wrist, the tip of his blade snaked past Valek's defenses and cut a path up Valek's right arm. Sharp pain registered for a moment, but he was too busy dodging the

MARIA V. SNYDER

King's next lunge to dwell on it. More cuts followed. Blood soaked his sleeves.

Then Valek miscalculated a strike and parried too late. The tip of the King's blade pierced his flesh near his left hip. Valek gasped as his body jerked. It felt as if he'd run full speed into the edge of a desk. Shock waves rippled through him, sending a cold skittery pulse to his extremities.

The King smirked as he drew back. "You have enough magic to counter mine. It's a shame the same can't be said for your fighting skills. Is there anything you'd like to confess before I kill you? I hear it can be quite…cathartic."

There was no way in hell this corrupt son of a bitch would live to see daylight. Valek envisioned his brothers. Imagining their ghosts standing here watching the fight, he drew strength from them and, it seemed, also advice. Vincent bared his teeth and made a stabbing motion. Valek returned his attention to the task at hand. The pain faded as he focused on what he'd worked so hard for.

"I do have a confession," Valek said. "I'm not a magician. I'm an assassin." Valek threw the sword down and pulled his knives—one for each hand. "I just forgot for a moment."

He surprised a laugh from the King. Then Valek attacked, and the King was no longer smiling. Even with magic pressing down on him, he kept a quick pace, forcing the King to backpedal. The man doggedly blocked the knives.

As the fight continued, sweat ran down the King's face as his responses slowed. Using magic appeared to be as draining as resisting it. The heaviness around Valek disappeared at the same time the King launched an energetic counteroffensive. The man was smart to concentrate his strength on his sword. Too bad for him that Valek's knife-fighting skills had been honed by five years of practice.

Without the presence of magic to slow him down, Valek

disarmed the King within a few moves. Valek pushed him against the wall, pressing the edge of one blade on the King's neck, and the other blade poked into his royal stomach just below the breastbone.

Panic reddened the King's face. "I can pay you ten times what your client offered."

"Not interested."

"I'll make you a general."

"No."

"My daughter! You can marry her and become a prince."

"Aren't you a swell dad. Sorry, but I've met your brat of a daughter. That would be worse than death."

"I'll give you anything."

"Good. After you die, I want you to explain to my three brothers why your soldiers murdered them in *your* name." Valek stabbed his knife up into the King's heart.

The King's magic exploded, propelling Valek back. The King of Ixia stumbled forward clutching the hilt of the knife. He gasped, "My blood…will…stain…your hands…forever." And collapsed.

Valek knelt next to the King and watched the life fade from his gaze. He listened for that last shuddering breath. And once the man died, Valek endured a tumult of emotions. Joy, relief and satisfaction spun around his racing heart. The euphoria rushed to his head. He sat back on his heels, overcome for a moment.

Now he could live his life. If he lived through the take-over, he'd be able to serve the Commander and purge Ixia of the King's rot.

But first, he needed to finish the job and eradicate the roots. Valek stood. All the aches and pains from the fight flared to life, demanding attention. He inspected the stab wound near his left hip bone. Blood oozed from the puncture. It hurt like crazy. At least it wasn't gushing and he could still move.

Focusing on the positive, he climbed out the window. Not much time left for him to visit the King's two children, three nephews, one sister-in-law and one brother before the King's corpse was discovered. While Valek had enjoyed thrusting his knife into the King's heart, he didn't relish this task.

He spidered from one royal's window to the next, easing the panes open and ghosting through bedrooms. Using the same poison he'd fed to Queen Jewel, Valek dripped five drops of My Love into their mouths, or their noses if they slept with their lips clamped shut. If they startled awake, he held his hand over their mouths for a few seconds. The fast-acting poison did the rest.

By the time he finished, the noises from the hallways had increased to panic levels with doors slamming, boots pounding and screams mixing with shouts of alarm. Despite exhaustion settling into all his muscles, Valek slipped out the prince's window and returned to his rooms. The outer door gaped open. Someone had searched them, and his skirts and few possessions were strewn on the floor. He secured the door.

Valek debated changing into Valma's nightgown to continue the ruse, but by this point either the Commander's forces would be successful or not, and in both cases Valma was no longer needed.

Instead, he peeled his blood-soaked sneak suit from his battered body, wincing as the dried patches ripped from his skin and the silky material tugged at the deeper cuts on his arms. He sponged off the gore. Red and purple bruises bloomed around the stab wound in his hip. He'd deal with that later.

Donning a pair of pants, Valek locked the bedroom door and collapsed into bed.

He slept for... He had no idea how long. But way too soon,

a loud crash jolted him from oblivion. In a blink of two very bleary eyes, four big, well-armed goons surrounded his bed. Cuts, bruises, blood spatters, disheveled hair and ripped tunics all evidence these men had been in a fight. But whose side?

"Is this him?" Bruiser One asked Bruiser Two.

"Yup."

"Grab him," Bruiser One ordered the others.

Too tired to resist, Valek allowed them to haul him from the bed. But once he was on his feet, he yanked his arms from Bruiser Three and Bruiser Four. "No need to carry me." He spread his hands. "I'm unarmed."

Bruiser One studied him. "Are you sure this is the guy who assassinated the King and his family? He looks—"

"Hold that insult," Valek interrupted. "If you value your life."

The man snorted.

"Come on. We're to report back to the throne room," Bruiser Two said.

They peered at Valek. He longed to return to his bed, but their postures said they weren't leaving without him. "Who are you reporting to?"

"The Commander."

Good news. "Then give me a minute to change."

After Valek dressed, the four bruisers escorted him to the throne room. He mulled over reasons why they acted as if he were the enemy. They could be recent recruits who had once been loyal to the King's family. While many citizens of Ixia hated the King, they wouldn't automatically be supporters of the Commander. He'd have to win their trust and loyalty. And Valek would be required to do the same with the soldiers. The idea would be more palatable once he was fully rested.

The throne room buzzed with activity. Servants ripped the tapestries from the walls, tearing the fabric with knives.

MARIA V. SNYDER

Groups of guards herded prisoners toward the Commander, who sat on the throne—a large garish chair made from gold. The overstuffed white cushion was reportedly sewn from snow-cat hide. Ambrose talked to the captives. When he finished, most of them knelt on one knee—probably swearing loyalty, while the others were taken away.

Valek approached with the bruisers by his side. The Commander's gaze flashed with joy. Giddy with his triumph, Ambrose jumped to his feet and hugged Valek for the first and only time.

"Well done, my boy. Well done." He thumped Valek on the back. "Where have you been?"

"He was sleeping," Bruiser Two said.

"How can you sleep? You should be celebrating. The takeover was a complete success!"

"He's pretty beat up," Bruiser One said.

"Did that bastard put up a fight?" Ambrose asked.

Valek glanced at his bruiser buddies. "What? No answer this time?"

They stared back.

"It was an intense match, sir. I'll give you a full report later," Valek said.

"Good idea. In the meantime, I have something for you." The Commander gestured to one of his advisers.

The woman picked up a silver platter with a cover. Odd. She presented it to the Commander. He removed the lid with a flourish, revealing Valek's favorite knife. Bright red blood coated the blade.

"We found it in the King's chest. I believe it is yours."

"Guess I need to clean it." Valek reached for the weapon.

"Won't work," Ambrose said.

"Excuse me?"

The Commander grabbed the cloth hanging over the woman's

arm. He picked up the knife and wiped the blade on the material. The blood clung to the metal. Not a drop stained the towel.

"I'm guessing it's magic." Ambrose handed the knife to Valek.

He ran a finger along the flat side. The blood avoided his skin, parting as he skimmed over the blade and re-pooling after his finger had passed. A stickiness pulsed from the weapon.

Valek laughed. "He cursed me with his dying breath. Said my hands would always be stained with his blood. Seems the curse attached to my knife instead." He tsked. "Such a shame. It was my favorite. What should I do with it now?"

"Put it on display in your office. So everyone who walks through those doors knows you are the King Killer."

And twenty-three years later, the King's blood still glistened in the lamplight.

Valek rushed around the next morning, organizing his teams for the mission, assembling supplies and explaining to Ari for the fourth time why Valek was leaving him behind.

"I know where the wagons disappeared in the foothills and where the factory is located," Ari said. "You'll need me."

"I need you here. And you can debrief Janco and Onora when they return."

"Then can we both catch up?" Ari asked in a hopeful tone.

"Not unless I send for you." Valek put a hand on Ari's shoulder when the big man's expression creased. "Ari, the castle's security has been lax, and I'm worried we still have gaps. Hedda trained Onora, but she could have trained more. I need you here."

"Yes, sir."

Valek watched his friend and hoped Janco returned soon. Ari wasn't quite Ari without his partner.

MARIA V. SNYDER

On his way back from visiting the stable, one of the gate's guards rushed up to Valek.

"Sir! There's—"

"I don't have time to deal with another messenger." Valek kept walking.

"It's not a messenger, sir."

He paused. "What, then?"

"It's...well...it's Kiki, sir. She's at the gate."

Did he hear that right? "Yelena's horse is at the gate?"

"Yes, sir. She is. And she brought...er...friends, sir."

28

JANCO

Janco watched Maren as she talked and drank Ixian white brandy with the smugglers in the warehouse. His colleague and friend appeared to be at ease with the others. She wore Sitian clothes and her long blond hair had been pulled back into a braid.

Maren's mystery mission for the Commander was no longer quite a mystery. Janco scratched at the scar below his ear. If Maren was working undercover in the smuggling operation, then why didn't the Commander inform the rest of them? Finding and stopping this gang had been their priority, so why the secrecy about Maren? He wished Ari was here. His partner would have an answer.

Fingers touched his arm and Janco about jumped out of his skin. A black shadow detached from the wall right next to him. Onora frowned. She jerked her head, indicating they should move deeper into the factory.

He retraced his steps, skirting a couple of vats and water pumps to reach the door to the stairwell.

Onora pushed it open, gestured him inside, then closed it behind them, plunging them into darkness. "Did you even discover where the smaller containers were headed?" Her question was hissed in a low whisper.

"Yeah, into Ixia." Before she could explode, he said, "We can learn that later. What if there was a magical illusion on this side, as well? You needed me."

She sighed, sounding a lot like Ari. "Do you recognize any of this equipment? Or what they're producing?"

"No. The smell is so familiar it's been driving me crazy. It's not cigars, that's for sure."

"Why not?"

"They'd be drying out the leaves, not soaking them or pulping them."

"Parchment?"

"Maybe, but what's illegal about that?"

"Nothing. But something's not right here. It feels...off."

Janco agreed. "Perhaps Maren can tell us what's going on."

"Maren, as in the Commander's missing adviser? She's here?"

"Yup. She's drinking with them."

Onora remained quiet for a few moments. "Do you think she switched sides? Who better to aid the smugglers than someone who is very familiar with Ixian security."

That would make sense if the person had been anyone other than Maren. Or Ari, or Yelena, or Valek. "Nope. She's loyal."

"Then why didn't the Commander tell us about her?"

"For a very good reason."

"You have no idea."

"It doesn't matter. I trust the Commander. That's all I need. And all you should need, too."

"All right," she said, but she chewed on her lower lip. "What do we do next?"

"I can see you!" he whispered.

"So?"

He glanced up. A faint light lit the upper level.

She pointed to the small pool of blackness underneath the stairs. They crouched close together. The light brightened as quiet footsteps sounded above. Janco concentrated. Only one person descended. The figure held a tiny metal lantern atop a post. Instead of the lantern hanging down, it resembled a torch, but without open flames.

When the cloaked figure reached the bottom, the person turned around and shone the dim light around the small space, revealing their hiding spot.

"Oh—"

Onora sprang forward. She rushed the intruder. The torch fell to the ground. Janco picked it up. He recognized it. The light was one of those small lanterns built with a long handle underneath to resemble a torch. It was called a lantorch—one of their gadgets. Onora scuffled with the person. They banged against the door and a knife clanged to the floor before Onora trapped the shorter figure in a double arm lock.

"Should I kill her before the others arrive?" Little Miss Assassin asked.

"No." Janco tugged the captive's hood back, revealing a familiar face with a very unfamiliar expression—fear. "Release her. It's Yelena. What are you doing here?"

Onora let Yelena go, but the assassin didn't look pleased.

Yelena smoothed her cloak. "Probably the same thing you are." She glanced at Onora.

"New recruit," Janco said.

Voices sounded on the other side of the door. "...heard something. I'm sure."

Time to go. Janco pointed up and the three of them climbed the steps to the second story. He led them to the storeroom. A grapple had been hooked over the windowsill and a rope hung to the ground. Yelena must have taken advantage of the

MARIA V. SNYDER

open window he'd left behind. He switched the light off as Onora climbed from the room.

They reached the ground and ran for cover. Voices yelled from above, calling out their location. Damn moon was too bright. The other smugglers poured from the warehouse and headed in their direction.

"This way." Yelena took the lead. She raced down the main road and away from the town.

Janco stayed close to her.

"Still too exposed," Onora said, glancing over her shoulder. "They're about a hundred feet behind us."

"There's a sharp bend." Yelena gestured. "Make a right into the woods as soon as we're hidden from view."

"Do you have a boat?" Onora asked.

Yelena didn't bother to reply even though Janco thought it was a really good question. With no leaves on the trees and only about twenty feet of forest between the road and the river, there weren't any hiding places.

Once around the bend, they plunged into the woods and, sure enough, a boat waited at the bank. It was one of those small skiffs with a canvas dome top. However, Yelena pointed to a huge ancient tree. It resembled one of those thousand-legged bugs.

"Climb up as high as you can," she ordered.

He paused. It had at least a million branches, which equaled about a million scratches. "But—"

"Trust me."

She'd gotten them out of a dozen tight spots in the past. He grabbed branches and scrambled higher. Onora had disappeared. Janco assumed she was higher in the tree, but who knew with her and her creepy chameleon power.

Yelena untied the boat and pushed it into the current. Then she swung up behind him. She might have been raised in Ixia, but her Zaltana blood showed as she ascended with ease, passing him with a grin. When the branches bowed under their weight, they stopped. A twig poked in his ear and in a number of unmentionable places.

They didn't wait long before a group of six smugglers dashed into the woods.

"...heading for the river!"

"Look, a boat! Peeti, your crossbow. Quick."

"Light it!"

Bright orange bloomed below them. Then a twang sounded and a burning bolt shot over the water, hitting the boat dead center. The canvas dome caught fire. Peeti shot three more and soon the entire boat was engulfed in flames.

Damn. They meant business. And if anyone glanced up... Old timber burned fast and it wouldn't take long for Janco and his friends to turn into barbecue. He calculated the distance to the ground. If he landed on one of them, he might not break his legs.

"Let's go. We got them," one voice said.

"Not yet. Search the area. The boat could have been a decoy," another ordered.

Great. Janco never liked hiding. He'd rather duke it out, and his companions could each handle two opponents easily.

"No," Yelena whispered. "It's not the right time."

He frowned hard at her. She'd read his mind even though she knew how much he hated magic. Then again, that creepy crawly sensation crossing the back of his neck wasn't quite the same as... A bug! Ewww! Staying still required an immense effort. Janco concentrated on the men below, debated between being killed by smugglers versus being bitten. The bug crawled up into his hair. Okay, smugglers it was!

Yelena flicked the bug away. He smiled his thanks. She shook her head just like Ari did when exasperated with him.

MARIA V. SNYDER

Which was quite often, although he'd no clue why because his logic was undeniable.

Eventually, the search moved far enough away from their hiding place.

"We can't stay here much longer," Janco said. The bug might have friends.

"We should split up," Onora said. She sat on the branch right above him. "They're looking for three people."

Yelena agreed. "Let's meet at the Water Witch Inn. It's in Port Monroe, located about five miles downstream of here."

"See you there." Onora climbed down.

"She's quiet," Yelena said as they returned to solid ground.

Shuddering, Janco brushed off his hair and clothes. "Yeah, and she's good with a knife."

"Hopefully she won't need it tonight. See you at the Witch." Yelena turned to go, but Janco grabbed her arm.

He didn't like how she held herself as if afraid she'd break. And she'd entered the warehouse alone and without backup. That didn't jibe. Something wasn't right and Valek would kill him if he didn't stick with her. Ari, too.

"We'll go together," he said.

"But—"

"They're looking for three, not two."

She smiled. "All right, but we need to get to the other side of the river."

He glanced at the cold churning water. "We're gonna swim?"

"Not if I can help it. There's a bridge back in Lapeer."

"Lapeer? Is that the town we were just in?"

"Yup."

"What about the smugglers?"

"We'll worry about that then."

He released her and she led him along the bank, heading upstream until they reached the bridge. They climbed and peered over the embankment. A couple of smugglers walked along the main street. "Are you sure we need to cross?"

"Yes." She yanked her hood down and unwound her hair, letting the long black strands hang over her shoulders. "Follow my lead." She took his hand, lacing her fingers with his and winked.

Ah. He grinned. "I knew you'd come around eventually."

Yelena tugged him up onto the bridge's walking path. She pressed against his side, walking slow. "It's always been you, Janco. I've just been suppressing my true feelings."

"What about Valek?" He stared at her as if she were the only one in the world even though he longed to check if the goons had spotted them yet.

"Valek, smalek. He's way too serious."

They paused at the center of the bridge, taking in the view. Little diamonds of moonlight sparkled on the water. He pulled her into a hug before they moseyed to the other side.

"You'll leave Valek for me?" he asked.

"Yes. You just have to tell him we're running away together." She smirked.

"Ow." He pressed a hand to his heart. "Doused with ice-cold reality. All loving feelings gone. Sorry, sweetheart, you're not worth dying for."

"Are you sure it's not that pretty new recruit?" She made a left onto a trail, heading downstream.

"It's not. She'd probably rather kill me than kiss me."

"Oh?"

"Long story. I'll tell you about it later." The path cut between the river and the forest. "How many miles is it?"

"About five, but my horse can take us both."

Just as he realized why that didn't sound right, Yelena turned right and entered the woods. She hiked until they reached a grayish horse.

Oh no. Worried, he asked, "Where's Kiki?"

MARIA V. SNYDER

29

YELENA

Despite the near miss at the factory and being chased, my mood had improved. It might have been due to Janco's presence, but I'd never confess that to him. He'd gloat about it forever. Janco held on to my waist as The Madam trotted along the path that paralleled the twists and turns of the Sunworth river.

We reached Port Monroe an hour later. After I settled The Madam in the Water Witch's stable, we entered the common room just as the sun rose. We sat at a table opposite the door, ordered sweet cakes and tea. I needed at least a gallon of tea. Janco didn't seem to be his normal peppy self, either.

"Did Valek send you to investigate the Curare factory?" I asked before he could start with his questions.

"Curare!" He smacked his forehead. "Of course. That's why it smelled so familiar. It was driving me crazy."

I waited.

"Curare. Oh sh—"

"That's what I thought when I caught the scent. It took me a day to hone in on that factory. I waited until the night-time to learn who is responsible, and…well, you know the rest. If you didn't know they were producing Curare, then why were you there?"

Janco told me about tracking smugglers to Sitia. "…using magic to hide their routes. And we also discovered Maren's working undercover in the operation."

"Are you her backup?"

"No. The Commander didn't tell us where she was. Not even Valek."

That worried me. Did the Commander suspect there was an informer in Valek's corps?

Our food arrived and we both shoveled steaming sweet cakes into our mouths. I gulped my tea despite the hot temperature. The liquid burned all the way to my stomach and warmed me.

"Okay, your turn. Why are you here?" Janco asked.

I gave him the short version, which didn't include my lost magic. I'd tell him before we did anything dangerous.

"You think the people who rescued Ben are involved with the Curare factory?" he asked.

"I'm not sure. That's why I sneaked inside to see if there was any connection. But regardless of who is involved, we have to shut that place down."

"Yeah, I kinda figured you'd say that. Do you want to notify the Sitian authorities? Or take matters into our own hands?"

"And what can the two of us do?"

Janco's eyes lit up. "Burn the place down. Totally doable with the *three* of us. You're forgetting Little Miss Assassin, our newest recruit."

This was going to be good. "Little Miss Assassin?"

"She doesn't like to be called that."

"Gee, I wonder why."

"Onora's overly sensitive. But I'm working on her. Anyhoo,

she showed up one night." Janco launched into a detailed story of how Onora made an impression on the Commander. "…and she would have beaten Valek if she'd finished her training. If she wants Valek's job—"

"What does Valek think about all this?"

"He didn't say, but I think he'd be more than happy to let another take over the reins."

"I don't agree. He loves his job."

"He loves you more."

Janco didn't quite understand. For Valek, the Commander would always come first, and I'd accepted that…mostly. I'd admit there were times I'd wished it was different.

As Janco helped himself to my tea, I mulled over the information. With Ben locked in Wirral, he couldn't direct a smuggling operation. We really needed to get inside and find out who was in charge before we informed the authorities. Was it the mystery accomplice I couldn't remember?

The Sitian methods for raiding a place were far from subtle. Plus I didn't have any doubt the smugglers had paid off the town watch. Not with the place stinking of Curare. The watchman would tip them off and all the evidence would be gone before the authorities organized an attack.

"Thinking devious thoughts?" Janco asked.

"Not quite. I'd like to discover who's behind the factory, but after tonight, I'd bet they're scrambling to relocate or hide the evidence."

"Maren might know. We should find a way to contact her."

"Or wait for her to contact us," I said. "She probably recognized us. Either way, we should return to Lapeer and keep an eye on that factory. See who comes and goes."

"They'll be on guard, watching for us."

"Then we'll have to go in disguise. How attached are you to your hair, old man?"

Janco groaned. "How about we pretend to be newlyweds?"

"No." I glanced at the door. We'd been talking for a couple of hours. "Shouldn't Little Miss Assassin be here by now?"

"Maybe she had to make a detour to shake a tail."

"You're not worried?"

"Not at all. The girl was trained by the same lady who trained Valek, and she…"

"She what?"

"She just blends in, but I don't get that icky magic sensation around her. Did you feel it last night? Could she be one of those One-Trick Wonders?"

"Maybe. Did Valek sense any magic?"

"He didn't say. Can't you use your superpowers on her and get the skinny?"

"Uh…about that, Janco. I—"

"There she is."

His voice held more relief than his early comments about her implied. Interesting. I studied the young woman as she approached. Graceful with pretty, light gray eyes and a narrow face. Her lips were pressed together and a crease marked her forehead. She'd be beautiful without that dour expression. I doubted she cared.

"What took ya so long?" Janco asked.

She frowned at me before meeting his gaze. "I don't think it's a good idea to discuss Ixian business in front of a Sitian."

Janco laughed. "Yelena isn't Sitian or Ixian. She's just an ian—neutral."

"No one is neutral," Onora said.

"True. How could she not love Ixia more? She can't. Oh, stop scowling at me, Little Miss Assassin. I'm just gonna tell her everything anyway. This way, I won't mess up the details."

"So you admit you've messed up the details in the past?" I asked.

"No way, sweetheart."

Onora turned to me. "It's amazing he's lived this long."

"He grows on you. Sort of like a barnacle."

"Hey!" He pouted.

"Did you run into trouble?" I asked Onora, ignoring Janco.

"No. While you two were pretending to be lovebirds, I looped back to the factory. Everyone was outside hunting for us, so I figured no one would be looking inside."

Smart. A server came over to take Onora's breakfast order. She ordered eggs, toast and ham.

When the girl retreated, I asked, "Did you find anything?"

"I saw Maren loading up the wagon with those small casks, and I heard two men arguing in an office next to the main factory area. They didn't agree on whether to close the factory down or to relocate it. But they planned to load their inventory on barges and send it upstream to a warehouse in Sunworth. Isn't that the name of the river?"

"Yes, but it's named after a town in the foothills of the Emerald Mountains, where the river starts," I said.

"That jibes with our other intel about the disappearing wagons," Janco said. "Ari and the grunt planned to check it out on the Ixian side."

I considered. "Onora, did you see the men or hear any names?"

"No. When Maren left with the horses and wagon, I followed her."

Janco straightened. "Why?"

"I knew the smugglers' plans, but I didn't know her destination."

"And?" he asked.

"She's returning to Ixia."

"Through the tunnel we found?"

"No. Why would she? She's an adviser to the Commander and can cross the border without trouble."

"Except she's working undercover. That would tip the smugglers off," Janco said.

"Unless—"

"She's not a traitor," Janco growled at Onora.

"*Unless* things have gotten too hot for her."

I suppressed a smile. Onora might be young, but she had plenty of confidence.

"Speculation will only get us so far," I said, trying to break the tension. "If they're planning on moving their inventory then we need to raid the factory."

Janco glanced around the room. "Do you have an army I don't know about?"

"I'll talk to Lapeer's town watch. That might tip the smugglers off, but at this point we need to get a good look inside. There might be invoices and other documents that would indicate who is supplying them with the Curare vine." The vine grew in the Illiais Jungle, my clan's lands, and the Zaltanas were supposed to be guarding it for just this reason. Concern for my family pulsed in my heart. I'd have to send a message to my father, warning him of poachers.

"While you organize the watchmen, we'll keep an eye on the factory," Onora said. "We'll follow anyone who leaves before the raid."

"We?" Janco smirked. "Just can't get enough of my company, can you, sweetheart?"

Onora met my gaze.

"It's best to ignore him."

"Easier said than done," she muttered.

"Hear that, Yelena?" Janco bumped my arm with his elbow. "I'm irresistible."

After Onora finished her breakfast, we split up once again. I rode The Madam to Lapeer. The afternoon sun warmed my shoulders. To avoid falling asleep in the saddle, I mulled over all the information from Janco and Onora. What was in those casks Maren loaded into the wagon? Curare, probably. The significance of that hit me. So worried about who'd been producing the drug, I hadn't considered the ramifications of it being available to Ixians. The Sitian Council kept strict control of it for a reason.

If the criminal element in Ixia had access to Curare, then Valek and his corps would no longer have an advantage. My stomach churned just thinking about it. At least Maren managed to take some with her and out of circulation. Or had she? An evil thought popped into my head.

Maybe the Commander was a client. If Sitia ever attacked Ixia, they'd have the upper hand. Sitia had magicians, the super messengers and Curare. It made sense for the Commander to want to even the playing field a bit by importing Curare. Except Janco had said the Commander made finding and stopping the smugglers a priority. Why would he do that if he was benefiting from them? He wouldn't.

The tight knot in my chest eased. I spurred The Madam into a gallop and headed straight for the town's station house.

My arrival was initially met with some resistance, but having a reputation as a powerful Soulfinder pushed past the doubts. Handy. As predicted, it took a while for the captain to organize his forces. We had to wait for off-duty officers to report in and for everyone to be briefed. The delay allowed Janco and Onora to get into position, but it reduced our chances of catching anyone. Hopefully they'd trail whoever bailed. If that was the case, one of them would eventually return to let me know where the smugglers went.

"Speed is better than surprise," I said to Captain Fleming for the tenth time. "They already know we're coming."

Sure enough, the factory was empty by the time we arrived later that afternoon. I hoped Janco had witnessed the exodus. At least I had a couple of hours of sunlight left to search the place. Papers littering the office, drawers hanging open and scuffs on the floor were all evidence of their hasty exit. In the factory, not much remained behind except for the equipment. Not even one of those casks. The rooms on the second floor remained full of storage, and I suspected the boxes had been left over from the previous tenants.

I scanned a few of the documents, looking for information. The captain tsked over the vats of half-pulped Curare vines and insisted everything would be destroyed.

"Didn't you recognize the smell?" I asked.

"Nope. We're not allowed to carry Curare. That's only for the bigger cities." He assigned a man to collect all the papers to bring back to the station to analyze.

I righted an office chair and sat. Hard to believe they managed to empty the place in twelve hours. Perhaps they had a hidden storeroom and after all the commotion died down, they'd return for the rest of their stock. Maybe in a basement?

While the officers cataloged the equipment and inventoried the storage rooms' boxes, I searched for a hidden door. I ran my fingers along the walls in case an entrance had been concealed by a magical illusion. Soon my hands turned black with grime. After encountering a couple of dead ends, I found a small stairwell. At first, it appeared to go to only the second floor. However, an invisible metal seam marked the floor underneath the steps. Feeling my way, I discovered a square metal panel.

I triggered my switchblade and pried the edge of the panel up, revealing a hole of darkness. Another illusion? Digging in

MARIA V. SNYDER

my pack, I pulled out my lantorch and lit the filament, hoping I had enough oil to last awhile.

The light reflected off a metal ladder descending into the darkness. I waited, listening for any sounds from below. All remained quiet. I climbed down. When I reached the floor, I turned, shining the light around the space.

Bingo! Barrels lined the floor along with piles of boxes. Crates had been hastily stacked against the right wall. But no casks. On the far side was an opening into another room. I entered and spotted more barrels. The Commander's white brandy must sell well in Sitia.

A faint click sounded just as I was about to turn around to report my find to the captain. I hurried to the ladder, but the hatch above had been closed.

"I told him it wouldn't work," Ben said.

I spun. What I'd thought was a stack of crates was actually an illusion. Ben, another man, a woman and two goons stood in its place. The lady must be Rika, the magician who created the illusion. They had their weapons drawn, but appeared relaxed. Probably because they'd erected a null shield.

"Tell who?" I asked in a calm voice, although my heart recognized the danger and urged me to bolt.

Ben huffed in amusement. "You don't remember and yet you found us anyway. Amazing."

I bowed. "Thank you."

"How did you find us?"

"I didn't think you could clear out the entire factory in—"

"Not that. How did you know we were in *Lapeer*?"

No reason to lie. "A lucky guess."

"She's lying," one of the men said. "Why didn't you go west with your brother and the others?"

To admit to being locked in protective custody hurt too much. Instead, I said, "Your clues were too obvious. In fact, they all looped north and have surrounded the factory. You might as well surrender now."

Alarmed, Ben asked, "Drey, you said they headed west."

"They did," Drey the goon said. "She's bluffing."

Better than being called a liar. Progress. I acted unconcerned, but I inched toward the ladder. "Believe what you want."

"It doesn't matter. Once the town watch leaves the factory, Rika can hide us with her magic," Ben said.

Uh-oh. Even if Captain Fleming realized I'd disappeared, he couldn't see through a magical illusion. I slid into a fighting stance, keeping a firm grip on my switchblade.

"In the meantime," Ben said, "you're here and so am I. And do you know who's *not* here?"

"Your mother?"

"Cute. The Boss isn't here to save your life this time." Ben tightened his grip on his sword.

The Boss! Memories of being held down with Ben ready to plunge his knife into my stomach surged. But the Boss's identity remained elusive.

Rika touched his arm. "There's a good reason why he doesn't want her dead."

Ben rounded on her. "What else can we do? She won't stay away."

I moved closer to the ladder.

"Incapacitate her," Rika suggested. "Let the Boss decide."

Time for me to leave. I tossed my lantorch at them, grabbed the rungs and climbed.

"Tyen," Ben said.

Oh no. Tyen's magic could move large objects, including me. Except a cold dart pricked my neck. I yanked it from my skin, but it was too late.

"That doesn't work on her. Use one of the barrels."

As the room spun, I knew I was in big trouble. My foot slipped off the ladder and I slid back to the ground. Darkness pressed along the edges of my vision. Not Curare. A sleeping potion? Poison? A heavy object slammed into me, knocking me to the ground, sending me into oblivion.

I woke to the rumbling vibrations of wagon wheels over cobblestones. My head ached, pain ringed my wrists and ankles, and dry cotton filled my mouth. It didn't take long for me to learn the full extent of my predicament. Lying flat on my back in a wagon, I stared at a canvas covering that hung inches from my nose. No light shone through the fabric. Nighttime.

Gagged and tied spread-eagle to the sides of the wagon, I'd been effectively neutralized. Had they figured out the sleeping potion worked or did they assume the barrel had knocked me unconscious? Did it matter? Since I'd been bluffing people based on my reputation alone…yes, it did matter. Very much.

The only thing that kept me from panicking was the hope that Captain Fleming realized I was missing. Also Ben might be taking me to the same location as the other shipments where Janco and Onora should be. A thin hope, but better than nothing.

I marked time by the noise from the wheels. The jarring shake of cobblestones stopped and the crunch of gravel signaled we'd left the main streets of a town. Then the smooth, quiet hum of either a dirt or grass path meant we were in the countryside between towns. Keeping track of the cycles of noise, I'd counted three towns when we slowed after reaching the outskirts of the third town.

We turned left and lurched over uneven ground before hinges squeaked and what sounded like doors clicked shut. Lantern light cast shadows on the canvas covering. Voices talked, but not close enough for me to understand the words. The familiar jingle of a harness indicated someone worked at unhitching the team of horses. This stop could be our final destination. My stomach skittered. Bad choice of words.

The distant voices grew louder as the speakers moved toward my position. Ben and another man argued. The Boss? Something about his superior tone seemed familiar.

"...doesn't matter now. He knows what you're up to," Ben said. "He has plenty of inventory. Cut your losses and run."

"I'd planned to renegotiate, but now you've screwed that up, too."

"What else was I supposed to do?"

"Disappear like I ordered after I rescued you from Wirral," the Boss said.

"I endured three years of hell in that prison," Ben said. "And she put me there. She deserves to die."

"We've discussed this. If she dies, then the Master Magicians, the Sitian Council and Valek will all be breathing down our necks. Even if we're arrested, Valek will still find us and kill us. No. I have a better idea."

A better idea? I didn't like the sound of that. The wagon tilted as someone climbed onto it. The canvas was pulled away and there stood—

"Hello, Yelena. Remember me?"

30

VALEK

"Kiki's at the gate and she brought friends?" Valek asked the guard, just to ensure he'd heard the man right. He kept a tight grasp on his emotions. No sense worrying until he had all the facts.

"Yes, sir."

"Who's with her?"

"Ah...it would be best for you to see for yourself, sir."

"All right." Valek followed the guard back to the castle complex's main gate. Sure enough, Kiki stood on the other side with two riders. The last two people he'd expect, but not unwelcome, either. "Let them in," he ordered.

Kiki didn't wait. She cleared the gate with one leap, then butted his chest with her head. He stroked her neck, but his attention focused on Devlen and then Reema, sitting in front. She wore Yelena's cloak.

"While I'm glad to see you both, I'm curious why you're here," he said.

"It is a long story." Devlen dismounted. He helped Reema from the saddle.

She gazed at the castle with rapt attention. Kiki, on the

other hand, drooped with fatigue. Valek ran a hand down her legs, checking for hot spots.

"She kept a brisk pace and would not stop for long," Devlen said.

"Let's take care of Kiki and then we'll talk." Valek pulled Yelena's saddle from her back and carried it to the stable while Kiki plodded beside him.

Devlen and Reema trailed behind, gawking at the sights. Valek clamped down on the million questions boiling up his throat. The castle's Stable Master tsked over Kiki. He assigned her two favorite lads to attend to her. Satisfied, Valek led the others to his office.

Many of the household staff and soldiers stared at Devlen. Hard to blame them, considering his size and skin color. Unlike the pale Ixians, his bronzed skin stood out. Then add Sitian clothes, a powerful build, a scimitar hanging from his belt and a nasty-looking scar on his neck and he was the definition of intimidating. Devlen ignored the attention. He held Reema's hand.

Valek ushered them into his office. Ari sat at his desk, but jumped to his feet as soon as he spotted Valek.

"I just finished sketching the security around that warehouse," Ari said. Then he grinned. "Devlen! What brings you here?" He shook Devlen's hand. "Tired of beating up those wimpy Sitians and decided to come up here for a real fight?"

"I wish. I have been too busy trying to outsmart a crafty fox who finds new and unique ways to avoid going to school every morning," Devlen said. "Ari, meet my daughter, Reema."

Ari crouched down to her eye level. "Nice to meet you." He took her hand and pumped it once.

"Hello," she said, gazing at him in awe. "Ari as in 'Ari and Janco'?"

"Yup."

"I've heard *a lot* about you two."

Valek fought to keep a straight face.

Ari straightened. "Is that so? What have you been saying, Devlen?"

"Not me. Yelena. She tells Reema stories before bed. Seems the ones with you and Janco put Reema right to sleep."

"Ouch." But Ari laughed.

Yelena's name cut through Valek's amusement. "Ari, why don't you give Reema a tour? Make sure you show her the Commander's war room. She'll love seeing the stained glass."

"All right. Come on, Reema. I'll even show you where Janco likes to hide when he doesn't want to do paperwork."

Reema glanced at Devlen. He nodded and she hurried after Ari, already asking questions.

As soon as the door shut, Devlen said, "Yelena's fine—at least the last I heard."

Relief shot through him. He gestured to a chair. "Sit down. Would you like a drink?"

"Yes." Devlen plopped into the chair.

"Tea? Water? Or something stronger?"

"Stronger. It has been a long four days."

Valek poured two shots of whiskey and handed one to Devlen before sitting down behind his desk. Devlen drank his in one gulp. Valek followed suit and poured them both another.

"What's going on?" Valek asked.

Devlen tossed back the second shot. "Do you know about Ben Moon's escape?"

"Yes. And I received Yelena's message that he and his cohorts might be in Ixia. I dispatched agents to MD-5 but, so far, we haven't seen any sign of them."

"That's because they were in Fulgor. Now the authorities believe Ben and his gang are headed west."

"With Yelena and her colleagues chasing after?"

"No. Yelena is in the holding cells at the Fulgor security headquarters."

Valek stilled. "For a very good reason. Right?"

"To keep her safe."

"That's extreme."

Devlen sighed. "Did Yelena message you about her magic?"

A cold mist of fear settled on Valek. "No. What about her magic?"

As Devlen filled him in on Yelena's predicament, Valek employed every ounce of self-control not to interrupt. His emotions cycled from fear and worry to fury that she hadn't confided in him and then back through them all again at least twice more.

"...understand why Leif had her placed in protective custody?" Devlen asked.

"Yes." Valek was halfway to the door before he realized he'd even stood up. "Come on. She won't be locked in there for long." And she was a sitting duck. The Mosquito would be stupid not to use that golden opportunity to make another attempt to assassinate her. Irys's message about Yelena being vulnerable and the rumors Arbon heard made more sense now. He understood why Irys had been vague. She'd probably assumed Yelena had told Valek about losing her magic.

"Where are we going?" Devlen asked.

"To find Ari and then to Fulgor."

"What about Reema? According to Yelena, they threatened her life, too."

"That's why we need Ari."

He found them in the war room. As expected, Reema stared, mesmerized, at the tall stained-glass windows that ringed the round room.

She squealed when she spotted Devlen at the threshold.

"Daddy! You *have* to see this! It's fantastic!" Reema grabbed his arm and pulled him inside.

Valek gestured Ari into the hallway. He explained what was going on. "Devlen and I are going to Fulgor. You—"

"Are coming, too." Ari crossed his massive arms.

"No. You are going to protect Reema. I don't trust anyone else."

"Why not leave Devlen here to babysit her?" Ari demanded.

"He's Sitian and he's friends with Fulgor's security forces."

"What about the mission to the Soul Mountains?"

Ah hell. Valek had forgotten about it. He'd have to rearrange a number of things. Plus Kiki needed time to rest. She wouldn't let him leave without her. "I'll rendezvous with the teams in the foothills. They'll be on foot, while I'll have Onyx. Can you get Devlen something to eat and find him a place to catch a few hours of sleep?"

"Yes, sir." Ari frowned. "Where should Reema stay while she's here?"

"With you. Don't let her out of your sight."

"Wonderful." Ari's sarcastic tone sounded just like Janco's.

"She'll surprise you. Reema's a smart little scamp." Valek paused. "She reminds me of Yelena at times. They both had difficult childhoods, yet instead of breaking them, it made them stronger. Think of this not as babysitting duty, but encouraging a future recruit."

"Opal won't like that."

Valek grinned. "Opal doesn't have to know."

He left Ari to take care of their visitors while Valek rushed around and updated his team members on the new timeline and rendezvous point. Hopefully, he'd find Yelena, convince her to come with him and then figure out how to return her magic. The Commander would probably not be pleased with Valek's detour, but he didn't care. Nor did Valek plan to inform him of his change in itinerary. As long as Valek completed his mission and stopped the smugglers, the Commander would be happy.

A couple of hours after the sun set, Valek and Devlen mounted Onyx and Kiki and headed southeast through the Snake Forest. With Kiki in the lead, they kept a fast pace and only stopped to feed and rest the horses. As they traveled, Valek searched his memory for a name of a substance or poison that would block a magician's power. Other than Curare, nothing came to mind.

They crossed the Sitian border without encountering a single guard. No surprise. Kiki had an uncanny knack for avoiding the patrols, just like she knew the shortest route to any destination in Sitia and Ixia.

When Kiki veered to the right during their second day on the road, Valek thought she might be overtired. But she cut through the trees and onto another path. Kiki slowed as a wagon appeared, traveling toward them. Odd.

One person drove the team of horses. The driver's hood had been pulled down, hiding his or her face. Yanking on the reins, the driver stopped the wagon.

"What are you doing here?" the driver asked.

"I could ask you the same thing, Maren," Valek said.

"I'm returning from a mission for the Commander."

"What's in the wagon?"

"It's classified."

Valek bit down on a harsh reply. Nothing should be classified for him. But Devlen was with him.

"Are you out here for business or pleasure?" Maren glanced at Kiki.

"We're investigating a smuggling operation."

"Then you want to head east to Lapeer. The smugglers

have dug a tunnel under the border into Sitia a couple miles straight north of the town."

"How did—"

"I was undercover with them, but it got too hot for me, so I bugged out. But don't worry. Janco's there with some chick, and Yelena is sniffing around, too."

Valek tightened his grip on the reins. Why hadn't the Commander informed him of Maren's whereabouts? She had critical information about the smugglers. He kept his tone neutral as he thanked Maren for the intel.

She waved as she spurred her horses forward. Valek's curiosity urged him to follow her in order to take a peek at her cargo, but catching up to Yelena in Lapeer was a priority.

Kiki set off, presumably toward Lapeer. Had Kiki known Maren would have information about Yelena, or had she just smelled a familiar person and decided to investigate? He'd have to ask Yel... Oh. Without her magic, Yelena wouldn't be able to communicate with Kiki. His anger at his heart mate disappeared. Yelena must be devastated. No wonder she'd confided in Devlen and Opal. They'd endured the same hardship.

Valek and Devlen reached Lapeer two days later at midafternoon. Doing a quick recon of the town, Valek noticed guards posted around one of the warehouses and quite a bit of activity around the station house. While Devlen visited the authorities, Valek stabled the horses and then took a closer look at that warehouse.

He found a gap in their security and slipped into the building. While the equipment was unfamiliar, the smell slapped him in the face. Curare. They'd been manufacturing Curare. The smuggling operation, which he'd viewed as an annoyance, had transformed into a high-level threat to both Ixia and Sitia. No wonder the Commander had been so determined to shut it down.

Except…

Why wouldn't he tell Valek that Maren had been working undercover? They could have saved time with her intel.

Unless…

The answer shocked him. He stood in the middle of the room, not caring who might see him. It explained so much. Not everything, but the reason the Commander hadn't confided in Valek became clear.

Maren's wagon was loaded with Curare for the Commander. And now that the Commander had enough of the drug and probably insider knowledge on how to produce more, he'd sent Valek to shut the smugglers down. No point in having Curare if everyone had it—that wouldn't be a good strategy. And since Valek had "divided" loyalties, the Commander kept this part of the operation a secret so Valek wouldn't inform Yelena. He didn't trust Valek.

Not sure how he felt about the Commander's lack of faith, Valek finished scouting the building. All evidence suggested the place had been abandoned. He exited and hurried to join Devlen in the Log Jam Inn's common room for supper. Neither of them had eaten a hot meal in days.

"What did you discover?" Valek asked as he sat next to Devlen.

"That their corn pie is supposedly the best. I ordered one for you, too."

"You sound like Leif."

"I learned to ask the servers what their favorite dish is from him," Devlen said. "It takes all the guesswork out of ordering a meal."

"That is *one* good thing when traveling with Leif. The food is always better."

"True." Devlen scrunched his napkin between his hands. "I learned the smugglers are producing Curare." Guilt creased his face. "Yelena's father developed the drug to help people in pain, and the Daviian Warpers stole it and misused it. And now... Hell, I was a Warper. I was a part of all that. And just thinking about some street thug using Curare on my children..." He twisted the cloth into a tight rope.

"It can't be undone," Valek said. "It can't be contained. But we can fight it. There is an antidote, and Leif and Esau have been working on finding a way to mass-produce it. And more healers are using Curare to manage pain. A good thing. Besides, from what I hear about Reema and Teegan, the street thug will be the one in danger."

That surprised a laugh from Devlen. "Especially if they're together."

"That poor street thug won't know what hit him." He smiled.

The server arrived with two steaming corn pies and two mugs of ale. All conversation ceased as they inhaled the food. Not bad. The pie had chunks of chicken, potatoes and corn inside a flaky crust.

When they finished, Valek asked, "Did you learn anything else?"

"The smugglers had fled before the raid. But they think Yelena found a clue to their destination and followed them."

"Think?"

"She disappeared after the raid."

Valek wrapped his hands around the mug to keep them from grabbing Devlen's shirt and slamming him on the table. "Why didn't you tell me this sooner?"

"What could you do? They don't know which direction the smugglers headed. The horses need to rest. We need to eat."

He drew in a deep breath. "When was the raid?"

"Yesterday."

Valek considered. "Did they mention if Yelena was with anyone?"

"She was alone, which concerned the captain. He expected the Soulfinder to have an escort and did not believe her story about the factory at first."

Which meant Janco and Onora had kept a low profile. And there was a good chance they'd followed the smugglers. Did they head north to that tunnel Maren had mentioned? One way to find out.

Valek returned to the Log Jam Inn after finding the tunnel. The entrance had been hidden by magic and it had taken him four hours to discover its location. Pure exhaustion soaked into his bones, and he fumbled at the door, waking Devlen when he entered the room.

"Any signs of recent activity?" Devlen asked.

"No. It was last used about three or four days ago."

"That rules out north. And we know they did not go west or Kiki would have smelled Yelena. South?"

"Not with the Fulgor security forces searching for Ben Moon."

"Then that leaves east."

Of course. He groaned. "They have another tunnel near the mountains." Where he planned to rendezvous with his teams.

"You still had to check north just in case they crossed into Ixia and then headed east. Go to sleep, Valek. You will think clearer in the morning."

Except the morning came sooner than expected.

A slight noise woke him. He jumped to his feet with his knife in hand. Onora stood by the open window. Her skin and clothes appeared gray in the predawn light that framed her. She was barefoot and without a cloak despite the cold air streaming into the room.

"Too slow, Valek. I had plenty of time to reach you," she said.

"Why didn't you?" he asked.

"Then I'd have your job and I'd have to deal with Janco all the time."

He relaxed. "He'll grow on you."

"That's what everyone keeps telling me."

Devlen laughed from the other bed. "It would be difficult to find a person who has met Janco and did not wish to kill him right away."

"Who's he?" Onora asked, eyeing Devlen with suspicion.

Valek introduced her to the Sitian. He stood to shake her hand. She stepped back. He wore a pair of pants, but no shirt. And the man certainly kept in shape. Just like Captain Timmer. Devlen sensed her fear—and dropped his hand. Valek needed to have a chat with Onora about Timmer, but now wasn't the time or place.

"Do you have information for me?" he asked.

She pulled her gaze from Devlen and told Valek about her and Janco following a group of smugglers east through a number of small towns before they stopped in what appeared to be one of their hideouts. "A couple of wagons joined them a few hours later. When it was apparent they planned to stay, I left to update Yelena. She was supposed to remain in town. Do you know where she went?"

"No." The worry that had been simmering in his heart boiled over. He explained what they'd learned from Captain Fleming.

"She's either still in the factory, or she hid in one of the wagons that arrived later, or she's a captive," Onora said in a matter-of-fact tone.

"Still in the factory?" Devlen asked.

"Yes. These people have magic and they've been using illusions to conceal things. So why not use it to hide in the factory?"

It made sense. Wait out the raid and leave later. Or even during the raid. If you were hidden from sight, then you just had to make sure you didn't bump into anybody.

Devlen glanced at him. "Did you feel magic in the warehouse?"

"No, but I wasn't searching for it."

"Then we should return and do another sweep," Onora suggested.

"Good idea." Valek changed his shirt.

"What should I do?" Devlen asked.

"Take Kiki and head east. Yelena might be with the smugglers, and that's our destination regardless. We'll catch up."

After Devlen left, Valek stopped Onora.

She frowned at him. "We're wasting time."

"This won't take long. I need to trust you, Onora."

A wary expression crossed her face. "I'm here, helping. What more do you want?"

"Assurance that you won't attack Yelena again."

Onora pressed her lips together to cover her surprise.

"Why?" he asked.

"Orders."

Ah. "How long have you and the Commander been working together?"

"Six months."

"Do you have orders to kill her?"

"I *never* had orders to kill her."

"But the arrow was filled with a poison."

"No. It was filled with a harmless substance to make the attack appear to be more dire."

Powerful relief swept through his body. Nice to know his friend and Commander didn't wish his heart mate dead. Ex-

　　　　　　　MARIA V. SNYDER

cept...what had happened to Yelena's magic? "Did you prep the arrow yourself?"

"No. Why?"

"Who gave you the arrow?"

"The Commander."

Everything circled back to the Commander. Damn.

"The Commander said you'd figure it out. I didn't think it'd be this soon."

Valek planned to have a heart-to-heart talk with Ambrose as soon as they found Yelena. He shoved his swirling thoughts and emotions aside to concentrate on her.

Valek and Onora had no trouble entering the factory. This time Valek kept alert for evidence of magic.

"When Janco feels magic it hurts him. Is it like that for you?" Onora asked.

"No. For me, it's sticky. The magic presses against me, but can't penetrate my skin."

"Because of your immunity?"

"Yes."

"Can you see through an illusion like he does?"

"No. I only sense it through touch, and I have to guess what type of magic it is. Very frustrating at times."

Onora remained quiet as they searched the ground floor. Then she said, "If Sitia has all this magic, then why haven't they conquered Ixia?"

"Magic is a strong weapon. But like every weapon, there is a defense. Plus magicians are human. They can be bribed, tricked and coerced. They have their own agendas. Sitia had its hands full with rogue magicians who are more of a threat than Ixia."

"For now."

Valek turned to her. Had the Commander confided in her about the Curare? No emotion shone on her face.

When they entered a small stairwell, Valek sensed power emanating from the floor. He found a hatch. They descended and found Yelena's switchblade lying near the base of the ladder. Valek's heart lurched. She'd never leave it behind, which meant she'd been captured. Determined to return it to her, he tucked it into his belt.

He rushed to finish checking the basement. It was empty of goods and magic. And Yelena. They had taken her with them. Valek needed to find them.

Fast.

31

JANCO

Where was Onora? She should have been back by now. Janco circled the smuggler's farm another time. The place was big and surrounded by a chain-link fence, but he doubted any actual farming went on in there. Lots of barns, people and activity, but no cows, crops or farm equipment. Each hour that passed brought more wagons and sketchy-looking goons. Where was Onora?

Plus Janco thought he'd spotted that Ben Moon guy Yelena had talked about. The man resembled her description, and she'd suspected he might be involved. He thought about the fugitive. That rescue op from Wirral Prison would have cost a bundle. And what better way to raise money than smuggling? Selling Curare. No doubt you could collect lots and lots of gold for Curare.

He watched the compound from a low branch in a tree and kept track of people going into and between buildings, counting heads and guessing their jobs. The sun set and lanterns were lit—a good indication of which structures were occupied. Tired of waiting for Onora, Janco decided to sneak into the compound later and have a look around.

When the activity diminished, Janco ghosted along the

fence until he found a dark area out of sight from the main buildings. He climbed over the ten-foot-high fence. A weird tingle lingered on his palms. Janco rubbed them on his pants. Must be from the cold.

The first barn he explored smelled authentic. Yuck. Moldy straw bales mixed with crates of goods. The second place was even more uninteresting. However, hidden between two buildings was a strange-looking structure. The one-story-high oversize shed had been constructed with glass. Odd. Janco moved closer. Water beaded the glass on the inside. Dark leafy plants filled the interior. He circled it and found the entrance. Locked. But not for long.

Hot steamy air along with the rich earthy smells of the jungle puffed in his face when he opened the door. Janco entered. Various plants and bushes filled the room along with pools of water and two red-hot woodstoves. A thick vine wove through the foliage. The Curare vine.

This was bad. Really bad. If they were growing their own vines here, they could be growing them anywhere. He'd assumed they brought the vines up from the Illiais Jungle. That would be easier to stop than finding these little glass hothouses.

Time to leave. Janco exited the…jungle. He turned to relock the door and a sharp point pricked him in the back.

Three sharp points, actually.

"Hands up," a voice said.

Damn. Not much he could do. He spread his arms, but kept his hands low. They took his sword, knife and lock picks. Well, one set, anyway. Then manacled his hands behind his back. Pushing on his shoulder, they led him to another building. Not the chattiest bunch, either, which meant he'd been ambushed by a trio of grunts. A blow to his ego, for sure.

A number of people were inside the new building. The guy he guessed was Ben was there, but also another man he recognized, who stood inside a wagon. This had gone beyond bad. Janco was screwed.

"Well, well, well. Isn't this just a happy reunion? Yelena, guess who came to visit? Your friend...Janco, is it?"

"Pretty good memory for a dead guy," Janco said. He glanced around, but didn't see Yelena. She must be on the floor of the wagon and under a null shield, otherwise the jerk wouldn't be so cocky.

Owen Moon beamed at him. "I always remember the faces and names of my enemies. I don't want to forget to kill anyone."

32

YELENA

What little hope I had of being rescued shrank even more when Janco's sarcastic voice sounded. He'd been captured, too. And from his comments, he was as surprised as I had been upon seeing Owen Moon alive and well. Despite the Commander's message to the Sitian Council, informing them of Owen's execution four years ago. Why hadn't the Commander killed him? The answer flashed in my mind.

Owen had been busy working *for* the Commander. And it didn't take a genius to guess what he had been doing—learning how to manufacture Curare.

But why would the Commander wish to shut Owen down? Owen smirked at me. His posture like a hunter's, gloating over his kill. Cocky bastard. And I'd bet that particular personality trait of his was what had pissed the Commander off. He'd rescued his brother, alerting the Sitians, and I'd guess he was selling Curare to other interested parties. Yep, I'd wager more than a few gold coins that was what had happened.

Of course, it would have been useful to have figured this out sooner. Before I'd been tied to the wagon and gagged. The knowledge didn't help my situation. Nor Janco's.

"Where is your companion?" Owen asked Janco for the second time.

No answer. Janco would never tell him.

"Loris, jog his memory," Owen ordered.

Janco cried out. A thump sounded. "Nooo…" He groaned.

Helpless, I struggled against the ropes as I listened to Janco's distress increase as Loris pulled the information from Janco's mind. I'd been assaulted the same way when I'd first arrived at the Magician's Keep. Janco had another reason to hate magic. Right now, I hated it, too.

Janco yelped. Then grunted. More than a few moments passed.

"What's taking so long?" Owen demanded.

"His thoughts are…jumbled. Chaotic."

Go Janco!

"Crack a few ribs. That'll give him something to focus on."

I braced for the impact even though I wasn't the target. The thud echoed in my chest as Janco's breath whooshed out.

Another pause and then Loris said, "She returned to Lapeer to rendezvous with Yelena."

"What about Valek? Is he on the way?" Owen asked.

Valek! Reema and Devlen should have reached the castle by now. Devlen would have told him everything. Valek was probably angry at me. No, not probably. *Furious* would be the correct term. Although, keeping secrets was a part of both our jobs. Should I be upset with him for not telling me about Owen? Did Valek even know about him? Hopefully, I'd have a chance to ask him after Owen's arrest. Might as well think positive.

"Last time he talked to Valek, the assassin planned to remain at the castle, collecting information." Loris huffed in amusement. "He didn't have time to send a message to Valek about what he has discovered in Lapeer."

"Good. And the Commander? Any info on him?" Owen asked.

"Nothing new. The Commander is still intent on shutting down our smuggling routes into Ixia."

"Does Janco know how the Commander found out about our...side business?"

"No."

"Take him down to the cellar. Stake him down to the floor spread-eagle. These Ixians have weapons and lock picks hidden everywhere. It's best just to keep their hands and feet far apart."

"Yes, sir."

Sounds of a scuffle reached me along with another thud. Then nothing. Poor Janco.

"Send out a couple patrols," Owen ordered. "His companion will be back and we need to pick her up before she has a chance to send a report north."

"Yes, sir."

Owen looked down. "Now you'll get my full attention." He crouched beside me. "My hunting expedition inside your mind was very educational. While I'm not happy the memories I planted in your head didn't work, I discovered something very interesting about you." His expression was downright gleeful.

I'd panic. But I'd been in a state of ever-increasing panic since I woke up tied to the wagon and saw Owen. I was beyond mere panic and into the realms of mind-numbing terror at this point.

Owen stroked my throat. I recoiled from his touch.

"Oh, please." He pulled on the chain around my neck, tugging my octopus pendant free of my shirt.

Pain bit into my skin as he yanked the necklace, breaking the chain.

"Oops." Owen dropped it over the side of the wagon. It

MARIA V. SNYDER

shattered. He pressed his hand on my chest near the base of my throat.

An uncomfortable burning sensation spread throughout my body. The skin on my scalp crawled. Goose bumps rose despite the heat. A reaction to his magic? The strange conflicting feelings stopped as fast as they started.

Owen laughed. "Too bad I wasted perfectly good Theobroma on you when I didn't have to. You're just a regular girl now. How wonderful." He untied my gag, removing it.

Relief flowed into my cheeks and I worked my mouth and tongue to produce moisture.

He sat back on his heels. "What is blocking your magic?"

"I've no idea." My voice rasped. I told him about the attack in the woods. Why not? "At first, I thought it was one of Ben's cohorts."

"The plan was for everyone to lie low. Until my idiot brother lured you to our hideout in Fulgor. It wasn't us. Seems you're just a very unpopular girl," Owen said. "You shouldn't be surprised. And now someone has gone to considerable trouble to neutralize you with that attack in the woods. Your death will cause too much trouble. So that's a perfect solution—spread the word that you're powerless, and let another person target you. Or rather, dozens of others in your case. Too bad it won't work for me."

"Because I know too much."

"Right. And unless you want to swear loyalty to me…?"

"No."

"Thought so. But not to worry. This time when I erase your memories, I won't make the same mistake."

"Mistake?"

"I only erased a few hours of your life. This time, I'm going to erase everything. You won't even remember your name."

"That's…" Fear closed my throat.

"Clever. I know. Loris and Cilly are very talented with mental communication and the three of us make a great team. How do you think I stayed dead all these years?"

"When?"

"As soon as we catch your colleague. It'll be easier to do all three of you at once."

A momentary reprieve.

"Go ahead, ask," Owen said in his smug tone.

"Was it the Commander's idea?"

"Not at first. He was ready to send me to the noose, but I pleaded for my life. And argued that I could help him by getting him Curare. Actually, I should thank you, Yelena. Your efforts to change the Commander's mind about magicians in Ixia helped sway him."

Lovely. "And he funded your research."

"Yes."

"And you had to screw it up by rescuing your brother."

Anger flashed in his eyes. "I couldn't leave him in that hellhole."

"But you could leave your wife, Selene, in Dawnwood Prison?"

"She's a traitor."

"According to the Commander, so are you." As soon as the words left my mouth, I braced for his reaction.

He curled a fist, but didn't swing. "The fervor over Ben would have eventually died down."

"I was referring to you selling Curare to other customers. That's why the Commander is going to shut you down. You can erase our memories, but eventually, he'll send Valek and his corps after you."

Owen grinned, but the humor failed to reach his eyes. "Oh, don't you worry about me. I've discovered something big that will please the Commander, and all will be forgiven."

MARIA V. SNYDER

I didn't like the sound of that. "And that is?"

"Nice try, but I'm not stupid."

True. Overconfidence and greed would trip him up. If it hadn't already. "The Commander is not the forgiving type."

"I'm touched you're so concerned." Owen straightened. He called to his men. "Take her down with Janco. Secure her in the same manner." Hopping off the wagon, he disappeared from my view.

A couple of his goons untied me, but kept a firm hold. My stiff leg and arm muscles protested the movement as blood rushed to my hands and feet. I considered fighting the two men, but once I stood upright, I spotted a number of other guards in the building. And Ben leaned against the wall, watching with a satisfied smirk.

The musty smell of hay tickled my nose as they escorted me to a hatch in the wooden floor. The high-vaulted ceiling suggested that this building had once been a barn. I glanced out the window. Weak sunlight shone on the glass—early morning. If Owen's men didn't find Onora, we might be here awhile, which was a good thing. More time for... What? Not sure what I could do without my magic.

We walked down a ramp into the semidark dampness below. The root cellar had earthen walls and a hard-packed dirt floor. Two oversize musclemen sat in chairs near the base of the ramp. Daggers hung from their belts. Behind them was Janco.

"Can we gag this idiot?" one of the guards asked my companions. "He won't shut up and is driving us crazy."

Good news. If Janco had enough energy to harass his guards, it meant he wasn't as hurt as I'd feared.

The guy on my left shrugged. "Sure. The Boss shouldn't mind." He handed me off to the guard. "This one can join her friend."

"Yeah?" The guard's expression brightened as a slow smile spread, exposing broken teeth. "Can we play?"

My breath hitched. Fear bit into my guts.

"No."

I relaxed.

"Ah, too bad."

My two escorts left. Broken Teeth tugged me deeper into the cellar. Janco watched us, craning his head up, but he didn't say a word. His wrists and ankles had been tied with ropes. We stopped next to Janco. Four more metal stakes had been driven into the ground.

"Your room is ready," Broken Teeth said.

His partner chuckled. Sections of rope hung from his meaty hands. "Lie down," he ordered.

Broken Teeth pushed on my shoulder. "Come—"

I moved. Spinning and ducking under his arm, I snagged the man's dagger then stepped back. They wouldn't tie me down without a fight.

"Oh, she's feisty. I like that." Broken Teeth advanced. "Give me back my knife before you get hurt."

Broken Teeth lunged. I sidestepped and slashed at his stomach. He blocked my swing late and the blade cut across his forearm.

"Hey! We need help here!" the other guard yelled toward the hatch before he dropped the ropes and drew his dagger. He moved to swing in behind me.

Sparring with Broken Teeth, I countered his attacks and tried to avoid being trapped between the two men.

When boots pounded on the ramp, I knew my time was up. I faked a breakaway to the right, but then cut left, tripping over Janco. He grunted in pain when I landed on him.

"Sorry," I said right before the guards grabbed me.

I struggled, and it took four of them to secure me to the

MARIA V. SNYDER

stakes. When they finished, they nursed their bruises while I puffed with the effort, sweating. Broken Teeth found his weapon lying near Janco. Eventually, the extra guards left, leaving the original two. They returned to their seats. At least they hadn't gagged Janco yet.

"Not bad," Janco said to me in a low voice. "If the guards had manned up instead of crying for help, you would have had a decent shot."

"I tried to cut and run, but that didn't work as planned."

"Not entirely."

I glanced at Janco. He shot me a grin. When I had "tripped" over him, I'd slashed at the ropes near his right wrist, but I'd no idea if it was deep enough to cut through. From the gleam in his eyes and his comment, I guessed my attempt had met with some success. I hoped it was enough.

"Do they have you covered with a null shield? Damn thing screws everything up," Janco said.

The thought of explaining to him how I was even more helpless than he believed while tied spread-eagle to a dirt floor was too depressing. "Yeah. Don't count on my magic. How are you feeling?"

"Murderous. Just give me one minute with that magician and I'll show him how it feels to have things ripped from you."

"And your ribs?"

"Sore. They'll heal. I've cracked my ribs dozens of times. I imagine my bones resemble a messed-up spiderweb by this point."

"I'd prefer a broken bone than cracked ribs," I said. "You can't breathe or laugh or twist or sleep without pain."

"Yeah, but if you break your leg, then you can't walk. And a broken arm makes it harder to fight."

"You can't fight with cracked ribs."

"I can."

"Considering our present situation, I hope you're not exaggerating."

Janco didn't reply right away. "So what's Owen's plan?"

I explained about the memory wipe.

"I'd rather be killed." Janco sounded horrified.

"Oh, I don't know. I've some memories I'd be happy to forget." I mulled over Owen's confidence in regaining the Commander's trust. The Commander already had plenty of Curare. What else could Owen offer him? I mentioned it to Janco.

"Maybe he discovered a new drug from one of his jungle plants."

"His jungle plants? Is that a euphemism for something else?"

"No. He's growing the Curare vine in these…hot glass houses."

"He's growing it? That's…" I searched for a word to describe the magnitude of this news.

"Serious trouble for all of us?"

"To put it mildly."

"Yeah. That's why they got the drop on me. I was still reeling." Janco described what he'd found inside the hothouse before he was captured. "Do you recognize any of the other vegetation?"

"I'd have to see it."

"Maybe Owen will give us a tour before he scrambles our brains."

Trust Janco to put a positive spin on a bad situation. At least he was entertaining. We could be here awhile. "What are the chances of Owen's people catching Onora?"

"No chance. She's probably halfway to Ixia by now."

"Why do you think that?"

"She's smart. And she has no reason to be loyal to us. Ari would charge in here like a bull seeing a lady bull wearing red."

MARIA V. SNYDER

"There are no lady bulls."

"Sure there are. How do you think we get baby bulls?"

It required too much energy to explain about the bulls and the bees to Janco. "Ari would be caught right away."

"That's beside the point. Onora's like Valek—cold and calculating. Well, like him when he's not with you."

At least that meant we had some time to figure out a way to escape. I craned my neck. Janco met my gaze and tilted his head toward the guards, then cleared his throat. The guards kept their attention on the hatch, but checked on us from time to time. I nodded my understanding.

When both guards faced forward, Janco pulled his right wrist free. He dug in the waistband of his pants and withdrew a small knife. I watched the guards and signaled with a cough whenever one turned his head our way.

After twenty minutes or so, Janco called, "Hey, boneheads! I'm hungry. Ya got anything to eat?"

I glanced at him. He appeared to be still tied to the stakes. Janco continued to harass the guards. They threatened to gag him, but he increased his taunting until Broken Teeth stood up with a growl.

He approached and pulled a cloth from his pocket. "I've got a snotty hankie just for you." Broken Teeth leaned over.

Janco slashed at his throat with the small knife. The guard yelled, and then Janco grabbed the man's dagger and stabbed it into his stomach. Broken Teeth's partner raced up the ramp.

"Ah hell." Janco cut the ropes around his ankles, scrambled to his feet and sprinted after him.

I waited. Broken Teeth groaned, cursed and promised to kill Janco, but he didn't chase after him and, eventually, he slumped over. Unconscious or dead, I couldn't tell until the stench of offal reached me. Dead.

Nothing happened for a long time. Then shadows crossed

the hatch and four guards descended. I laid my head back and hoped they hadn't killed Janco. They untied me and marched me back to the main floor. Janco knelt on the ground surrounded by six guards who pointed their swords at him. Blood from a cut on his forehead spilled down his cheek. His hands were laced behind his neck.

"Sorry," he said, looking miserable.

"You tried," I said.

But he tilted his head to the left. Onora stood in the middle of another group of guards. Her pale face and wide eyes gave her the appearance of being nervous, but she scanned the room as if assessing weaknesses. I copied her. At least two dozen of Owen's smugglers filled the area along with Owen, Ben and his three magician friends. Oh joy.

"Take them to the stables," Owen ordered.

We tried to resist, but they dragged us into the daylight and to the stable. The large wooden building had two rows of stalls. But these were fully enclosed, with bars on the top half to prevent horses from jumping. Or to keep a person contained inside.

Pushed into a stall, I tumbled to the straw-coated floor. By the time I gained my feet, the door had locked shut. Janco occupied the one to my left and Onora stood in the stall to my right.

Owen consulted with Cilly and Loris.

I asked Onora, "How did they catch you?"

"Tactical error." She paced the six-foot-square space and twisted the end of her shirt.

If she was digging for lock picks, she'd better hurry. I lowered my voice. "Did you send a message?"

"No time."

"Couldn't you at least lie to me?"

MARIA V. SNYDER

"Oh. Uh…I did send a message, and now the entire Ixian army is camped outside this compound."

"You're a lousy liar."

"My one flaw," she joked.

"One?" Janco choked. "I know at least a dozen. You're terrible at avoiding capture, following orders—"

"I can say the same for you. What part of 'wait for me before you go inside' didn't you understand?"

Owen interrupted them. He approached my stall as Loris stood in front of Janco's and Cilly took up position outside Onora's. Unease swirled. I backed away, until I hit the wall.

"Now," Owen ordered.

I opened my mouth, but a hot knifing pain pierced my head, stripping away my resistance and willpower. It felt as if my soul was being ripped into a thousand pieces. Horror at losing myself welled and built until I could no longer stand the pressure. I screamed.

33

VALEK

Yelena's scream stabbed right through Valek's heart. He moved without thought. Devlen grabbed his arm, stopping him.

"Wait for it," Devlen said.

They crouched in the woods just outside the fence. Town watchmen surrounded the complex. Captain Fleming had gone above and beyond, recruiting as many soldiers from the local towns that he could in mere hours.

When Yelena screamed again, Valek growled. "What is she waiting for?"

"The right opportunity."

Valek had put a great deal of trust into Onora. When the assassin had volunteered to be captured, Valek initially resisted the idea. But then he agreed she had the best chance. However, now he questioned his decision.

Many agonizing minutes passed.

"There," Devlen said. "Smoke."

Valek whistled and the signal repeated on both sides. He waited just long enough for the message to reach all the soldiers. Then he and Devlen and the watchmen all climbed over the fence. Magic clung to the metal links. Hell.

"They know we're coming," he shouted to both sides.

"How?" Devlen asked as he joined him.

"Magic woven through the fence."

"Then we better hurry."

They raced toward the building leaking smoke. It had been a stable. Men poured out, coughing with tears running down their cheeks. The watchmen engaged them, but Valek bypassed them, slipping inside. He crouched low, staying under the cloud. Glass shards from Onora's smoke bombs crunched under his boots.

Through the gray haze, he spotted Onora and Janco fighting a trio of guards.

"Where's Yelena?" Valek asked.

"Owen has her," Janco shouted. "They disappeared. That way." He pointed right as he ducked under an opponent's sword.

"Owen?"

"Ben's not-so-dead brother."

He'd think about Owen's rise from the dead later. Yelena first. Valek followed Janco's directions. At the end of the row of stalls was a corridor. The smoke thinned as he ghosted down the hall and into a training ring.

Owen pulled a hatch open in the center. Yelena lay nearby. She pressed her hands to her head and moaned in pain.

Valek drew his knives and ran toward them. Owen spotted the movement and Valek slammed into an invisible wall. The impact dazed him for a second. A null shield blocked him. Magic couldn't pierce it, but objects could. He flipped his weapons, grabbing the blades, and aimed at Owen. The shield tightened and knocked into his hands just as he threw the weapons. They missed. One struck the soft dirt near Yelena and the other sailed past. The shield pressed around him, trapping his arms.

"Wow," Owen said. "It's true. The infamous Valek can be stopped by a simple null shield. That information was worth every gold coin I spent for it." He glanced at Yelena. "I planned to use her as a hostage, but she'll only slow me down." Owen knelt next to her. "I'll just finish what I started." Touching her forehead with two fingers, he closed his eyes.

Yelena jerked. In a panic, Valek struggled against the invisible force wrapped around him, but it didn't budge. Without her magic, she wouldn't survive. That word, *survive*, sparked a memory. She'd survived before back when she didn't know she had power.

Valek yelled, "Fight him. Come on, Yelena. You don't need magic. You survived Mogkan and Reyad. Come on. Fight. Survive!"

34

YELENA

I'd been torn apart. Pieces of me littered the ground. I felt like a stuffed toy whose stuffing had been ripped out. Owen dug for more. The sharp pain gouged and it hurt to form a thought. Mindless, I burrowed deeper into the tiny bit left, but it crumbled and soon nothing of me would remain.

Valek's strident voice cut through my haze of pain. I didn't understand all the words, but his emotions flowed into me like pure energy. And one word burned brighter. *Survive.* I could do that. I'd done it many times before.

Concentrating on the image of me as an empty toy, I gathered the clumps and crammed them into my mind, body and soul. Owen worked to drag them away, but I collected them just as fast. Survive. All I needed to do was survive. He'd get tired eventually, while Valek's encouragement strengthened my efforts.

The attack increased in intensity, but I persisted, harvesting the pieces of me. My skull ached, and pain seared my skin and burned my muscles. Memories of the agony I suffered when I'd crossed into the fire world surfaced. I'd survived that without the help of my magic. Other recollections of survival rose unbidden. I'd endured Mogkan's torture and lived through Reyad's assault.

Owen yelled and power slammed into me. White light sparked behind my eyelids as pain exploded inside my head. I kept a tight grip on all I'd worked so hard to collect.

Another bolt of agony sliced through me. I fought to remain awake and teetered on the edge, enduring, surviving until the attack stopped. A cool hand touched my hot skin. Safe. I relaxed, letting a blackness wash over me.

I woke to a soft voice and a touch on my cheek. Opening my eyes required effort since my lids weighed a hundred pounds each. The lantern light seemed overly bright, but I squinted and my exertions were rewarded with a wonderful sight. Valek.

He sat on the edge of my bed, holding my hand and stroking my face with his fingers. The small room gave no clues as to where we were. But I didn't really care at this point.

His worried expression disappeared into a smile. "How are you feeling?"

"Like a chew toy for a pack of snow cats." My voice rasped and my throat burned with thirst.

Valek let go and I mewled like a kitten.

"I'm not leaving, love. Here." He handed me a glass filled with a yellowish-colored liquid with bits of green floating in it. "Drink it all."

Raising the glass up to my lips required too much energy. "Is this one of Leif's concoctions?"

"Yes." Valek supported me and guided my hand.

I gulped the lukewarm drink. It tasted like honey grass. "Is he here? And where are we exactly?"

"He's here. Along with Opal and another magician. They arrived a couple hours after the ruckus and have been helping with the cleanup. We are in a bedroom of the compound's farmhouse."

I finished the potion despite the bits of green clinging to my teeth. Leif's restoratives might not taste good, but they worked. "I'm still mad at them. Leif especially."

"I'm grateful Leif's here. Besides the drinks, he aided in your mental recovery. Owen had done considerable damage." All softness left Valek's face. "When I catch up to him, I'm going to personally ensure he stays dead."

Not good. "He escaped?"

"Yes. He dropped down through the hatch and secured it on the inside. It led to a tunnel. By the time we broke in, he was long gone."

"Did you know he was still alive?"

"No, love. The Commander hadn't confided in me about him, the Curare or Maren's involvement."

"Perhaps he thought you'd tell me. It's a game changer."

"Perhaps." Valek didn't appear convinced.

"What are you going to do?"

Pain and betrayal creased his expression and he suddenly appeared to be exhausted. "I need to talk to him. Find out why he's keeping things from me and determine if he still trusts me."

I squeezed his hand. It would be a difficult conversation. "What about the others? Did anyone else escape?"

"We caught Loris, Cilly and Ben Moon. The others got away. I promise Ben won't live for long."

"Don't kill him. We can use him as bait. Owen rescued him before and may again."

"You sound just like the others."

Which reminded me. "How are Janco and Onora doing?"

"They're bickering like brother and sister."

In other words, fine. "Reema and Devlen?"

"Devlen is coordinating with the authorities. Reema is safe in Ixia with Ari. And before you ask, Kiki is impatiently waiting for you in the local inn's stable."

Good. I told Valek about Owen's confidence regarding the Commander's continuing support. "Maybe something growing in the hothouse."

"Leif's already compiling an inventory of the plants."

And what he couldn't identify, our father would know. "There might be more of those hothouses in Sitia. This isn't the end."

"It never is."

Depressing but true. "I'm sorry."

"Nothing you can do about it. It's the way of the world."

"No. I'm sorry for not telling you about…you know. I didn't want to worry you."

Valek pulled the glass from my grip, set it on the table, then took both my hands in his. "When we're apart, I worry about you. Even when I know you're fine and doing some boring research for Bain or visiting your parents, I worry. Even though you are more than capable of taking care of yourself, I worry."

"I *was* capable."

"You still are. Owen couldn't break you."

"If it wasn't for you, he would have. Your voice gave me the strength."

"You used your own strength. I just reminded you that it was already within you."

I didn't know if I agreed with him or not. "Then it's a good thing you showed up in time. How did you find us?"

"Later. You need your rest."

He leaned in and kissed me lightly on the lips then tried to let go of my hands.

I wouldn't release him. "Stay."

"All right."

MARIA V. SNYDER

I scooched over, making room on the bed. Valek kicked off his boots, removed a number of weapons and then stretched next to me. I snuggled against him, breathing in his scent. Safe and warm. My eyes drifted shut.

"Yelena?"

"Hmm?"

"I'd like you to stay with me while we figure out how to unblock your magic. We're stronger together."

"All right."

He laughed. "I thought I'd have more of a fight."

"I'm too tired to argue."

"Then I should take advantage of the situation."

I cracked one eye open. "And?"

"I'd like you to stay with me forever."

My heart jolted with surprise. Wide-awake, I pushed up to my elbow. "Is that a proposal?" I demanded.

"Uh…no. Not at all. Because that would be very unromantic."

"Right."

"Guess I should find a better time and place?"

"There's no guessing about it."

The smell of wet dog intruded on my dreams. They weren't the best dreams, but far better than the stink of damp puppy.

"Go away," I said without opening my eyes.

"No," Leif said.

An image of him crossing his arms and setting his square jaw formed in my mind. It'd be easier to get rid of a splinter driven deep under my skin than my brother. I opened my eyes. Sure enough, that Zaltana stubbornness stiffened his posture. He held a cup of steaming liquid—wet-dog tea.

"If that's your idea of a peace offering, then I'm going to declare war," I said.

"Valek has charged me with your care. Since you haven't been eating, you need to drink this to regain your strength." He handed it to me.

It had been a couple of days since I last woke, but my body still ached, I had no energy and my stomach remained unsettled. The encounter with Owen had left me feeling raw and exposed. Even the blankets chafed against my skin. Sunlight reflected off the window's glass.

I sipped the tea. It tasted better than it smelled. "Happy? Now go away."

Leif stayed by my bed. "Yelena, how many times do I need to apologize? I was following orders and you were going to put yourself in harm's way."

"That's what I do. It's my job so others like Reema are safe."

"I agree. Except now you need to be more cautious and have backup."

I changed the subject and asked about the plants in the hothouse.

"The ones I recognized all have medicinal applications, but there're a few that I can't identify. Father's coming to help."

"Are any of them like Curare, with extraordinary properties?"

"Valek asked about that, too. They're good for fevers and coughs and constipation. Nothing significant. Maybe our father will discover what Owen was talking about."

"Can you ask him about my problem? He might know if a poison caused it."

"Does this mean you forgive me?"

I huffed. "Oh, all right, but only because you're my brother."

"Gee, Yelena, don't get all mushy on me."

"You'll talk to Father?"

"Of course. Now finish your tea."

Holding my breath, I managed another swallow. "How did you know we were here?"

Leif plopped into the chair next to my bed. "After realizing we'd been duped, we trudged back to Fulgor with our tails between our legs. Captain Alden pounced as soon as we arrived, and Hale and I hightailed it back to the Second Chance Inn. I talked to the staff, visited the Clever Fox stables and followed your scent."

"My scent?"

"It's hard for me to explain as it's not really a smell, but rather a primal certainty that you went in a certain direction. Plus Rusalka and Garnet acted as if they knew where they were going. Opal said the Sandseed horses think of us as part of their herd, and they're very protective of the members of their herd."

Leif chatted until I finished my tea. My stomach growled with hunger for the first time in days. My brother jumped to his feet and hurried to fetch me a bowl of soup.

Janco arrived with the promised bowl.

"I see your talents are being put to good use," I teased.

"Real funny." He handed it to me.

I sniffed it. Chicken noodle. Yum.

Janco settled into the chair. "You look better. When Valek carried you up here, I'd thought I'd have to get a shovel and start digging."

"Thanks, I think. How about you? How're the ribs?"

"Tender."

"And your head?"

He scowled. "Other than feeling like my brain has been sliced and diced, fed to a cat and horked out along with a giant hair ball, I'm peachy."

"So back to normal?"

"Normal? I think I've lost track of what normal feels like. Do you know what I want for my birthday?"

"For magic to disappear forever?"

"You know me so well."

"You may have your wish. Whatever is blocking my magic might be the next weapon against magicians. In the hands of the wrong people, they could make magic disappear forever."

Janco stared out the window. "Magic sucks and I hate it, but I wouldn't do that to a magician."

"Really? How about the magicians like Owen? What about them?"

"Tempting. Maybe after they've been tried and convicted of abusing their powers."

"Now you sound like a Sitian."

Janco gasped in mock horror. "Forget I said that! We should kill them all. Every one. Better?"

"Yes, very Ixian."

"Whew!"

Once I started eating full meals, my energy returned after another day.

Valek arrived that evening with my pack slung over his shoulder. "Found this stuffed in the corner of a wagon." He put it on the bed. "And I've been meaning to give this to you." He tossed me my switchblade.

I caught it in midair. "Thanks. I thought I'd lost it." Turning it over in my hands, I examined the handle, running my finger over the silver symbols Janco had etched into it over eight years ago. The symbols meant "sieges weathered, fight together, friends forever." Janco, Ari and Valek had certainly proved this true time after time. And I hoped they'd continue to do so. Which reminded me...

"I found out who sent the assassin after me," I said to Valek.

MARIA V. SNYDER

He stilled. "Tell me."

I detailed my encounter with Kynan, aka The Mosquito. "I still don't know who attacked me in the woods."

Valek's scowl deepened. "Do you think this Bruns Jewelrose is taking advantage of your condition?"

"Probably. My demise could be used as an example. There are a number of Sitians who wish the Council had more power over magicians. The recent ruckus about Opal keeping control of who is given those magic detectors is just one of many skirmishes."

"A visit to Bruns Jewelrose will have to wait until we've figured out how to get your magic back. I doubt the assassin will target you when you're with me. And if he does..." Valek touched the hilt of his knife. "I will be more than happy to take care of him."

"If I don't reach him first."

Valek laughed. "That's my girl. I'd like to leave in the morning. Will you be strong enough to travel?"

"Yes." I opened my pack and sorted through the contents. Ooh...clean clothes. "I need to bathe. Is there—"

"There's a big tub downstairs." Heat burned in Valek's gaze. "I'll be more than happy to assist you."

"Mighty nice of you."

"Not at all. I aim to please."

I laughed. Unable to find my soap and hair wash, I dumped the rest of the stuff onto the bed. My money pouch jingled. Darts and vials of Curare and other potions rolled. And— I gasped.

"What's wrong?" Valek asked.

Holding up a long tube filled with a white liquid, I calculated the last time... Shocked, I stared at Valek.

"What's wrong? Tell me, love." He moved closer.

"This is Moon potion."

"And?"

"And I was supposed to take it after…but, but…it didn't come. I was so busy…I didn't even think…"

"What didn't come? You're not making sense."

My hands shook. "I'm pregnant."

★ ★ ★ ★ ★

ACKNOWLEDGEMENTS

This book would not have been written if not for my readers.

I was quite happy with how Yelena and Valek's story ended in *Fire Study* and I was excited to move on to new stories and characters. However, my very persistent readers kept asking me to write more. I've been inundated with e-mails, messages, comments on my Facebook page and heartfelt requests at my book signings since 2008. So a gigantic thanks to all of you for pushing me to write more. I had a blast getting reacquainted with Yelena, Valek and the other characters in the Study world! While I was certain my loyal readers would understand the backstory and relationships in this book, I worried a new reader would be lost. However, thanks to some helpful feedback from Joelle Swift, I'm confident the story won't confuse a newbie. Also, a big thanks to Judi Fleming, who not only encourages me to write, but her expertise in horses and a zillion other things has been most useful in ensuring I get 'it' right. And I can't forget Natalie Bejin, who helped me by creating the most wonderful and organised spreadsheet of all the characters in the world of Ixia and Sitia. Thanks so much, Natalie!

I cannot write an acknowledgement without thanking my editor, Mary-Theresa Hussey, and agent, Robert Mecoy. Both have been vital in my career and I can't thank you enough! I also want to thank all the amazing people at Harlequin. Your hard work behind the scenes to produce my books doesn't go unnoticed and I brag about you to my writer friends all the time.

And no acknowledgments of mine are complete without a huge thank-you to my husband, son and daughter. You guys rock!

CHOOSE:
A QUICK DEATH...
OR A SLOW POISON...

About to be executed for murder, Yelena is offered the chance to become a food taster. She'll eat the best meals, have rooms in the palace—and risk assassination by anyone trying to kill the Commander of Ixia.

But disasters keep mounting as rebels plot to seize Ixia and Yelena develops magical powers she can't control. Her life is threatened again and choices must be made. But this time the outcomes aren't so clear...

www.miraink.co.uk

THEY DESTROYED HER WORLD. BUT SHE'S THEIR ONLY HOPE...

Avry's power to heal the sick should earn her respect in the plague-torn land of Kazan. Instead she is feared and blamed for spreading the plague.

When Avry uses her forbidden magic, she faces the guillotine. Until a dark, mysterious man rescues her from her prison cell. His people need Avry's magic to save their dying prince.

Saving the prince is certain to kill Avry. Now she must choose—use her healing touch to show the ultimate mercy or die a martyr to a lost cause?

IN JULIE KAGAWA'S GROUND-BREAKING MODERN FANTASY SERIES, DRAGONS WALK AMONG US IN HUMAN FORM

Long ago, dragons were hunted to near extinction by the Order of St George. Hiding in human form and increasing their numbers in secret, the dragons of Talon have become strong and cunning, and they're positioned to take over the world with humans none the wiser.

Trained to infiltrate society, Ember wants to live the teen experience before taking her destined place in Talon. But destiny is a matter of perspective and a rogue dragon will soon challenge everything Ember has been taught.

www.miraink.co.uk

WE'LL EITHER DESTROY THEM FOR GOOD, OR THEY'LL DESTROY US

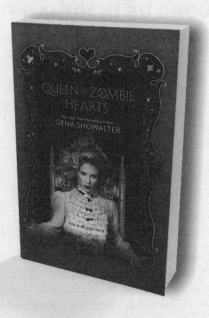

Alice 'Ali' Bell thinks the worst is behind her. She's ready to take the next step with boyfriend Cole Holland, the leader of the zombie slayers... until Anima Industries, the agency controlling the zombies, launches a sneak attack, killing four of her friends. It's then she realises that humans can be more dangerous than monsters...and the worst has only begun.

www.miraink.co.uk